大学文科英汉双语教材系列

A Series of Bilingual English / Chinese Humanities Te

丛书主编 / 孙 逊 孙景尧

黄铁池 孙 建 /编著

A Study of
European and American Classical Short Stories

欧美小说名篇研读

上海教育出版社

大学文科英汉双语教材系列
编 委 会 名 单

总　序

Preface

　　改革开放以来,随着国门的打开,我国掀起了一股持久的学习外语和外国文化的热潮,大学外语类专业成为很多年轻人的首选。这股"外语热",从一个侧面反映了我国改革开放所走过的历程,而且至今也还没有成为过去。

　　但文化交流总是双向的,随着我国国力的强盛,当今世界又开始涌动学习汉语的热潮,大学对外汉语专业也随之成为年轻人的新宠。外语和汉语,外国文化和中国文化的双向交流,正以前所未有的深度和广度,在全球范围内相竞相生,相激相荡。

　　面对世界的"汉语热",我国大学中文系的使命何在? 这是摆在大学中文系师生面前的一个迫切问题。我们当然有理由为世界的"汉语热"感到自豪,但我们更不能放松和忘记的是自身的母语学习和中国传统文化的教学与普及。大学中文系,顾名思义,是学习中国语言和文学的学术殿堂。教好、学好母语和中国文学,是中文系师生神圣的职责和使命。不可否认,由于"外语热"的持续升温,一个时期以来,我们对母语的学习有放松和忽略的迹象:好像这年头,只要学好了外语,就可以走遍天下都不怕;而中国人懂汉语是自然习得的,汉语还有什么好学的? 以致各种语法、文字错误满天飞。与汉语学习同样存在问题的是中国文学和文化的学习:现在很多年轻人对本国传统的东西不感兴趣,文学和影视作品喜欢外国的,连过节也爱过洋节日;课堂教学和课外阅读只背文学基本原理和文学史,记住一些条条杠杠,或只读"图",不读书,要读也读一些时尚流行书。凡此种种,都是当前大学中文系教学中存在的问题。为此,我们可透过世界的"汉语热",反观汉语和中国文化学习的重要性,使我们的学生真正明白:自己首先要尊重本国的语言文学和文化,即使是中国人,要学好中文也是不容易的,通晓中国文化更是艰巨。这就需要我们通过精心的课程设置,确保大学中文系学生学好中文、精通中文;同时,也需要同学们刻苦读书,多读经典、多读原著,要想学好中文,必须有几部中国文化的原典在肚子里打底。

　　在引导学生学好母语和中国文化的同时,当然也不能忽略对外语与外国文化的学习。我们处在一个开放的时代,在这个时代里,不与外部世界交流和沟通,是培养不出符合现代社会需求的专门人才的。因此,在学好母语和中国文化的同时,学好外语和外国文化也是至关重要的。这里就涉及双语教学和多元文化的学习问题。有一个时期,我们经常听到这样的议论:母语还没有学好,搞什么双语教学?认为双语教学根本就没有必要。直到今天,也还不时可以听到这类议论。其实,即便是中文系学生,会讲外语,能够掌握跨文化交际能力,也是非常重要的。例如,不懂外语也可教对外汉语,但会讲外语的对外汉语老师肯定会更受欢迎,这里有个高下之别、文野之别、粗细之别。即使不从事对外汉语教学,会讲外语,粗知一些外国文化也会使你如虎添翼。特别是随着我国更多地融入国际社会,跨国公司、大型企业和重点中学都需要具有跨文化交际能力的专业人才。至于有些人担心:母语还没有学好,如何能学好外语?这也是多余的,我们很多老一辈的学者和今天年轻的专业人士都不同程度地做到了这一点。只是语言文化学习是一个长期的过程,永无止境,我们不可能一下子就尽善尽美,但必须朝着这个目标坚持不懈地努力。

中文学科是一个有着悠久学术传统和积淀的学科,在长期的办学过程中,积累了丰富的经验,有着许多行之有效的做法,这些经验和做法今后一定会坚持下去。但时代在飞速发展,世界范围内兴起的"汉语热",既为大学中文系的办学注入了新的活力,提供了难得的历史机遇,同时也提出了更高的要求。我们正可在继承以往经验和做法的基础上,探索一条适应新的时代变化和需求的办学路子,其中包括:如何更好地夯实汉语言文学的基础,引导学生认真地阅读原著和原典,而不是只会死记硬背文学基本原理和文学史里的一些条条杠杠;如何引导学生在学好专业的同时学好外语,精心设置一套适合大学中文系学习的双语教材和课程,培养学生成为具有跨文化交际能力的汉语言文学工作者;以及如何在实践、实习环节,组织学生在不走出国门的前提下,通过参与国际学术文化交流的服务工作,通过国际合作办学中的远程网络教学,锻炼学生的实战能力。总之,大学中文系如何更好地适应世界"汉语热"而调整办学思路,这方面正有着大量的工作等着我们去做。

大学中文系承担着传承和传播汉语言文化的历史使命。如果说,旧中国的贫穷落后使我们的先辈徒有满腹经纶,无法实现他们的抱负;改革开放前的闭关自锁又使我们缚住了自己的手脚,坐失了许多与世界文化交流与交融的良机;那么今天,国家的富强,民族的兴盛,终于使我们迎来了这千载难逢的一次历史性机遇。作为个中之人,我们既由衷地感到自豪,更真切地感到有一份沉甸甸的责任。

正是基于以上思考,我们在以往实践的基础上,尝试编写这套"大学文科英汉双语教材系列"。它与通常的英语教材或中文教材的不同之处是,重在"研读"且又是"双语"对照。这里的"双语",就是教材的文本是英文原著,在原文旁加上中文批注,以起到导读英文原著的作用;所谓"研读",就是借助解读分析英语原文,着力于直接具体地领会并"拿来"西方作家与学者的运思过程、表述特点、传统心理、价值观念和美学思想等传统文化精神,以便既能从中学习研究问题、发现问题和解决问题的方法,又能有效提高沟通"自我"与"他者"的能力。这在全球化的今天,对人文学科的大学生来说,是十分必要的。

与此同时,我们还考虑到当下教学的实际需要,即对大多数中文系学生来说,他们经过长达十来年的英语学习,并又过了英语的四级和六级考试,理应在阅读英文原著方面不成问题。然而,根据多年教学实践,我们遗憾地发现,不少学生很少或很不善于阅读英文原著,尤其是学术论著。这是因为,一方面同他们经历了多年应试教育而形成的惯式有关,另一方面也是他们未能适应和掌握大学自学和治学规律所致,而缺乏阅读研究学术论著的具体方法指导和实践训练,则是其最主要的原因。因此我们这套由8本组成的系列双语教材,即《英美诗歌名篇研读》《欧美散文名篇研读》《欧美小说名篇研读》《西方古典文论要著研读》《西方现当代文论要著研读》《西方比较文学要著研读》《当代欧美汉学要著研读》和《当代西方语言学要著研读》,既有文学作品,又有语言学和文学的理论和研究论著,并同课程设置的主干课程配套。

本书的编写体例和使用方法,由于同一般著作不太一样,因此也须略作说明。在每篇正文之前,均有导读,对作者及其事业专长、主要贡献,对选文的主要内容和价值意义等,以中文予以简要介绍。书中英语正文旁,都有中文的批点:或对原文的论点论旨论据、逻辑论述的层次结构、所用的方法和特点等,予以点评或解释;或对作品的思想观念、艺术魅力、情节结构、感情抒写和写作技巧等,予以评论和赏析,以起导读深究作用。对原文难句、难词的翻译或解释,均放在每页的脚注;而原文的原注也一概附上,以供读者查阅参考。

从20世纪80年代末起,我们先给研究生编选了《比较文学经典要著研读》并讲授此课,后又扩大到本科生的多门课程。十多年来,我们和学生们都感到教学相长,双赢互益。有些高校同行闻讯之后,来人或来函索取。上海教育出版社的领导和编辑,欣然愿意帮助出版,以供教学参考和传播之用。我们在此十分感谢大家的关心与支持,但我们又深知本书还存在诸多不尽如人意的地方,也还有因我们水平所限而难以克服的差错,我们真诚祈望专家学者和广大读者的批评指正。

孙　逊　孙景尧

2009 年 10 月于上海

注，以起到导读英文原著的作用；所谓"研读"，就是借助解读分析英语原文，着力于直接具体地领会并"拿来"西方作家与学者的运思过程、表述特点、传统心理、价值观念和美学思想等传统文化精神，以便既能从中学习研究问题、发现问题和解决问题的方法，又能有效提高沟通"自我"与"他者"的能力。这在全球化的今天，对人文学科的大学生来说，是十分必要的。

与此同时，我们还考虑到当下教学的实际需要，即对大多数中文系学生来说，他们经过长达十来年的英语学习，并又过了英语的四级和六级考试，理应在阅读英文原著方面不成问题。然而，根据多年教学实践，我们遗憾地发现，不少学生很少或很不善于阅读英文原著，尤其是学术论著。这是因为，一方面同他们经历了多年应试教育而形成的惯式有关，另一方面也是他们未能适应和掌握大学自学和治学规律所致，而缺乏阅读研究学术论著的具体方法指导和实践训练，则是其最主要的原因。因此我们这套由8本组成的系列双语教材，即《英美诗歌名篇研读》《欧美散文名篇研读》《欧美小说名篇研读》《西方古典文论要著研读》《西方现当代文论要著研读》《西方比较文学要著研读》《当代欧美汉学要著研读》和《当代西方语言学要著研读》，既有文学作品，又有语言学和文学的理论和研究论著，并同课程设置的主干课程配套。

本书的编写体例和使用方法，由于同一般著作不太一样，因此也须略作说明。在每篇正文之前，均有导读，对作者及其事业专长、主要贡献，对选文的主要内容和价值意义等，以中文予以简要介绍。书中英语正文旁，都有中文的批点：或对原文的论点论旨论据、逻辑论述的层次结构、所用的方法和特点等，予以点评或解释；或对作品的思想观念、艺术魅力、情节结构、感情抒写和写作技巧等，予以评论和赏析，以起导读深究作用。对原文难句、难词的翻译或解释，均放在每页的脚注；而原文的原注也一概附上，以供读者查阅参考。

从20世纪80年代末起，我们先给研究生编选了《比较文学经典要著研读》并讲授此课，后又扩大到本科生的多门课程。十多年来，我们和学生们都感到教学相长，双赢互益。有些高校同行闻讯之后，来人或来函索取。上海教育出版社的领导和编辑，欣然愿意帮助出版，以供教学参考和传播之用。我们在此十分感谢大家的关心与支持，但我们又深知本书还存在诸多不尽如人意的地方，也还有因我们水平所限而难以克服的差错，我们真诚祈望专家学者和广大读者的批评指正。

孙　逊　孙景尧

2009年10月于上海

目 录
Contents

前言
Foreword

　　要为中国读者选一本外国短篇小说集,看似寻常,实则不易。虽然类似的集子几乎随处可得,但细细看来总有不少局限之处。就连最权威的《诺顿短篇小说精粹》也非样板,单单长达几千页,重似厚砖的篇幅已令人却步。事实上,作为一部世界性的经典小说集,不免要照顾方方面面,上下几百年、周围一大片。这样的集子,显然不符合我们的本旨。至于其他的版本,虽各有特点,但也有不尽适用之处。于是,我们试图为这套教材编写一本别有样式的双语小说集,在各个集子的基础上选用篇幅适当,题材广泛,地域、国家众多的短篇小说的精华,汇成一册,与读者共享。

　　作为"大学文科英汉双语教材系列"丛书之一,本书也与其他分册一样,除了正文的英文外,每篇文章都有中文的导读、旁批、难字难句的注释和最后的问题与思考,为具有一定英语水平的大学生与普通读者提供一些阅读上的方便。

　　当然,短篇小说作为文学中最具影响力的一部分,它的魅力不仅仅在语言上,读者欣赏这些故事也不会单纯地停留在内容与情节上。一个训练有素的读者,往往会把文学作品看成一个整体,它可传达的文化编码诸如社会思想意识、艺术技巧、情节结构、心理层次等都是我们需要细细品味的地方。因此,本书如果能让读者得到一些语言上的帮助从而对文学名著产生共鸣,将是值得庆幸的。一个例子是,一位大三中文系的学生对美国作家辛格的短篇小说《市场街的斯宾诺莎》被各种小说集和文学教材所选中表示不解。这样一个不温不火的故事和一位年近古稀的老学究,他的故事何以打动了亿万读者?通过双语教材中的导读与脚注,这位同学反复阅读了原著,终于尝到了经典名作所带来的狂喜:这位终日沉溺于斯宾诺莎伦理学中的老博士最后从冰冷的生活中挣扎出来而给人启示多多。显然,这不仅仅是对一部作品的认识,更重要的是他找到了一种阅读的方式与门径。

　　参与本书选编的有任菊秀博士、俞曦霞博士,博士生贺江、王刚以及复旦大学的研究生江雨斯、吴雨穹等人,在此一并感谢。

黄铁池　孙　建

2014 年 6 月

A Hunger Artist

饥饿艺术家

卡夫卡

【导读】

弗兰茨·卡夫卡(Franz Kafka,1883—1924),奥地利小说家,西方现代主义文学奠基者之一。卡夫卡成功地掌握了现代语言艺术,革新了文学观念,后世的许多现代主义文学流派,如"荒诞派戏剧"、法国的"新小说"等都把卡夫卡奉为自己的鼻祖。

卡夫卡1883年生于布拉格,他的父母均为犹太血统。父亲是一间妇女用品商店的店主,从小对他进行严厉的管教。1901年卡夫卡读完高级文科中学,进入布拉格德语大学攻读法律,1906年取得法学博士学位。实习一年后,他进入布拉格劳动事故保险公司任职,直到1922年病退为止。1924年卡夫卡卒于维也纳附近的基尔疗养院。

从中学起,卡夫卡就喜欢阅读斯宾诺莎(Benedictus Spinoza)、尼采(Friedrich Wilhelm Nietzsche)、达尔文(Charles Robert Darwin)、豪普特曼(Gerhart Hauptmann)、易卜生(Henrik Johan Ibsen)等一些欧洲近现代的哲学家和文学家的作品。上大学后,他对德国戏剧家赫贝尔(Hebbel)、克莱斯特(Kleist),奥地利的诗人霍夫曼斯塔尔(Hofmannstahl, Hugo Von)等感兴趣。1902年,他认识了马克斯·布罗德(Max Brod),并在其鼓励下从事写作。卡夫卡终身未婚。

从1902年至1912年,是卡夫卡的早期写作时期,只有一本散文小说集《观察》,共收18篇作品,以及一个未完成的长篇《乡村婚事》。1912年是卡夫卡创作的高潮期,成名作和代表作《变形记》(*Metamorphosis*)和《判决》都是在这一年问世的。1912年至逝世前,他写出了许多短篇,如《司炉》(1913)、《在流放地》(*In the Penal Colony*,1914)、《为某科学院写的一份报告》(1917)、《乡村医生》(1919)、《饥饿艺术家》(*A Hunger Artist*,1922)等。他还写了三部未完成的长篇:《失踪者》(1912—1914)、《审判》(*The Trial*,1914—1918)和《城堡》(*The Castle*,1922)。此外,卡夫卡还写过大量的书信和日记,如《致父亲》(1919)堪称向父辈文化宣战的檄文。他的小说主要运用象征手法,揭示了一种荒诞的充满非理性色彩的景象,并充满了忧郁和孤独的情绪。

中篇小说《变形记》是卡夫卡的成名作和代表作,最能体现"卡夫卡"小说的基本特征:不在真实的摹写中追求再现式的逼真,而是以象征式的表现追求真实中的荒诞、荒诞中的真实。主人公是某公司的旅行推销员格里高尔。一天早晨,他一觉醒来发现自己变成了一只大甲虫。他十分着急,因为他是这个家庭的主要经济支柱。他的变形,引起了父母及妹妹的恐慌。刚开始他们还能照顾他,可是随着日子一天天过去,家里人对他也日渐疏远,渐至十分厌恶。而此时,家庭的经济状况也每况愈下,大家都在为生活忙于奔波。父母空出几间房子租出去,把多余的家具都塞到格里高尔的房间。再后来,房客们发现了他,要求退房。竟连刚开始对他还不错的妹妹也气愤地要把他弄走。绝望的格里高尔在一天晚上,怀着对家人的温柔和爱意,告别了这个世界。格里高尔死后,他的家人迁入新居,很快忘却了那段有格里高尔这只变形虫的不好的岁月,开始了他们新的生活。卡夫卡用意识流的手法和神话象征的模式表现了真实而荒诞的世界,通过人变成大甲虫的荒诞故事,展现了现代人丧失自我,在绝望中挣扎的精神状态。

《饥饿艺术家》是卡夫卡最后一卷小说集的标题小说,小说中饥饿艺术家自愿钻进牢笼,呆在那里,表现他真正的自我。他想让人们承认他是独一无二的艺术家,可是公众先是误解他,后来又怠慢他,不理会他。不过,饥饿艺术家在弥留之际公开告知世人自己的骗局,说他不值得受到赞赏,他只是个畸形人,世界上找不到他可吃的食物。因此,除了忍饥挨饿,别无他法。

《饥饿艺术家》是灵与肉的悖缪:饥饿艺术家的艺术达到最高境界之日,就是他的生命消失之时。卡夫卡用他那"圣经式"的笔法以及现实主义的表现手法展现了一个艺术家的生存境遇和人生的荒诞。

A Hunger Artist

Translated by Willa and Edwin Muir

During these last decades the interest in professional fasting① has markedly diminished②. It used to pay very well to stage such great performances under one's own management, but today that is quite impossible. We live in a different world now. At one time the whole town

---

① fasting:禁食。
② diminished:淡薄,冷落。

took a lively① interest in the hunger artist; from day to day of his fast the excitement mounted; everybody wanted to see him at least once a day; there were people who bought season② tickets for the last few days and sat from morning till night in front of his small barred③ cage; even in the nighttime there were visiting hours, when the whole effect was heightened by torch flares; on fine days the cage was set out in the open air, and then it was the children's special treat④ to see the hunger artist; for their elders he was often just a joke that happened to be in fashion, but the children stood open-mouthed, holding each other's hands for greater security, marveling⑤ at him as he sat there pallid⑥ in black tights, with his ribs sticking out so prominently, not even on a seat but down among straw on the ground, sometimes giving a courteous⑦ nod, answering questions with a constrained smile or perhaps stretching an arm through the bars so that one might feel how thin it was, and then again withdrawing deep into himself, paying no attention to anyone or anything, not even to the all-important striking of the clock that was the only piece of furniture in his cage, but merely staring into vacancy with half-shut eyes, now and then taking a sip from a tiny glass of water to moisten⑧ his lips.

Besides casual onlookers there were also relays of permanent watchers selected by the public, usually

即使是在夜间观众也络绎不绝,在火把的照耀下,别有一番情趣;用来说明当时饥饿艺术家的表演非常轰动。

大人们看主要是图个消遣、追赶时髦。可孩子们截然不同,他们看到这位身穿黑色紧身衣,脸色异常苍白,全身瘦骨嶙峋的饥饿艺术家时神情紧张,目瞪口呆。为了壮胆,他们相互牵着手,饥饿艺术家甚至连椅子都不屑一顾,只是一屁股坐到铺在笼子里的干草上。

任何人对他都变得不复存在,连笼子里那个对他至关重要的钟鸣(笼子里唯一的陈设就是时钟)他也充耳不闻,只是那双几乎紧闭的双眼茫然地望着前方出神。

---

① lively：强烈的。
② season：长期的。
③ barred：铁栅栏的,上了栓的。
④ treat：对待,看法。
⑤ marvel：惊叹。
⑥ pallid：苍白的,病态的。
⑦ courteous：礼貌的。
⑧ moisten：弄湿,滋润。

有些值夜班的看守就很马虎，他们坐在远离饥饿艺术家的某个角落里埋头玩牌，故意给他一个进食的机会。他们总认为，饥饿艺术家绝对有妙招搞点存货填填肚子。碰到这样的看守，饥饿艺术家真是苦不堪言。这里饥饿艺术家对不相信他的那些看守的肤浅做法感到无法忍受。

butchers, strangely enough, and it was their task to watch the hunger artist day and night, three of them at a time, in case he should have some secret recourse① to nourishment②. This was nothing but a formality, instigated to reassure the masses③, for the initiates④ knew well enough that during his fast the artist would never in any circumstances, not even under forcible compulsion, swallow the smallest morsel⑤ of food; the honor of his profession forbade it. Not every watcher, of course, was capable of understanding this, there were often groups of night watchers who were very lax⑥ in carrying out their duties and deliberately huddled together in a retired corner to play cards with great absorption, obviously intending to give the hunger artist the chance of a little refreshment, which they supposed he would draw from some private hoard⑦. Nothing annoyed the artist more than these watchers; they made him miserable; they made his fast seem unendurable; sometimes he mastered his feebleness sufficiently to sing during their watch for as long as he could keep going, to show them how unjust⑧ their suspicions were. But that was of little use; they only wondered at his cleverness in being able to fill his mouth even while singing. Much more to his taste were the watchers who sat close up to the bars, who were not content with the dim night lighting of the hall but focused him in the full glare of the electric pocket torch given

---

① recourse：求助。
② nourishment：进食。
③ a formality, instigated to reassure the masses：让群众安心的一种形式。
④ initiates：内行，行家。
⑤ morsel：（尤其指食物）小块。
⑥ lax：松懈的。
⑦ hoard：储藏。
⑧ unjust：冤枉，不公平。

them by the impresario①. The harsh light did not trouble him at all，in any case he could never sleep properly，and he could always drowse a little②，whatever the light，at any hour，even when the hall was thronged③ with noisy onlookers. He was quite happy at the prospect of spending a sleepless night with such watchers; he was ready to exchange jokes with them，to tell them stories out of his nomadic④ life，anything at all to keep them awake and demonstrate to them again that he had no eatables in his cage and that he was fasting as not one of them could fast⑤. But his happiest moment was when the morning came and an enormous breakfast was brought for them，at his expense，on which they flung themselves with the keen appetite of healthy men after a weary night of wakefulness. Of course there were people who argued that this breakfast was an unfair attempt to bribe⑥ the watchers，but that was going rather too far⑦，and when they were invited to take on a night's vigil⑧ without a breakfast，merely for the sake of the cause⑨，they made themselves scarce，although they stuck stubbornly to their suspicions.

Such suspicions，anyhow，were a necessary accompaniment⑩ to the profession of fasting. No one could possibly watch the hunger artist continuously，day and night，and so no one could produce first-hand

然而他感到最幸福的是，当天亮以后，他掏腰包让人给他们送来丰盛的早餐，看着这些壮汉们在熬了一个通宵以后，以健康人的旺盛食欲狼吞虎咽。这种情景和饥饿艺术家的不用监督就不吃饭形成对比。

---

① impresario：演出经理，主要指意大利等一些国家的歌剧团、乐团等的演出的主办人、导演或指挥。
② drowse a little：打个小盹儿。
③ be thronged with：挤满。
④ nomadic：漂泊生涯的。
⑤ he was fasting as not one of them could fast：他们之中谁也比不上他禁食的本领。
⑥ bribe：行贿。
⑦ going rather too far：太离谱了，无稽之谈。
⑧ vigil：守夜。
⑨ cause：事业。
⑩ necessary accompaniment：不可避免的事情，这里说饥饿艺术家的本领总会受到人们的怀疑。

evidence that the fast had really been rigorous① and continuous; only the artist himself could know that, he was therefore bound to be the sole completely satisfied spectator of his own fast. Yet for other reasons he was never satisfied; it was not perhaps mere fasting that had brought him to such skeleton thinness that many people had regretfully② to keep away from his exhibitions, because the sight of him was too much for them, perhaps it was dissatisfaction with himself that had worn him down. For he alone knew, what no other initiate knew, how easy it was to fast. It was the easiest thing in the world. He made no secret of this③, yet people did not believe him, at the best they set him down as modest④, most of them, however, thought he was out for publicity or else was some kind of cheat who found it easy to fast because he had discovered a way of making it easy, and then had the impudence⑤ to admit the fact, more or less. He had to put up with all that, and in the course of time had got used to it, but his inner dissatisfaction always rankled, and never yet, after any term of fasting — this must be granted to his credit — had he left the cage of his own free will. The longest period of fasting was fixed by his impresario at forty days, beyond that term he was not allowed to go, not even in great cities, and there was good reason for it, too. Experience had proved that for about forty days the interest of the public could be stimulated⑥ by a steadily increasing pressure of advertisement, but after that the town began to lose interest, sympathetic

点出饥饿艺术家执着于饥饿表演的真实原因：并非因为饥饿是最容易的事情，而是因为对于自己的不满，对现状的不满，而这种不满最终导致他瘦骨嶙峋。

而他又那么厚颜无耻，居然遮遮掩掩地说出断绝饮食是易如反掌的事情。这一切流言蜚语他都得忍下去，他对此已经习以为常。但在他的内心，这种不满意始终折磨着他，每逢饥饿表演期满，他没有一次是自觉自愿地离开笼子的。

---

① rigorous：严格意义上的，一点漏洞也没有。
② regretfully：懊悔地，遗憾地，惋惜地。
③ He made no secret of this：他自己对此直言不讳。
④ at the best they set him down as modest：善意的说法是说他谦虚。
⑤ impudence：厚颜无耻。
⑥ stimulate：激发。

support began notably to fall off; there were of course local variations① as between one town and another or one country and another, but as a general rule forty days marked the limit. So on the fortieth day the flower-bedecked② cage was opened, enthusiastic spectators filled the hall, a military band played, two doctors entered the cage to measure the results of the fast, which were announced through a megaphone③, and finally two young ladies appeared, blissful④ at having been selected for the honor, to help the hunger artist down the few steps leading to a small table on which was spread a carefully chosen invalid repast⑤. And at this very moment the artist always turned stubborn. True, he would entrust his bony⑥ arms to the outstretched helping hands of the ladies bending over him, but stand up he would not. Why stop fasting at this particular moment, after forty days of it? He had held out for a long time, an illimitably long time, why stop now, when he was in his best fasting form, or rather, not yet quite in his best fasting form? Why should he be cheated of the fame he would get for fasting longer, for being not only the record hunger artist of all time, which presumably he was already, but for beating his own record by a performance beyond human imagination, since he felt that there were no limits to his capacity for fasting? His public pretended to admire him so much, why should it have so little patience with him; if he could endure fasting longer, why shouldn't the public endure it? Besides, he was tired, he was comfortable sitting in the

写出饥饿艺术家在饥饿表演四十天到期时不得不被阻止时的心理感受。他觉得还不够，还不能体现他的最佳表演。

---

① variations：区别。
② flower-bedecked：四周插满鲜花。
③ megaphone：扩音器。
④ blissful：有幸的，幸运的。
⑤ invalid repast：病号饭。
⑥ bony：皮包骨头的。

他抬了下头望了望表面上如此和蔼,事实上却很残酷的两位女士的眼神。这里说女士残酷是因为她们扶着他,让他走到桌前吃饭,而这正好和他的饥饿表演是矛盾的。

于是饥饿艺术家完全任其摆布,他的脑袋耷拉到胸前,就好像它一滚到哪里,就莫名其妙地停住不动了。他的身体已经掏空,他的腿出于自卫的本能紧紧地夹在一起,但两脚擦着地面,仿佛不是脚踏实地。此处把饥饿艺术家经过饥饿表演之后骨瘦如柴的身体状况写得惟妙惟肖。

这里写出了当饥饿

straw, and now he was supposed to lift himself to his full height and go down to a meal the very thought of which gave him a nausea① that only the presence of the ladies kept him from betraying, and even that with an effort. And he looked up into the eyes of the ladies who were apparently so friendly and in reality so cruel, and shook his head, which felt too heavy on its strengthless neck. But then there happened again what always happened. The impresario came forward, without a word — for the band made speech impossible — lifted his arms in the air above the artist, as if inviting Heaven to look down upon this creature here in the straw, this suffering martyr②, which indeed he was, although in quite another sense; grasped him around the emaciated③ waist, with exaggerated caution④, so that the frail⑤ condition he was in might be appreciated; and committed him to the care of the blenching⑥ ladies, not without secretly giving him a shaking so that his legs and body tottered and swayed⑦. The artist now submitted completely; his head lolled on his breast as if it had landed there by chance; his body was hollowed out; his legs in a spasm of self-preservation clung each other at the knees, yet scraped on the ground as if it were not really solid ground, as if they were only trying to find solid ground; and the whole weight of his body, a featherweight after all, relapsed onto one of the ladies, who, looking around for help and panting⑧ a little — this

① nausea:恶心。
② martyr:殉道者。
③ emaciated:细的,消瘦的。
④ exaggerated caution:过分小心翼翼。
⑤ frail:极容易破碎的。
⑥ blenching:苍白的。
⑦ tottered and swayed:左右摇摆不停。
⑧ panting:气喘吁吁。

post of honor was not at all what she had expected it to be — first stretched her neck as far as she could to keep her face at least free from contact with the artist, then finding this impossible, and her more fortunate companion not coming to her aid but merely holding extended in her own trembling hand the little bunch of knucklebones① that was the artist's, to the great delight of the spectators burst into tears and had to be replaced by an attendant who had long been stationed in readiness. Then came the food, a little of which the impresario managed to get between the artist's lips, while he sat in a kind of half-fainting trance②, to the accompaniment③ of cheerful patter④ designed to distract to public's attention for the artist's condition; after that, a toast⑤ was drunk to the public, supposedly prompted by a whisper from the artist in the impresario's ear; the band confirmed it with a mighty flourish⑥, the spectators melted⑦ away, and no one had any cause to be dissatisfied with the proceedings, no one except the hunger artist himself, he only, as always.

So he lived for many years, with small regular intervals of recuperation, in visible glory, honored by the world, yet in spite of that, troubled in spirit, and all the more troubled because no one would take his trouble seriously. What comfort could he possibly need? What more could he possibly wish for? And if some good-

艺术家真的落在她身上的时候,那位庆幸的女士的光荣感和幸运感一下子变得无影无踪,换来的是无尽的苦恼、逃避与挣扎。前后态度变化极大。

就这样:表演,休息,休息,表演,他度过了许多岁月,表面上光彩照人,名扬四海,尽管如此,他的心情常常是阴郁的,并且有增无减,因为没有一个人能够认真地去体察他的心情。

① little bunch of knucklebones:一小把骨头,写出了饥饿艺术家的手直接就是干枯的一小把骨头,没有肉。
② half-fainting trance:近乎昏厥的半眠状态。
③ accompaniment:伴随。
④ patter:行话,顺口溜。
⑤ toast:干杯。
⑥ confirmed it with mighty flourish:起劲的奏乐助兴。
⑦ melted:散去。

他就会勃然大怒，像一只凶猛的野兽吓人地摇晃着栅栏。写出了当饥饿艺术家被说成他的悲伤可能就是因为饥饿的原因时，他那强烈的愤怒。

natured① person, feeling sorry for him, tried to console him by pointing out that his melancholy was probably caused by fasting, it could happen, especially when he had been fasting for some time, that he reacted with an outburst of fury and to the general alarm began to shake the bars of his cage like a wild animal. Yet the impresario had a way of punishing these outbreaks which he rather enjoyed putting into operation. He would apologize publicly for the artist's behavior, which was only to be excused, he admitted, because of the irritability caused by fasting; a condition hardly to be understood by well-fed people; then by natural transition he went on to mention the artist's equally incomprehensible② boast that he could fast for much longer than he was doing; he praised the high ambition, the good will, the great self-denial③ undoubtedly implicit④ in such a statement; and then quite simply countered it by bringing out photographs, which were also on sale to the public, showing the artist on the fortieth day of a fast lying in bed almost dead from exhaustion. This perversion of the truth, familiar to the artist though it was, always unnerved him afresh and proved too much for him. What was a consequence of the premature⑤ ending of his fast was here presented as the cause of it! To fight against this lack of understanding, against a whole world of non-understanding, was impossible. Time and again in good faith he stood by the bars listening to the impresario, but as soon as the photographs appeared he always let go and sank with a

他总是虔诚地、如饥似渴地抓着栅栏，认真地听经理说的每一句话，但当经理展示照片时，他每次都松开栅栏，唉声叹气地坐回到草堆上，刚刚受到抚慰的观众又重新围过来观看他的表演。

---

① good-natured：好心肠的，心地善良的。

② incomprehensive：难以理解的。

③ self-denial：自我否定的。

④ implicit：含蓄的。

⑤ premature：未成熟的。

groan back onto his straw, and the reassured public could once more come close and gaze at him.

A few years later when the witnesses of such scenes called them to mind①, they often failed to understand themselves at all. For meanwhile the aforementioned② change in public interest had set in③; it seemed to happen almost overnight④; there may have been profound causes for it, but who was going to bother about that⑤; at any rate the pampered⑥ hunger artist suddenly found himself deserted on fine day by the amusement seekers⑦, who went streaming past him to other more favored attractions. For the last time the impresario hurried him over half Europe to discover whether the old interest might still survive here and there; all in vain; everywhere, as if by secret agreement, a positive revulsion from professional fasting was in evidence. Of course it could not really have sprung up so suddenly as all that⑧, and many premonitory⑨ symptoms which had not been sufficiently remarked⑩ or suppressed during the rush and glitter of success now came retrospectively⑪ to mind, but it was now too late to take any countermeasures⑫. Fasting would surely come into fashion again at some future date, yet that was no comfort for those living in the present. What, then, was the hunger artist to do? He had

演出经理带着他又一次跋涉了半个欧洲，以便看看是否能在某个地方找回昔日的狂热和兴趣，然而一无所获，好像人们私下达成了某种默契，到处笼罩着厌恶饥饿表演的气氛。这儿写出了曾经流行一时的饥饿艺术表演已经不能再引起大家的兴趣了。

---

① called them to mind：回忆。
② aforementioned：被提及的，前述的。
③ set in：发生。
④ overnight：突其如来的。
⑤ bother about that：深究其原因。
⑥ pampered：饮食过量的。
⑦ amusement seeker：追求娱乐者，喜欢热闹的人。
⑧ it could not really have sprung up so suddenly as all that：冰冻三尺，非一日之寒。
⑨ premonitory：先兆，苗头。
⑩ sufficiently remarked：足够的重视。
⑪ retrospectively：追溯。
⑫ countermeasure：对策。

最终他告别了演出经理——他人生旅途上无与伦比的伙伴,而被一个庞大的马戏团招聘了去,为了避免再受刺激,他甚至连合同都没瞥上一眼。

这里把饥饿艺术家和动物、器具的更新和补充联系在一起,表明这时饥饿艺术家和动物、器具一样,只是人们用来表演的工具,根本没被当成一个人。

这里把饥饿艺术家的雄心勃勃与执着和世人对他的付之一笑作对比,暗示了饥饿艺术家的悲哀。

been applauded by thousands in his time and could hardly come down to showing himself in a street booth① at village fairs②, and as for adopting another profession, he was not only too old for that but too fanatically devoted to fasting③. So he took leave of the impresario, his partner in an unparalleled career, and hired himself to a large circus; in order to spare his own feelings he avoided reading the conditions of his contract.

A large circus with its enormous traffic④ in replacing and recruiting⑤ men, animals, and apparatus⑥ can always find a use for people at any time, even for a hunger artist, provided of course that he does not ask too much, and in this particular case anyhow it was not only the artist who was taken on but his famous and long-known name as well, indeed considering the peculiar nature⑦ of his performance, which was not impaired⑧ by advancing age, it could not be objected that here was an artist past his prime, no longer at the height of his professional skill, seeking a refuge in some quiet corner of a circus; on the contrary, the hunger artist averred⑨ that he could fast as well as ever, which was entirely credible, he even alleged that if he were allowed to fast as he liked, and this was at once promised him without more ado⑩, he could astound⑪ the world by establishing a record never yet

① booth:摊棚。
② fairs:集市,乡村集市。
③ fanatically devoted to fasting:对饥饿表演如痴如狂。
④ traffic:交易市场。
⑤ recruit:招聘。
⑥ apparatus:器具。
⑦ peculiar nature:独特性质。
⑧ impaired:影响。
⑨ averred:宣告,保证。
⑩ ado:费力。
⑪ astound:震撼,震惊。

achieved，a statement that certainly provoked a smile①
among the other professionals，since it left out of account
the change in public opinion②，which the hunger artist in
his zeal conveniently forgot.

He had not，however，actually lost his sense of the
real situation and took it as a matter of course that he and
his cage should be stationed，not in the middle of the ring
as a main attraction，but outside，near the animal cages，
on a site that was after all easily accessible. Large and
gaily③ painted placards④ made a frame for the cage and
announced what was to be seen inside it. When the public
came thronging out in the intervals⑤ to see the animals，
they could hardly avoid passing the hunger artist's cage
and stopping there for a moment，perhaps they might
even have stayed longer，had not those pressing behind
them in the narrow gangway⑥，who did not understand
why they should be held up on their way towards the
excitements of the menagerie⑦，made it impossible for
anyone to stand gazing for any length of time. And that
was the reason why the hunger artist，who had of course
been looking forward to these visiting hours as the main
achievement of his life，began instead to shrink from
them. At first he could hardly wait for the intervals；it
was exhilarating⑧ to watch the crowds come streaming his
way，until only too soon — not even the most obstinate⑨

---

① provoked a smile：付之一笑，一笑置之。
② it left out of account the change in public opinion：和当今的观众趣味不合。
③ gaily：喜气洋洋的，华丽的。
④ placards：广告，宣传画。
⑤ intervals：幕间休息。
⑥ gangway：通道。
⑦ menagerie：野兽(尤其是指在笼子中用于马戏团表演的野兽)。
⑧ exhilarating：欣喜若狂的，令人兴奋的。
⑨ obstinate：顽固不化的，顽固的。

self-deception①, clung to almost consciously, could hold out against the fact — the conviction was borne in upon him that these people, most of them, to judge from their actions, again and again, without exception, were all on their way to the menagerie. And the first sight of them from a distance remained the best. For when they reached his cage he was at once deafened② by the storm of shouting and abuse③ that arose from the two contending factions④, which renewed themselves continuously, of those who wanted to stop and stare at him — he soon began to dislike them more than the others — not out of real interest but only out of obstinate self-assertiveness⑤, and those who wanted to go straight on to the animals. When the first great rush was past, the stragglers came along, and these, whom nothing could have prevented from stopping to look at him as long as they had breath, raced past with long strides, hardly even glancing at him, in their haste to get to the menagerie in time. And all too rarely did it happen that he had a stroke of luck, when some father of a family fetched up before him with his children, pointed a finger at the hunger artist, and explained at length⑥ what the phenomenon meant, telling stories of earlier years when he himself had watched similar but much more thrilling performances, and the children, still rather uncomprehending, since neither inside or outside school had they been sufficiently prepared for this lesson — what did they care about fasting? — yet showed by the brightness of their intent

等到大批人群过去,又有一些人姗姗来迟。他们只要有兴趣在饥饿艺术家面前停留,是不会再有人妨碍他们的了。但这些人为了能及时看到兽场,迈着大步,匆匆走过,甚至连瞥也不瞥一眼。写出了人们对于饥饿艺术家的漠视。

---

① self-deception：自欺欺人。
② deafen：被很大的声音淹没(把……震聋)。
③ abuse：谩骂。
④ factions：派别。
⑤ self-assertiveness：自作主张,坚持己见。
⑥ at length：详细的。

eyes that new and better times might be coming. Perhaps，said the hunger artist to himself many a time，things would be a little better if his cage were set not quite so near the menagerie. That made it too easy for people to make their choice，to say nothing of what he suffered from the stench① of the menagerie，the animals? Restlessness② by night，the carrying past of raw lumps of flesh for the beasts of prey，the roaring at feeding times，depressed him continually. But he did not dare to lodge③ a complaint with the management；after all，he had the animals to thank for the troops of people who passed his cage，among whom there might always be one here and there to take an interest in him，and who could tell where they might seclude him④ if he called attention to his existence and thereby to the fact that，strictly speaking，he was only an impediment⑤ on the way to the menagerie.

A small impediment，to be sure，one that grew steadily less. People grew familiar with the strange idea that they could be expected，in times like these，to take an interest in a hunger artist，and with this familiarity the verdict went out against him. He might fast as much as he could，and he did so；but nothing could save him now，people passed him by. Just try to explain to anyone the art of fasting! Anyone who has no feeling for it cannot be made to understand it. The fine placards grew dirty and illegible⑥，they were torn down；the little notice board showing the number of fast days achieved，which at first was changed carefully every day，had long stayed at the

这里写出人们对一直在表演的饥饿艺术家的冷落。从前赫赫有名的艺术家如今却落到这个下场，让人悲叹。

---

① stench：臭气，恶臭。
② restlessness：闹腾（夜间动物老是不停地闹腾）。
③ lodge：提出申诉。
④ where they might seclude him：谁知道人们将会把他塞到哪个角落。
⑤ impediment：障碍。
⑥ illegible：模糊的，看不清的。

假如有一天，一个游手好闲的家伙，他把笼子上的旧数字奚落一番并说这是骗人的玩意，他的话才是真正的人的冷漠和天生的恶意所能虚构的最愚蠢的谎言，因为饥饿艺术家的劳动是诚恳的，他没有欺骗别人，倒是这个世界欺骗了他。

same figure, for after the first few weeks even this small task seemed pointless to the staff; and so the artist simply fasted on and on, as he had once dreamed of doing, and it was no trouble to him, just as he had always foretold, but no one counted the days, no one, not even the artist himself, knew what records he was already breaking, and his heart became heavy. And when once in a while some leisurely① passer-by stopped, made merry over the old figure on the board and spoke of swindling②, that was in its way the stupidest lie ever invented by indifference and inborn③ malice, since it was not the hunger artist who was cheating, he was working honestly, but the world was cheating him of his reward.

Many more days went by, however, and that too came to an end. An overseer's eye fell on the cage one day and he asked the attendants why this perfectly good cage should be left standing there unused with dirty straw inside it; nobody knew, until one man, helped out by the notice board, remembered about the hunger artist. They poked into the straw with sticks and found him in it. Are you still fasting? Asked the overseer, when on earth do you mean to stop? "Forgive me, everybody," whispered the hunger artist; only the overseer, who had his ear to the bars, understood him. "Of course," said the overseer, and tapped his forehead with a finger to let the attendants know what state the man was in, "we forgive you." "I always wanted you to admire my fasting," said the hunger artist. "We do admire it," said the overseer, affably④.

---

① leisurely：游手好闲的，悠闲的。
② swindling：骗人的玩意。
③ inborn：天生的。
④ affably：迁就的，原词的意思是殷勤的、和蔼的，但是文中暗示他们并不是很赞同饥饿表演，只是看到饥饿艺术家的执着表演不忍心表达自己心中的真实看法。

"But you shouldn't admire it," said the hunger artist. "Well then we don't admire it," said the overseer, "but why shouldn't we admire it?" "Because I have to fast, I can't help it," said the hunger artist. "What a fellow you are," said the overseer, "and why can't you help it?" "Because," said the hunger artist, lifting his head a little and speaking, with his lips pursed, as if for a kiss, right into the overseer's ear, so that no syllable might be lost, "Because I couldn't find the food I liked. If I had found it, believe me, I should have made no fuss and stuffed myself like you or anyone else." These were his last words, but in his dimming eyes remained the firm though no longer proud persuasion that he was still continuing to fast.

"Well, clear this out now①!" said the overseer, and they buried the hunger artist, straw and all. Into the cage they put a young panther②. Even the most insensitive felt it refreshing to see this wild creature leaping around the cage that had so long been dreary③. The panther was all right. The food he liked was brought to him without hesitation by the attendants; he seemed not even to miss his freedom; his noble body, furnished④ almost to the bursting point with all that it needed, seemed to carry freedom around with it too; somewhere in his jaws it seemed to lurk⑤; and the joy of life streamed with such ardent⑥ passion from his throat that for the onlookers it was not easy to stand the shock of it. But they braced⑦

① clear this out now：整理整理吧。
② panther：美洲豹。
③ dreary：闲置很久的。
④ furnished：这里指供应、提供的意思。
⑤ lurk：隐藏。
⑥ ardent：强烈的。
⑦ braced：使自己站稳。

因为我只能挨饿，没有其他办法。这里引出了饥饿艺术家为什么坚持饥饿表演的原因，为说明他是因为没有其他办法才进行饥饿表演做了铺垫。

多么奇怪啊！

因为我找不到适合我胃口的食物，假如我找到这样的食物，请相信我，我不会这样惊动视听，并像你，像大家一样，吃得饱饱的。

themselves，crowded around the cage，and did not ever want to move away.

【思考题】

1. 饥饿艺术家是个怎样的艺术家？小说里为什么称他是一个殉道士？

2. 为什么饥饿表演最终受到观众的冷落？从中反映出观众对待饥饿表演怎样的态度？

3. 从本小说可以看出卡夫卡的作品具有怎样的荒诞派风格？

The Hitchhiking Game

搭车游戏

米兰·昆德拉

【导读】

米兰·昆德拉(Milan Kundera，1929—　　)，捷克小说家，生于捷克布尔诺市的一个中产阶级家庭，父亲是知名钢琴家。昆德拉自幼跟随父亲学习钢琴弹奏，而后到音乐学院接受过正规的音乐创作学习。他的作品也处处透露出音乐对他的影响。少年时代，昆德拉开始广泛阅读世界文学名著。青年时代，写过诗和剧本，画过画，搞过音乐并从事过电影教学。总之，用他自己的话说："我曾在艺术领域里四处摸索，试图找到我的方向。"50 年代初，他作为诗人登上文坛，出版过《人，一座广阔的花园》(1953)、《独白》(1957)以及《最后一个五月》等诗集。但诗歌创作并不是昆德拉的长远追求。1967 年，他的第一部长篇小说《玩笑》在捷克出版，获得巨大成功，从此确定了昆德拉小说创作的发展道路。然而，1968 年苏联入侵捷克，《玩笑》被列为禁书。昆德拉失去了自己当时在电影学院的职务，文学创作也难以进行下去。1975 年，他携妻子离开捷克到法国定居。

移居法国后，他很快便成为法国读者最喜爱的外国作家之一。他的绝大多数作品，如《笑忘录》(1978)、《生命不能承受之轻》(1984)、《不朽》(1990)等都是首先在法国走红，然后才引起世界文坛的瞩目。他曾多次获得国际文学奖，并多次被提名为诺贝尔文学奖的候选人。

除小说外，昆德拉还出版过三本论述小说艺术的文集，其中《小说的艺术》(1986)以及《背叛的遗嘱》(1993)在世界各地流传甚广。

昆德拉原先一直用捷克语进行创作。但近年来，他开始尝试用法语写作，已出版了《缓慢》(1995)和《身份》(1997)两部小说。

在小说人物的塑造上，昆德拉非常重视词语的选择，而不是对人物进行单纯的外貌描写。故事叙述语言简练，节奏流畅，借助电影拍摄的手法，场景切割准确并且留给读者清晰的视觉阅读体验。在《小说的艺术》一书中，昆德拉提到，读者的想象会自然而然地完善作者的视野。作为作者应该抓住故事的核心，外貌甚至人物的内心活动都不能构成理解小说的关键，其核心在于人物性格中某一特殊品质的深化。昆德拉小说创作的这一特点也是他的作品受世界各地的读者广泛追捧的重要原因之一。

昆德拉最负盛名的小说《生命不能承受之轻》以 1968 年苏联入侵捷克,捷克知识分子大量逃亡海外欧洲为背景,讲述了一男两女(托马斯与特丽莎、萨丽娜)情感交织的爱情故事。主人公托马斯原本是布拉格一位出色的外科大夫,他生性轻浮,追求个人精神的绝对自由,有众多的情人,后来对酒吧女招待特丽莎一见钟情,并与她携手走进了自己的第二段婚姻。但是婚后托马斯依然本性难改,到处拈花惹草,这让特丽莎非常痛苦。画家萨丽娜就是托马斯众多情人当中的一个,与托马斯保持着长时间的性关系,托马斯把她当作最理解自己的人,因此招来特丽莎最多的嫉妒。后来战争爆发,在战乱中托马斯丢掉了工作,历经曲折,最后和妻子定居乡下,成了一名卡车司机。妻子本以为从此家庭生活可以走向平静,不料他们的生命也走到了尽头,最终两人双双死于卡车车祸。故事绝不是一个简单的三角性爱故事,而是由三个人爱情的纠缠带出了作者对政治、文化、人类生命的省思和嘲讽。在苏联入侵捷克的时期,民主改革的气息被压榨专政代替,普通知识分子在动荡的社会中命运起伏波折,然而生命之轻也无法阻挡人们对于爱的追求——爱人之爱、朋友之爱、祖国之爱,小说的主人公在面对自己感情生活起起伏伏、悲欢离合的同时,始终坚持的是对民主的追求,反对"媚俗"的坚定信仰,以及对生命意义的寻找。任何欲望之下,每个人对各种类型的爱都有自己选择的权利,爱赋予个人以责任,唯有责任存在,生命的重量才堪比泰山。

本书选文《搭车游戏》选自昆德拉 1969 年出版的短篇小说集《好笑的爱》,故事讲述的是一对年轻情侣在假期驾车出游时,出于不同的目的(女方出于对男友嫉妒的猜疑,男方出于对打破常规生活的渴望),双方不自觉地滑入扮演陌生人的游戏。女孩扮演起在路上想要诱惑司机的搭车女郎,而男孩则扮演开车的司机。女孩在角色扮演时完全释放出了潜藏在心里的放荡诱惑的一面,出于嫉妒,也或许出于天性,但终究在衣裳褪去之后还原了最真实的自己,那个简单、害羞、忠诚的姑娘。而男孩在面对女友扮演的角色时,愤怒不已,他似乎看到了女孩最真实的面目——放荡的,无所顾忌的,这和他以前遇到的女孩子毫无区别,这让他失望,愤怒,同时这种愤怒被转化为了粗暴的肉欲。激情过后,等待他们的是对彼此的失望,还是和好如初,作者为我们留下了想象的空间。

《搭车游戏》体现的主题旨在表现两性关系之间的一种权利斗争,这种斗争是在个人深处的政治和社会环境下必然形成的,并且到最后个人的斗争必然受控于社会环境而以失败告终,在昆德拉的其他作品中也经常体现这样的主题。批评家莫瑞斯对于故事的结局曾给予这样的评价:"故事的最后,男女主人翁意识到在追求自由的过程中他们其实已经陷入自己原本想要逃离的专制,这种专制已经变成了现实政治环境的一面镜子。"昆德拉自己也谈到,现代社会已经变成了极权主义者的暴政和极端的怀疑主义,这两者就像一场搭车游戏,"昆德拉所迷惑的是人类命运的本质……他认为,斯大林主义甚至比法西斯还要危险,因为它已经在慢慢转向自己宣扬的反面:从爱和人性到残暴……"(《新共和国周刊》)。

  故事的另一特点在于昆德拉将其深层次的主题隐喻藏于故事的玩笑、幽默与游戏之中。这也是昆德拉在写作中善于使用的技巧,以反讽手法、幽默的语调描绘人类境况。他的作品表面轻松,实质沉重;表面随意,实质精致;表面通俗,实质充满了人生智慧。

The Hitchhiking Game

I

The needle on the gas gauge① suddenly dipped toward empty and the young driver of the sports car declared that it was maddening how much gas the car ate up. "See that we don't run out of gas again," protested the girl (about twenty-two), and reminded the driver of several places where this had already happened to them. The young man replied that he wasn't worried, because whatever he went through with her had the charm of adventure for him. The girl objected; whenever they had run out of gas on the highway it had, she said, always been an adventure only for her. The young man had hidden and she had had to make ill use of her charms by thumbing a ride② and letting herself be driven to the nearest gas station, then thumbing a ride back with a can of gas. The young man asked the girl whether the drivers who had given her a ride had been unpleasant, since she spoke as if her task had been a hardship. She replied (with awkward flirtatiousness) that some-times they had been very pleasant but that it hadn't done her any good as she had

> eat up: 吃光,耗尽,在这里比喻跑车胃口太大,很耗油。

---

①   gas gauge: 汽油表。
②   thumb a ride: 搭车。

been burdened with the can and had had to leave them before she could get anything going. "Pig," said the young man. The girl protested that she wasn't a pig, but that he really was. God knows how many girls stopped him on the highway, when he was driving the car alone! Still driving, the young man put his arm around the girl's shoulders and kissed her gently on the forehead. He knew that she loved him and that she was jealous. Jealousy isn't a pleasant quality, but if it isn't overdone (and if it's combined with modesty), apart from its inconvenience there's even something touching① about it. At least that's what the young man thought. Because he was only twenty-eight, it seemed to him that he was old and knew everything that a man could know about women. In the girl sitting beside him he valued precisely what, until now, he had met with least in women: purity.

小伙子自认为是情场老手。

The needle was already on empty, when to the fight the young man caught sight of a sign, announcing that the station was a quarter of a mile ahead. The girl hardly had time to say how relieved she was before the young man was signaling left and driving into a space in front of the pumps. However, he had to stop a little way off, because beside the pumps was a huge gasoline truck with a large metal tank and a bulky hose, which was refilling the pumps. "We'll have to wait," said the young man to the girl and got out of the car. "How long will it take?" he shouted to the man in overalls②. "Only a moment," replied the attendant, and the young man said:"I've heard that one before." He wanted to go back and sit in the car, but he saw that the girl had gotten out the other side. "I'll

---

① touching：此处指高兴，令人欢喜的。
② in overalls：身着工装。

take a little walk in the meantime," she said. "Where to?" the young man asked on purpose, wanting to see the girl's embarrassment. He had known her for a year now but she would still get shy in front of him. He enjoyed her moments of shyness, partly because they distinguished her from the women he'd met before, partly because he was aware of the law of universal transience, which made even his girl's shyness a precious thing to him.

指人生短促。

II

The girl really didn't like it when during the trip (the young man would drive for several hours without stopping) she had to ask him to stop for a moment somewhere near a clump of trees. She always got angry when, with feigned surprise, he asked her why he should stop. She knew that her shyness was ridiculous and old-fashioned. Many times at work she had noticed that they laughed at her on account of it and deliberately provoked her. She always got shy in advance at the thought of how she was going to get shy. She often longed to feel free and easy about her body, the way most of the women around her did. She had even invented a special course in self-persuasion: she would repeat to herself that at birth[①] every human being received one out of the millions of available bodies, as one would receive an allotted room out of the millions of rooms in an enormous hotel. Consequently, the body was fortuitous and impersonal, it was only a ready-made, borrowed thing. She would repeat this to herself in different ways, but she could never manage to feel it. This mind-body dualism was alien to her. She was too much one with her body; that is why she always felt such anxiety about it.

小伙子明知故问。

女孩越害怕害羞就越容易害羞。

身体皮肉只是现成的借用之物。

女孩无法将身体和思想统一到一块儿。

---

① at birth：从生下来开始。

23

She experienced this same anxiety even in her relations with the young man，whom she had known for a year and with whom she was happy，perhaps because he never separated her body from her soul and she could live with him wholly. In this unity there was happiness，but fight behind the happiness lurked suspicion，and the girl was full of that①. For instance，it often occurred to her that the other women（those who weren't anxious）were more attractive and more seductive and that the young man，who did not conceal the fact that he knew this kind of woman well，would someday leave her for a woman like that.（True，the young man declared that he'd had enough of② them to last his whole life，but she knew that he was still much younger than he thought.）She wanted him to be completely hers and she to be completely his，but it often seemed to her that the more she tried to give him everything，the more she denied him something：the very thing that a light and superficial love or a flirtation gives to a person. It worried her that she was not able to combine seriousness with lightheartedness.

But now she wasn't worrying and any such thoughts were far from her mind. She felt good. It was the first day of their vacation（of their two-week vacation，about which she had been dreaming for a whole year），the sky was blue（the whole year she had been worrying about whether the sky would really be blue），and he was beside her. At his，"Where to？" she blushed，and left the car without a word. She walked around the gas station，which was situated beside the highway in total isolation，surrounded by fields. About a hundred yards away（in the

女孩觉得可以对小伙子托付终身。

逢场作戏的调情。

---

① be full of that：充分意识到这一点。
② had enough of：对某事感到厌倦，无法再容忍下去。

direction in which they were traveling), a wood began. She set off for① it, vanished behind a little bush, and gave herself up to her good mood. (In solitude it was possible for her to get the greatest enjoyment from the presence of the man she loved. If his presence had been continuous, it would have kept on disappearing. Only when alone was she able to hold on to it.)

When she came out of the wood onto the highway the gas station was visible. The large gasoline truck was already pulling out and the sports car moved forward toward the red turret of the pump. The girl walked on along the highway and only at times looked back to see if the sports car was coming. At last she caught sight of it. She stopped and began to wave at it like a hitchhiker waving at a stranger's car. The sports car slowed down and stopped close to the girl. The young man leaned toward the window, rolled it down, smiled, and asked, "Where are you headed, miss?" "Are you going to Bystritsa?" asked the girl, smiling flirtatiously at him. "Yes, please get in," said the young man, opening the door. The girl got in and the car took off.

III

The young man was always glad when his girl friend was gay. This didn't happen too often; she had a quite tiresome job in an unpleasant environment, many hours of overtime without compensatory leisure and, at home, a sick mother. So she often felt tired. She didn't have either particularly good nerves or self-confidence and easily fell into a state of anxiety and fear. For this reason he welcomed every manifestation of her gaiety with the

女孩从树林中走出,跑车已经加好油,游戏开始。

---

① set off for: 前往。

25

tender solicitude① of a foster parent. He smiled at her and said: "I'm lucky today. I've been driving for five years, but I've never given a ride to such a pretty hitchhiker."

The girl was grateful to the young man for every bit of flattery; she wanted to linger for a moment in its warmth and so she said, "You're very good at lying."

"Do I look like a liar?"

"You look like you enjoy lying to women," said the girl, and into her words there crept unawares a touch of the old anxiety, because she really did believe that her young man enjoyed lying to women. The girl's jealousy often irritated the young man, but this time he could easily overlook it for, after all, her words didn't apply to him but to the unknown driver. And so he just casually inquired, "Does it bother you?"

"If I were going with you, then it would bother me," said the girl and her words contained a subtle, instructive message for the young man; but the end of her sentence applied only to the unknown driver, "but I don't know you, so it doesn't bother me."

"Things about her own man always bother a woman more than things about a stranger" (this was now the young man's subtle, instructive message to the girl), "so seeing that we are strangers, we could get on well together."

The girl purposely didn't want to understand the implied meaning of his message, so she now addressed the unknown driver exclusively:

"What does it matter, since we'll part company in a little while②?"

女孩之前的疑虑爬上心头。

① solicitude：爱怜的担忧情绪。
② part company in a little while：萍水相逢。

26

"Why?" asked the young man.

"Well，I'm getting out at Bystritsa."

"And what if I get out with you?"

At those words the girl looked up at him and found that he looked exactly as she imagined him in her most agonizing hours of jealousy. She was alarmed at how he was flattering her and flirting with her（an unknown hitchhiker），and how becoming it was to him. Therefore she responded with defiant provocativeness，"What would you do with me，I wonder?"

女孩猜测男友对别的搭车者也是这样的腔调。

"I wouldn't have to think too hard about what to do with such a beautiful woman，" said the young man gallantly and at this moment he was once again speaking far more to his own girl than to the figure of the hitchhiker.

But this flattering sentence made the girl feel as if she had caught him at something①，as if she had wheedled② a confession out of him with a fraudulent trick. She felt toward him a brief flash of intense hatred and said，"Aren't you rather too sure of yourself③?"

女孩对男孩轻佻自信的言语很不愉快，接着反唇相讥。

The young man looked at the girl. Her defiant face appeared to him to be completely convulsed. He felt sorry for her and longed for her usual，familiar expression（which he used to call childish and simple）. He leaned toward her，put his arm around her shoulders，and softly spoke the name with which he usually addressed her and with which he now wanted to stop the game.

But the girl released herself and said："You're going a bit too fast!"

---

① catch him at something：抓住把柄。

② wheedled：用甜言蜜语哄骗。

③ Aren't you rather too sure of yourself? 你自我感觉也太好了吧?

At this rebuff① the young man said: "Excuse me, miss," and looked silently in front of him at the highway.

IV

The girl's pitiful jealous, however, left her as quickly as it had come over her. After all, she was sensible and knew perfectly well that all this was merely a game. Now it even struck her as a little ridiculous that she had repulsed her man out of a jealous rage. It wouldn't be pleasant for her if he found out why she had done it. Fortunately women have the miraculous ability to change the meaning of their actions after the event. Using this ability, she decided that she had repulsed him not out of anger but so that she could go on with the game, which, with its whimsicality, so well suited the first day of their vacation.

事后找别的原因来解释自己的行为。

So again she was the hitchhiker, who had just repulsed the overenterprising② driver, but only so as to slow down his conquest and make it more exciting. She half turned toward the young man and said caressingly:

不想让（搭车司机）这么快得手。

"I didn't mean to offend you, mister!"

"Excuse me, I won't touch you again," said the young man.

He was furious with the girl for not listening to him and refusing to be herself when that was what he wanted. And since the girl insisted on continuing in her role, he transferred his anger to the unknown hitchhiker whom she was portraying. And all at once he discovered the character of his own part: he stopped making the gallant remarks with which he had wanted to flatter his girl in a roundabout way③, and began to play the tough guy who

① rebuff：断然回绝。
② overenterprising：胆量过人。
③ roundabout way：拐弯抹角的方式。

treats women to the coarser aspects of his masculinity: willfulness, sarcasm, self-assurance.

男人天性中粗暴的一面：任性、刻薄、狂妄。

This role was a complete contradiction of the young man's habitually solicitous approach to the girl. True, before he had met her, he had in fact behaved roughly rather than gently toward women. But he had never resembled a heartless tough guy, because he had never demonstrated either a particularly strong will or ruthlessness. However, if he did not resemble such a man, nonetheless he had longed to at one time. Of course it was a quite naïve desire, but there it was. Childish desires withstand all the snares of the adult mind and often survive into ripe old age. And this childish desire quickly took advantage of the opportunity to embody itself in the proffered role.

渴望扮演一次粗野的角色。

意为再年长成熟的人也会有幼稚的念头。

小伙子的幼稚念头马上就可以在他现在扮演的角色中得到验证。

The young man's sarcastic reserve① suited the girl very well — it freed her from herself. For she herself was, above all, the epitome of jealousy. The moment she stopped seeing the gallantly seductive young man beside her and saw only his inaccessible face, her jealousy subsided. The girl could forget herself and give herself up to her role.

男友的冷漠反而平息了女孩心中的嫉妒情绪，这也正是她满心期待的男友对于别的搭车女郎的态度。

Her role? What was her role? It was a role out of② trashy literature. The hitchhiker stopped the car not to get a ride, but to seduce the man who was driving the car. She was an artful seductress, cleverly knowing how to use her charms. The girl slipped into this silly, romantic part with an ease③ that astonished her and held her spellbound④.

---

① reserve：想法，念头。
② out of：超越。
③ with an ease：轻易地。
④ spellbound：茫然不知所措。

V

There was nothing the young man missed in his life more than light-heartedness①, The main road of his life was drawn with implacable precision. His job didn't use up merely eight hours a day, it also infiltrated the remaining time with the compulsory boredom of meetings and home study, and, by means of the attentiveness of his countless male and female colleagues, it infiltrated the wretchedly little time he had left for his private life as well. This private life never remained secret and sometimes even became the subject of gossip and public discussion. Even two weeks' vacation didn't give him a feeling of liberation and adventure; the gray shadow of precise planning lay even here. The scarcity of summer accommodations in our country compelled him to book a room in the Tatras six months in advance, and since for that he needed a recommendation from his office, its omnipresent brain thus did not cease knowing about him even for an instant.

循规蹈矩的生活。

平淡琐碎的生活阴影无处不在，让他一刻不得安息。

He had become reconciled to② all this, yet all the same from time to time the terrible thought of the straight road would overcome him — a road along which he was being pursued, where he was visible to everyone, and from which he could not turn aside. At this moment that thought returned to him. Through an odd and brief conjunction of ideas the figurative road③ became identified with the real highway along which he was driving — and this led him suddenly to do a crazy thing.

眼前这条笔直的高速公路跟自己循规蹈矩的思想之路交汇在了一起。

"Where did you say you wanted to go?" he asked the girl.

---

① light-heartedness：轻松自在。
② become reconcile to：甘心接受。
③ figurative road：比喻心灵路程。

"To Banska Bystrita," she replied.

"And what are you going to do there?"

"I have a date there."

"Who with?"

"With a certain gentleman."

The car was just coming to a large crossroads. The driver slowed down so he should read the road signs, then turned off to the right.

"What will happen if you don't arrive for that date?"

"It would be your fault and you would have to take care of me."

"You obviously didn't notice that I turned off in the direction of Nove Zamky."

"Is that true? You've gone crazy!"

"Don't be afraid, I'll take care of you," said the young man.

So they drove and chatted thus the driver and the hitchhiker who did not know each other.

The game all at once went into a higher gear. The sports car was moving away not only from the imaginary goal of Banska Bystritsa, but also from the real goal, toward which it had been heading in the morning: the Tatras and the room that had been booked. Fiction was suddenly making an assault upon real life. The young man was moving away from himself and from the implacable straight road, from which he had never strayed until now.

作者如同导演一般在这里向读者宣布，好戏进行到了下一幕。

小说总是给现实生活以打击。

小伙子偏离的不仅是一成不变的道路，也是自己长期以来循规蹈矩的生活。

VI

When they drove into Nove Zamky it was already getting dark.

The young man had never been here before and it took him a while to orient① himself. Several times he

①　orient：使适应。

stopped the car and asked the passerby directions to the hotel. Several streets had been dug up①, so that the drive to the hotel, even though it was quite close by (as all those who had been asked asserted), necessitated so many detours and roundabout routes that it was almost a quarter of an hour before they finally stopped in front of it. The hotel looked unprepossessing, but it was the only one in town and the young man didn't feel like driving on. So he said to the girl, "Wait here," and got out of the car.

Out of the car he was, of course, himself again. And it was upsetting for him to find himself in the evening somewhere completely different from his intended destination — the more so because no one had forced him to do it and as a matter of fact he hadn't even really wanted to. He blamed himself for this piece of folly, but then became reconciled to it. The room in the Tatras could wait until tomorrow and it wouldn't do any harm of they celebrated the first day of their vacation with something unexpected.

更令他不开心的是……

He walked through the restaurant — smoky, noisy, and crowded — and asked for the reception desk. They sent him to the back of the lobby near the staircase, where behind a glass panel a superannuated blonde was sitting beneath a board full of keys. With difficulty, he obtained the key to the only room left.

The girl, when she found herself alone, also threw off her role. She didn't feel ill-humored, though, at finding herself in an unexpected town. She was so devoted to the young man that she never had doubts about anything he did, and confidently entrusted every moment of her life to him. On the other hand the idea once again

---

① dig up: (路面)翻修。

popped into her mind that perhaps — just as she was now doing — other women had waited for her man in his car, those women whom he met on business trips. But surprisingly enough this idea didn't upset her at all now. In fact, she smiled at the thought of how nice it was that today she was this other woman, this irresponsible, indecent other woman, one of those women of whom she was so jealous. It seemed to her that she was cutting them all out[①], that she had learned how to use their weapons; how to give the young man what until now she had not known how to give him: lightheartedness, shamelessness, and dissoluteness. A curious feeling of satisfaction filled her, because she alone had the ability to be all women and in this way (she alone) could completely captivate her lover and hold his interest.

此时姑娘的嫉妒之心已经不复存在,她觉得自己也拥有其他放荡女人的秘密武器——诱惑的魅力,心中充满了自信。

The young man opened the car door and led the girl into the restaurant. Amid the din, the dirt, and the smoke he found a single, unoccupied table in a corner.

VII

"So how are you going to take care of me now?" asked the girl provocatively.

"What would you like for an aperitif?"

The girl wasn't too fond of alcohol, still she drank a little wine and liked vermouth[②] fairly well. Now, however, she purposely said: "Vodka."

"Fine," said the young man. "I hope you won't get drunk on me."

"And if I do?" said the girl.

The young man did not reply but called over a waiter and ordered two vodkas and two steak dinners. In a

---

① cut them all out：把她们抛到了九霄云外。
② vermouth：苦艾酒。

moment the waiter brought a tray with two small glasses and placed it in front of them.

The man raised his glass, "To you!"

"Can't you think of a wittier toast?"

Something was beginning to irritate him about the girl's game. Now sitting face to face with her, he realized that it wasn't just the words which were turning her into a stranger, but that her whole persona had changed, the movements of her body and her facial expression, and that she unpalatably and faithfully resembled that type of woman whom he knew so well and for whom he felt some aversion.

And so (holding his glass in his raised hand), he corrected his toast: "O. K., then I won't drink to you, but to your kind, in which are combined so successfully the better qualities of the animal and the worse aspects of the human being."

"By 'kind' do you mean all women?" asked the girl.

"No, I mean only those who are like you."

"Anyway it doesn't seem very witty to me to compare a woman with an animal."

"O. K.," the young man was still holding his glass aloft, "then I won't drink to your kind, but to your soul. Agreed? To your soul, which lights up① when it descends from your head into your belly, and which goes out when it rises back up to your head."

The girl raised her glass. "O. K., to my soul, which descends into my belly."

"I'll correct myself once more," said the young man. "To your belly, into which your soul descends."

"To my belly," said the girl, and her belly (now that

---

① lights up: (灵魂)放光。

they had named it specifically), as it were, responded to the call; she felt every inch of it.

Then the waiter brought their steaks and the young man ordered them another vodka and some water (this time they drank to the girl's breasts), and the conversation continued in this peculiar, frivolous tone. It irritated the young man more and more how well able the girl was to become the lascivious miss. If she was able to do it so well, he thought, it meant that she really was like that. After all, no alien soul had entered into her from somewhere in space. What she was acting now was she herself; perhaps it was the part of her being which had formerly been locked up and which the pretext of the game had let out of its cage. Perhaps the girl supposed that by means of the game she was disowning herself, but wasn't it the other way around? Wasn't she becoming herself only through the game? Wasn't she freeing herself through the game? No, opposite him was not sitting a strange woman in his girl's body; it was his girl, herself, no one else. He looked at her and felt growing aversion toward her.

However, it was not only aversion. The more the girl withdrew from him psychically, the more he longed for her physically. The alien quality of her soul drew attention to her body, yes, as a matter of fact it turned her body into a body for him as if until now it had existed for the young man hidden within clouds of compassion, tenderness, concern, love, and emotion, as if it had been lost in these clouds (yes, as if this body had been lost!). It seemed to the young man that today he was seeing his girl's body for the first time.

After her third vodka and soda the girl got up and said flirtatiously, "Excuse me."

杯酒下肚，肚子发热，似乎真的给了她祝酒词一种回应。

小伙子对女友放荡的行为感到厌恶，然而心理上越厌恶，身体的情欲却越强烈。

35

The young man said, "May I ask you where you are going, miss?"

"To piss, if you'll permit me," said the girl and walked off between the tables back toward the plush screen.

VIII

She was pleased with the way she had astounded the young man with this word, which — in spite of all its innocence — he had never heard from her. Nothing seemed to her truer to the character of the woman she was playing than this flirtatious emphasis placed on the word in question①. Yes, she was pleased, she was in the best of moods. The game captivated her. It allowed her to feel what she had not felt till now: a feeling of happy-go-lucky irresponsibility②.

She, who was always uneasy in advance about her every next step, suddenly felt completely relaxed. The alien life in which she had become involved was a life without shame, without biographical specifications③, without past or future, without obligations. It was a life that was extraordinarily free. The girl, as a hitchhiker, could do anything, everything was permitted her. She could say, do, and feel whatever she liked. She walked through the room and was aware that people were watching her from all the tables. It was a new sensation, one she didn't recognize: indecent joy caused by her body. Until now she had never been able to get rid of the fourteen-year-old girl within herself who was ashamed of her breasts and had the disagreeable feeling that she was indecent, because they stuck out from her body and were

她的身体带给别人的非分之想。

---

① the word in question: 谈及的，讨论中的。
② irresponsibility: 逍遥自在，毫无负担的感觉。
③ without biographical specifications: 没有任何档案记载。

visible. Even though she was proud of being pretty and having a good figure, this feeling of pride was always immediately curtailed by shame. She rightly suspected that feminine beauty functioned above all as sexual provocation and she found this distasteful. She longed for her body to relate only to the man she loved. When men stared at her breasts in the street it seemed to her that they were invading a piece of her most secret privacy which should belong only to herself and her lover. But now she was the hitchhiker, the woman without a destiny. In this role she was relieved of the tender bonds of her love and began to be intensely aware of her body. And her body became more aroused the more alien the eyes watching it.

女孩吸引的陌生目光越多,她的身体就越散发出诱惑的魅力。

She was walking past the last table when an intoxicated man, wanting to show off his worldliness, addressed her in French: "Combien, mademoiselle?"

法语,意为多少钱,小姐(彻底把她当成街头卖身的女郎)。

The girl understood. She thrust out her breasts and fully experienced every movement of her hips, then disappeared behind the screen.

IX

It was a curious[1] game. This curiousness was evidenced, for example, in the fact that the young man, even though he himself was playing the unknown driver remarkably well, did not for a moment stop seeing his girl in the hitchhiker. And it was precisely this that was tormenting. He saw his girl seducing a strange man, and had the bitter privilege of being present, of seeing at close quarters[2] how she looked and of hearing what she said when she was cheating on him (when she had cheated on him, when she would cheat on him). He had the paradoxical

充满讽刺意味的一句话,男孩眼睁睁地看着女友与陌生人调情的一举一动,这种滋味痛苦而无奈。

---

① curious: 难以理喻的。
② at close quarters: 接近地。

honor of being himself the pretext of her unfaithfulness.

This was all the worse because he worshipped rather than loved her. It had always seemed to him that her inward nature was real only within the bounds of fidelity and purity, and that beyond these bounds it simply didn't exist. Beyond these bounds she would cease to be herself, as water ceases to be water beyond the boiling point. When he now saw her crossing this horrifying boundary with nonchalant elegance, he was filled with anger.

姑娘扮演这种放荡角色的若无其事更增加了男友的愤怒。

The girl came back from the rest room and complained: "A guy over there asked me: Combien, mademoiselle?"

"You shouldn't be surprised," said the young man, "after all, you look like a whore."

"Do you know that it doesn't bother me in the least?"

"Then you should go with the gentleman!"

"But I have you."

"You can go with him after me. Go and work out something with him."

"I don't find him attractive."

"But in principle you have nothing against it, having several men in one night."

"Why not, if they're good-looking."

"Do you prefer them one after the other or at the same time?"

"Either way," said the girl.

The conversation was proceeding to still greater extremes of rudeness; it shocked the girl slightly but she couldn't protest. Even in a game there lurks a lack of freedom; even a game is a trap for the players. If this had not been a game and they had really been two strangers, the hitchhiker could long ago have taken offense[①] and

---

① take offense：生气。

left. But there's no escape from a game. A team cannot flee from① the playing field before the end of the match, chess pieces cannot desert the chessboard: the boundaries of the playing field are fixed. The girl knew that she had to accept whatever form the game might take, just because it was a game. She knew that the more extreme the game became, the more it would be a game and the more obediently she would have to play it. And it was futile to evoke good sense and warn her dazed soul that she must keep her distance from the game and not take it seriously. Just because it was only a game her soul was not afraid, did not oppose the game, and narcotically sank deeper into it.

The young man called the waiter and paid. Then he got up and said to the girl, "We're going."

"Where to?" The girl feigned surprise.

"Don't ask, just come on," said the young man.

"What sort of way is that to talk to me?"

"The way I talk to whores," said the young man.

X

They went up the badly lit staircase. On the landing below the second② floor a group of intoxicated men was standing near the rest room. The young man caught hold of the girl from behind so that he was holding her breast with his hand. The men by the rest room saw this and began to call out. The girl wanted to break away, but the young man yelled at her: "Keep still!" The men greeted this with general ribaldry and addressed several dirty remarks to the girl. The young man and the girl reached the second floor he opened the door of their room and

---

① flee from: 从……逃出来。
② below the second: 不到第二楼。

switched on the light.

It was a narrow room with two beds, a small table, a chair, and a washbasin. The young man locked the door and turned to the girl. She was standing facing him in a defiant pose with insolent sensuality[1] in her eyes. He looked at her and tried to discover behind her lascivious expression the familiar features which he loved tenderly.

It was as if he were looking at two images through the same lens, at two images superimposed one upon the other with the one showing through the other. These two images showing through each other were telling him that everything was in the girl, that her soul was terrifyingly amorphous, that it held faithfulness and unfaithfulness, treachery and innocence, flirtatiousness and chastity. This disorderly jumble seemed disgusting to him, like the variety to be found in a pile of garbage. Both images continued to show through each other and the young man understood that the girl differed only on the surface from other women, but deep down was the same as they: full of all possible thoughts, feelings, and vices, which justified all his secret misgivings and fits of jealousy. The impression that certain outlines delineated her as an individual was only a delusion to which the other person, the one who was looking, was subject — namely himself. It seemed to him that the girl he loved was a creation of his desire, his thoughts, and his faith and that the real girl now standing in front of him was hopelessly alien, hopelessly ambiguous. He hated her.

"What are you waiting for? Strip," he said.

The girl flirtatiously bent her head and said, "Is it necessary?"

女孩灵魂下潜藏的是令人吃惊的两面性,变化多端,难以揣测。

在小伙子的眼中,女友性格中的杂糅因素似乎是垃圾堆里的腥臊杂物,只叫他感到恶心。

以前在小伙子心中,姑娘的形象是单一而纯粹的。

---

① with insolent sensuality：欲火涌动。

The tone in which she said this seemed to him very familiar; it seemed to him that once long ago some other woman had said this to him, only he no longer knew which one. He longed to humiliate her. Not the hitchhiker, but his own girl. The game merged with life. The game of humiliating the hitchhiker became only a pretext for humiliating his girl. The young man had forgotten that he was playing a game. He simply hated the woman standing in front of him. He stared at her and took a fifty-crown bill from his wallet. He offered it to the girl. "Is that enough?"

游戏进行到现在，已经假戏真做了。

The girl took the fifty crowns and said: "You don't think I'm worth much."

The young man said: "You aren't worth more."

The girl nestled up① against the young man. "You can't get around me like that! You must try a different approach, you must work a little!"

She put her arms around him and moved her mouth toward his. He put his fingers on her mouth and gently pushed her away. He said: "I only kiss women I love."

"And you don't love me?"

"No."

"Whom do you love?"

"What's that got to do with you? Strip!"

XI

She had never undressed like this before. The shyness, the feeling of inner panic, the dizziness, all that she had always felt when undressing in front of the young man (and she couldn't hide in the darkness), all this was gone. She was standing in front of him self-confident, insolent, bathed in light, and astonished at where she had

---

① nestled up: 依偎。

41

all of a sudden discovered the gestures, heretofore① unknown to her, of a slow, provocative striptease. She took in his glances②, slipping off each piece of clothing with a caressing movement and enjoying each individual stage of this exposure.

> 享受衣服一层一层褪去的快感。

But then suddenly she was standing in front of him completely naked and at this moment it flashed through③ her head that now the whole game would end, that, since she had stripped off her clothes, she had also stripped away her dissimulation④, and that being naked meant that she was now herself and the young man ought to come up to her now and make a gesture with which he would wipe out⑤ everything and after which would follow only their most intimate love-making. So she stood naked in front of the young man and at this moment stopped playing the game. She felt embarrassed and on her face appeared the smile, which really belonged to her — a shy and confused smile.

> 恨让他的七情六欲都消失殆尽。

But the young man didn't come to her and didn't end the game. He didn't notice the familiar smile. He saw before him only the beautiful, alien body of his own girl, whom he hated. Hatred cleansed his sensuality of any sentimental coating. She wanted to come to him, but he said: "Stay where you are, I want to have a good look at you." Now he longed only to treat her like a whore. But the young man had never had a whore and the ideas he had about them came from literature and hearsay. So he turned to these ideas and the first thing he recalled was the

---

① heretofore：迄今为止。
② took in his glances：暗送秋波。
③ flash through：掠过，闪过。
④ dissimulation：虚伪的掩饰。
⑤ wipe out：消灭，彻底摧毁。

image of a woman in black underwear (and black stockings) dancing on the shiny top of a piano. In the little hotel room there was no piano, there was only a small table covered with a linen cloth leaning against the wall. He ordered the girl to climb up on it. The girl made a pleading gesture, but the young man said, "You've been paid."

When she saw the look of unshakable obsession in the young man's eyes, she tried to go on with the game, even though she no longer could and no longer knew how. With tears in her eyes she climbed onto the table. The top was scarcely three feet square and one leg was a little bit shorter than the others so that standing on it the girl felt unsteady.

But the young man was pleased with the naked figure, now towering above① him, and the girl's shy insecurity merely inflamed his imperiousness. He wanted to see her body in all positions and from all sides, as he imagined other men had seen it and would see it. He was vulgar and lascivious. He used words that she had never heard from him in her life. She wanted to refuse, she wanted to be released from the game. She called him by his first name, but he immediately yelled at her that she had no fight to address him so intimately. And so eventually in confusion and on the verge of tears, she obeyed, and bent forward and squatted according to the young man's wishes, saluted, and then wiggled her hips as she did the Twist② for him. During a slightly more violent movement, when the cloth slipped beneath her feet and she nearly fell, the young man caught her and dragged her to the bed.

---

① tower above：远远高出。
② Twist：摇摆舞。

He had intercourse with her. She was glad that at least now finally the unfortunate game would end and they would again be the two people they had been before and would love each other. She wanted to press her mouth against his. But the young man pushed her head away and repeated that he only kissed women he loved. She burst into loud sobs. But she wasn't even allowed to cry, because the young man's furious passion gradually won over her body, which then silenced the complaint of her soul. On the bed there were soon two bodies in perfect harmony, two sensual bodies, alien to each other. This was exactly what the girl had most dreaded all her life and had scrupulously avoided till now: love-making without emotion or love. She knew that she had crossed the forbidden boundary, but she proceeded across it without objections and as a full participant — only somewhere, far off① in a corner of her consciousness, did she feel horror at the thought that she had never known such pleasure, never so much pleasure as at this moment — beyond the boundary.

角色扮演带来的精神的疏离却给身体带来了前所未有的激情。女孩明白,她已经轻易地跨越了自己的道德边界。

XII

Then it was all over. The young man got up off the girl and, reaching out for the long cord hanging over the bed, switched off the light. He didn't want to see the girl's face. He knew that the game was over, but didn't feel like returning to their customary relationship. He feared this return. He lay beside the girl in the dark in such a way that their bodies would not touch.

After a moment he heard her sobbing quietly. The girl's hand diffidently childishly touched his. It touched, withdrew, then touched again, and then a pleading,

---

① far off: 遥远的。

sobbing voice broke the silence, calling him by his name and saying, "I am me, I am me . . . ."

The young man was silent, he didn't move, and he was aware of the sad emptiness of the girl's assertion, in which the unknown was defined in terms of the same unknown quantity.

小伙子觉得女孩的哭泣包含着空虚,这一切显得莫名其妙。

And the girl soon passed from sobbing to loud crying and went on endlessly repeating this pitiful tautology①: "I am me, I am me, I am me . . . ."

The young man began to call compassion to his aid (he had to call it from afar, because it was nowherenear at hand), so as to be able to calm the girl. There were still thirteen days' vacation before them.

[1969]

游戏结束,男孩和女孩都在激情之后呈现的哀伤忧虑之中慢慢寻回真实的自己。

【思考题】

1. 请从女孩的角色扮演和心理转变的整个过程来分析她本质上究竟是什么样的人?

2. 请从故事恋人关系的转换中思考社会的专制带给人精神的压迫和角色定义的强制性,以及这些影响如何导致最终游戏滑向难以逆转的尴尬境地?

---

① tautology:无谓的重复。

The Guest

不速之客

阿尔贝·加缪

【导读】

阿尔贝·加缪（Albert Camus，1913—1960），法国存在主义哲学家、小说家、戏剧家、评论家，1913 年 11 月 7 日生于阿尔及利亚的蒙多维——法属阿尔及利亚，在北非的贫民窟中度过了艰难的童年。他是 1957 年诺贝尔文学奖得主，二战之后在巴黎从事过记者、剧作家和小说家等多种职业。1942 年的小说处女作《局外人》让他在圈内崭露头角并获得广泛关注。如同他的作品《不速之客》中的主人公一样，加缪在 1940—1942 的两年间在阿尔及利亚做一名教师。在此期间，他加入了法国抵抗组织，积极而秘密地从事抵抗运动直到二战结束。从少年时代起，贫穷与死亡的阴影就与加缪长相伴，这使加缪更能深切地体会人生的荒谬与荒诞，在他的一生中，无论是他的作品还是他的现实人生，都在与荒诞作斗争。戏剧在他一生的创作中占有重要地位。主要剧本有《误会》(1944)、《卡利古拉》(1945)、《戒严》(1948)和《正义》(1949)等。1957 年，他因为"作为一个艺术家和道德家，通过一个存在主义者对世界荒诞性的透视，形象地体现了现代人的道德良知，戏剧性地表现了自由、正义和死亡等有关人类存在的最基本的问题"，被授予诺贝尔文学奖。1960 年，加缪在一次车祸中不幸身亡。

加缪是存在主义哲学流派小说的代表人物，创作特色是用白描手法极其客观地表现人物的一言一行。文笔简洁、明快、朴实，保持传统的优雅笔调和纯正风格。在短暂的创作生涯中，他赢得了远远超过前辈的荣誉。他的哲学及其文学作品对后期的荒诞派戏剧和新小说影响很大。

《不速之客》是加缪作品中具有代表意义的一篇短篇小说，发表于 1957 年，收录在短篇小说集《流放和王国》中。小说主人公达鲁在被迫与一名阿尔及利亚杀人犯一昼夜的相处过程中，始终用自己人道主义的行为方式及态度对待这名罪犯，使之感受到了做人的尊严。达鲁和罪犯都在自己的两难处境中，在身不由己的情况下，进行了自由选择，并承担了自己行为所带来的后果。这样，他们都成了存在主义的英雄，使人性的尊严在荒谬的宇宙中发出夺目的光辉。这篇小说，语言简洁而明晰，用第三人称的视角娓娓道来，看似平淡而自然的叙述中,昭示了主人公进退维谷、犹豫而微妙的心理变化过程,牵动着读者的心。

加缪的存在主义哲学观在这篇小说中有着深刻的体现,在这个荒谬的世界中,很多痛苦和绝望是难以克服的,而达鲁和罪犯都被固有的命运所限制,虽然,他们不能自由地作出人生选择,却一直在逆境中选择对命运进行默默抗争。这是一种积极的态度,号召人们即使在空虚和挫败中也要寻求生存的意义,为自己的尊严和自由呐喊并寻找出路,并且,永远都不放弃生存下去的希望。

The Guest

Translated by Justin O'Brien

The schoolmaster was watching the two men climb toward him. One was on horseback①, the other on foot. They had not yet tackled the abrupt② rise leading to the schoolhouse③ built on the hillside. They were toiling onward, making slow progress in the snow, among the stones, on the vast expanse of the high, deserted plateau④. From time to time the horse stumbled⑤, without hearing anything yet, he could see the breath issuing from the horse's nostrils⑥. One of the men, at least, knew the region. They were following the trace although it had disappeared days ago under a layer of dirty white snow. The schoolmaster calculated that it would take them half an hour to get onto the hill. It was cold; he went back into the school to get a sweater.

He crossed the erupt, frigid⑦ classroom. On the blackboard the four rivers of France, drawn with four

简单一句话,暗示了两人身份的差别。

困顿的环境,艰难的跋涉。

温度之低,可见一斑。

---

① horseback:马背。
② abrupt:陡峭的。
③ schoolhouse:小学或乡村学校的校舍。
④ plateau:高原。
⑤ stumbled:踉跄;蹒跚而行。
⑥ nostrils:鼻孔。
⑦ frigid:极冷的。

different colored chalks, had been flowing toward their estuaries① for the past three days. Snow had suddenly fallen in mid-October after eight months of drought without the transition of rain, and the twenty pupils, more or less, who lived in the villages scattered over the plateau had stopped coming. With fair weather they would return. Daru now heated only the single room that was his lodging, adjoining the classroom and giving also onto the plateau to the east. Like the class windows, his window looked to the south. On that side the school was a few kilometers from the point where the plateau began to slope toward the south. In clear weather could be seen the purple mass of the mountain range where the gap opened onto the desert.

交代了为什么学校如此的冷清——原来，漫长的大雪天阻碍了学生前来上课。

Somewhat warmed, Daru returned to the window from which he had first seen the two men: They were no longer visible. Hence they must have tackled the rise. The sky was not so dark, for the snow had stopped falling during the night. The morning had opened with a dirty light which had scarcely become brighter as the ceiling of clouds lifted. At two in the afternoon it seemed as if the day were merely beginning. But still this was better than those three days when the thick snow was falling amidst unbroken darkness with little gusts of wind that rattled the double door of the classroom. Then Daru had spent long hours in his room, leaving it only to go to the shed and feed the chickens or get some coal. Fortunately the delivery truck from Tadjid, the nearest village to the north, had brought his supplies two days before the blizzard②. It would return in forty-eight hours.

对清晨光景的描写,呈现了一幅乍明还暗的图景。

---

① estuaries：河口。
② blizzard：暴风雪。

Besides, he had enough to resist a siege, for the little room was cluttered with bags of wheat that the administration left as a stock to distribute to those of his pupils whose families had suffered from the drought. Actually they had all been victims because they were all poor. Every day Daru would distribute a ration to the children. They had missed it, he knew, during these bad days. Possibly one of the fathers or big brothers would come this afternoon and he could supply them with grain. It was just a matter of carrying them over to the next harvest. Now shiploads of wheat were arriving from France and the worst was over. But it would be hard to forget that poverty, that army of ragged ghosts wandering in the sunlight, the plateaus burned to a cinder① month after month, the earth shriveled② up little by little, literally scorched, every stone bursting into dust under one's foot. The sheep had died then by thousands and even a few men, here and there, sometimes without anyone's knowing.

In contrast with such poverty, he who lived almost like a monk in his remote schoolhouse nonetheless satisfied with the little he had and with the rough life, had felt like a lord with his whitewashed walls, his narrow couch, his unpainted shelves, his well, and his weekly provision of water and food. And suddenly this snow, without warning, without the foretaste of rain. This is the way the region was, cruel to live in, even without men — who didn't help matters either. But Daru had been born here. Everywhere else, he felt exiled.

He stepped out onto the terrace in front of the

简洁而干净的语言,展示的却是一幅生灵涂炭的残忍景象。

---

① cinder: (煤炭、木头等的)余烬。
② shriveled: (因热力、严寒、干燥、年老等)枯萎,皱缩。

借达鲁之眼描写阿拉伯人的狼狈情状。

细节的描写，于不经意间体现出巴尔杜齐的善良细心。

schoolhouse. The two men were now halfway up the slope. He recognized the horseman as Balducci, the old gendarme① he had known for a long time. Balducci was holding on the end of a rope an Arab who was walking behind him with hands bound and head lowered. The gendarme waved a greeting to which Daru did not reply, lost as he was in contemplation of the Arab dressed in a faded blue jellaba, his feet in sandals② but covered with socks of heavy raw wool, his head surmounted by a narrow, short cheche. They were approaching. Balducci was holding back his horse in order not to hurt the Arab, and the group was advancing slowly.

时刻不忘自己的职责。人物的性格在这些细节间就体现出来了。

Within earshot③, Balducci shouted:"One hour to do the three kilometers from El Ameur!" Daru did not answer. Short and square in his thick sweater, he watched them climb. Not once had the Arab raised his head. "Hello," said Daru when they got up onto the terrace④. "Come and warm Up." Balducci painfully got down from his horse without letting go of the rope. From under his bristling mustache⑤ he smiled at the schoolmaster. His little dark eyes, deep-set under a tanned forehead, and his mouth surrounded with wrinkles made him look attentive⑥ and studious. Dam took the bridle, led the horse to the shed, and came back to the two men, who were now waiting for him in the school. He led them into his room. "I am going to heat up the classroom," he said. "We'll be more comfortable there." When he entered the room again Balducci was on the couch. He had undone the

---

① gendarme：宪兵，警官。
② sandals：凉鞋。
③ earshot：在听力所及范围之内。
④ terrace：露台，平台，屋顶。
⑤ mustache：短而硬的胡子。
⑥ attentive：彬彬有礼的。

rope tying him to the Arab, who had squatted near the stove. His hands still bound, the cheche pushed back on his head, he was looking toward the window. At first Daru noticed only his huge lips, fat, smooth, almost Negroid; yet his nose was straight, his eyes were dark and full of fever. The cheche revealed an obstinate forehead and, under the weathered skin now rather discolored① by the cold, the whole face had a restless and rebellious look that struck Daru when the Arab, turning his face toward him, looked him straight in the eyes. "Go into the other room," said the schoolmaster, "and I'll make you some mint tea." "Thanks," Balducci said. "What a chore! How I long for retirement." And addressing his prisoner in Arabic:"Come on, you." The Arab got up and, slowly, holding his bound wrists in front of him, went into the classroom.

With the tea, Daru brought a chair. But Balducci was already enthroned on the nearest pupil's desk and the Arab had squatted② against the teacher's platform facing the stove, which stood between the desk and the window. When he held out the glass of tea to the prisoner, Daru hesitated at the sight of his bound hands. "He might perhaps be untied." "Sure," said Balducci.

"That was for the trip." He started to get to his feet. But Daru, setting the glass on the floor, had knelt beside the Arab. Without saying anything, the Arab watched him with his feverish③ eyes. Once his hands were free, he rubbed his swollen④ wrists against each other, took the glass of tea, and sucked up the burning liquid in swift little

---

① discolored：变色的，发黑的。
② squatted：蹲坐，蹲姿。
③ feverish：狂热的，兴奋的。
④ swollen：浮肿的，肿胀的。

sips.

"Good," said Daru, "And where are you headed?"

Balducci withdrew his mustache from the tea. "Here, son."

"Odd pupils! And you're spending the night?"

"No. I'm going back to El Ameur. And you will deliver this fellow to Tinguit. He is expected at police headquarters."

Balducci was; looking at Daru with a friendly little smile.

出乎意料，无法拒绝的客人。

"What's this story?" asked the schoolmaster. "Are you pulling my leg?"

"No, son. Those are the orders."

"The orders? I'm not ..." Daru hesitated, not wanting to hurt the old Corsican①. "I mean, that's not my job."

"What! What's the meaning of that? In wartime people do all kinds of jobs."

"Then I'll wait for the declaration of war?"

Balducci nodded.

"O. K. But the orders exist and they concern you too. Things are brewing, it appears. There is talk of a forthcoming revolt. We are mobilized, in a way."

Daru still had his obstinate② look.

"Listen, son," Balducci said. "I like you and you must understand. There's only a dozen of us at El Ameur to patrol throughout the whole territory of a small department and I must get back in a hurry. I was told to hand this guy over to you and return without delay. He couldn't be kept there. His village was beginning to stir;

---

① Corsican：科西嘉人。

② obstinate：顽固的，不屈服的。

they wanted to take him back. You must take him to Tinguit tomorrow before the day is over. Twenty kilometers shouldn't faze① a husky② fellow like you. After that，all will be over. You'll come back to your pupils and your comfortable life."

Behind the wall the horse could be heard snorting③ and pawing the earth. Daru was looking out the window. Decidedly，the weather was clearing and the light was increasing over the snowy plateau. When all the snow was melted④，the sun would take over again and once more would burn the fields of stone. For days，still，the unchanging sky would shed its dry light on the solitary expanse where nothing had any connection with man.

"After all，" he said，turning around toward Balducci，"what did he do?" And，before the gendarme had opened his mouth，he asked："Does he speak French?"

"No，not a word. We had been looking for him for a month，but they were hiding him. He killed his cousin."

"Is he against us?"

"I don't think so. But you can never be sure."

"Why did he kill?"

"A family squabble，I think. One owed the other grain，it seems. It's not at all clear in short，he killed his cousin with a billhook. You know，like a sheep，kreezk!"

Balducci made the gesture of drawing a blade across his throat and the Arab，his attention attracted，watched him with a sort of anxiety. Daru felt a sudden wrath against the man，against all men with their rotten spite，

通过描写对话,巧妙地展示了谈话的艺术,先提出自己的困难,再强调命令不能拒绝,然后恭维对方的能力完成任务不成问题,最后保证回来以后可以继续正常的生活。

---

① faze：折磨,使某人显得狼狈。
② husky：高大强壮的。
③ snorting：喷鼻息。
④ melted：(雪的)融化。

最初的愤怒来得是如此简单，只因为对生命的热爱。

their tireless hates, their blood lust.

But the kettle was singing on the stove. He served Balducci more tea, hesitated, then served the Arab again, who, a second time, drank avidly. His raised arms made the jellaba① fall open and the schoolmaster saw his thin, muscular chest.

"Thanks, kid," Balducci said. "And now, I'm off."

He got up and went toward the Arab, taking a small rope from his pocket.

"What are you doing?" Daru asked dryly.

Balducci, disconcerted, showed him the rope.

"Don't bother."

The old gendarme hesitated. "It's up to you. Of course, you are armed?"

"I have my shotgun②."

"Where?"

"In the trunk."

"You ought have it near your bed."

"Why? I have nothing to fear."

"You're crazy, son. If there's an uprising, no one is safe, we're all in the same boat."

此话昭示了他善恶分明的态度，同时也有自己的原则和判断。

"I'll defend myself, I'll have time to see them coming."

"Balducci began to laugh, then suddenly the mustache covered the white teeth. "You'll have time? O. K. That's just what I was saying. You have always been a little cracked. That's why I like you, my son was like that."

At the same time he took out his revolver③ and put it on the desk.

"Keep it, I don't need two weapons from here to El

---

① jellaba：（阿拉伯人的）连帽宽袍。
② shotgun：猎枪，霰弹枪。
③ revolver：左轮手枪。

Ameur. "

The revolver shone against the black paint of the table. When the gendarme turned toward him, the schoolmaster caught the smell of leather and horseflesh①.

"Listen, Balducci," Daru said suddenly, "every bit of this disgusts me, and first of all your fellow here. But I won't hand him over. Fight, yes, if I have to. But not that. "

The old gendarme stood in front of him and looked at him severely.

"You're being a fool," he said slowly, "I don't like it either. You don't get used to putting a rope on a man even after years of it, and you're even ashamed — yes, ashamed. But you can't let them have their way. "

"I won't hand him over," Daru said again.

"It's an order, son, and I repeat it. "

"That's right. Repeat to them what I've said to you: I won't hand him over. "

Balducci made a visible② effort to reflect. He looked at the Arab and at Daru. At last he decided.

"No, I won't tell them anything. If you want to drop us, go ahead; I'll not denounce③ you. I have an order to deliver the prisoner and I'm doing so. And now you'll just sign this paper for me. "

"There's no need. I'll not deny that you left him with me. "

"Don't be mean with me. I know you'll tell the truth. You're from hereabouts and you are a man. But you must sign, that's the rule. "

Daru opened his drawer, took out a little square

---

① horseflesh：马肉。
② visible：显而易见的。
③ denounce：揭发；告发。

bottle of purple ink, the red wooden penholder with the "sergeant-major"① pen he used for making models of penmanship②, and signed. The gendarme carefully folded the paper and put it into his wallet. Then he moved toward the door.

"I'll see you off," Daru said.

"No," said Balducci. "There's no use being polite. You insulted③ me."

He looked at the Arab, motionless in the same spot, sniffed peevishly④, and turned away toward the door. "Good-bye, son," he said. The door shut behind him. Balducci appeared suddenly outside the window and then disappeared: His footsteps where muffled by the snow. The horse stirred on the other side of the wall and several chickens fluttered in fright. A moment later Balducci reappeared outside the window leading the horse by the bridle. He walked toward the little rise without turning around and disappeared from sight with the horse following him. A big stone could be heard bouncing down. Daru walked back toward the prisoner, who, without stirring, never took his eyes off him. "Wait," the schoolmaster said in Arabic and went toward the bedroom, as he was going through the door, he had a second thought, went to the desk, took the revolver, and stuck it in his pocket. Then, without looking back, he went into his room.

谨慎地收起了武器,达鲁并不是毫无心机的滥好人。

For some time he lay on his couch watching the sky gradually close over, listening to the silence. It was this silence that had seemed painful to him during the first

---

① sergeant-major:"军士长"。
② penmanship:书写,字迹。
③ insulted:侮辱,冒犯。
④ peevishly:急躁地。

days here, after the war. He had requested a post in the little town at the base of the foothills① separating the upper plateaus from the desert. There, rocky walls, green and black to the north, pink and lavender② to the south, marked the frontier of eternal summer. He had been named to a post farther north, on the plateau itself. In the beginning, the solitude and the silence had been hard for him on these wastelands③ peopled only by stones. Occasionally, furrows④ suggested cultivation, but they had been dug to un-cover a certain kind of stone good for building. The only plowing here was to harvest rocks. Elsewhere a thin layer of soil accumulated in the hollows would be scraped out to enrich paltry village gardens. This is the way it was: bare rock covered three quarters of the region. Towns sprang up, flourished, then disappeared; men came by, loved one another or fought bitterly, then died. No one in this desert, neither he nor his guest, mattered. And yet, outside this desert neither of them, Daru knew, could have really lived.

寂静使他不安与痛苦。

When he got up, no noise came from the classroom. He was amazed at the unmixed⑤ joy he derived from the mere thought that the Arab might have fled and that he would be: alone with no decision to make. But the prisoner was there. He had merely stretched out between the stove and the desk. With eyes open, he was staring at the ceiling. In that position, his thick lips were particularly noticeable⑥, giving him a pouting⑦ look.

寓深刻的道理于简单的文字中——生活的艰难恰恰在于枯燥的重复。

---

① foothills：小丘。
② lavender：淡紫色。
③ wastelands：荒原，荒地。
④ furrows：犁沟。
⑤ unmixed：未掺杂的，纯粹的。
⑥ noticeable：显著的，显而易见的。
⑦ pouting：板着脸的，不高兴的。

"Come," said Daru. The Arab got up and followed him. In the bedroom, the schoolmaster pointed to a chair near the table under the window. The Arab sat down without taking his eyes off Daru.

"Are you hungry?"

"Yes," the prisoner said.

Daru set the table for two. He took flour and oil, shaped a cake in a frying-pan, and lighted the little stove that functioned on bottled gas. While the cake was cooking, he went out to the shed to get cheese, eggs, dates, and condensed milk①. When the cake was done he set it on the window sill to cool, heated some condensed milk diluted② with water, and beat up the eggs into an omelette③. In one of his motions he knocked against the revolver stuck in his right pocket. He set the bowl down, went into the classroom, and put the revolver in his desk drawer. When he came back to the room, night was failing. He put on the light and served the Arab. "Eat," he said. The Arab took a piece of the cake, lifted it eagerly to his mouth, and stopped short.

"And you?" he asked.

"After you. I'll eat too."

The thick lips opened slightly. The Arab hesitated, then bit into the cake determinedly.

The meal Over, the Arab looked at the schoolmaster. "Are you the judge?"

"No, I'm simply keeping you until tomorrow."

"Why do you eat with me?"

"I'm hungry."

The Arab fell silent. Daru got up and went out. He

最顺理成章的原因反而是最难以相信的原因。

---

① condensed milk：炼乳，炼奶。
② diluted：稀释，变稀薄。
③ omelette：煎蛋卷，煎蛋饼。

brought back a folding bed from the shed; set it up between the table and the stove, perpen dicular to his own bed. From a large suitcase which, upright in a corner, served as a shelf for papers, he took two blankets and arranged them on the camp bed. Then he stopped, felt useless, and sat down on his bed. There was nothing more to do or to get ready He had to look at this man. He looked at him, therefore, trying to imagine his face bursting with rage. He couldn't do so. He could nothing but the dark yet shining eyes and the animal mouth.

精心准备的食物、床铺,人性的善良在简单的动作中闪耀着光芒。

"Why did you kill him?" he asked in a voice whose hostile tone surprised him.

给我一个宽恕你的理由。

The Arab looked away. "He ran away. I ran after him."

He raised his eyes to Daru and they were full of a sort of woeful interrogation①. "Now what will they do to me?"

"Are you afraid?"

He stiffened②, turning his eyes away.

"Are you sorry?"

The Arab stared at him openmouthed. Obviously he did not understand. Daru's annoyance was growing. At the same time he felt awkward and self-conscious with his big body wedged between the two beds.

"Lie down there," he said impatiently. "That's your bed."

The Arab didn't move. He called to Dana:

"Tell me!"

The schoolmaster looked at him.

---

① interrogation: 疑问,质问。
② stiffened: 变僵硬。

59

"Is the gendarme coming back tomorrow?"

"I don't know."

"Are you coming with us?"

"I don't know. Why?"

The prisoner got up and stretched out on top of the blankets, his feet toward the window. The light from the electric bulb shone straight into his eyes and he closed them at once.

"Why?" Daru repeated, standing beside the bed.

The Arab opened his eyes under the blinding light and looked at him, trying not to blink.

"Come with us," he said.

In the middle of the night, Daru was still not asleep. He had gone to bed after undressing completely; he generally slept naked. But when he suddenly realized that he had nothing on, he hesitated. He felt vulnerable and the temptation① came to him to put his clothes back on. Then he shrugged his shoulders; after all, he wasn't a child and, if need be, he could break his adversary in two. From his bed he could observe him, lying on his back, still motionless with his eyes closed under the harsh② light. When Daru turned out the light, the darkness seemed to coagulate③ all of a sudden. Little by little, the night came back to life in the window where the starless sky was stirring gently. The schoolmaster soon made out the body lying at his feet. The Arab still did not move, but his eyes seemed open. A faint wind was prowling around the schoolhouse. Perhaps it would drive away the clouds and the sun would reappear.

脱下又穿上的，仅仅是衣服么？

---

① temptation：诱惑，引诱。
② harsh：刺目的，刺眼的。
③ coagulate：凝结，凝固。

During the night the wind increased. The hens fluttered① a little and then were silent. The Arab turned over on his side with his back to Daru, who thought he heard him moan. Then he listened for his guest's breathing, become heavier and more regular. He listened to that breath so close to him and mused without being able to go to sleep. In this room where he had been sleeping alone for a year, this presence bothered him. But it bothered him also by imposing on him a sort of brotherhood he knew well but refused to accept in the present circumstances. Men who share the same rooms, soldiers or prisoners, develop a strange alliance② as if, having cast off their armor with their clothing, they fraternized every evening, over and above their differences, in the ancient community of dream and fatigue. But Daru shook himself; he didn't like such musings, and it was essential to sleep.

A little later, however, when the Arab stirred slightly, the schoolmaster was still not asleep. When the prisoner made a second move, he stiffened, on the alert. The Arab was lifting himself slowly on his arms with almost the motion of a sleepwalker③. Seated upright in bed, he waited motionless without turning his head toward Daru, as if he were listening attentively. Daru did not stir; it had just occurred to him that the revolver was still in the drawer of his desk. It was better to act at once. Yet he continued to observe the prisoner, who, with the same slithery④ motion, put his feet on the ground, waited again, then began to stand up slowly. Daru was about to

---

① fluttered: 振翼，拍翅膀。
② alliance: 联盟，同盟。
③ sleepwalker: 梦游者。
④ slithery: 滑溜的。

call out to him when the Arab began to walk, in a quite natural but extraordinary silent way. He was heading toward the door at the end of the room that opened into the shed. He lifted the latch① with precaution and went out, pushing the door behind him but without shutting it. Daru had not stirred. "He is running away," he merely thought. "Good riddance②? Yet he listened attentively. The hens were not fluttering; the guest must be on the plateau. A faint sound of water reached him, and he didn't know what it was until the Arab again stood framed in the doorway, closed the door carefully, and came back to bed without a sound. Then Daru turned his back on him and fell asleep. Still later he seemed, from the depths of his sleep, to hear furtive steps around the schoolhouse. "I'm dreaming! I'm dreaming!" he repeated to himself. And he went on sleeping.

相比较之下，达鲁还是更希望囚犯逃走吧。

When he awoke, the sky was clear; the loose window let in a cold, pure air. The Arab was asleep, hunched up under the blankets now, his mouth open, utterly relaxed. But when Daru shook him, he started dreadfully, staring at Daru with wild eyes as if he had never seen him and such a frightened expression that the schoolmaster stepped back. "Don't be afraid. It's me. You must eat." The Arab nodded and said yes. Calm had returned to his face, but his expression was vacant and listless.

细节描写，是在烘云托月地暗示他之前总是被粗暴地唤醒。

The coffee was ready. They drank it seated together on the folding bed as they munched③ their pieces of the cake. Then Daru led the Arab under the shed and showed him the faucet④ where he washed. He went back into the

---

① latch：门锁。
② riddance：摆脱，清除。
③ munched：津津有味地嚼。
④ faucet：水龙头，旋塞。

room, folded the blankets and the bed, made his own bed and put the room in order. Then he went through the classroom and out onto the terrace. The sun was already rising in the blue sky; a soft bright light was bathing the deserted plateau. On the ridge the snow was melting in spots. The stones were about to reappear. Crouched[①] on the edge of the plateau, the schoolmaster looked at the deserted expanse[②]. He thought of Balducci. He had hurt him, for he had sent him off in a way as if he didn't want to be associated with him. He could hear the gendarme's farewell and, without knowing why, he felt strangely empty and vulnerable. At that moment, from the other side of the schoolhouse, the prisoner coughed. Daru listened to him almost despite himself and then, furious, threw a pebble[③] that whistled through the air before sinking into the snow. That man's stupid crime revolted him, but to hand him over was contrary to honor. Merely thinking of it made him smart with humiliation. And he cursed at one and the same time his own people who had sent him this Arab and the Arab too who had dared to kill and not managed to get away. Daru got up, walked, in a circle on the terrace, waited motionless, and then went back into the schoolhouse.

细腻的描写，道出了他的善良，在意着身边人的感受。

复杂而矛盾的心情。

The Arab, leaning over the cement floor of the shed, was washing his teeth with two fingers. Daru looked at him and said:"Come." He went back into the room ahead of the prisoner. He slipped a hunting-jacket on over his sweater and put on walking-shoes. Standing, he waited until the Arab had put on his cheche and sandals. They went into the classroom and the schoolmaster pointed to

① crouched：蹲伏，蜷伏。
② expanse：广袤，广阔的区域。
③ pebble：鹅卵石。

the exit, saying: "Go ahead." The fellow didn't budge. "I'm coming," said Daru. The Arab went out. Daru went back into the room and made a package of pieces of rusk, dates, and sugar. In the classroom, before going out, he hesitated a second in front of his desk, then crossed the threshold and locked the door. "That's the way," he said. He started toward the east, followed by the prisoner. But, a short distance from the schoolhouse, he thought he heard a slight sound behind them. He retraced his steps and examined the surroundings of the house; there was no one there. The Arab watched him without seeming to understand. "Come on," said Daru.

预示着某些意外的事要发生了。

They walked for an hour and rested beside a sharp peak of limestone①. The snow was melting faster and faster and the sun was drinking up the puddles at once, rapidly cleaning the plateau, which gradually dried and vibrated like the air itself. When they resumed walking, the ground rang under their feet. From time to time a bird rent the space in front of them with a joyful cry. Daru breathed in deeply the fresh morning light. He felt a sort of rapture② before the vast familiar expanse, now almost entirely yellow under its dome③ of blue sky. They walked an hour or more, descending toward the south. They reached a level height made up of crumbly④ rocks. From there on, the plateau sloped down, eastward toward a low plain where there were a few spindly⑤ trees and, to the south, toward outcroppings of rock that gave the landscape a chaotic⑥ look.

---

① limestone: 石灰岩, 石灰石。
② rapture: 痴迷, 狂喜。
③ dome: 穹顶, 圆顶。
④ crumbly: 脆的, 易碎的。
⑤ spindly: 细长的, 纤弱的。
⑥ chaotic: 无序的, 杂乱无章的。

Daru surveyed the two directions. There was nothing but the sky on the horizon. Not a man could be seen. He turned toward the Arab, who was looking at him blankly. Daru held out the package to him. "Take it," he said "There are dates, bread, and sugar. You can hold out for two days. Here are a thousand francs① too." The Arab took the package and the money but kept his full hands at chest level as if he didn't know what to do with what was being given him. "Now look," the schoolmaster said as he pointed in the direction of the east, "there's the way to Tinguit. You have a two-hour walk. At Tinguit you'll find the administration and the police. They are expecting you." The Arab looked toward the east, still holding the package and the money against his chest. Daru took his elbow and turned him rather roughly toward the south. At the foot of the height on which they stood could be seen a faint path. "That's the trail across the plateau. In a day's walk from here you'll find pasturelands and the first nomads. They'll take you in and shelter you according to their law." The Arab had now turned toward Daru and a sort of panic was visible in his expression. "Listen," he said. Daru shook his head, "No, be quiet. Now I'm leaving you." He turned his back on him, took two long steps in the direction of the school, looked hesitantly at the motionless Arab, and started off again. For a few minutes he heard nothing but his own step resounding on the cold ground and did not turn his head. A moment later, however, he turned around. The Arab was still there on the edge of the hill, his arms hanging now, and he was looking at the schoolmaster. Daru felt something rise in his throat. But he swore with impatience, waved

---

① francs：法郎（货币单位）。

65

vaguely, and started off again. He had already gone some distance when he again stopped and looked. There was no longer anyone on the hill.

读者不禁会问,囚犯选择了哪一条路呢?

Daru hesitated. The sun was now rather high in the sky and was beginning to beat down on his head. The schoolmaster retraced his steps, at first somewhat uncertainly, then with decision. When he reached the little hill, he was bathed in sweat. He climbed it as fast as he could and stopped, out of breath, at the top. The rock-fields to the south stood out sharply against the blue sky, but on the plain to the east a steamy heat was already rising. And in that slight haze, Daru, with heavy heart, made out the Arab walking slowly on the road to prison.

答案揭晓。

A little later, standing before the window of the classroom, the schoolmaster was watching the clear light bathing the whole surface of the plateau, but he hardly saw it. Behind him on the blackboard, among the winding French rivers, sprawled the clumsily chalked-up[①] words he had just read: "You handed over our brother. You will pay for this." Daru looked at the sky, the plateau, and, beyond, the invisible lands stretching all the way to the sea. In the vast landscape he had loved so much, he was alone.   [1957]

文章的最后,又一次点题:在这世上,真正善良的人总是孤独和不被理解的。

【思考题】

1. 学校里为什么只有达鲁一个人?

2. 达鲁并不是军人,巴尔杜齐为什么给他下命令?他又为什么难以拒绝?

3. 达鲁对犯人的第一印象是什么?后来又是如何改变的?

4. 小说中多次以细节描写的方式刻画了达鲁的人物性

---

① chalked-up: 记下的,已有的。

格,请试着找出并分析这些细节的意义。

5. 在中国历史上,也曾经有人有与小说中达鲁类似的行为,不过规模可是大多了——放了上百人的囚犯,你知道是谁么?

The Dead

死　者

詹姆斯·乔伊斯

【导读】

　　詹姆斯·乔伊斯(James Joyce，1882—1941)，1882 年 2 月 2 日出生在爱尔兰首都都柏林，被认为是 20 世纪最有影响力的作家之一，其作品对现代小说的创作起着里程碑的作用，最负盛誉的是他的小说《尤利西斯》(1922)，其他主要作品还有短篇小说集《都柏林人》(1916)、小说《青年艺术家画像》(1914)和《芬尼根的守灵夜》(1939)。

　　乔伊斯一生大部分时间都在国外度过，而他童年在爱尔兰生活的经历对他的小说创作产生了深远影响。

　　乔伊斯的父亲是破产的中产阶级，母亲是虔诚的天主教徒。乔伊斯出生的时候，爱尔兰还是英国的殖民地，战乱不断，民不聊生。他有一大群弟弟妹妹，但他父亲偏爱这个才华横溢的长子，他从小就被送进教会学校接受天主教教育，学习成绩出众，并表现出非凡的文学才能。1898 年乔伊斯进入都柏林大学学习语言，特别是英语、法语和意大利语，同时在戏剧和文学圈表现也非常活跃。1903 年从都柏林大学毕业以后，乔伊斯前往法国学习医学，不久因为语言问题而放弃。1904 年，乔伊斯因母亲癌症病危归国，在爱尔兰停留了短暂时间，彻底与天主教决裂，在此期间遇见了他的妻子诺拉。处理完母亲的后事不久，乔伊斯和妻子私奔到欧洲大陆，开始了自行的流亡，而后辗转生活于瑞士、意大利、法国。1941 年 1 月 13 日卒于瑞士苏黎世。其间，曾回爱尔兰停留过短暂时间，但因为对自己国家政治宗教的腐败现状感到失望而很快离开，继续流亡的生活。

　　乔伊斯的文学生涯始于他 1904 年开始创作的短篇小说集《都柏林人》。这本短篇小说集包含的十五个小故事都是描写都柏林呆滞、麻痹的社会现象。这些故事都以主人公的顿悟贯穿始终，这是乔伊斯在创作中独有的写作手法，旨在表现主人公由某一件事情的激发而产生的意识突然觉醒。乔伊斯阐述了这本书的创作原则："我的宗旨是要为我国的道德和精神史写下自己的一章。"这实际上也成了他一生文学追求的目标。在乔伊斯眼中，处于大英帝国和天主教会双重压迫下的爱尔兰是一个不可救药的国家，而都柏林则是它"瘫痪的中心"，在这个城市里麻木苦闷的人们深陷其中,彷徨不安。小说集中的故事人物从青年、仆人、政客,到自负的中产阶级,构成了20世纪初都柏林生活的广阔画面。

詹姆斯·乔伊斯于1904年母亲逝世之后在都柏林开始创作长篇小说《青年艺术家画像》,1914年完稿于意大利的里雅斯特,历时10年。小说有强烈的自传色彩,主要描写都柏林青年斯蒂芬·迪达勒斯童年、少年及青年的心理成长历程,在这个过程中,主人公面临来自各方面的压制——家庭的束缚、宗教传统和狭隘的民族主义,经历过叛逆、流浪、寻找,最终他成功挣脱了妨碍自己发展的这些影响因素,去追求艺术的自我觉醒。小说主人公的原型其实就是乔伊斯自己,青年斯蒂芬对艺术的执着追求就是乔伊斯一生努力奋斗、挣脱束缚、寻求自身解放的精神写照。小说中运用的贯穿始终的写作技巧,例如意识流和内心独白,也被乔伊斯广泛地运用到日后小说的创作当中。

乔伊斯享有盛名的长篇意识流小说《尤利西斯》(1922)讲述了一个平凡的小人物——广告经纪人利奥波德·布卢姆于1904年6月16日这平凡的一天在都柏林的活动记录。小说的题目取自希腊神话中的奥德修斯(其拉丁名为尤利西斯),而《尤利西斯》的内容和结构则借用了荷马史诗《奥德赛》的框架,把布卢姆一天18小时在都柏林的游荡比作奥德修斯10年的海上漂泊,使《尤利西斯》具有了现代史诗的概括性。《尤利西斯》中主要人物有三个,除代表庸人主义的主人公布卢姆外,还有他的妻子,因一直不满意丈夫庸碌无为而到处招蜂引蝶的莫莉以及离家出走寻找自己精神之父的青年斯蒂芬·迪达勒斯(这个人物是《青年艺术家画像》中主人公形象的延续,其形象和经历也与乔伊斯本人有着诸多相似之处)。小说通过这三个人一天的生活,把他们的全部历史、精神生活和内心世界表现得淋漓尽致。故事的结尾,布卢姆和斯蒂芬相遇,他们在彼此身上找到了各自精神上所缺乏的东西,斯蒂芬找到了父亲,布卢姆"找回"了已经夭折的儿子。而妻子在半睡半醒中经历了一系列的思考,决定再给丈夫一次机会,继续他们已经维持了10来年的夫妻生活。

《尤利西斯》的巨大成功让爱尔兰人甚至把小说中故事发生的日期6月16日定为"布卢姆日",该节日后来成为爱尔兰仅次于国庆日(3月17日圣巴特里克节)的大节日。

长篇小说《芬尼根的守灵夜》是乔伊斯最后一部长篇小说,故事以都柏林近郊一家酒店老板以及他的家人(妻子、孩子、母亲)的潜意识和梦幻为线索,是一部用梦幻的语言写成的梦幻的作品。小说完全抛弃了故事情节和人物描写的传统写作手法约束,语言奇特而晦涩,作者把全人类的经验看做支离破碎的片段。文字大量使用双关语、外国语言、自造词汇,并将其与历史、心理和宗教宇宙观的幻象相融合,喻示爱尔兰乃至全人类的历史、全宇宙的运动。

乔伊斯另著有诗集《室内乐集》和剧本《流亡者》等。

本书选用的短篇小说《死者》是小说集《都柏林人》的最后一篇,是全书最长也被认为是最好的一篇。故事讲述的是男主人公加布里埃尔带着自己的妻子格莉塔像往年一样参加姨妈家已经连续举行了30年的周年舞会,时间是在1904年1月的第一周,应该是为庆祝1月6日的主显节。而后全文用近百分之八十的篇幅长篇累牍地描绘了这场舞会的各种细节,从舞会前的准备工作,到客人的陆续到来,再到舞会结束后的用餐情况,直至清晨客人纷纷散去。其中着重描写了加布里埃尔在社会交往过程中的不安全感,以及他为处理自己的社交忧虑用的种种方法。在加布里埃尔和妻子从舞会回到旅馆的途中,文章才峰回路转。妻子因为舞会上听到的一首歌曲而感慨万千,回忆起了多年前伤感的往事,并在旅馆里告诉丈夫在自己心中封存了多时的私密爱情,此时,无论是对妻子还是对丈夫来说,蛰伏多年的情感以这种方式复苏,是意想不到的。听了妻子的故事,加布里埃尔开始反思之前举止可笑的自己,反思结婚多年却似乎并不了解的妻子,反思过去和现在,以及已经逝去的人。主人公的这种顿悟是模糊的,我们无法确知这是主人公瞬间情感的触动还是自此他就能从自己的渺小和不安全感中脱离。

对于小说的题目《死者》,批评家们一直以来对其所指进行着持续的讨论,有些人认为它就是故事中格莉塔死去的初恋情人,另外一些人则认为死者暗指舞会上除加布里埃尔以外的所有人,甚至是所有在麻木中生活的爱尔兰人。结尾部分,主人公觉醒准备开始一次向西的旅行,这既可以和死亡联系起来,也可以说寓意着新生活的开始。同样,结尾对于雪的刻画,像是死亡的帷幕笼罩着整个爱尔兰,又像是宇宙的净化,将它降落之处覆盖的人的心灵予以净化,开启他们新的生活篇章。

The Dead

LILY, the caretaker's daughter, was literally① run off her feet②. Hardly had she brought one gentleman into the little pantry behind the office on the ground floor and helped him off with his overcoat than the wheezy hall-door bell clanged again and she had to scamper along the

---

① literally:简直是,不夸张地。
② run off one's feet:忙得脚不着地。

bare hallway① to let in another guest. It was well for her she had not to attend to the ladies also. But Miss Kate and Miss Julia had thought of that and had converted the bathroom upstairs into a ladies' dressing-room. Miss Kate and Miss Julia were there, gossiping and laughing and fussing②, walking after each other③ to the head of the stairs, peering down over the banisters and calling down to Lily to ask her who had come.

It was always a great affair, the Misses Morkan's annual dance. Everybody who knew them came to it, members of the family, old friends of the family, the members of Julia's choir, any of Kate's pupils that were grown up enough④, and even some of Mary Jane's pupils too. Never once had it fallen flat. For years and years it had gone off⑤ in splendid style⑥, as long as anyone could remember; ever since Kate and Julia, after the death of their brother Pat, had left the house in Stoney Batter and taken Mary Jane, their only niece, to live with them in the dark, gaunt house on Usher's Island, the upper part of which they had rented from Mr. Fulham, the corn-factor⑦ on the ground floor. That was a good thirty years ago if it was a day. Mary Jane, who was then a little girl in short clothes, was now the main prop of the household⑧, for she had the organ in Haddington Road. She had been through the Academy and gave a pupils' concert every year in the upper room of the Antient

舞会没有一次不是
尽欢而散。

整整 30 年了,情况
依旧如此。

---

① bare hallway：空荡荡的过道。
② fussing：没事儿瞎忙。
③ each other：轮番。
④ grow up enough：已经长大成人的学生。
⑤ go off：举行。
⑥ in splendid style：指舞会开办得很成功。
⑦ corn-factor：做粮食生意的人。
⑧ household：家里的台柱。

Concert Rooms. Many of her pupils belonged to the better-class families on the Kingstown and Dalkey line. Old as they were, her aunts also did their share①. Julia, though she was quite grey, was still the leading soprano in Adam and Eve's, and Kate, being too feeble to go about much, gave music lessons to beginners on the old square piano in the back room. Lily, the caretaker's daughter, did housemaid's work for them. Though their life was modest, they believed in eating well; the best of everything: diamond-bone sirloins②, three-shilling tea and the best bottled stout③. But Lily seldom made a mistake in the orders, so that she got on well with her three mistresses. They were fussy, that was all. But the only thing they would not stand was back answers④.

没落中产阶级竭力维持的体面生活,例如精致的晚餐。

Of course, they had good reason to be fussy on such a night. And then it was long after ten o'clock and yet there was no sign of Gabriel and his wife. Besides they were dreadfully afraid that Freddy Malins might turn up screwed⑤. They would not wish for worlds that any of Mary Jane's pupils should see him under the influence; and when he was like that it was sometimes very hard to manage him. Freddy Malins always came late, but they wondered what could be keeping Gabriel, and that was what brought them every two minutes to the banisters to ask Lily had Gabriel or Freddy come.

"O, Mr. Conroy," said Lily to Gabriel when she opened the door for him, "Miss Kate and Miss Julia thought you were never coming. Good-night, Mrs.

---

① did their share: 尽自己的一份力。
② diamond-bone sirloins: 带棱形骨头的牛腰肉。
③ bottled stout: 瓶装黑啤酒。
④ be back answers: 顶嘴。
⑤ screwed: 喝醉酒的,头脑不清醒的。

Conroy."

"I'll engage① they did," said Gabriel, "but they forget that my wife here takes three mortal hours to dress herself."

He stood on the mat, scraping the snow from his galoshes, while Lily led his wife to the foot of the stairs and called out:

"Miss Kate, here's Mrs. Conroy."

Kate and Julia came toddling down the dark stairs at once. Both of them kissed Gabriel's wife, said she must be perished alive②, and asked was Gabriel with her.

"Here I am as right as the mail③, Aunt Kate! Go on up. I'll follow," called out Gabriel from the dark.

He continued scraping his feet vigorously while the three women went upstairs, laughing, to the ladies' dressing-room. A light fringe of snow lay like a cape on the shoulders of his overcoat and like toecaps on the toes of his galoshes; and, as the buttons of his overcoat slipped with a squeaking noise through the snow-stiffened frieze④, a cold, fragrant air from out-of-doors escaped from crevices and folds.

"Is it snowing again, Mr. Conroy?" asked Lily.

She had preceded him into the pantry to help him off with his overcoat. Gabriel smiled at the three syllables she had given his surname and glanced at her. She was a slim; growing girl, pale in complexion and with hay-coloured hair. The gas in the pantry made her look still paler. Gabriel had known her when she was a child and used to sit on the lowest step nursing a rag doll.

---

① engage：肯定，料定，保证。
② be perished alive：活活被冻坏了。
③ as right as the mail：跟邮件一样准时。
④ slipped with a squeaking noise through the snow-stiffened frieze：咯吱咯吱地解开大衣上冻硬的纽扣。

"Yes, Lily," he answered, "and I think we're in for a night of it. ①"

He looked up at the pantry ceiling, which was shaking with the stamping and shuffling of feet on the floor above, listened for a moment to the piano and then glanced at the girl, who was folding his overcoat carefully at the end of a shelf.

"Tell me. Lily," he said in a friendly tone, "do you still go to school?"

"O no, sir," she answered. "I'm done schooling this year and more."

"O, then," said Gabriel gaily, "I suppose we'll be going to your wedding one of these fine days with your young man, eh?"

The girl glanced back at him over her shoulder and said with great bitterness:

"The men that is now is only all palaver and what they can get out of you."

莉莉认为男人都不可靠,会把女人身上能骗走的东西都骗走。

Gabriel coloured, as if he felt he had made a mistake and, without looking at her, kicked off his galoshes and flicked actively with his muffler at his patent-leather shoes.

加布里埃尔在舞会社交中遭遇的第一次尴尬对话,他之后的化解方式也叫人深感诧异。

He was a stout, tallish young man. The high colour② of his cheeks pushed upwards even to his forehead, where it scattered itself in a few formless patches of pale red; and on his hairless face there scintillated restlessly the polished lenses and the bright gilt rims of the glasses which screened③ his delicate and restless eyes. His glossy black hair was parted in the middle and brushed in a long curve behind his ears where it curled slightly beneath the groove

① I think we're in for a night of it: 我看还得下一整夜呢。
② high colour: 血色红润。
③ screened: 遮掩。

left by his hat.

When he had flicked lustre into his shoes he stood up and pulled his waistcoat down more tightly on his plump body. Then he took a coin rapidly from his pocket.

"O Lily," he said, thrusting it into her hands, "it's Christmas-time, isn't it? Just ... here's a little ..."

He walked rapidly towards the door.

"O no, sir!" cried the girl, following him. "Really, sir, I wouldn't take it."

"Christmas-time! Christmas-time!" said Gabriel, almost trotting to the stairs and waving his hand to her in deprecation.

The girl, seeing that he had gained the stairs①, called out after him:

"Well, thank you, sir."

He waited outside the drawing-room door until the waltz should finish, listening to the skirts that swept against it and to the shuffling of feet. He was still discomposed by the girl's bitter and sudden retort. It had cast a gloom over him which he tried to dispel by arranging his cuffs and the bows of his tie. He then took from his waistcoat pocket a little paper and glanced at the headings he had made for his speech. He was undecided about the lines from Robert Browning, for he feared they would be above the heads of his hearers②. Some quotation that they would recognise from Shakespeare or from the Melodies would be better. The indelicate clacking of the men's heels and the shuffling of their soles reminded him that their grade③ of culture differed from his. He would only make himself ridiculous by quoting poetry to them

---

① gained the stairs: 走下楼梯。
② be above the heads of his hearers: 超出听话人的知识水平。
③ grade: 层次,文化等级。

which they could not understand. They would think that he was airing① his superior education. He would fail with② them just as he had failed with the girl in the pantry. He had taken up a wrong tone. His whole speech was a mistake from first to last, an utter failure.

Just then his aunts and his wife came out of the ladies' dressing-room. His aunts were two small, plainly dressed old women. Aunt Julia was an inch or so the taller. Her hair, drawn low over the tops of her ears, was grey; and grey also, with darker shadows, was her large flaccid face. Though she was stout in build③ and stood erect, her slow④ eyes and parted lips gave her the appearance of a woman who did not know where she was or where she was going. Aunt Kate was more vivacious. Her face, healthier than her sister's, was all puckers and creases, like a shrivelled red apple, and her hair, braided in the same old-fashioned way, had not lost its ripe nut colour.

They both kissed Gabriel frankly. He was their favourite nephew the son of their dead elder sister, Ellen, who had married T. J. Conroy of the Port and Docks.

"Gretta tells me you're not going to take a cab back to Monkstown tonight, Gabriel," said Aunt Kate.

"No," said Gabriel, turning to his wife, "we had quite enough of that last year, hadn't we? Don't you remember, Aunt Kate, what a cold Gretta got out of it? Cab windows rattling all the way, and the east wind blowing in after we passed Merrion. Very jolly it was. Gretta caught a dreadful cold."

Aunt Kate frowned severely and nodded her head at

---

① airing: 炫耀。
② fail with: 社交不成功,打交道失败。
③ be stout in build: 体格结实。
④ slow: 形容眼神迟钝。

every word.

"Quite right, Gabriel, quite right," she said. "You can't be too careful①."

"But as for Gretta there," said Gabriel, "she'd walk home in the snow if she were let."

Mrs. Conroy laughed.

"Don't mind him, Aunt Kate," she said. "He's really an awful bother, what with green shades for Tom's eyes at night② and making him do the dumb-bells, and forcing Eva to eat the stirabout③. The poor child! And she simply hates the sight of it④! ... O, but you'll never guess what he makes me wear now!"

She broke out into a peal of laughter and glanced at her husband, whose admiring and happy eyes had been wandering from her dress to her face and hair. The two aunts laughed heartily, too, for Gabriel's solicitude was a standing joke⑤ with them.

加布里埃尔对家人过于细致的关怀。

"Galoshes!" said Mrs. Conroy. "That's the latest. Whenever it's wet underfoot I must put on my galoshes. Tonight even, he wanted me to put them on, but I wouldn't. The next thing he'll buy me will be a diving suit."

Gabriel laughed nervously and patted his tie reassuringly, while Aunt Kate nearly doubled herself⑥, so heartily did she enjoy the joke. The smile soon faded from Aunt Julia's face and her mirthless eyes were directed towards her nephew's face. After a pause she asked:

化解自己社交尴尬的时候,加布里埃尔总是有很多小动作。

"And what are galoshes, Gabriel?"

---

① You can't be too careful. 仔细一点是不会错的。
② for Tom's eyes at night: 为了儿子视力健康。
③ stirabout: 麦片粥。
④ hates the sight of it: 一见(麦片粥)就讨厌。
⑤ standing joke: 常令人发笑的笑料。
⑥ nearly doubled oneself: 笑得都直不起腰来了。

"Galoshes, Julia!" exclaimed her sister. "Goodness me, don't you know what galoshes are? You wear them over your ... over your boots, Gretta, isn't it?"

"Yes," said Mrs. Conroy. "Guttapercha things①. We both have a pair now. Gabriel says everyone wears them on the Continent."

"O, on the Continent," murmured Aunt Julia, nodding her head slowly.

Gabriel knitted his brows and said, as if he were slightly angered:

"It's nothing very wonderful, but Gretta thinks it very funny because she says the word reminds her of Christy Minstrels②."

"But tell me, Gabriel," said Aunt Kate, with brisk tact. "Of course, you've seen about the room. Gretta was saying ..."

"O, the room is all right," replied Gabriel. "I've taken one in the Gresham."

"To be sure," said Aunt Kate, "by far the best thing to do. And the children, Gretta, you're not anxious about them?"

"O, for one night," said Mrs. Conroy. "Besides, Bessie will look after them."

"To be sure," said Aunt Kate again. "What a comfort it is to have a girl like that, one you can depend on! There's that Lily, I'm sure I don't know what has come over her lately. She's not the girl she was at all."

Gabriel was about to ask his aunt some questions on this point, but she broke off③ suddenly to gaze after her

---

① Guttapercha things：古塔胶一类的东西做的。
② Christy Minstrels：克瑞斯蒂剧团：19 世纪美国人乔治·克瑞斯蒂在纽约创办的一种剧团，有白人扮演黑人演唱黑人歌曲，直到 20 世纪初，人们仍习惯称这种剧团为"克瑞斯蒂"剧团。
③ broke off：突然停止。

sister, who had wandered down the stairs and was craning her neck over the banisters.

"Now, I ask you," she said almost testily, "where is Julia going? Julia! Julia! Where are you going?"

Julia, who had gone half way down one flight, came back and announced blandly:

"Here's Freddy."

At the same moment a clapping of hands and a final flourish① of the pianist told that the waltz had ended. The drawing-room door was opened from within and some couples came out. Aunt Kate drew Gabriel aside hurriedly and whispered into his ear:

"Slip down②, Gabriel, like a good fellow and see if he's all right, and don't let him up if he's screwed. I'm sure he's screwed. I'm sure he is."

Gabriel went to the stairs and listened over the banisters. He could hear two persons talking in the pantry. Then he recognised Freddy Malins' laugh. He went down the stairs noisily③.

"It's such a relief," said Aunt Kate to Mrs. Conroy, "that Gabriel is here. I always feel easier in my mind when he's here ... Julia, there's Miss Daly and Miss Power will take some refreshment. Thanks for your beautiful waltz, Miss Daly. It made lovely time."

A tall wizen-faced④ man, with a stiff grizzled moustache and swarthy skin, who was passing out with his partner, said:

"And may we have some refreshment, too, Miss Morkan?"

---

① a final flourish:（演奏）最后一段装饰性的乐章。
② slip down:溜下楼去。
③ noisily:形容脚步很重。
④ wizen-faced:面容干瘪。

"Julia," said Aunt Kate summarily, "and here's Mr. Browne and Miss Furlong. Take them in, Julia, with Miss Daly and Miss Power."

"I'm the man for the ladies," said Mr. Browne, pursing his lips ① until his moustache bristled and smiling in all his wrinkles②. "You know, Miss Morkan, the reason they are so fond of me is —"

He did not finish his sentence, but, seeing that Aunt Kate was out of earshot, at once led the three young ladies into the back room. The middle of the room was occupied by two square tables placed end to end, and on these Aunt Julia and the caretaker were straightening and smoothing a large cloth. On the sideboard were arrayed dishes and plates, and glasses and bundles of knives and forks and spoons. The top of the closed square piano served also as a sideboard for viands and sweets. At a smaller sideboard in one corner two young men were standing, drinking hop-bitters③.

Lead his charges thither, 冲到那边。这是布朗先生向女宾们献殷勤的举动。

Mr. Browne led his charges thither and invited them all, in jest④, to some ladies' punch⑤, hot, strong and sweet. As they said they never took anything strong, he opened three bottles of lemonade for them. Then he asked one of the young men to move aside, and, taking hold of the decanter⑥, filled out for himself a goodly measure of whisky. The young men eyed him respectfully while he took a trial sip.

"God help me," he said, smiling, "it's the doctor's orders."

---

① pursing his lips：噘嘴。
② smiling in all his wrinkles：形容笑得满脸皱纹都出来了。
③ hop-bitters：苦味蛇麻子啤酒。
④ in jest：诙谐地。
⑤ ladies' punch：女宾用的混合甜饮。
⑥ decanter：有玻璃塞的细颈酒瓶。

His wizened face broke into a broader smile, and the three young ladies laughed in musical echo to his pleasantry, swaying their bodies to and fro, with nervous jerks of their shoulders. The boldest said:

"O, now, Mr. Browne, I'm sure the doctor never ordered anything of the kind."

Mr. Browne took another sip of his whisky and said, with sidling mimicry:

"Well, you see, I'm like the famous Mrs. Cassidy, who is reported to have said: 'Now, Mary Grimes, if I don't take it, make me take it, for I feel I want it.'"

His hot face had leaned forward a little too confidentially and he had assumed a very low Dublin accent so that the young ladies, with one instinct, received his speech in silence. Miss Furlong, who was one of Mary Jane's pupils, asked Miss Daly what was the name of the pretty waltz she had played; and Mr. Browne, seeing that he was ignored, turned promptly to the two young men who were more appreciative.

A red-faced young woman, dressed in pansy, came into the room, excitedly clapping her hands and crying:

"Quadrilles①! Quadrilles!"

Close on her heels② came Aunt Kate, crying:

"Two gentlemen and three ladies, Mary Jane!"

"O, here's Mr. Bergin and Mr. Kerrigan," said Mary Jane. "Mr. Kerrigan, will you take Miss Power? Miss Furlong, may I get you a partner, Mr. Bergin. O, that'll just do now."

"Three ladies, Mary Jane," said Aunt Kate.

The two young gentlemen asked the ladies if they

---

① quadrilles：（由四队或四队以上舞伴组成的老式）方阵舞。
② close on her heels：形容凯特姨妈紧跟进来。

might have the pleasure, and Mary Jane turned to Miss Daly.

"O, Miss Daly, you're really awfully good, after playing for the last two dances, but really we're so short of ladies tonight."

"I don't mind in the least①, Miss Morkan."

"But I've a nice partner for you, Mr. Bartell D'Arcy, the tenor. I'll get him to sing later on. All Dublin is raving about him."

"Lovely voice, lovely voice!" said Aunt Kate.

As the piano had twice begun the prelude to the first figure Mary Jane led her recruits quickly from the room. They had hardly gone when Aunt Julia wandered slowly into the room, looking behind her at something.

"What is the matter, Julia?" asked Aunt Kate anxiously. "Who is it?"

Julia, who was carrying in a column of table-napkins, turned to her sister and said, simply, as if the question had surprised her:

"It's only Freddy, Kate, and Gabriel with him."

In fact right behind her Gabriel could be seen piloting② Freddy Malins across the landing. The latter, a young man of about forty, was of Gabriel's size and build, with very round shoulders. His face was fleshy and pallid, touched with colour only at the thick hanging lobes of his ears and at the wide wings of his nose③. He had coarse features④, a blunt nose, a convex and receding brow⑤, tumid and protruded lips. His heavy-lidded eyes and the

---

① I don't mind in the least：一点儿也不介意。

② piloting：带领。

③ His face was fleshy and pallid, touched with colour only at the thick hanging lobes of his ears and at the wide wings of his nose：此句形容弗雷迪面色苍白,只有耳垂和鼻翼上有些血色。

④ coarse features：相貌粗俗。

⑤ a blunt nose, a convex and receding brow：形容弗雷迪额头生得奇怪,凸出又向后缩进。

disorder of his scanty hair made him look sleepy. He was laughing heartily in a high key at a story which he had been telling Gabriel on the stairs and at the same time rubbing the knuckles of his left fist backwards and forwards into his left eye.

弗雷迪的出场，相貌丑陋，一副酒醉的邋遢形象。

"Good-evening, Freddy," said Aunt Julia.

Freddy Malins bade the Misses Morkan good-evening in what seemed an offhand fashion① by reason of the habitual catch in his voice and then, seeing that Mr. Browne was grinning at② him from the sideboard, crossed the room on rather shaky legs and began to repeat in an undertone the story he had just told to Gabriel.

一向说话声音都是嗄声嗄气的。

"He's not so bad, is he?" said Aunt Kate to Gabriel.

Gabriel's brows were dark but he raised them quickly and answered:

"O, no, hardly noticeable."

"Now, isn't he a terrible fellow!" she said. "And his poor mother made him take the pledge③ on New Year's Eve. But come on, Gabriel, into the drawing-room."

Before leaving the room with Gabriel she signalled to Mr. Browne by frowning and shaking her forefinger in warning to and fro. Mr. Browne nodded in answer and, when she had gone, said to Freddy Malins:

"Now, then, Teddy, I'm going to fill you out a good glass of lemonade just to buck you up④."

Freddy Malins, who was nearing the climax of his story, waved the offer aside⑤ impatiently but Mr. Browne, having first called Freddy Malins' attention to a

---

① offhand fashion：态度随意。
② grin at：咧嘴笑。
③ take the pledge：发誓戒酒。
④ buck sb. up：提神。
⑤ waved the offer aside：拒绝提议。

disarray in his dress, filled out and handed him a full glass of lemonade. Freddy Malins' left hand accepted the glass mechanically, his right hand being engaged in the mechanical readjustment of his dress. Mr. Browne, whose face was once more wrinkling with mirth, poured out[①] for himself a glass of whisky while Freddy Malins exploded, before he had well reached the climax of his story, in a kink of high-pitched bronchitic laughter[②] and, setting down his untasted and overflowing glass, began to rub the knuckles of his left fist backwards and forwards into his left eye, repeating words of his last phrase as well as his fit of laughter would allow him.

Gabriel could not listen while Mary Jane was playing her Academy piece, full of runs and difficult passages, to the hushed drawing-room. He liked music but the piece she was playing had no melody for him and he doubted whether it had any melody for the other listeners, though they had begged Mary Jane to play something. Four young men, who had come from the refreshment-room to stand in the doorway at the sound of the piano[③], had gone away quietly in couples after a few minutes. The only persons who seemed to follow the music were Mary Jane herself, her hands racing along the key-board or lifted from it at the pauses like those of a priestess in momentary imprecation, and Aunt Kate standing at her elbow to turn the page.

Gabriel's eyes, irritated by the floor, which glittered with beeswax under the heavy chandelier, wandered to the wall above the piano. A picture of the balcony scene in *Romeo and Juliet* hung there and beside it was a picture

机械地整理衣服。

形容玛丽弹琴停顿时举起的两只手像女术士进行诅咒时的动作。

---

① poured out：倾吐，诉说。
② high-pitched bronchitic laughter：高声的咳嗽般的大笑。
③ at the sound of the piano：意为听到琴声。

of the two murdered princes in the Tower① which Aunt Julia had worked in red, blue and brown wools when she was a girl. Probably in the school they had gone to as girls that kind of work had been taught for one year. His mother had worked for him as a birthday present a waistcoat of purple tabinet②, with little foxes' heads upon it, lined with brown satin and having round mulberry buttons. It was strange that his mother had had no musical talent though Aunt Kate used to call her the brains carrier③ of the Morkan family. Both she and Julia had always seemed a little proud of their serious and matronly sister. Her photograph stood before the pierglass④. She held an open book on her knees and was pointing out something in it to Constantine who, dressed in a man-o-war suit, lay at her feet. It was she who had chosen the name of her sons for she was very sensible of the dignity of family life. Thanks to her, Constantine was now senior curate in Balbrigan⑤ and, thanks to her, Gabriel himself had taken his degree in the Royal University. A shadow passed over his face as he remembered her sullen opposition to his marriage. Some slighting phrases she had used still rankled in his memory; she had once spoken of Gretta as being country cute⑥ and that was not true of Gretta at all. It was Gretta who had nursed her during all her last long illness in their house at Monkstown.

He knew that Mary Jane must be near the end of her piece for she was playing again the opening melody with runs of scales after every bar and while he waited for the

---

① Tower：伦敦古堡是座监狱，理查三世在古堡中杀害了两位王子，详见莎士比亚的《理查三世》。
② purple tabinet：紫色波纹毛葛背心。
③ brains carrier：智囊。
④ pierglass：穿衣镜。
⑤ Balbrigan：巴尔不里干，都柏林郡北部沿海的一个镇名。
⑥ being country cute：乡下人似的做作。

end the resentment died down① in his heart. The piece ended with a trill of octaves in the treble② and a final deep octave in the bass③. Great applause greeted Mary Jane as, blushing and rolling up her music nervously, she escaped from the room. The most vigorous clapping came from the four young men in the doorway who had gone away to the refreshment-room at the beginning of the piece but had come back when the piano had stopped.

Lancers were arranged. Gabriel found himself partnered with Miss Ivors. She was a frank-mannered talkative young lady, with a freckled face and prominent brown eyes. She did not wear a low-cut bodice④ and the large brooch which was fixed in the front of her collar bore on it an Irish device and motto.

When they had taken their places she said abruptly:

"I have a crow to pluck with you⑤."

"With me?" said Gabriel.

She nodded her head gravely.

"What is it?" asked Gabriel, smiling at her solemn manner.

"Who is G. C.?" answered Miss Ivors, turning her eyes upon him.

Gabriel coloured and was about to knit his brows, as if he did not understand, when she said bluntly:

"O, innocent Amy⑥! I have found out that you write for *The Daily Express*. Now, aren't you ashamed of yourself?"

"Why should I be ashamed of myself?" asked

① died down: 消逝。
② treble: 高音部八度颤音。
③ bass: 低音部八度音阶。
④ low-cut bodice: 女式低领紧身胸衣。
⑤ I have a crow to pluck with you: 意为"我有件事情要跟你问明白"。
⑥ innocent Amy: 天真无邪的小姑娘。

Gabriel, blinking his eyes and trying to smile.

"Well, I'm ashamed of you," said Miss Ivors frankly. "To say you'd write for a paper like that. I didn't think you were a West Briton①."

A look of perplexity② appeared on Gabriel's face. It was true that he wrote a literary column every Wednesday in *The Daily Express*, for which he was paid fifteen shillings. But that did not make him a West Briton surely. The books he received for review were almost more welcome than the paltry cheque. He loved to feel the covers and turn over the pages of newly printed books. Nearly every day when his teaching in the college was ended he used to wander down the quays to the second-hand booksellers, to Hickey's on Bachelor's Walk, to Web's or Massey's on Aston's Quay, or to O'Clohissey's in the bystreet. He did not know how to meet③ her charge. He wanted to say that literature was above politics. But they were friends of many years' standing and their careers had been parallel④, first at the University and then as teachers: he could not risk a grandiose phrase⑤ with her. He continued blinking his eyes and trying to smile and murmured lamely that he saw nothing political in writing reviews of books.

性格善良却显得软弱的加布里埃尔面对朋友的指责并不做有力的辩驳。

When their turn to cross had come he was still perplexed and inattentive. Miss Ivors promptly took his hand in a warm grasp and said in a soft friendly tone:

"Of course, I was only joking. Come, we cross now."

---

① West Briton：西布立吞人：古代盎格鲁—撒克逊人入侵以前住在不列颠岛上的凯尔特族人，后被迫退入西部山地，逐渐形成近代威尔士人。故西布立吞人即指威尔士人。此处艾弗丝只是讽刺加布里埃尔的行为不像个爱尔兰人。

② a look of perplexity：困惑的表情。

③ meet：应对，回答。

④ their careers had been parallel：彼此的经历相似。

⑤ grandiose phrase：长篇大论。

When they were together again she spoke of the University question and Gabriel felt more at ease. A friend of hers had shown her his review of Browning's poems. That was how she had found out the secret, but she liked the review immensely. Then she said suddenly:

"O, Mr. Conroy, will you come for an excursion to the Aran Isles① this summer? We're going to stay there a whole month. It will be splendid out in the Atlantic. You ought to come. Mr. Clancy is coming, and Mr. Kilkelly and Kathleen Kearney. It would be splendid for Gretta too if she'd come. She's from Connacht②, isn't she?"

"Her people are," said Gabriel shortly.

> 省略句,意为"她老家是那儿的"。

"But you will come, won't you?" said Miss Ivors, laying her arm hand eagerly on his arm.

"The fact is," said Gabriel, "I have just arranged to go —"

"Go where?" asked Miss Ivors.

"Well, you know, every year I go for a cycling tour with some fellows and so —"

"But where?" asked Miss Ivors.

"Well, we usually go to France or Belgium or perhaps Germany," said Gabriel awkwardly.

"And why do you go to France and Belgium," said Miss Ivors, "instead of visiting your own land?"

"Well," said Gabriel, "it's partly to keep in touch with the languages and partly for a change."

> 这句话似乎道出了常年生活在国外而不愿回爱尔兰定居的作者的心声。

"And haven't you your own language to keep in touch with — Irish?" asked Miss Ivors.

"Well," said Gabriel, "if it comes to that, you know, Irish is not my language."

---

① the Aran Isles:阿兰岛:大西洋中的一个小岛名,在爱尔兰岛东北。
② Connacht:康诺特,爱尔兰的一个省。

Their neighbours had turned to listen to the cross-examination①. Gabriel glanced right and left nervously and tried to keep his good humour under the ordeal which was making a blush invade his forehead②.

"And haven't you your own land to visit," continued Miss Ivors, "that you know nothing of, your own people, and your own country?"

"O, to tell you the truth," retorted Gabriel suddenly, "I'm sick of my own country, sick of it!"

"Why?" asked Miss Ivors.

Gabriel did not answer for his retort had heated him.

"Why?" repeated Miss Ivors.

They had to go visiting together and, as he had not answered her, Miss Ivors said warmly:

"Of course, you've no answer."

Gabriel tried to cover his agitation by taking part in the dance with great energy. He avoided her eyes for he had seen a sour expression on her face. But when they met in the long chain③ he was surprised to feel his hand firmly pressed. She looked at him from under her brows for a moment quizzically until he smiled. Then, just as the chain was about to start again, she stood on tiptoe and whispered into his ear:

"West Briton!"

When the lancers were over Gabriel went away to a remote corner of the room where Freddy Malins' mother was sitting. She was a stout feeble old woman with white hair. Her voice had a catch in it like her son's and she stuttered slightly. She had been told that Freddy had come and that he was nearly all right. Gabriel asked her

终于对责问作出强烈的回应,却没有说出自己的理由,再次选择逃避。

加布里埃尔之前的反驳现在使他感到激动。

---

① cross-examination：盘问。
② make a blush invade his forehead：因为紧张而额头泛起红晕。
③ in the long chain：连成一串的跳舞的人。

whether she had had a good crossing. She lived with her married daughter in Glasgow and came to Dublin on a visit once a year. She answered placidly that she had had a beautiful crossing and that the captain had been most attentive to her. She spoke also of the beautiful house her daughter kept in Glasgow，and of all the friends they had there. While her tongue rambled on① Gabriel tried to banish from② his mind all memory of the unpleasant incident with Miss Ivors. Of course the girl or woman，or whatever she was，was an enthusiast but there was a time for all things. Perhaps he ought not to have answered her like that. But she had no right to call him a West Briton before people，even in joke. She had tried to make him ridiculous before people，heckling③ him and staring at him with her rabbit's eyes.

He saw his wife making her way towards him through the waltzing couples. When she reached him she said into his ear：

"Gabriel. Aunt Kate wants to know won't you carve the goose as usual. Miss Daly will carve the ham and I'll do the pudding."

"All right，" said Gabriel.

"She's sending in the younger ones first as soon as this waltz is over so that we'll have the table to ourselves."

"Were you dancing?" asked Gabriel.

"Of course I was. Didn't you see me? What row④ had you with Molly Ivors?"

"No row. Why? Did she say so?"

"Something like that. I'm trying to get that Mr.

加布里埃尔的心理描写，他还在为刚才与艾弗丝的争论而恼怒，认为无论她是个什么样的人，有些话也不是在任何时候任何场合都能说的。

---

① rambled on：漫谈下去。
② banish from：消除，排除。
③ heckling：激烈质问。
④ row：争吵。

D'Arcy to sing. He's full of conceit①, I think."

"There was no row," said Gabriel moodily, "only she wanted me to go for a trip to the west of Ireland and I said I wouldn't."

His wife clasped her hands excitedly and gave a little jump.

"O, do go, Gabriel," she cried. "I'd love to see Galway again."

"You can go if you like," said Gabriel coldly.

She looked at him for a moment, then turned to Mrs. Malins and said:

"There's a nice husband for you, Mrs. Malins."

While she was threading her way back across② the room Mrs. Malins, without adverting to③ the interruption, went on to tell Gabriel what beautiful places there were in Scotland and beautiful scenery. Her son-in-law brought them every year to the lakes and they used to go fishing. Her son-in-law was a splendid fisher. One day he caught a beautiful big fish and the man in the hotel cooked it for their dinner.

Gabriel hardly heard what she said. Now that supper was coming near he began to think again about his speech and about the quotation. When he saw Freddy Malins coming across the room to visit his mother, Gabriel left the chair free for him and retired into the embrasure of the window. The room had already cleared and from the back room came the clatter of plates and knives. Those who still remained in the drawing room seemed tired of dancing and were conversing quietly in little groups. Gabriel's warm trembling fingers tapped the cold pane of

意为"你瞧这个丈夫有多好",此处是对丈夫冷漠的讽刺。

① be full of conceit：自以为了不起。
② threading one's way back across：穿梭行走。
③ advert to：注意到。

the window. How cool it must be outside! How pleasant it would be to walk out alone, first along by the river and then through the park! The snow would be lying on the branches of the trees and forming a bright cap on the top of the Wellington① Monument. How much more pleasant it would be there than at the supper-table!

再次陷入社交尴尬状态的加布里埃尔此时的注意力暂时转移到了外面世界的景色之中。

He ran over② the headings of his speech: Irish hospitality, sad memories, the Three Graces, Paris③, the quotation from Browning. He repeated to himself a phrase he had written in his review: "One feels that one is listening to a thought-tormented music④." Miss Ivors had praised the review. Was she sincere? Had she really any life of her own behind all her propagandism⑤? There had never been any ill-feeling⑥ between them until that night. It unnerved⑦ him to think that she would be at the supper-table, looking up at him while he spoke with her critical quizzing eyes. Perhaps she would not be sorry to see him fail in his speech. An idea came into his mind and gave him courage. He would say, alluding to Aunt Kate and Aunt Julia: "Ladies and Gentlemen, the generation which is now on the wane⑧ among us may have had its faults but for my part I think it had certain qualities of hospitality, of humour, of humanity, which the new and very serious and hypereducated⑨ generation that is growing up around us seems to me to lack." Very good: that was one for Miss

① Wellington：威灵顿(1769—1852)，英国统帅。在反对拿破仑战争中，为反法联盟统帅之一，以指挥滑铁卢战役闻名。
② ran over：匆匆回顾。
③ Paris：帕里斯，希腊神话中，由特洛伊王子帕里斯判断三位女神哪一位最美丽，后引起特洛伊战争。
④ thought-tormented music：扰人心绪的音乐。
⑤ propagandism：宣传。
⑥ ill-feeling：敌意，坏印象。
⑦ unnerved：感到不安。
⑧ be on the wane：正在衰退。
⑨ hypereducated：受教育太多。

Ivors. What did he care that his aunts were only two ignorant old women?

A murmur in the room attracted his attention. Mr. Browne was advancing from the door, gallantly escorting Aunt Julia, who leaned upon his arm, smiling and hanging her head[①]. An irregular musketry of applause escorted her also as far as the piano and then, as Mary Jane seated herself on the stool, and Aunt Julia, no longer smiling, half turned so as to pitch her voice fairly into the room, gradually ceased. Gabriel recognised the prelude. It was that of an old song of Aunt Julia's — *Arrayed for the Bridal*. Her voice, strong and clear in tone, attacked with great spirit the runs which embellish the air and though she sang very rapidly she did not miss even the smallest of the grace notes. To follow the voice, without looking at the singer's face, was to feel and share the excitement of swift and secure flight. Gabriel applauded loudly with all the others at the close of the song and loud applause was borne in from the invisible supper-table. It sounded so genuine that a little colour struggled into Aunt Julia's face as she bent to replace in the musicstand the old leather-bound songbook that had her initials on the cover. Freddy Malins, who had listened with his head perched sideways to hear her better, was still applauding when everyone else had ceased and talking animatedly to his mother who nodded her head gravely and slowly in acquiescence. At last, when he could clap no more, he stood up suddenly and hurried across the room to Aunt Julia whose hand he seized and held in both his hands, shaking it when words failed him or the catch in his voice proved too much for him.

---

① hanging her head: 低垂着头。

"I was just telling my mother," he said, "I never heard you sing so well, never. No, I never heard your voice so good as it is to-night. Now! Would you believe that now? That's the truth. Upon my word and honour① that's the truth. I never heard your voice sound so fresh and so ... so clear and fresh, never."

Aunt Julia smiled broadly and murmured something about compliments as she released her hand from his grasp. Mr. Browne extended his open hand② towards her and said to those who were near him in the manner of a showman introducing a prodigy to an audience:

"Miss Julia Morkan, my latest discovery!"

He was laughing very heartily at this himself when Freddy Malins turned to him and said:

弗雷狄讽刺布朗先生这种大献殷勤的行为,认为他的发现并不高明。

"Well, Browne, if you're serious you might make a worse discovery. All I can say is I never heard her sing half so well as long as I am coming here. And that's the honest truth."

"Neither did I," said Mr. Browne. "I think her voice has greatly improved."

Aunt Julia shrugged her shoulders and said with meek pride③:

"Thirty years ago I hadn't a bad voice as voices go④."

"I often told Julia," said Aunt Kate emphatically, "that she was simply thrown away⑤ in that choir. But she never would be said by me."

She turned as if to appeal to the good sense of the others against a refractory child while Aunt Julia gazed in

---

① upon my word and honour:用自己的信誉担保。
② extended his open hand:手心摊开。
③ meek pride:温柔而自傲。
④ as voices go:跟一般的嗓音相比。
⑤ throw away:不被重视。

front of her, a vague smile of reminiscence① playing on her face.

"No," continued Aunt Kate, "she wouldn't be said or led by anyone, slaving there in that choir night and day, night and day. Six o'clock on Christmas morning! And all for what?"

"Well, isn't it for the honour of God, Aunt Kate?" asked Mary Jane, twisting round on the piano-stool and smiling.

Aunt Kate turned fiercely on her niece and said:

"I know all about the honour of God, Mary Jane, but I think it's not at all honourable for the Pope to turn out the women out of the choirs that have slaved there all their lives and put little whipper-snappers of boys② over their heads. I suppose it is for the good of the Church if the Pope does it. But it's not just, Mary Jane, and it's not right."

She had worked herself into a passion and would have continued in defence of her sister for it was a sore subject with her but Mary Jane, seeing that all the dancers had come back, intervened pacifically:

"Now, Aunt Kate, you're giving scandal to③ Mr. Browne who is of the other persuasion④."

Aunt Kate turned to Mr. Browne, who was grinning at this allusion to his religion, and said hastily:

"O, I don't question the Pope's being right. I'm only a stupid old woman and I wouldn't presume to do such a thing. But there's such a thing as common everyday politeness and gratitude. And if I were in Julia's place I'd

从凯特姨妈为茱莉亚姨妈打抱不平的一席话中其实也可见作者对爱尔兰宗教制度的不满。

---

① smile of reminiscence: 缅怀往昔的笑容。
② little whipper-snappers of boys: 妄自尊大的小男孩。
③ give scandal to: 惹某人生气。
④ other persuasion: 宗教信仰不同。

tell that Father Healey straight up to his face ..."

"And besides, Aunt Kate," said Mary Jane, "we really are all hungry and when we are hungry we are all very quarrelsome."

"And when we are thirsty we are also quarrelsome," added Mr. Browne.

"So that we had better go to supper," said Mary Jane, "and finish the discussion afterwards."

On the landing outside the drawing-room Gabriel found his wife and Mary Jane trying to persuade Miss Ivors to stay for supper. But Miss Ivors, who had put on her hat and was buttoning her cloak, would not stay. She did not feel in the least hungry and she had already overstayed her time①.

"But only for ten minutes, Molly," said Mrs. Conroy. "That won't delay you."

"To take a pick itself②," said Mary Jane, "after all your dancing."

"I really couldn't," said Miss Ivors.

"I am afraid you didn't enjoy yourself at all," said Mary Jane hopelessly.

"Ever so much, I assure you," said Miss Ivors, "but you really must let me run off now."

"But how can you get home?" asked Mrs. Conroy.

"O, it's only two steps③ up the quay."

Gabriel hesitated a moment and said:

"If you will allow me, Miss Ivors, I'll see you home④ if you are really obliged to go."

But Miss Ivors broke away from them.

---

① overstay her time：超过了逗留的时间。
② to take a pick itself：就吃一点。
③ only two steps：走几步路就到了。
④ see you home：送您回去。

"I won't hear of it," she cried. "For goodness' sake go in to your suppers and don't mind me. I'm quite well able to take care of myself."

"Well, you're the comical① girl, Molly," said Mrs. Conroy frankly.

"*Beannacht libh*②," cried Miss Ivors, with a laugh, as she ran down the staircase.

Mary Jane gazed after her, a moody puzzled expression on her face, while Mrs. Conroy leaned over the banisters to listen for the hall-door. Gabriel asked himself was he the cause of her abrupt departure. But she did not seem to be in ill humour③: she had gone away laughing. He stared blankly down the staircase.

At the moment Aunt Kate came toddling④ out of the supper-room, almost wringing her hands in despair.

"Where is Gabriel?" she cried. "Where on earth is Gabriel? There's everyone waiting in there, stage to let⑤, and nobody to carve the goose!"

"Here I am, Aunt Kate!" cried Gabriel, with sudden animation⑥, "ready to carve a flock of geese, if necessary."

A fat brown goose lay at one end of the table and at the other end, on a bed of creased paper strewn with sprigs of parsley, lay a great ham, stripped of its outer skin and peppered over with crust crumbs, a neat paper frill round its shin and beside this was a round of spiced beef. Between these rival ends ran parallel lines of side-dishes: two little minsters of jelly, red and yellow; a

① comical：怪里怪气的。
② *beannacht libh*：晚安, 亲爱的。
③ be in ill humour：情绪不快。
④ toddling：跌跌撞撞地走。
⑤ stage to let：虚位以待。
⑥ with sudden animation：突然活跃起来。

shallow dish full of blocks of blancmange and red jam, a large green leaf-shaped dish with a stalk-shaped handle, on which lay bunches of purple raisins and peeled almonds, a companion dish on which lay a solid rectangle of Smyrna figs, a dish of custard topped with grated nutmeg, a small bowl full of chocolates and sweets wrapped in gold and silver papers and a glass vase in which stood some tall celery stalks. In the centre of the table there stood, as sentries to a fruit-stand which upheld a pyramid of oranges and American apples, two squat old-fashioned decanters of cut glass, one containing port and the other dark sherry. On the closed square piano a pudding in a huge yellow dish lay in waiting and behind it were three squads of bottles of stout and ale and minerals, drawn up according to the colours of their uniforms, the first two black, with brown and red labels, the third and smallest squad white, with transverse green sashes.

Gabriel took his seat boldly at the head of the table and, having looked to the edge of the carver, plunged his fork firmly into the goose. He felt quite at ease now for he was an expert carver and liked nothing better than to find himself at the head of a well-laden table.

"Miss Furlong, what shall I send you?" he asked. "A wing or a slice of the breast?"

"Just a small slice of the breast."

"Miss Higgins, what for you?"

"O, anything at all, Mr. Conroy."

While Gabriel and Miss Daly exchanged plates of goose and plates of ham and spiced beef① Lily went from guest to guest with a dish of hot floury potatoes wrapped in a white napkin. This was Mary Jane's idea and she had

加布里埃尔在此时似乎感觉到了自我的存在。

---

① spiced beef：五香牛肉。

also suggested apple sauce for the goose but Aunt Kate had said that plain roast goose① without any apple sauce had always been good enough for her and she hoped she might never eat worse. Mary Jane waited on her pupils and saw that they got the best slices and Aunt Kate and Aunt Julia opened and carried across from the piano bottles of stout and ale for the gentlemen and bottles of minerals for the ladies. There was a great deal of confusion and laughter and noise, the noise of orders and counter-orders②, of knives and forks, of corks and glass-stoppers. Gabriel began to carve second helpings③ as soon as he had finished the first round without serving himself. Everyone protested loudly so that he compromised by taking a long draught of stout for he had found the carving hot work④. Mary Jane settled down quietly to her supper but Aunt Kate and Aunt Julia were still toddling round the table, walking on each other's heels, getting in each other's way and giving each other unheeded orders. Mr. Browne begged of them to sit down and eat their suppers and so did Gabriel but they said there was time enough, so that, at last, Freddy Malins stood up and, capturing Aunt Kate, plumped her down on her chair amid general laughter.

When everyone had been well served Gabriel said, smiling:

"Now, if anyone wants a little more of what vulgar people call stuffing let him or her speak."

A chorus of voices invited him to begin his own supper and Lily came forward with three potatoes which she had reserved for him.

---

① roast goose: 不加任何作料的烤鹅。
② counter-orders: 让菜声。
③ helpings: 一份量的事物。
④ hot work: 费劲的工作。

"Very well," said Gabriel amiably, as he took another preparatory draught, " kindly forget my existence, ladies and gentlemen, for a few minutes."

He set to his supper and took no part in the conversation with which the table covered Lily's removal of the plates. The subject of talk was the opera company which was then at the Theatre Royal. Mr. Bartell D'Arcy, the tenor, a dark-complexioned young man with a smart moustache, praised very highly the leading contralto of the company but Miss Furlong thought she had a rather vulgar style of production①. Freddy Malins said there was a Negro chieftain singing in the second part of the Gaiety pantomime who had one of the finest tenor voices he had ever heard.

"Have you heard him?" he asked Mr. Bartell D'Arcy across the table.

"No," answered Mr. Bartell D'Arcy carelessly.

"Because," Freddy Malins explained, "now I'd be curious to hear your opinion of him. I think he has a grand voice."

"It takes Teddy to find out the really good things," said Mr. Browne familiarly to the table.

"And why couldn't he have a voice too?" asked Freddy Malins sharply. "Is it because he's only a black?"

Nobody answered this question and Mary Jane led the table back to the legitimate opera②. One of her pupils had given her a pass for *Mignon*③. Of course it was very fine, she said, but it made her think of poor Georgina Burns. Mr. Browne could go back farther④ still, to the old

---

① vulgar style of production：表演风格俗气。
② legitimate opera：正统歌剧。
③ *Mignon*：《迷娘》,歌德原著,法国马思耐谱为歌剧的名作。
④ go back farther：指谈到过去的许多事情。

Italian companies that used to come to Dublin — Tietjens, Ilma de Murzka, Campanini, the great Trebelli, Giuglini, Ravelli, Aramburo. Those were the days, he said, when there was something like singing to be heard in Dublin. He told too of how the top gallery of the old Royal used to be packed night after night①, of how one night an Italian tenor had sung five encores to *Let me like a Soldier Fall*, introducing a high C every time, and of how the gallery boys would sometimes in their enthusiasm unyoke the horses from the carriage of some great prima donna② and pull her themselves through the streets to her hotel. Why did they never play the grand old operas now, he asked, *Dinorah*, *Lucrezia Borgia*? Because they could not get the voices to sing them: that was why.

追忆往昔都柏林歌剧的繁荣,更衬托出如今的萧条景象。

"Oh, well," said Mr. Bartell D'Arcy, "I presume there are as good singers to-day as there were then."

"Where are they?" asked Mr. Browne defiantly.

"In London, Paris, Milan," said Mr. Bartell D'Arcy warmly. "I suppose Caruso, for example, is quite as good, if not better than any of the men you have mentioned."

"Maybe so," said Mr. Browne. "But I may tell you I doubt it strongly."

"O, I'd give anything to hear Caruso sing," said Mary Jane.

"For me," said Aunt Kate, who had been picking a bone, "there was only one tenor. To please me, I mean. But I suppose none of you ever heard of him."

"Who was he, Miss Morkan?" asked Mr. Bartell D'Arcy politely.

---

① be packed night after night:每天晚上都客满,这是对都柏林过去歌剧繁荣的回忆。

② prima donna:歌剧女演员。

"His name," said Aunt Kate, "was Parkinson. I heard him when he was in his prime and I think he had then the purest tenor voice that was ever put into a man's throat."

"Strange," said Mr. Bartell D'Arcy. "I never even heard of him."

"Yes, yes, Miss Morkan is right," said Mr. Browne. "I remember hearing of old Parkinson but he's too far back① for me."

"A beautiful, pure, sweet, mellow English tenor," said Aunt Kate with enthusiasm.

Gabriel having finished, the huge pudding was transferred to the table. The clatter of forks and spoons began again. Gabriel's wife served out spoonfuls of the pudding and passed the plates down the table. Midway down they were held up by Mary Jane, who replenished them with raspberry or orange jelly or with blancmange and jam. The pudding was of Aunt Julia's making and she received praises for it from all quarters②. She herself said that it was not quite brown enough③.

"Well, I hope, Miss Morkan," said Mr. Browne, "that I'm brown enough for you because, you know, I'm all brown④."

All the gentlemen, except Gabriel, ate some of the pudding out of compliment to Aunt Julia. As Gabriel never ate sweets the celery had been left for him. Freddy Malins also took a stalk of celery and ate it with his pudding. He had been told that celery was a capital thing for the blood and he was just then under doctor's care.

---

① he's too far back：他(唱歌的时代)离得太远太远了。
② from all quarters：从四面八方。
③ not quite brown enough：烤得不够黄。
④ I'm brown：布朗说的是句俏皮话，因为布朗(brown)在英语里作"黄褐色"解。

Mrs. Malins, who had been silent all through the supper, said that her son was going down to Mount Melleray in a week or so. The table then spoke of Mount Melleray, how bracing the air was down there, how hospitable the monks were and how they never asked for a penny-piece from their guests.

"And do you mean to say," asked Mr. Browne incredulously, "that a chap can go down there and put up there as if it were a hotel and live on the fat of the land and then come away without paying anything?"

锦衣玉食、奢侈的生活。这里是指到寺庙大吃大喝。

"O, most people give some donation to the monastery when they leave." said Mary Jane.

"I wish we had an institution like that in our Church," said Mr. Browne candidly.

He was astonished to hear that the monks never spoke, got up at two in the morning and slept in their coffins. He asked what they did it for.

"That's the rule of the order," said Aunt Kate firmly.

"Yes, but why?" asked Mr. Browne.

Aunt Kate repeated that it was the rule, that was all. Mr. Browne still seemed not to understand. Freddy Malins explained to him, as best he could, that the monks were trying to make up for the sins committed by all the sinners in the outside world. The explanation was not very clear for Mr. Browne grinned and said:

作者花笔墨叙述这座众人口中的山中寺庙,其实也是在暗讽爱尔兰宗教腐败的现状。山中僧人的清贫克制与天主教会的奢侈敛财形成强烈对比。

"I like that idea very much but wouldn't a comfortable spring bed① do them as well as a coffin?"

"The coffin," said Mary Jane, "is to remind them of their last end."

As the subject had grown lugubrious it was buried in a silence of the table during which Mrs. Malins could be

---

① spring bed: 弹簧床。

heard saying to her neighbour in an indistinct undertone：

"They are very good men, the monks, very pious men."

The raisins and almonds and figs and apples and oranges and chocolates and sweets were now passed about the table and Aunt Julia invited all the guests to have either port or sherry. At first Mr. Bartell D'Arcy refused to take either but one of his neighbours nudged him and whispered something to him upon which he allowed his glass to be filled. Gradually as the last glasses were being filled the conversation ceased. A pause followed, broken only by the noise of the wine and by unsettlings of chairs. The Misses Morkan, all three, looked down at the tablecloth. Someone coughed once or twice and then a few gentlemen patted the table gently as a signal for silence. The silence came and Gabriel pushed back his chair.

加布里埃尔再次表现出他在公众场合的紧张情绪。

The patting at once grew louder in encouragement and then ceased altogether. Gabriel leaned his ten trembling fingers on the tablecloth and smiled nervously at the company①. Meeting a row of upturned faces② he raised his eyes to the chandelier. The piano was playing a waltz tune and he could hear the skirts sweeping against the drawing-room door. People, perhaps, were standing in the snow on the quay outside, gazing up at the lighted windows and listening to the waltz music. The air was pure there. In the distance lay the park where the trees were weighted with snow. The Wellington Monument wore a gleaming cap of snow that flashed westward over the white field of Fifteen Acres.

He began：

---

① company：在场的各位。
② a row of upturned faces：一排仰起的脸庞。

"Ladies and Gentlemen, it has fallen to my lot[1] this evening, as in years past, to perform a very pleasing task but a task for which I am afraid my poor powers as a speaker are all too inadequate."

"No, no!" said Mr. Browne.

加布里埃尔在此自谦自己的演讲能力不够。

"But, however that may be, I can only ask you to-night to take the will for the deed and to lend me your attention for a few moments while I endeavour to express to you in words what my feelings are on this occasion.

"Ladies and Gentlemen, it is not the first time that we have gathered together under this hospitable roof, around this hospitable board. It is not the first time that we have been the recipients — or perhaps, I had better say, the victims — of the hospitality of certain good ladies."

He made a circle in the air with his arm and paused. Everyone laughed or smiled at Aunt Kate and Aunt Julia and Mary Jane who all turned crimson with pleasure[2]. Gabriel went on more boldly:

"I feel more strongly with every recurring year that our country has no tradition which does it so much honour and which it should guard so jealously as that of its hospitality. It is a tradition that is unique as far as my experience goes (and I have visited not a few places abroad) among the modern nations. Some would say, perhaps, that with us it is rather a failing than anything to be boasted of[3]. But granted even that, it is, to my mind, a princely failing[4], and one that I trust will long be cultivated among us. Of one thing, at least, I am sure. As

---

① fall to my lot：意指重大的职责落到了自己身上。
② all turned crimson with pleasure：因高兴而笑得满脸绯红。
③ be boasted of：自夸,吹嘘。
④ princely failing：高贵的弱点。

long as this one roof shelters the good ladies aforesaid —
and I wish from my heart it may do so for many and many
a long year to come — the tradition of genuine warm-
hearted courteous Irish hospitality①, which our
forefathers have handed down to us and which we in turn
must hand down to our descendants, is still alive
among us."

A hearty murmur of assent ran round the table. It
shot through Gabriel's mind② that Miss Ivors was not
there and that she had gone away discourteously, and he
said with confidence in himself:

"Ladies and Gentlemen,

"A new generation is growing up in our midst③, a
generation actuated by new ideas and new principles. It is
serious and enthusiastic for these new ideas and its
enthusiasm, even when it is misdirected, is, I believe, in
the main sincere. But we are living in a skeptical and, if I
may use the phrase, a thought-tormented age, and
sometimes I fear that this new generation, educated or
hypereducated as it is, will lack those qualities of
humanity, of hospitality, of kindly humour which
belonged to an older day. Listening tonight to the names
of all those great singers of the past it seemed to me, I
must confess, that we were living in a less spacious age.
Those days might, without exaggeration, be called
spacious days, and if they are gone beyond recall④ let us
hope, at least, that in gatherings such as this we shall still
speak of them with pride and affection, still cherish in our

从加布里埃尔的祝
酒词中吐露出作者对爱
尔兰现状的忧虑。

---

① the tradition of genuine warm-hearted courteous Irish hospitality：真诚、热心、殷勤的爱尔兰式的好客
传统。
② shot through Gabirel's mind：突然想到。
③ in our midst：在我们之中。
④ go beyond recall：一去不复返。

hearts the memory of those dead and gone great ones whose fame the world will not willingly let die."

"Hear，hear!" said Mr. Browne loudly.

"But yet，" continued Gabriel，his voice falling into a softer inflection，"there are always in gatherings such as this sadder thoughts that will recur to our minds: thoughts of the past，of youth，of changes，of absent faces that we miss here tonight. Our path through life is strewn with① many such sad memories，and were we to brood upon② them always we could not find the heart to go on bravely with our work among the living. We have all of us living duties and living affections which claim，and rightly claim，our strenuous endeavours③.

"Therefore，I will not linger on the past④. I will not let any gloomy moralising intrude upon⑤ us here to-night. Here we are gathered together for a brief moment from the bustle and rush of our everyday routine. We are met here as friends，in the spirit of good fellowship，as colleagues，also to a certain extent，in the true spirit of *camaraderie*⑥，and as the guests of — what shall I call them? — the Three Graces of the Dublin musical world ⑦."

The table burst into applause and laughter at this allusion. Aunt Julia vainly asked each of her neighbours in turn to tell her what Gabriel had said.

"He says we are the Three Graces，Aunt Julia，" said Mary Jane.

---

① be strewn with：铺满，充满。
② brood upon：对过去的事物念念不忘。
③ strenuous endeavours：奋发努力。
④ linger on the past：回忆过去徘徊不前。
⑤ intrude upon：侵扰。
⑥ in the true spirit of *camaraderie*：有着真正的志同道合精神的同志。
⑦ the Three Graces of the Dublin musical world：这是加布里埃尔对此次宴会三位女主人的赞美，将她们称为"都柏林音乐世界的三位女神"。

Aunt Julia did not understand but she looked up, smiling, at Gabriel, who continued in the same vein:

"Ladies and Gentlemen,

"I will not attempt to play to-night the part that Paris played on another occasion. I will not attempt to choose between them. The task would be an invidious one and one beyond my poor powers. For when I view them in turn, whether it be our chief hostess herself, whose good heart, whose too good heart, has become a byword with all who know her, or her sister, who seems to be gifted with perennial youth① and whose singing must have been a surprise and a revelation to us all to-night, or, last but not least, when I consider our youngest hostess, talented, cheerful, hard-working and the best of nieces, I confess, Ladies and Gentlemen, that I do not know to which of them I should award the prize."

Gabriel glanced down at his aunts and, seeing the large smile on Aunt Julia's face and the tears which had risen to Aunt Kate's eyes, hastened to his close②. He raised his glass of port gallantly, while every member of the company fingered a glass expectantly, and said loudly:

"Let us toast them all three together. Let us drink to their health, wealth, long life, happiness and prosperity and may they long continue to hold the proud and self-won position which they hold in their profession and the position of honour and affection which they hold in our hearts."

All the guests stood up, glass in hand, and turning towards the three seated ladies, sang in unison③, with Mr. Browne as leader:

① perennial youth: 永不凋谢的青春。
② hastened to his close: 赶忙结束讲话。
③ in unison: 一致地。

"For they are jolly gay fellows,

For they are jolly gay fellows,

For they are jolly gay fellows,

Which nobody can deny."

Aunt Kate was making frank use[①] of her handkerchief and even Aunt Julia seemed moved. Freddy Malins beat time[②] with his pudding-fork and the singers turned towards one another, as if in melodious conference, while they sang with emphasis:

"Unless he tells a lie,

Unless he tells a lie,

Then, turning once more towards their hostesses, they sang:

For they are jolly gay fellows,

For they are jolly gay fellows,

For they are jolly gay fellows,

Which nobody can deny."

The acclamation which followed was taken up beyond the door of the supper-room by many of the other guests and renewed time after time, Freddy Malins acting as officer with his fork on high.

The piercing morning air came into the hall where they were standing so that Aunt Kate said:

"Close the door, somebody. Mrs. Malins will get her death of cold."

"Browne is out there, Aunt Kate," said Mary Jane.

"Browne is everywhere," said Aunt Kate, lowering her voice.

Mary Jane laughed at her tone.

"Really," she said archly, "he is very attentive."

---

① make frank use：毫不掩饰地使用。

② beat time：打拍子。

"He has been laid on here like the gas," said Aunt Kate in the same tone, "all during the Christmas."

She laughed herself this time good-humouredly① and then added quickly:

"But tell him to come in, Mary Jane, and close the door. I hope to goodness he didn't hear me."

At that moment the hall-door was opened and Mr. Browne came in from the doorstep, laughing as if his heart would break. He was dressed in a long green overcoat with mock astrakhan② cuffs and collar and wore on his head an oval fur cap. He pointed down the snow-covered quay from where the sound of shrill prolonged whistling was borne in.

"Teddy will have all the cabs in Dublin out," he said.

Gabriel advanced from the little pantry behind the office, struggling into his overcoat and, looking round the hall, said:

"Gretta not down yet?"

"She's getting on her things, Gabriel," said Aunt Kate.

"Who's playing up there?" asked Gabriel.

"Nobody. They're all gone."

"O no, Aunt Kate," said Mary Jane. "Bartell D'Arcy and Miss O'Callaghan aren't gone yet."

"Someone is fooling at③ the piano anyhow," said Gabriel.

Mary Jane glanced at Gabriel and Mr. Browne and said with a shiver:

"It makes me feel cold to look at you two gentlemen

---

① good-humouredly：心情愉快地。
② mock astrakhan：仿阿斯特拉罕羔羊皮的。
③ be fooling at：乱弹一气。

muffled up① like that. I wouldn't like to face your journey home at this hour."

"I'd like nothing better this minute," said Mr. Browne stoutly, "than a rattling fine walk in the country or a fast drive with a good spanking goer between the shafts."

"We used to have a very good horse and trap at home," said Aunt Julia sadly.

每当回忆过去,姨妈就会变得伤感。

"The never-to-be-forgotten② Johnny," said Mary Jane, laughing.

Aunt Kate and Gabriel laughed too.

"Why, what was wonderful about Johnny?" asked Mr. Browne.

"The late lamented③ Patrick Morkan, our grandfather, that is," explained Gabriel, "commonly known in his later years as the old gentleman, was a glue-boiler④."

"O, now, Gabriel," said Aunt Kate, laughing, "he had a starch mill."

"Well, glue or starch," said Gabriel, "the old gentleman had a horse by the name of Johnny. And Johnny used to work in the old gentleman's mill, walking round and round in order to drive the mill. That was all very well; but now comes the tragic part about Johnny. One fine day the old gentleman thought he'd like to drive out with the quality⑤ to a military review in the park."

"The Lord have mercy on his soul⑥," said Aunt Kate compassionately.

---

① muffled up：形容衣服穿得厚重，包裹得严实。
② never-to-be-forgotten：永远都忘不掉的。
③ lamented：已故的。
④ glue-boiler：做熬胶生意的人。
⑤ quality：意为上流人士的架势。
⑥ the Lord have mercy on his soul：上帝怜悯他的灵魂吧。

"Amen," said Gabriel. "So the old gentleman, as I said, harnessed Johnny and put on his very best tall hat and his very best stock collar and drove out in grand style from his ancestral mansion somewhere near Back Lane, I think." Everyone laughed, even Mrs. Malins, at Gabriel's manner and Aunt Kate said:

此处依然是形容祖父驾车出行的架势很大。

"O, now, Gabriel, he didn't live in Back Lane, really. Only the mill was there."

"Out from the mansion of his forefathers," continued Gabriel, "he drove with Johnny. And everything went on beautifully until Johnny came in sight of King Billy's statue, and whether he fell in love with the horse King Billy sits on or whether he thought he was back again in the mill, anyhow he began to walk round the statue."

Gabriel paced in a circle round the hall in his galoshes amid the laughter of the others.

"Round and round he went," said Gabriel, "and the old gentleman, who was a very pompous① old gentleman, was highly indignant. 'Go on, sir! What do you mean, sir? Johnny! Johnny! Most extraordinary conduct②! Can't understand the horse!'"

The peal of laughter which followed Gabriel's imitation of the incident was interrupted by a resounding knock at the hall-door. Mary Jane ran to open it and let in Freddy Malins. Freddy Malins, with his hat well back on his head and his shoulders humped with cold, was puffing and steaming after his exertions.

形容因寒冷和劳累而喘气,冒出热气。

"I could only get one cab," he said.

"O, we'll find another along the quay," said Gabriel.

"Yes," said Aunt Kate. "Better not keep Mrs. Malins

---

① pompous：傲慢的,自视清高的。
② most extraordinary conduct：真是莫名其妙。

standing in the draught①."

Mrs. Malins was helped down the front steps by her son and Mr. Browne and，after many manoeuvres②, hoisted into the cab. Freddy Malins clambered in after her and spent a long time settling her on the seat，Mr. Browne helping him with advice. At last she was settled comfortably and Freddy Malins invited Mr. Browne into the cab. There was a good deal of confused talk③，and then Mr. Browne got into the cab. The cabman settled his rug over his knees，and bent down for the address④. The confusion grew greater and the cabman was directed differently by Freddy Malins and Mr. Browne，each of whom had his head out through a window of the cab. The difficulty was to know where to drop Mr. Browne along the route，and Aunt Kate，Aunt Julia and Mary Jane helped the discussion from the doorstep with cross-directions and contradictions and abundance of laughter. As for Freddy Malins he was speechless with laughter. He popped his head in and out of the window every moment to the great danger of his hat⑤，and told his mother how the discussion was progressing，till at last Mr. Browne shouted to the bewildered cabman above the din of everybody's laughter：

关于布朗先生在哪儿下车的问题大家都在七嘴八舌地讨论,且相互矛盾,弄得大家笑个不停。聚会的气氛似乎到这里说再见的时候才摆脱刚才在室内的沉闷,变得轻松自在起来。

"Do you know Trinity College?"

"Yes，sir，" said the cabman.

"Well，drive bang up against Trinity College gates，" said Mr. Browne，"and then we'll tell you where to go. You understand now?"

开车撞到三一学院的墙上去。这是布朗先生的玩笑话。

---

① standing in the drought：站在风口上。
② after many manoeuvres：费了好些周折。
③ a good deal of confused talk：指说了一大通乱七八糟的话。
④ bent down for the address：车夫弯下腰问他们去哪儿。
⑤ the great danger of his hat：他的帽子冒着极大的风险。

"Yes，sir，" said the cabman.

"Make like a bird for Trinity College."

"Right，sir，" said the cabman.

The horse was whipped up and the cab rattled off① along the quay amid a chorus of laughter and adieus.

Gabriel had not gone to the door with the others. He was in a dark part of the hall gazing up the staircase. A woman was standing near the top of the first flight，in the shadow also. He could not see her face but he could see the terra-cotta and salmon-pink panels② of her skirt which the shadow made appear black and white. It was his wife. She was leaning on the banisters，listening to something. Gabriel was surprised at her stillness and strained his ear to listen③ also. But he could hear little save④ the noise of laughter and dispute on the front steps，a few chords struck on the piano and a few notes of a man's voice singing.

He stood still in the gloom of the hall，trying to catch the air that the voice was singing and gazing up at his wife. There was grace and mystery in her attitude as if she were a symbol of something. He asked himself what is a woman standing on the stairs in the shadow，listening to distant music，a symbol of. If he were a painter he would paint her in that attitude. Her blue felt hat would show off⑤ the bronze of her hair against the darkness and the dark panels of her skirt would show off the light ones. *Distant Music* he would call the picture if he were a painter.

The hall-door was closed；and Aunt Kate，Aunt Julia

从这里开始，加布里埃尔的注意力从自己的社交焦虑中转移到了爱妻身上。

---

① the cab rattled off：指马车隆隆地奔了出去。
② salmon-pink panels：赤褐色和橙红色的拼花。
③ strained his ear to listen：竖起耳朵听。
④ save：除……之外。
⑤ show off：衬托。

and Mary Jane came down the hall, still laughing.

"Well, isn't Freddy terrible?" said Mary Jane. "He's really terrible."

Gabriel said nothing but pointed up the stairs towards where his wife was standing. Now that the hall-door was closed the voice and the piano could be heard more clearly. Gabriel held up his hand for them to be silent. The song seemed to be in the old Irish tonality and the singer seemed uncertain both of his words and of his voice. The voice, made plaintive by distance and by the singer's hoarseness, faintly illuminated the cadence of the air with words expressing grief:

歌声隐隐地传出了节奏和吐露悲痛的句子。

"O, the rain falls on my heavy locks

And the dew wets my skin,

My babe lies cold . . ."

"O," exclaimed Mary Jane. "It's Bartell D'Arcy singing and he wouldn't sing all the night. O, I'll get him to sing a song before he goes."

"O, do, Mary Jane," said Aunt Kate.

Mary Jane brushed past the others① and ran to the staircase, but before she reached it the singing stopped and the piano was closed abruptly.

"O, what a pity!" she cried. "Is he coming down, Gretta?"

Gabriel heard his wife answer yes and saw her come down towards them. A few steps behind her were Mr. Bartell D'Arcy and Miss O'Callaghan.

"O, Mr. D'Arcy," cried Mary Jane, "it's downright mean of you to break off like that when we were all in raptures② listening to you."

你这样做太不应该了。

① brushed past the others: 擦过其他人走过。
② be all in raptures: 狂热地，欢喜地。

"I have been at him all the evening," said Miss O'Callaghan, "and Mrs. Conroy, too, and he told us he had a dreadful cold and couldn't sing."

"O, Mr. D'Arcy," said Aunt Kate, "now that was a great fib① to tell."

"Can't you see that I'm as hoarse as a crow?" said Mr. D'Arcy roughly.

He went into the pantry hastily and put on his overcoat. The others, taken aback by his rude speech, could find nothing to say②. Aunt Kate wrinkled her brows and made signs to the others to drop the subject. Mr. D'Arcy stood swathing his neck carefully and frowning.

"It's the weather," said Aunt Julia, after a pause.

"Yes, everybody has colds," said Aunt Kate readily, "everybody."

"They say," said Mary Jane, "we haven't had snow like it for thirty years; and I read this morning in the newspapers that the snow is general all over Ireland."

"I love the look of snow," said Aunt Julia sadly.

"So do I," said Miss O'Callaghan. "I think Christmas is never really Christmas unless we have the snow on the ground."

"But poor Mr. D'Arcy doesn't like the snow," said Aunt Kate, smiling.

Mr. D'Arcy came from the pantry, fully swathed and buttoned, and in a repentant tone told them the history of his cold. Everyone gave him advice and said it was a great pity and urged him to be very careful of his throat in the night air. Gabriel watched his wife, who did not join in

---

① a great fib: 很妙的小谎。

② The others, taken aback by his rude speech, could find nothing to say. 由于达西先生的回答粗鲁, 大家都无言以对。

the conversation. She was standing right under the dusty fanlight and the flame of the gas lit up the rich bronze of her hair, which he had seen her drying at the fire a few days before. She was in the same attitude and seemed unaware of the talk about her. At last she turned towards them and Gabriel saw that there was colour on her cheeks and that her eyes were shining. A sudden tide of joy went leaping out of his heart①.

"Mr. D'Arcy," she said, "what is the name of that song you were singing?"

"It's called *The Lass of Aughrim*," said Mr. D'Arcy, "but I couldn't remember it properly. Why? Do you know it?"

"*The Lass of Aughrim*," she repeated. "I couldn't think of the name."

"It's a very nice air②," said Mary Jane. "I'm sorry you were not in voice③ tonight."

"Now, Mary Jane," said Aunt Kate, "don't annoy Mr. D'Arcy. I won't have him annoyed."

Seeing that all were ready to start she shepherded them to the door, where good-night was said:

"Well, good-night, Aunt Kate, and thanks for the pleasant evening."

"Good-night, Gabriel. Good-night, Gretta!"

"Good-night, Aunt Kate, and thanks ever so much. Good-night, Aunt Julia."

"O, good-night, Gretta, I didn't see you."

"Good-night, Mr. D'Arcy. Good-night, Miss O'Callaghan."

"Good-night, Miss Morkan."

---

① went leaping out of his heart: 从心底涌出。
② very nice air: 歌的曲调很优美。
③ be not in voice: 嗓子不好。

"Good-night, again."

"Good-night, all. Safe home①."

"Good-night. Good-night."

The morning was still dark. A dull, yellow light brooded over② the houses and the river; and the sky seemed to be descending. It was slushy underfoot; and only streaks and patches of snow③ lay on the roofs, on the parapets of the quay and on the area railings. The lamps were still burning redly in the murky air and, across the river, the palace of the Four Courts stood out menacingly against the heavy sky.

She was walking on before him with Mr. Bartell D'Arcy, her shoes in a brown parcel tucked under one arm and her hands holding her skirt up from the slush. She had no longer any grace of attitude, but Gabriel's eyes were still bright with happiness. The blood went bounding along his veins; and the thoughts went rioting through his brain④, proud, joyful, tender, valorous.

加布里埃尔在独自对妻子的注视下，头脑里的爱意和情欲越来越强烈，以致血液也在身体里奔涌了起来。

She was walking on before him so lightly and so erect that he longed to run after her noiselessly, catch her by the shoulders and say something foolish and affectionate into her ear. She seemed to him so frail that he longed to defend her against something and then to be alone with her. Moments of their secret life together burst like stars upon his memory. A heliotrope envelope was lying beside his breakfast-cup and he was caressing it with his hand. Birds were twittering in the ivy and the sunny web of the curtain was shimmering along the floor: he could not eat for happiness. They were standing on the crowded platform

形容清晨的帷幕渐渐拉开，阳光遍洒。

---

① safe home：一路平安。
② brooded over：笼罩。
③ streaks and patches of snow：一道一道的河，一片一片的雪。
④ went rioting through his brain：思潮起伏。

and he was placing a ticket inside the warm palm of her glove. He was standing with her in the cold, looking in through a grated window at a man making bottles in a roaring furnace. It was very cold. Her face, fragrant in the cold air, was quite close to his; and suddenly he called out to the man at the furnace:

"Is the fire hot, sir?"

But the man could not hear with the noise of the furnace. It was just as well. He might have answered rudely.

A wave of yet more tender joy escaped from his heart and went coursing in warm flood along his arteries. Like the tender fire of stars moments of their life together, that no one knew of or would ever know of, broke upon[①] and illumined his memory. He longed to recall to her those moments, to make her forget the years of their dull existence together and remember only their moments of ecstasy. For the years, he felt, had not quenched his soul or hers. Their children, his writing, her household cares had not quenched all their souls' tender fire[②]. In one letter that he had written to her then he had said:"Why is it that words like these seem to me so dull and cold? Is it because there is no word tender enough to be your name?"

Like distant music these words that he had written years before were borne towards him from the past[③]. He longed to be alone with her. When the others had gone away, when he and she were in the room in the hotel, then they would be alone together. He would call her softly:

"Gretta!"

---

① broke upon: 突然出现。
② souls' tender fire: 心灵的柔情之火。
③ towards him from the past:（多年前的字句）从过去向他袭来。

Perhaps she would not hear at once: she would be undressing. Then something in his voice would strike her. She would turn and look at him ...

At the corner of Winetavern Street they met a cab. He was glad of its rattling noise as it saved him from conversation. She was looking out of the window and seemed tired. The others spoke only a few words, pointing out some building or street. The horse galloped along wearily under the murky morning sky, dragging his old rattling box after his heels, and Gabriel was again in a cab with her, galloping to catch the boat, galloping to their honeymoon.

乔伊斯意识流小说中主人公的典型特征再度显现,比起与周围人的交流,他们更注重与自己心灵的对话,思考是他们生活中重要的一部分,也是故事得以展开的中心线索。

As the cab drove across O'Connell Bridge Miss O'Callaghan said:

"They say you never cross O'Connell Bridge without seeing a white horse."

"I see a white man this time," said Gabriel.

"Where?" asked Mr. Bartell D'Arcy.

Gabriel pointed to the statue, on which lay patches of snow. Then he nodded familiarly to it and waved his hand.

"Good-night, Dan," he said gaily.

When the cab drew up[①] before the hotel, Gabriel jumped out and, in spite of Mr. Bartell D'Arcy's protest, paid the driver. He gave the man a shilling over his fare. The man saluted and said:

"A prosperous New Year to you, sir."

"The same to you," said Gabriel cordially.

She leaned for a moment on his arm in getting out of the cab and while standing at the curbstone, bidding the others good-night. She leaned lightly on his arm, as

---

① drew up: 停下。

lightly as when she had danced with him a few hours before. He had felt proud and happy then, happy that she was his, proud of her grace and wifely carriage①. But now, after the kindling again of so many memories, the first touch of her body, musical and strange and perfumed, sent through him a keen pang of lust②. Under cover of her silence he pressed her arm closely to his side; and, as they stood at the hotel door, he felt that they had escaped from their lives and duties, escaped from home and friends and run away together with wild and radiant hearts to a new adventure.

An old man was dozing in a great hooded chair in the hall. He lit a candle in the office and went before them to the stairs. They followed him in silence, their feet falling in soft thuds on the thickly carpeted stairs. She mounted the stairs③ behind the porter, her head bowed in the ascent, her frail shoulders curved as with a burden④, her skirt girt tightly about her. He could have flung his arms about her hips and held her still, for his arms were trembling with desire to seize her and only the stress of his nails against the palms of his hands held the wild impulse of his body in check⑤. The porter halted on the stairs to settle his guttering candle. They halted, too, on the steps below him. In the silence Gabriel could hear the falling of the molten wax into the tray and the thumping of his own heart against his ribs⑥.

The porter led them along a corridor and opened a door. Then he set his unstable candle down on a toilet-

---

① grace and wifely carriage：作为妻子的得体举止。
② keen pang of lust：一阵强烈的情欲。
③ mounted the stairs：上楼。
④ with a burden：好像有东西压在背上。
⑤ in check：受到控制。
⑥ the thumping of his own heart against his ribs：自己的心脏撞到肋骨上的砰砰声。

table and asked at what hour they were to be called in the morning.

"Eight," said Gabriel.

The porter pointed to the tap of the electric-light and began a muttered apology, but Gabriel cut him short[1].

"We don't want any light. We have light enough from the street. And I say," he added, pointing to the candle, "you might remove that handsome article, like a good man."

The porter took up his candle again, but slowly, for he was surprised by such a novel idea. Then he mumbled good-night and went out. Gabriel shot the lock to.

A ghastly light from the street lamp lay in a long shaft from one window to the door. Gabriel threw his overcoat and hat on a couch and crossed the room towards the window. He looked down into the street in order that his emotion might calm a little. Then he turned and leaned against a chest of drawers with his back to the light. She had taken off her hat and cloak and was standing before a large swinging mirror[2], unhooking her waist. Gabriel paused for a few moments, watching her, and then said:

"Gretta!"

She turned away from the mirror slowly and walked along the shaft of light towards him. Her face looked so serious and weary that the words would not pass Gabriel's lips[3]. No, it was not the moment yet.

"You looked tired," he said.

"I am a little," she answered.

"You don't feel ill or weak?"

---

[1] cut him short：打断说话。
[2] swinging mirror：转动的穿衣镜。
[3] the words would not pass Gabriel's lips：无法开口说话。

"No, tired, that's all."

She went on to the window and stood there, looking out. Gabriel waited again and then, fearing that diffidence① was about to conquer him, he said abruptly:

"By the way, Gretta!"

"What is it?"

"You know that poor fellow Malins?" he said quickly.

"Yes. What about him?"

"Well, poor fellow, he's a decent sort of chap②, after all," continued Gabriel in a false③ voice. "He gave me back that sovereign I lent him, and I didn't expect it, really. It's a pity he wouldn't keep away from that Browne, because he's not a bad fellow, really."

He was trembling now with annoyance. Why did she seem so abstracted? He did not know how he could begin. Was she annoyed, too, about something? If she would only turn to him or come to him of her own accord④! To take her as she was would be brutal. No, he must see some ardour in her eyes first. He longed to be master of her strange mood.

"When did you lend him the pound?" she asked, after a pause.

Gabriel strove to restrain himself from breaking out into brutal language about the sottish Malins and his pound. He longed to cry to her from his soul, to crush her body against his, to overmaster her. But he said:

"O, at Christmas, when he opened that little Christmas-card shop in Henry Street."

---

① diffidence：羞怯。
② decent sort of chap：正派人。
③ false：形容声音不自然，做作。
④ of her own accord：自愿地，主动地。

He was in such a fever of rage and desire that he did not hear her come from the window. She stood before him for an instant, looking at him strangely. Then, suddenly raising herself on tiptoe① and resting her hands lightly on his shoulders, she kissed him.

"You are a very generous person, Gabriel," she said.

Gabriel, trembling with delight at her sudden kiss and at the quaintness of her phrase, put his hands on her hair and began smoothing it back, scarcely touching it with his fingers. The washing had made it fine and brilliant. His heart was brimming over with② happiness. Just when he was wishing for it she had come to him of her own accord. Perhaps her thoughts had been running with his. Perhaps she had felt the impetuous desire that was in him, and then the yielding mood had come upon her. Now that she had fallen to him so easily, he wondered why he had been so diffident.

He stood, holding her head between his hands. Then, slipping one arm swiftly about her body and drawing her towards him, he said softly:

"Gretta, dear, what are you thinking about?"

She did not answer nor yield wholly to his arm. He said again, softly:

"Tell me what it is, Gretta. I think I know what is the matter. Do I know?"

She did not answer at once. Then she said in an outburst of tears:

"O, I am thinking about that song, *The Lass of Aughrim*."

She broke loose from③ him and ran to the bed and,

---

① tiptoe：踮起脚尖。
② be brimming over with：充满，溢满。
③ broke loose from：从……中挣脱出来。

throwing her arms across the bed-rail, hid her face. Gabriel stood stockstill for a moment in astonishment and then followed her. As he passed in the way of the chevalglass he caught sight of himself in full length①, his broad, well-filled shirtfront, the face whose expression always puzzled him when he saw it in a mirror, and his glimmering gilt-rimmed eyeglasses. He halted a few paces from her and said:

"What about the song? Why does that make you cry?"

She raised her head from her arms and dried her eyes with the back of her hand like a child. A kinder note than he had intended went into his voice.

"Why, Gretta?" he asked.

"I am thinking about a person long ago who used to sing that song."

"And who was the person long ago?" asked Gabriel, smiling.

"It was a person I used to know in Galway when I was living with my grandmother," she said.

The smile passed away② from Gabriel's face. A dull anger began to gather again at the back of his mind③ and the dull fires of his lust began to glow angrily in his veins.

"Someone you were in love with?" he asked ironically.

"It was a young boy I used to know," she answered, "named Michael Furey. He used to sing that song, *The Lass of Aughrim*. He was very delicate."

Gabriel was silent. He did not wish her to think that he was interested in this delicate boy.

"I can see him so plainly," she said, after a moment.

---

① in full length: 全部身形。
② passed away: 消逝。
③ at the back of his mind: 思想深处。

"Such eyes as he had: big, dark eyes! And such an expression in them — an expression!"

"O, then, you are in love with him?" said Gabriel.

"I used to go out walking with him," she said, "when I was in Galway."

A thought flew across Gabriel's mind.

"Perhaps that was why you wanted to go to Galway with that Ivors girl?" he said coldly.

She looked at him and asked in surprise:

"What for?"

Her eyes made Gabriel feel awkward. He shrugged his shoulders and said:

"How do I know? To see him, perhaps."

She looked away from him along the shaft of light towards the window in silence.

"He is dead," she said at length①. "He died when he was only seventeen. Isn't it a terrible thing to die so young as that?"

"What was he?" asked Gabriel, still ironically.

"He was in the gasworks," she said.

Gabriel felt humiliated by the failure of his irony and by the evocation of this figure from the dead, a boy in the gasworks. While he had been full of memories of their secret life together, full of tenderness and joy and desire, she had been comparing him in her mind with another. A shameful consciousness of his own person assailed him. He saw himself as a ludicrous figure, acting as a pennyboy② for his aunts, a nervous, well-meaning③ sentimentalist, orating to vulgarians and idealising his own clownish lusts, the pitiable fatuous fellow he had caught a glimpse of in

---

① at length: 最后，终于。
② pennyboy: 为大人跑腿赚零花钱的小孩。
③ well-meaning: 善意的，好心的。

the mirror. Instinctively he turned his back more to the light lest she might see the shame that burned upon his forehead.

He tried to keep up his tone of cold interrogation, but his voice when he spoke was humble and indifferent.

"I suppose you were in love with this Michael Furey, Gretta," he said.

"I was great with him at that time," she said.

Her voice was veiled and sad. Gabriel, feeling now how vain it would be to try to lead her whither he had purposed, caressed one of her hands and said, also sadly:

"And what did he die of so young, Gretta? Consumption①, was it?"

"I think he died for me," she answered.

A vague terror seized Gabriel at this answer, as if, at that hour when he had hoped to triumph, some impalpable and vindictive being was coming against him, gathering forces against him in its vague world. But he shook himself free of it② with an effort of reason and continued to caress her hand. He did not question her again, for he felt that she would tell him of herself. Her hand was warm and moist: it did not respond to his touch, but he continued to caress it just as he had caressed her first letter to him that spring morning.

"It was in the winter," she said, "about the beginning of the winter when I was going to leave my grandmother's and come up here to the convent. And he was ill at the time in his lodgings in Galway and wouldn't be let out, and his people in Oughterard were written to. He was in decline, they said, or something like that. I never knew

加布里埃尔终于开始看清自己的真实面孔。顿悟从这里开始。

---

① consumption：肺痨。
② free of it：甩开（恐惧）。

127

rightly."

She paused for a moment and sighed.

"Poor fellow," she said. "He was very fond of me and he was such a gentle boy. We used to go out together, walking, you know, Gabriel, like the way they do in the country. He was going to study singing only for his health. He had a very good voice, poor Michael Furey."

"Well; and then?" asked Gabriel.

"And then when it came to the time for me to leave Galway and come up to the convent he was much worse and I wouldn't be let see him so I wrote him a letter saying I was going up to Dublin and would be back in the summer, and hoping he would be better then."

She paused for a moment to get her voice under control, and then went on:

"Then the night before I left, I was in my grandmother's house in Nuns' Island, packing up①, and I heard gravel thrown up against the window. The window was so wet I couldn't see, so I ran downstairs as I was and slipped out the back into the garden and there was the poor fellow at the end of the garden, shivering."

"And did you not tell him to go back?" asked Gabriel.

"I implored of② him to go home at once and told him he would get his death in the rain. But he said he did not want to live. I can see his eyes as well! He was standing at the end of the wall where there was a tree."

"And did he go home?" asked Gabriel.

"Yes, he went home. And when I was only a week in the convent he died and he was buried in Oughterard,

---

① packing up: 收拾行李。
② implored of: 请求,恳求。

where his people came from. O, the day I heard that, that he was dead!"

She stopped, choking with sobs[①], and, overcome by emotion, flung herself face downward on the bed, sobbing in the quilt. Gabriel held her hand for a moment longer, irresolutely, and then, shy of intruding on[②] her grief, let it fall gently and walked quietly to the window.

She was fast asleep.

Gabriel, leaning on his elbow, looked for a few moments unresentfully on her tangled hair and half-open mouth, listening to her deep-drawn breath. So she had had that romance in her life: a man had died for her sake. It hardly pained him now to think how poor a part he, her husband, had played in her life. He watched her while she slept, as though he and she had never lived together as man and wife. His curious eyes rested long upon her face and on her hair, and, as he thought of what she must have been then, in that time of her first girlish beauty, a strange, friendly pity for her entered his soul. He did not like to say even to himself that her face was no longer beautiful, but he knew that it was no longer the face for which Michael Furey had braved death.

Perhaps she had not told him all the story. His eyes moved to the chair over which she had thrown some of her clothes. A petticoat string dangled to the floor. One boot stood upright, its limp upper fallen down: the fellow of it lay upon its side. He wondered at his riot of emotions of an hour before. From what had it proceeded? From his aunt's supper, from his own foolish speech, from the wine and dancing, the merry-making when saying good-night in

---

①   choking with sobs: 因哭泣而哽咽。
②   intruding on: 打扰。

加布里埃尔的心理活动中想到了亲人之死。从这里可以看出，文章的题目"死者"，并不单指妻子的初恋情人迈克尔·富里，还有那些虽然活着，但思想和身体已经走向坟墓的人。

shades：此刻，加布里埃尔感到自己和妻子也成为了世间的影子、幽灵，存在的意义因彼此心灵的隔阂而变得虚空而飘渺。

the hall, the pleasure of the walk along the river in the snow. Poor Aunt Julia! She, too, would soon be a shade with the shade of Patrick Morkan and his horse. He had caught that haggard look upon her face for a moment when she was singing *Arrayed for the Bridal*. Soon, perhaps, he would be sitting in that same drawing-room, dressed in black, his silk hat on his knees. The blinds would be drawn down and Aunt Kate would be sitting beside him, crying and blowing her nose and telling him how Julia had died. He would cast about in his mind for some words that might console her, and would find only lame and useless ones. Yes, yes: that would happen very soon.

The air of the room chilled his shoulders. He stretched himself cautiously along under the sheets and lay down beside his wife. One by one, they were all becoming shades. Better pass boldly into that other world, in the full glory of some passion, than fade and wither dismally with age. He thought of how she who lay beside him had locked in her heart for so many years that image of her lover's eyes when he had told her that he did not wish to live.

Generous tears[①] filled Gabriel's eyes. He had never felt like that himself towards any woman, but he knew that such a feeling must be love. The tears gathered more thickly in his eyes and in the partial darkness he imagined he saw the form of a young man standing under a dripping tree. Other forms were near. His soul had approached that region where dwell the vast hosts of the dead. He was conscious of, but could not apprehend, their wayward and

---

① generous tears：大量的泪水。

flickering existence①. His own identity was fading out② into a grey impalpable world：the solid world itself，which these dead had one time reared and lived in，was dissolving and dwindling.

A few light taps upon the pane made him turn to the window. It had begun to snow again. He watched sleepily the flakes③，silver and dark，falling obliquely against the lamplight. The time had come for him to set out on his journey westward. Yes，the newspapers were right：snow was general all over Ireland. It was falling on every part of the dark central plain，on the treeless hills，falling softly upon the Bog of Allen and，farther westward，softly falling into the dark mutinous Shannon waves. It was falling，too，upon every part of the lonely churchyard on the hill where Michael Furey lay buried. It lay thickly drifted on the crooked crosses and headstones，on the spears of the little gate，on the barren thorns. His soul swooned slowly as he heard the snow falling faintly through the universe and faintly falling，like the descent of their last end，upon all the living and the dead.

既可以理解为死亡之旅，也可以说是自我的净化之旅。

【思考题】

1. 思考小说主人公的心理转变线索，及这些转变如何实现最后的顿悟？

2. 思考最后一段对雪景的描写包含的深层含义。

---

① flickering existence：变幻无常，时隐时现的存在。
② fade out：渐渐消逝。
③ flakes：雪花。

And of Clay Are We Created

我们都是泥做的

伊莎贝尔·阿连德

【导读】

　　伊莎贝尔·阿连德(Isabel Allende，1942—　)，被誉为"穿裙子的加西亚·马尔克斯"。她继承了"拉美文学"的传统，擅长用流行拉美的魔幻现实主义手法来创作，作品中充满了女性的敏感和浓烈的激情，表现出倡导民主、自由、进步，抨击独裁专制的思想。

　　伊莎贝尔·阿连德1942年生于秘鲁首都利马。父亲是托马斯·阿连德，任智利驻利马的外交官。她三岁时，父母离异，在外祖父母家度过了童年。她对他们如父母般亲近，尤其依恋外祖父——一个超自然的神秘主义信仰者。当母亲与一个名叫拉蒙的外交官结婚后，全家人离开了智利，先后在玻利维亚、中东和欧洲生活过。她于15岁回到了智利。1959年开始从事新闻记者的工作，凭着知识分子的良知和正义感，她撰写了不少批评社会丑恶的文章。作为一名女权主义者，她为一家激进妇女杂志写文章，后来拥有了自己的电视节目。1970年，她父亲的第一个堂兄萨尔瓦多·阿连德·诺森斯博士(Salvador Allende Gossens)成为第一个被自由选举为智利总统的马列主义者。三年后，智利三军和警察部队在奥古斯塔斯·皮诺切特·乌加特(Augusto Pinochet Ugarte)将军的领导下发动武装叛乱，其伯父被暗杀。在美国的支持下，智利建立了军事专政，阿连德和她的家人逃往委内瑞拉，她感觉"我的生活被切成了碎片，不得不再重新开始"。

　　1981年，伊莎贝尔·阿连德99岁高龄的外祖父决定绝食自杀。她开始创作一部以外祖父的回忆为基础的小说，一个虚构家族几代人的编年史。于是就有了震惊世界文坛的长篇小说《幽灵之家》(*The House of the Spirits*)(1982)。她自己曾说过："我很幸运，我来自一个古怪的家庭。一群讨人喜欢的疯子构成了我们这个奇妙门第。他们几乎启发我写了我的全部长篇小说。有了我家的这些亲人，就不再需要想象，他们为我提供了魔幻现实主义的一切素材。"她的作品更多的是基于真实而非虚构，"因为真实一向比我的想象力的任何产物都更美好"。她曾经说，"在拉丁美洲，我们崇尚梦幻、激情、神秘、情绪，所有这些对我们的生活很重要，在文学世界里也举足轻重——我们对家族的理解、对宗教的理解、对迷信的理解……

拉丁美洲每天都在发生一些神奇的事——这不是我们虚构的"。

《幽灵之家》展现了埃斯特万·特鲁埃瓦家族从 20 世纪初到七八十年代的历史，分为四个时期：早期、幽灵时代、混乱时期、真理时刻和尾声。早期和幽灵时代讲述了埃斯特万·特鲁埃瓦通过开发金矿积累原始资本，用暴力和强权控制庄园，振兴农村。这个时期，埃斯特万·特鲁埃瓦强暴了管家佩德罗·加西亚第二的姐姐潘洽，她的儿子埃斯特万·加西亚埋下了向特鲁埃瓦家族复仇的火种。发财后的埃斯特万·特鲁埃瓦投身政治，并当上了议员，其女布兰卡与庄园管家的儿子佩德罗·加西亚第三相恋，因为身份的悬殊和佩德罗·加西亚第三鼓吹马克思主义的政治倾向而遭到埃斯特万·特鲁埃瓦的激烈反对。埃斯特万·特鲁埃瓦砍下了佩德罗·加西亚第三的三根手指，佩德罗·加西亚第三不得不开始逃亡并秘密地参与左派激进运动。不久布兰卡生下了阿尔芭——一个最终割断了家族的过去，将其连向未来的女孩。混乱时期，埃斯特万·特鲁埃瓦与政敌们明争暗斗，两个儿子也站在了他的对立面上。党派斗争激烈，学生运动此起彼伏，右派制造了经济混乱，造成了经济的衰退。最后军人们发动了政变，以血腥镇压和专制统治结束了一切。特鲁埃瓦家族受到了重创，埃斯特万·特鲁埃瓦失去了一个儿子——海格，阿尔芭也在这次流血政变中受尽了侮辱。最后，被捕后的阿尔芭在祖母幽灵的帮助下，挺了过来，埃斯特万·特鲁埃瓦救出了孙女。他们回到了原来平静的生活中，开始记录下这段历史。

阿尔芭的祖父埃斯特万·特鲁埃瓦是贯穿全篇的中心人物，脾气暴躁、意志坚强。为了赢得未婚妻罗莎的爱情，他只身前往深山开采金矿，即使后来罗莎死去，仍然无法忘怀。他有强烈的个人野心，为了满足自己的欲望，他经常强抢农庄的妇女。而他的仇恨和他的爱情来得一样浓烈，他可以毫不犹豫地砍掉女儿情人的三根手指，但在生死关头不顾一切地去搭救这位雇工的儿子、危险的政敌。他的粗暴和蛮横让他冲过道德底线，但是暴躁之后，他终能冷静地检讨，选择正确的道路。

阿连德在《幽灵之家》中融入了个人的亲身经历，但作品并不是对于家族生活的实录。对于她来说，写作是一种保存记忆的绝望企图。她是一个永恒的流浪者。记忆像她的衣服碎片一样丢在路上。走过了这么多路以后，原始的根从她的身上脱落下来。她写作是为了滋养现在漂浮在空气中的根。

除了给阿连德带来巨大知名度的《幽灵之家》外，阿连德紧接着发表了《爱和阴影》(*Of Love and Shadows*)(1986)和《伊娃·鲁娜》(*Eva Luna*)(1988)，及一部短篇小说集《伊娃·鲁娜的故事》(*The Stories of Eva Luna*)(1991)。《我们都是泥做的》(*And of Clay Are We Created*)是这本小说集的最后一篇。在这篇短篇小说中，阿连德用她惯用的超越虚构的真实笔调，尽可能地为地震中被困却无法被救出的女孩阿苏珊娜张目。读后我们可以感觉到,阿连德坐在我们身边就像她陪伴着罗尔夫·卡利(Rolf Carlé)一样,以平静悲伤却不绝望的方式来表现生命复现的根本主题——记忆永存,所以生命永恒。正如小说中罗尔夫·卡利把作家讲故事的技巧与《一千零一夜》的女主角莎拉嘉德相提并论:"你用文字思考;对你来说,语言是你编织的无穷无尽的丝线,仿佛在你讲述时你就创造了生活。"

And of Clay Are We Created

Translated by Margaret Sayers Peden

巨大的坟场遍布着死亡的气息:孤儿的啼哭和伤者的哀号。执着求生的女孩阿苏珊娜·莉莉与之形成鲜明的对比。

They discovered the girl's head protruding from the mud pit①, eyes wide open, calling soundlessly. She had a First Communion② name, Azucena Lily. In that vast cemetery where the odor of death was already attracting vulture's③ from far away, and where the weeping of orphans and wails of the injured filled the air, the little girl obstinately clinging to life became the symbol of the tragedy. The television cameras transmitted so often the unbearable image of the head budding like a black squash from the clay④ that there was no one who did not recognize her and know her name. And every time we saw her on the screen, right behind her was Rolf Carlé, who had gone there on assignment, never suspecting that he would find a fragment of his past, lost thirty years before⑤.

First a subterranean⑥ sob rocked the cotton fields, curling them like waves of foam. Geologists⑦ had set up

---

① the girl's head protruding from the mud pit:女孩的头露在泥坑外。
② First Communion:是罗马天主教的一种仪式,叫"初次圣礼",一般是七八岁的儿童初次领食圣餐,表示正式被罗马天主教接受。
③ vulture:秃鹰。
④ the head budding like a black squash from the clay:脑袋像泥土里长出来的黑倭瓜。
⑤ never suspecting that he would find a fragment of his past, lost thirty years before:从未曾料到会从尘封三十年的岁月中拾回某些记忆的碎片。
⑥ subterranean:地表下的。
⑦ geologist:地质学家。

their seismographs① weeks before and dictated that the heat of the eruption could detach the eternal ice from the slopes of the volcano②, but no one heeded their warnings; they sounded like the tales of frightened old women. The towns in the valley went about③ their daily life, deaf to the moaning of the earth④, until that fateful Wednesday night in November when a prolonged roar announced the end of the world, and walls of snow broke loose, rolling in an avalanche⑤ of clay, stones, and water that descended on the villages and buried them beneath unfathomable meters of telluric⑥ vomit⑦. As soon as the survivors emerged from the paralysis⑧ of that first awful terror, they could see that houses, plazas, churches, white cotton plantations, dark coffee forests, cattle pastures⑨— all had disappeared. Much later, after soldiers and volunteers had arrived to rescue the living and try to assess the magnitude of the cataclysm⑩, it was calculated that beneath the mud lay more than twenty thousand human beings and an indefinite number of animals putrefying⑪ in a viscous⑫ soup. Forests and rivers had also been swept away, and there was nothing to be seen but an immense desert of mire⑬.

When the station called before dawn, Rolf Carlé and

地壳地底下的流体的运动暗示着灾难的到来,但村民对地质学家的警告置若罔闻,认为这是老妇人的危言耸听。

地震后的惨状。

透过作者第一次介绍罗尔夫·卡利,当时他并不认为这次的采访非常特别。

---

① seismograph：地震仪。
② dictated that the heat of the eruption could detach the eternal ice from the slopes of the volcano：火山喷发的热量会融化山坡上终年不化的冰。detach from：脱离。
③ go about：从事。
④ deaf to the moaning of the earth：对大地的呻吟充耳不闻。
⑤ avalanche：雪崩。
⑥ telluric：地球上的。
⑦ vomit：呕吐物。
⑧ paralysis：瘫痪。
⑨ pasture：牧场。
⑩ assess the magnitude of the cataclysm：计算灾难级别。
⑪ putrefy：腐烂，化脓。
⑫ viscous：黏稠的。
⑬ mire：污泥，污沼。

I were together. I crawled out of bed, dazed with sleep①, and went to prepare coffee while he hurriedly dressed. He stuffed his gear in the green canvas backpack he always carried, and we said goodbye, as we had so many times before. I had no presentiments②. I sat in the kitchen, sipping my coffee and planning the long hours without him, sure that he would be back the next day.

He was one of the first to reach the scene, because while other reporters were fighting their way to the edges of that morass③ in jeeps, bicycles, or on foot, each getting there however he could, Rolf Carlé had the advantage of the television helicopter, which flew him over the avalanche. We watched on our screens the footage④ captured by his assistant's camera, in which he was up to his knees in muck⑤, a microphone in his hand, in the midst of a bedlam of lost children, wounded survivors, corpses, and devastation⑥. The story came to us in his calm voice. For years he had been a familiar figure in newscasts, reporting live at the scene of battles and catastrophes with awesome tenacity⑦. Nothing could stop him, and I was always amazed at his equanimity⑧ in the face of danger and suffering; it seemed as if nothing could shake his fortitude or deter his curiosity. Fear seemed never to touch him, although he had confessed to me that he was not a courageous man, far from it. I belive that the lens of the camera had a strange effect on him, it

罗尔夫·卡利，一位资深的记者，有着不为危险所吓倒的勇气、无法被阻挡的好奇心，甚至能够在镜头面前如同置身事外般沉着，但是这次采访让这位硬汉流露了真情。

---

① dazed with sleep：睡得迷迷糊糊地。
② presentiment：不祥预感。
③ morass：沼泽。
④ footage：电视电影的连续镜头。
⑤ he was up to his knees in muck：膝盖以下全部陷在泥沼里。
⑥ in the midst of a bedlam of lost children, wounded survivors, corpses, and devastation：置身于迷失的孩子、受伤的生还者、尸体和废墟交织在一起的乱哄哄场面中。bedlam：混乱的场景。
⑦ tenacity：不屈不挠。
⑧ equanimity：镇静。

was as if it transported him to a different time from which he could watch events without actually participating in them. When I knew him better, I came to realize that this fictive distance seemed to protect him from his own emotions.

Rolf Carlé was in on the story of Azucena from the beginning. He filmed the volunteers who discovered her, and the first person who tried to reach her; his camera zoomed in① on the girl, her dark face, her large desolate eyes, the plastered-down tangle of her hair②. The mud was like quicksand③ around her, and anyone attempting to reach her was in danger of sinking. They threw a rope to her that she made no effort to grasp until they shouted to her to catch it; then she pulled a hand from the mire and tired to move, but immediately sank a little deeper. Rolf threw down his knapsack④ and the rest of his equipment and waded into the quagmire⑤, commenting for his assistant's microphone that it was cold and that one could begin to smell the stench⑥ of corpse.

"What's your name?" he asked the girl, and she told him her flower name. "Don't move, Azucena," Rolf Carlé directed, and kept talking to her, without a thought for what he was saying, just to distract her, while slowly he worked his way forward in mud to his waist. The air around him seemed as murky⑦ as the mud.

It was impossible to reach her from the approach he was attempting, so he retreated and circled around where

第一次正面写到女孩的样子，黑色的脸，大而凄凉的双眼，因泥浆而结成一团的头发。

救援的艰难：她周围的烂泥就像流沙一样，任何人想靠近她的尝试都可能让她下沉。而事实上，她抓绳的举动让自己下陷得更深了。

① zoom in：用摄影机的变距镜头将画面推进，特写。
② the plastered-down tangle of her hair：因泥浆而结成一团的头发。
③ quicksand：流沙。
④ knapsack：背包。
⑤ wade into the quagmire：蹚进沼泽中。
⑥ stench：恶臭。
⑦ murky：黑暗的，混浊的。

seemed to be firmer footing. When finally he was close enough, he took the rope and tired it beneath her arms, so they could pull her out. He smiled at her with that smile that crinkles his eyes and makes him look like a little boy; he told her that everything was fine, that he was here with her now, that soon they would have her out. He signaled the others to pull, but as soon as the cord tensed, the girl screamed. They tried again, and her shoulders and arms appeared, but they could move her no farther; she was trapped. Someone suggested that her legs might be caught in① the collapsed walls of her house, but she said it was not just rubble②, that she was also held by the bodies of her brothers and sisters clinging to her legs.

罗尔夫·卡利尝试着把小女孩救出来,但她被倒下的墙壁、石块甚至是兄弟姐妹的尸体压住了。

"Don't worry, we'll get you out of here." Rolf promised. Despite the quality of the transmission, I could hear his voice break, and I loved him more than ever. Azucena looked at him, but said nothing.

罗尔夫·卡利给了女孩"生"的承诺,他会竭尽全力。其实只需要一只水泵,她就得救了。

During those first hours Rolf Carlé exhausted all the resources of his ingenuity to rescue her. He struggled with poles and ropes, but every tug③ was an intolerable torture for the imprisoned girl. It occurred to him to use one of the poles as lever④ but got no result and had to abandon the idea. He talked a couple of soldiers into⑤ working with him for a while, but they had to leave because so many other victims were calling for help. The girl could not move, she barely could breathe, but she did not seem desperate, as if an ancestral resignation⑥ allowed her to accept her fate. The reporter, on the other hand, was

---

① be caught in:陷入。
② rubble:碎石。
③ tug:猛拉。
④ lever:杠杆。
⑤ talk into:说服。
⑥ ancestral resignation:家族中顺从性格。

determined to snatch her from death. Someone brought him a tire, which he placed beneath her arms like a life buoy①, and then laid a plank② near the hole to hold his weight and allow him to stay closer to her. As it was impossible to remove the rubble blindly, he tried once or twice to dive toward her feet, but emerged frustrated, covered with mud, and spitting gravel. He concluded that he would have to have a pump to drain the water, and radioed a request for one, but received in return a message that there was no available transport and it could not be sent until the next morning.

"We can't wait that long!" Rolf Carlé shouted, but in the pandemonium③ no one stopped to commiserate④. Many more hours would go by before he accepted that time had stagnated and reality had been irreparably distorted⑤.

过了很长时间,罗尔夫·卡利不得不接受女孩无法被救出的事实,但是他还是没有放弃尝试。

A military doctor came to examine the girl, and observed that her heart was functioning well and that if she did not get too cold she could survive the night.

"Hang on⑥, Azucena, we'll have the pump tomorrow," Rolf Carlé tried to console⑦ her.

"Don't leave me alone," she begged.

"No, of course I won't leave you."

Someone brought him coffee, and he helped the girl drink it, sip by sip⑧. The warm liquid revived her and she

小姑娘讲述她如花的生命,如此年轻、鲜活,却即将转瞬即逝,让罗尔夫·卡利唏嘘不已。

---

① life buoy：救生圈。
② plank：厚板。
③ pandemonium：混乱的场面。
④ commiserate：同情,怜悯。
⑤ Many more hours would go by before he accepted that time had stagnated and reality had been irreparably distorted. 时间停滞了,现实扭曲了,毫无办法,待到他认可这一点时,又过去了好几个小时。Stagnate：停滞；distort：扭曲。
⑥ hang on：坚持住。
⑦ console：安慰。
⑧ sip by sip：一小口一小口地。

began telling him about her small life, about her family and her school, about how things were in that little bit of world before the volcano had erupted. She was thirteen, and she had never been outside her village. Rolf Carlé, buoyed by a premature optimism, was convinced that everything would end well: the pump would arrive, they would drain the water, move the rubble, and Azucena would be transported by helicopter to a hospital where she would recover rapidly and where he could visit her and bring her gifts. He thought, She's already too old for dolls, and I don't know what would please her; maybe a dress. I don't know much about women, he concluded, amused, reflecting that although he had known many women in his lifetime, none had taught him these details. To Pass the hours; he began to tell Azucena about his travels and adventures as a news-hound①, and when he exhausted his memory, he called upon imagination, inventing things he thought might entertain her. From time to time she dozed, but he kept talking in the darkness, to assure her that he was still there and to overcome the menace② of uncertainty.

That was a long night.

Many miles away, I watched Rolf Carlé and the girl on a television screen. I could not bear the wait at home, so I went to National Television, where I often spent entire nights with Rolf editing programs. There, I was near his world, and I could at least get a feeling of what he lived through during those three decisive days. I called all the important people in the city, senators, commanders of

罗尔夫·卡利被一种错误的乐观所误导,幻想一切苦难都会结束,小姑娘一定会被平安救出的。

罗尔夫·卡利鼓励女孩,帮助她活过今夜,但是她的情况不容乐观。

① news-hound：［俚语］新闻记者。
② menace：威胁。

140

the armed forces①, the North American ambassador②, and the president of National Petroleum③, begging them for a pump to remove the silt④, but obtained only vague promise. I began to ask for urgent help on radio and television, to see if there wasn't some who could help us. Between calls I would run to the newsroom to monitor the satellite transmissions that periodically brought new details of the catastrophe. While reporters selected scenes with most impact for the news report, I searched for footage that featured Azucena's mudpit. The screen reduced the disaster to a single plane and accentuated the tremendous distance that separated me from Rolf Carlé; nonetheless, I was there with him. The child's every suffering hurt me as it did him; I felt his frustration, his impotence⑤. Faced with the impossibility of communicating with him, the fantastic idea came to me that if I tried, I could reach him by force of mind⑥ and in that way give him encouragement. I concentrated until I was dizzy — a frenzied and futile activity⑦. At times I would be overcome with compassion and burst out crying; at other times, I was so drained⑧ I felt as if I were staring through a telescope at the light of a star dead for a million years.

I watched that hell on the first morning broadcast; cadavers⑨ of people and animals awash⑩ in the current of

在电视机旁边关注这一切的作者向一切她认识的大人物求助,但得到的只是空头支票。一泵难求!

---

① commanders of the armed forces：武装部队的长官。
② North American ambassador：北美大使。
③ the president of National Petroleum：国家石油部长。
④ silt：淤泥。
⑤ impotence：无力感。
⑥ force of mind：精神力量。
⑦ I concentrated until I was dizzy — a frenzied and futile activity. 我全神贯注直到晕眩——只是一件狂躁而无意义的事。
⑧ drained：耗尽,筋疲力尽。
⑨ cadaver：尸首。
⑩ awash：被淹没的。

new rivers formed overnight from the melted snow. Above the mud rose the tops of trees and the bell towers of a church where several people had taken refuge and were patiently awaiting rescue teams. Hundreds of soldiers and volunteers from the Civil Defense① were clawing through rubble searching for survivors, while long rows of ragged specters② awaited their turn for a cup of hot broth③. Radio networks announced that their phones were jammed with calls from families offering shelter to orphaned children. Drinking water was in scarce supply, along with gasoline and food. Doctors, resigned to amputating arms and legs without anesthesia④, pled that at least they be sent serum and painkillers and antibiotics⑤; most of roads, however, were impassable, and worse wore the bureaucratic⑥ obstacles that stood in the way. To top it all⑦, the clay contaminated⑧ by bodies threatened the living with an outbreak of epidemics⑨.

灾区环境恶劣,缺医少药,幸存者们仍有着生命危险。但是官僚主义却让一切雪上加霜。正是这个直接导致了阿苏珊娜·莉莉的死亡。

Azucena was shivering⑩ inside the tire that held her above the surface. Immobility and tension had greatly weakened her, but she was conscious and could still be heard when a microphone was held out to her. Her tone was humble, as if apologizing for all the fuss⑪. Rolf Carlé had a growth of beard, and dark circles beneath his eyes; he looked near exhaustion. Even from that enormous

阿苏珊娜·莉莉谦卑、歉意的语气让人心疼。

---

① Civil Defense:民防部。
② specter:衣衫褴褛的难民。原意为幽灵。
③ hot broth:热汤。
④ doctors, resigned to amputating arms and legs without anesthesia:医生拒绝在没有麻醉的情况下实施截肢手术。
⑤ serum and painkillers and antibiotics:血清、镇痛剂和抗生素。
⑥ bureaucratic:官僚主义的。
⑦ to top it all:最紧要的是。
⑧ contaminate:污染。
⑨ epidemic:流行病。
⑩ shiver:哆嗦,发抖。
⑪ fuss:忙乱。

distance I could sense the quality of his weariness, so different from the fatigue of other adventures. He had completely forgotten the camera; he could not look at the girl through a lens any longer. The pictures we were receiving were not his assistant's but those of other reporters who had appropriated Azucena, bestowing on① her the pathetic responsibility of embodying② the horror of what had happened in that place. With the first light Rolf tried again to dislodge③ the obstacles that held the girl in her tomb, but he had only his hands to work with; he did not dare use a tool for fear of injuring her. He fed Azucena a cup of the cornmeal mush④ and bananas the Army was distributing, but she immediately vomited it up. A doctor stated that she had a fever, but added that there was little he could do: antibiotics were being reserved for cases of gangrene⑤. A priest also passed by and blessed her, hanging a medal of the Virgin around her neck. By evening a gentle, persistent drizzle began to fall.

"The sky is weeping," Azucena murmured, and she, too, began to cry.

"Don't be afraid," Rolf begged. "You have to keep your strength up⑥ and be calm. Everything will be fine. I'm with you, and I'll get you out somehow."

Reporters returned to photograph Azucena and ask her the same questions, which she no longer tried to answer. In the meanwhile, more television and movie teams arrived with spools of cable, tapes, film, videos, precision lenses, recorders, sound consoles, lights,

罗尔夫·卡利也已经到了精疲力竭的边缘,他的疲倦与其他人的劳累是完全不同的。其他记者看阿苏珊娜·莉莉,只是把她当成传达恐怖灾难的工具。而罗尔夫·卡利是为了她的生命在争斗。

夜晚到来了,开始下起渐渐沥沥的蒙蒙细雨,暗示着阿苏珊娜·莉莉心情的阴郁和即将到来的死亡。

世界各地的记者们纷纷到来,大费周章地运来了各种先进的设备以便记录阿苏珊娜·莉莉的最后一刻,却没有人想到运送一个简单的水泵来拯救她的生命。人们愿意逼真地看着她死,而不是遥远地帮助她生。

---

① bestow on: 赠予。
② embody: 使具体化。
③ dislodge: 移除。
④ cornmeal mush: 玉米粥。
⑤ gangrene: 坏疽。
⑥ keep strength up: 保存体力。

reflecting screens, auxiliary motors, cartons of supplies electricians, sound technicians, and cameramen①: Azucena's face was beamed② to millions of screens around the world. And all the while Rolf Carlé kept pleading for a pump. The improved technical facilities bore results, and National Television began receiving sharper pictures and clearer sound; the distance seemed suddenly compressed, and I had the horrible sensation that Azucena and Rolf were by my side, separated from me by impenetrable③ glass. I was able to follow events hour by hour; I knew everything my love did to wrest the girl from④ her prison and help her endure her suffering; I overheard⑤ fragments of what they said to one another and could guess the rest; I was present when she taught Rolf to pray, and when he distracted her with the stories I had told him in a thousand and one nights⑥ beneath the white mosquito netting of our bed.

When darkness came on the second day, Rolf tried to sing Azucena to sleep with old Austrian folk songs he had learned from his mother, but she was far beyond sleep⑦. They spent most of the night talking, each in a stupor⑧ of exhaustion and hunger, and shaking with cold. That night, imperceptibly⑨, the unyielding floodgates⑩ that

---

① more television and movie teams arrived with spools of cable, tapes, film, videos, precision lenses, recorders, sound consoles, lights, reflecting screens, auxiliary motors, cartons of supplies electricians, sound technicians, and cameramen：更多的电视和电影队伍带了一轴轴的电缆、胶片、录像带、精密的镜头、话筒、音响控制板、灯光、反光板、辅助发电机、成箱的供给物、发电机、声音技术员和摄影师。

② beam：照射，传送。

③ impenetrable：不能穿过的。

④ wrest from：抢夺。

⑤ overhear：无意中听到。

⑥ a thousand and one nights：《一千零一夜》的故事。

⑦ far beyond sleep：睡不着，无法安然入睡。

⑧ stupor：恍惚。

⑨ imperceptibly：不知不觉。

⑩ floodgate：尘封已久的记忆闸门。

had contained Rolf Carlé's past for so many years began to open, and the torrent① of all that had lain hidden in the deepest and most secret layers of memory poured out②, leveling before it the obstacles③ that had blocked his consciousness for so long. He could not tell it all to Azucena; she perhaps did not know there was a world beyond the sea or time previous to her own; she was not capable of imagining Europe in the years of the war. So he could not tell her of defeat, nor of the afternoon the Russians had led them to the concentration camp④ to bury prisoners dead from starvation. Why should he describe to her how the naked bodies piled like a mountain of firewood resembled fragile china⑤? How could he tell this dying child about ovens and gallows⑥? Nor did he mention the night that he had seen his mother naked, shod in stiletto-heeled red boots⑦, sobbing with humiliation⑧. There was much he did not tell, but in those hours he relived for the first time all the things his mind had tried to erase. Azucena had surrendered her fear to him and so, without wishing it, had obliged Rolf to confront his own⑨. There, beside that hellhole of mud, it was impossible for Rolf to flee from⑩ himself any longer, and the visceral terror⑪ he had lived as a boy suddenly invaded

---

① torrent：激流。
② pour out：涌出。
③ obstacles：[医]业障。
④ concentration camp：集中营。
⑤ the naked bodies piled like a mountain of firewood resembled fragile china：赤裸的如同瓷器般易碎的尸体像柴火般堆积如山。
⑥ ovens and gallows：此处指焚化炉和绞刑架。
⑦ shod in stiletto-heeled red boots：穿着红色细高跟鞋。
⑧ sobbing with humiliation：极度羞愧地啜泣着。
⑨ obliged Rolf to confront his own：迫使罗尔夫面对自己。
⑩ flee from：逃避。
⑪ visceral terror：内心深处的恐惧。

him. He reverted to① the years when he was the age of Azucena, and younger, and, like her, found himself trapped in a pit without escape, buried in life, his head barely above ground; he saw before his eyes the boots and legs of his father, who had removed his belt and was whipping it in the air with the never-forgotten hiss of a viper coiled to strike②. Sorrow flooded through him, intact and precise, as if it had lain always in his mind, waiting. He was once again in the armoire③ where his father locked him to punish him for imagined misbehavior, there where for eternal hours he had crouched④ with his eyes closed, not to see the darkness, with his hands over his ears, to shut out⑤ the beating of his heart, trembling, huddled⑥ like a cornered animal.

讲述罗尔夫·卡利被唤醒的童年记忆,他同阿苏珊娜·莉莉一样有着被遗弃的绝望和面临死亡的恐惧。

Wandering in the mist of his memories he found his sister Katharina, a sweet, retarded⑦ child who spent her life hiding, with the hope that her father would forget the disgrace of her having been born. With Katharina, Rolf crawled beneath the dining room table, and with her hid there under the long white tablecloth, two children forever embraced, alert⑧ to footsteps and voices. Katharina's scent melded with his own sweat, with aromas⑨ of cooking, garlic, soup, freshly baked bread, and the unexpected odor of putrescent clay⑩. His sister's

---

① revert to：回归到。

② before his eyes the boots and legs of his father, who had removed his belt and was whipping it in the air with the never-forgotten hiss of a viper coiled to strike：他的眼前出现了他父亲的靴子和腿,他解开皮带在空中快速地抽动,发出令人难忘的嘶嘶声,就像一条盘旋着伺机出击的蝰蛇。viper：毒蛇。

③ armoire：装饰精美的大衣橱。

④ crouch：蜷缩。

⑤ shut out：把……关在外面。

⑥ huddle：蜷缩。

⑦ retarded：弱智。

⑧ alert：警惕,提防。

⑨ aroma：芳香。

⑩ unexpected odor of putrescent clay：突如其来的腐烂的泥土味。

hand in his, her frightened breathing, her silk hair against his cheek, the candid① gaze of her eyes. Katharina ... Katharina materialized before him, floating on the air like a flag, clothed in the white tablecloth, now a winding sheet②, and at last he could weep for her death and for the guilt of having abandoned her. He understood then that all his exploits③ as a reporter, the feats④ that had won him such recognition and fame, were merely an attempt to keep his most ancient fears at bay, a stratagem for taking refuge behind a lens to test whether reality was more tolerable from that perspective. He took excessive risks as an exercise of courage, training by day to conquer the monsters that tormented⑤ him by night. But he had come face to face with the moment of truth; he could not continue to escape his past. He was Azucena; he was buried in the clay mud; his terror was not the distant emotion of an almost forgotten childhood, it was claw sunk in his throat⑥. In the flush⑦ of his tears he saw his mother, dressed in black and clutching her imitation-crocodile pocketbook⑧ to her bosom; just as he had last seen her on the dock⑨ when she had come to put him on the boat to South America. She had not come to dry his tears, but to tell him to pick up a shovel⑩: the war was over and now they must bury the dead.

罗尔夫·卡利认识到摄影机的镜头只是他用来逃避自己的避风港。

---

① candid：率真的。
② winding sheet：裹尸布。
③ exploit：英勇的行为。
④ feat：功绩。
⑤ torment：折磨。
⑥ his terror was not the distant emotion of an almost forgotten childhood, it was claw sunk in his throat：他的害怕并不是快要遗忘了的童年的遥远情绪,而是现在扼紧咽喉的利爪。
⑦ flush：冲洗,一阵情感。
⑧ clutching her imitation-crocodile pocketbook：紧抓着仿鳄鱼皮手包。
⑨ dock：码头。
⑩ shovel：铲子。

"Don't cry. I don't hurt anymore. I'm fine."Azucena said when dawn came.

"I'm not crying for you," Rolf Carlé smiled. "I'm crying for myself. I hurt all over."

The third day in the valley of the cataclysm began with a pale light filtering through storm clouds①. The President of the Republic visited the area in his tailored safari jacket② to confirm that this was the worst catastrophe of the century; the country was in mourning③; sister nations had offered aid; he had ordered a state of siege④; the Armed Forces would be merciless, anyone caught stealing or committing other offenses would be shot on sight⑤. He added that it was impossible to remove all the corpses or count the thousands who had disappeared; the entire valley would be declared holy ground, and bishops would come to celebrate a solemn mass for the souls of the victims⑥. He went to the Army field tents to offer relief in the form of vague promises to crowds of the rescued⑦, then to the improvised⑧ hospital to offer a word of encouragement to doctors and nurses worn down⑨ from so many hours of tribulations⑩. Then he asked to be taken to see Azucena, the little girl the whole world had seen. He waved to her with a limp statesman's hand, and microphones recorded his emotional voice and paternal

总统的到来并没有改变阿苏珊娜·莉莉的命运。

---

① a pale light filtering through storm clouds：一束苍白的光透过乌云。
② in his tailored safari jacket：穿着剪裁讲究的猎装夹克。
③ mourning：哀悼。
④ ordered a state of siege：下令戒严状态。
⑤ shoot on sight：当场击毙。
⑥ bishops would come to celebrate a solemn mass for the souls of the victims：主教会来为受难的亡灵做庄严的弥撒。
⑦ in the form of vague promises to crowds of the rescued：用含糊的诺言安慰大批的生还者。
⑧ improvised：临时的。
⑨ wear down：精疲力竭。
⑩ tribulation：苦难。

tone① as he told her that her courage had served as an example to the nation. Rolf Carlé interrupted to ask for a pump, and the President assured him that he personally would attend to the matter. I caught a glimpse of② Rolf for a few seconds kneeling beside the mudpit. On the evening news broadcast，he was still in the same position；and I，glued to③ the screen like a fortuneteller④ to her crystal ball，could tell that something fundamental had changed in him. I knew somehow that during the night his defenses had crumbled and he had given in to⑤ grief；finally he was vulnerable. The girl had touched a part of him that he himself had no access to，a part he had never shared with me. Rolf had wanted to console her，but it was Azucena who had given him consolation.

I recognized the precise moment at which Rolf gave up the fight and surrendered to the torture of watching the girl die. I was with them，three days and two nights，spying on⑥ them from the other side of life. I was there when she told him that in all her thirteen years no boy had ever loved her and that it was a pity to leave this world without knowing love. Rolf assured her that he loved her more than he could ever love anyone，more than he loved his mother，more than his sister，more than all the women who had slept in his arms，more than he loved me，his life companion，who would have given anything to be trapped in that well in her place，who would have exchanged her life for Azucena's，and I watched as he leaned down to kiss her poor forehead，consumed by a sweet，sad emotion

罗尔夫·卡利仍然为了阿苏珊娜·莉莉的生命而做最后的努力。

罗尔夫·卡利意识到让阿苏珊娜·莉莉归于死亡的平静是最好的选择，虽然这个决定让他痛不欲生。

---

① paternal tone：父亲般的语调。
② a glimpse of：瞥见。
③ glue to：［非正式］似胶般固着于（某事物）。
④ fortuneteller：占卜者。
⑤ give in to：屈服于。
⑥ spy on：窥视。

he could not name①. I felt how in that instant both were saved from despair, how they were freed from the clay, how they rose above the vultures and helicopters, how together they flew above the vast swamp of corruption and laments②. How, finally, they were able to accept death. Rolf Carlé prayed in silence that she would die quickly, because such pain cannot be borne.

水泵终于有着落了,可是阿苏珊娜·莉莉——不该陨落的生命之花已经陷入泥沼,无可挽回了。

By then I had obtained a pump and was in touch with a general who had agreed to ship it the next morning on a military cargo plane③. But on the night of that third day, beneath the unblinking focus of quartz lamps④ and the lens of a hundred cameras, Azucena gave up, her eyes locked with that of the friend who had sustained her to the end⑤. Rolf Carlé removed the life buoy, closed her eyelids, held her to his chest for a few moments, and then let her go. She sank slowly, a flower in the mud.

目睹这一切的普通人和罗尔夫·卡利一样,不可能忘记,因为我们彼此血脉相连。

You are back with me, but you are not the same man. I often accompany you to the station and we watch the videos of Azucena again; you study them intently⑥, looking for something you could have done to save her, something you did not think of in time. Or maybe you study them to see yourself as if in a mirror, naked. Your cameras lie forgotten in a closet; you do not write or sing; you sit long hours before the window, staring at the

---

① consumed by a sweet, sad emotion he could not name:充溢着他难以言表的甜蜜而悲伤的情绪。consume:使充满……情感。

② I felt how in that instant both were saved from despair, how they were freed from the clay, how they rose above the vultures and helicopters, how together they flew above the vast swamp of corruption and laments. 我能感受到此刻他们是如何在这一瞬间从绝望中解脱,如何从泥沙中逃离,如何超越过秃鹫和直升机,如何一起飞过这片腐烂的沼泽和悲伤。

③ military cargo plane:军用运输机。

④ quartz lamp:石英灯。

⑤ her eyes locked with those of the friend who had sustained her to the end:她的双眼一直盯着那位坚守到最后的朋友的眼睛。

⑥ intently:专心地。

mountains. Beside you，I wait for you to complete the voyage into yourself，for the old wounds to heal. I know that when you return from your nightmares①，we shall again walk hand in hand，as before.

【思考题】

1. 小说中主人公记者罗尔夫·卡利在整个灾难事件过程中表现出不同于一般职业记者之处，请具体展开谈谈。

2. 小说中主人公女孩阿苏珊娜最终还是在大批全球媒体的镜头下无助地死去，这表达了作者怎样的社会道德立场和态度？

3. 这篇小说的叙事手段与传统意义上的新闻报道有何不同？小说表现了作家怎样独特的叙事艺术特色？

---

① nightmare：噩梦，恶梦。

Town and Country Lovers

城市和乡村的恋人们

纳丁·戈迪默

【导读】

纳丁·戈迪默（Nadine Gordimer，1923——　），南非白人女作家。她从南非吸取了大量的现实主义素材，创作出史诗般壮丽的作品，揭露了南非种族隔离政策的残忍，成为 1991 年诺贝尔文学奖得主。

戈迪默 1923 年生于约翰内斯堡附近一座名叫斯普林斯的矿业小城。她是犹太移民的后裔，父亲来自立陶宛，母亲是英国人。戈迪默从小就具有很强的独立性，醉心于读书写故事。15 岁那年，她在当地的一家文学杂志上发表了第一篇短篇小说，从此开始了笔耕生涯。在漫长的写作生涯中，戈迪默先后写了 10 部长篇小说和 200 多篇短篇小说以及其他一批评论、杂文等。戈迪默的作品已被译成 20 余种文字出版，蜚声世界文坛。

戈迪默的前期作品主要以现实主义笔法揭露南非种族主义的罪恶，着重刻画这一社会中的黑人与白人的种种心态，控诉种族主义制度对人性的扭曲。她的第一个短篇小说集《面对面》（Face to Face）出版于 1949 年，20 世纪 50 年代出版的《蛇的低语》（The Soft Voice of the Serpent，1952）、《六英尺土地》（Six Feet of the Country，1956），60 年代出版的《星期五的足迹》（Friday's Footprint，1960）和《不宜发表》（Not for Publication，1965）等短篇小说集都受到了评论界的高度赞扬。这一时期的长篇小说有《缥缈岁月》（The Lying Days，1953）、《陌生人的世界》（A World of Strangers，1958）、《恋爱时节》（Occasion for Loving，1963）、《逝去的资产阶级世界》（The Late Bourgeois World，1966）。1970 年出版的长篇小说《贵宾》（A Guest of Honour），被评论界看作她前、后期创作的分界线。

70 年代以来戈迪默又先后出版了《自然资源保护论者》（The Conservationist，1974）、《伯格的女儿》（Burger's Daughter，1979）、《朱利的族人》（July's People，1981）、《自然变异》（A Sport of Nature，1987）、《我儿子的故事》（My Son's Story，1990）、《没有陪伴我》（None to Accompany Me，1994）等长篇小说。短篇小说集有《利文斯顿的伙伴》（Livingstone's Companions，1970）、《小说选集》（Selected Stories，1975）、《士兵的拥抱》（A Soldier's Embrace，1980）及《跳跃》（Jump: And

Other Stories，1991)等。戈迪默的评论文集有《基本姿态：创作、政治及地域》（*The Essential Gesture: Writing，Politics and Places*，1988)和《写作与存在》（*Writing and Being: The Charles Eliot Norton Lectures*，1995)。戈迪默的后期作品除了继续展现南非的社会现实外，明显地加入了对南非未来命运的"预言"成分，创作手法也更为成熟和多样，每部作品都各具特色。

《贵客》是戈迪默的第五部长篇小说，也是她早期创作中最优秀的长篇代表作。主人公布雷是个生长在非洲的白人，应邀回到刚刚独立的祖国参加庆典。他是 10 年前被驱逐出境的，昔日的战友慕韦塔已经担任总统，其他人也担任了高级官员。但是，当他遇到革命功臣的老友施因扎，却发现他只是一个劳工组织者。不久，布雷便发现，施因扎认为慕韦塔已经背离了初衷，成为与过去的白人政权一样腐败的领导人，因而发动了全国总罢工，慕韦塔派兵镇压。布雷这位被请回国的贵客则在混乱之中被打死。《贵客》的价值就在于，通过黑人在建立政权、巩固政权过程中出现的激烈冲突，表现了人类实现美好理想的艰难。

《自然资源保护论者》是又一部以经典的现代小说技巧写成的优秀长篇。小说情节很简单：白人工业巨子梅林买下了一个方圆 400 英亩的农场，每逢周末和假日，他就去农场巡视一番。梅林认为他有必要将保护自然资源的观念传授给当地黑人，与当地的黑人产生了根本性的冲突。他是以土地所有者的身份同黑人交往的，因此成为黑人故土的掠夺者；他以保护土地原有状况的姿态自居，因此成为保护旧秩序、阻碍黑人独立的绊脚石；他无法应付大自然的变化，在暴风雨袭击时不得不逃走，又证明了他原本就是无力去保护自然的。梅林最后的出逃以及不得不将土地交给黑人的结局说明，他的存在和南非的白人政权一样，是违反自然的，不合时宜的。

《朱利的族人》将故事情节置于动荡的社会背景之中，通过处在重大变化中的黑人—白人关系，表现了作者对南非未来的预言。书中的主人公是白人斯梅尔斯夫妇及三个孩子。他们在国家爆发内战时，由黑人男佣朱利护送逃到朱利的家乡。那是个穷乡僻壤，贫穷程度超出斯梅尔斯夫妇的想象。他们虽有朱利的悉心照顾，却无法适应贫穷的生活。他们与同住一处的黑人无法沟通，黑人也不能理解这些拥有一切的白人何以无处可去。斯梅尔斯一家生活在恐惧和忧虑之中，最后同救过他们的朱利也闹起了矛盾，爆发了争吵。最后斯梅尔斯一家不得已寄希望于美国人，希望离开南非。这是一部基于现实的想象之作。它是悲剧性的，但不悲观，南非未来的希望就在孩子们身上。

　　戈迪默的短篇小说创作同样十分出色。她的早期短篇写得精巧、细腻,已经显露了"惊人的才华"。后期的短篇则以日趋成熟的技巧和冷峻深刻的思想而广受赞誉。《士兵的拥抱》(1980 年)就是她后期短篇小说的代表作。收入集子中的短篇《城市和乡村的恋人们》也颇有代表性。

　　第一个短篇描述一位当地黑人女孩和在南非工作的白人地质学家从相识、同居、相知相爱到被发现、被迫分开、形同陌路这一过程,描述了他们爱情的悲剧。

　　这篇小说继承了作者早期爱情故事的主题,并被赋予一种冷峻的气质,勾勒出一幅种族隔离制度下黑人女性悲惨的境遇与生存状况图景,揭露了种族隔离政策残酷无情的本质。

　　第二个短篇描述白人农场主儿子和黑人雇工女儿从小青梅竹马,结下真挚友谊并发展成自然的两性之爱,但怀孕后的黑人姑娘为了生下孩子而与别人结婚,两人为了孩子发生争执,导致孩子不幸夭折,后两人对簿公堂,白人农场主儿子被判无罪的故事。

　　这个短篇最发人深省之处是揭示了黑人姑娘在整个事件过程中始终逆来顺受,毫无反抗地接受种族偏见和财富门第给她爱情带来的毁灭性打击,而白人农场主儿子面对两人无法结合的残酷现实也未有任何积极抗争,这进一步暴露了南非社会种族问题作为一个社会毒瘤已经根深蒂固的严峻现状。

Town and Country Lovers

I

　　Dr. Franz-Josef von Leinsdorf[1] is a geologist absorbed in his work; wrapped up in it[2], as the saying goes — year after year the experience of this work enfolds him, swaddling[3] him away from the landscapes, the cities, and the people, wherever he lives: Peru, New Zealand, the United States. He's always been like that, his mother could confirm from their native Austria[4]. There, even as a handsome small boy he presented only

点出了弗兰兹—约瑟夫·冯·雷恩斯多夫博士的工作经历和生活习惯。

---

① Dr. Franz-Josef von Leinsdorf:弗兰兹-约瑟夫·冯·雷恩斯多夫博士,人名。
② wrapped up in it:心无旁骛。
③ swaddle:束缚,用襁褓包。
④ Austria:奥地利。

his profile to her: turned away to① his bits of rock and stone. His few relaxations have not changed much since then. An occasional skiing trip, listening to music, reading poetry — Rainer Maria Rilke once stayed in his grandmother's hunting lodge in the forests of Styria② and the boy was introduced to Rilke's poems while very young.

Layer upon layer③, country after country, wherever his work takes him — and now he has been almost seven years in Africa. First the Cote d'Ivoire④, and for the past five years, South Africa. The shortage of skilled manpower brought about his recruitment⑤ here. He has no interest in the politics of the countries he works in. His private preoccupation-within-the-preoccupation⑥ of his work has been research into underground watercourses⑦, but the mining company that employs him in a senior though not executive capacity is interested only in mineral discovery. So he is much out in the field — which is the veld⑧, here — seeking new gold, copper, platinum, and uranium deposits⑨. When he is at home — on this particular job, in this particular country, this city — he lives in a two-roomed flat in a suburban block with a landscaped garden, and does his shopping at a supermarket conveniently across the street. He is not married — yet. That is how his colleagues, and the typists and secretaries at the mining company's head office, would define his situation. Both men and women would

展现了冯·雷恩斯多夫博士的相貌情况和婚姻状态。

---

① turned away to：转过身去。
② Styria：施蒂里亚州。
③ Layer upon layer：一个地层又一个地层。
④ Cote d'Ivoire：象牙海岸。
⑤ recruitment：人才招募。
⑥ private preoccupation-within-the-preoccupation：个人兴趣。
⑦ watercourse：河道。
⑧ veld：草原。
⑨ gold, copper, platinum, and uranium deposits：金矿、铜矿、铂矿和铀矿。

describe him as a good-looking man, in a foreign way, with the lower half of his face dark and middle-aged (his mouth is thin and curving, and no matter how close-shaven his beard shows like fine shot embedded in the skin① round mouth and chin) and the upper half contradictorily young, with deep-set② eyes (some would say grey, some black), thick eyelashes and brows. A tangled gaze: through which concentration and gleaming thoughtfulness perhaps appear as fire and languor③. It is this that the women in the office mean when they remark he's not unattractive. Although the gaze seems to promise, he has never invited any one of them to go out with him. There is the general assumption he probably has a girl who's been picked for him, he's bespoken④ by one of his own kind, back home in Europe where he comes from. Many of these well-educated Europeans have no intention of becoming permanent immigrants; neither the remnant of white colonial life⑤ nor idealistic involvement with Black Africa appeals to them.

One advantage, at least, of living in underdeveloped or half-developedcountries is that flats are serviced. All Dr. von Leinsdorf has to do for himself is buy his own supplies and cook an evening meal if he doesn't want to go to a restaurant. It is simply a matter of dropping in to the supermarket on his way from his car to his flat after work in the afternoon. He wheels a trolley up and down the shelves, and his simple needs are presented to him in the form of tins, packages, plastic-wrapped meat, cheeses,

写出了冯·雷恩斯多夫博士目光的魅力: 蒙眬迷茫,透过目光不时现出专注的神色和炯炯闪光的沉思,如火焰,又似倦怠。

---

① fine shot embedded in the skin: 嵌入皮肤里的细铅砂。
② deep-set: (眼睛)深陷的。
③ languor: 倦怠。
④ bespoken: 预订。
⑤ the remnant of white colonial life: 苟延残喘地在殖民地过白人的生活。

fruit and vegetables，tubes，bottle … At the cashier's①
counters where customers must converge and queue there
are racks of small items uncategorized，for last-minute
purchase. Here，as the coloured girl cashier punches the
adding machine，he picks up cigarettes and perhaps a
packet of salted nuts or a bar of nougat②. Or razor-
blades③，when he remembers he's running short④. One
evening in winter he saw that the cardboard display was
empty of the brand of blades⑤ he preferred，and he drew
the cashier's attention to this. These young coloured girls
are usually pretty unhelpful，taking money and punching
their machines in a manner that asserts with the time-
serving obstinacy of the half-literate the limit of any
responsibility towards customers，but this one ran an alert
glance over the selection of razor-blades，apologized that
she was not allowed to leave her post，and said she would
see that the stock was replenished⑥"next time. " A day or
two later she recognized him，gravely，as he took his turn
before her counter — "I ahssed them，but it's out of
stock. You can't get it. I did ask about it⑦. " He said this
didn't matter. "When it comes in，I can keep a few
packets for you. " He thanked her.

　　He was away with the prospectors the whole of the
next week. He arrived back in town just before nightfall
on Friday，and was on his way from car to flat with his
arms full of briefcase，suitcase，and canvas bags when
someone stopped him by standing timidly in his path. He

写出了收款的有色
姑娘具体的工作形态,
她们只是机械地收钱按
键,一副半文盲的经久
不变的呆板嘴脸,表示
她们没有责任回应顾客
更多的要求,引出下文
的女主人公与这些姑娘
形成对比,这才有了两
个人的第一次相遇。

---

① cashier：出纳。
② nougat：杏仁糖。
③ razor-blades：剃须刀。
④ run short：快用完了。
⑤ blades：刀片。
⑥ replenish：补充。
⑦ I did ask about it：我确实问过了。

was about to dodge round① unseeingly on the crowded pavement but she spoke. "We got the blades in now. I didn't see you in the shop this week, but I kept some for when you come. So ..."

He recognized her. He had never seen her standing before, and she was wearing a coat. She was rather small and finely-made, for one of them. The coat was skimpy but no big backside jutted②. The cold brought an apricot③-graining of warm colour to her cheekbones, beneath which a very small face was quite delicately hollowed, and the skin was smooth, the subdued satiny colour of certain yellow wood④. That crepey hair, but worn drawn back flat and in a little knot pushed into one of the cheap wool chignons⑤ that (he recognized also) hung in the miscellany of small goods⑥ along with the razor-blades, at the supermarket. He said thanks, he was in a hurry, he'd only just got back from a trip — shifting the burdens he carried, to demonstrate. "Oh shame." She acknowledged his load. "But if you want I can run in and get it for you quickly. If you want."

He saw at once it was perfectly clear that all the girl meant was that she would go back to the supermarket, buy the blades, and bring the packet to him there where he stood, on the pavement. And it seemed that it was this certainty that made him say, in the kindly tone of assumption used for an obliging underling⑦, "I live just across there — Atlantis — that flat building. Could you

---

写出了姑娘的外貌形态，她身材不高，匀称窈窕。外套质地粗陋，但背部没明显地鼓出来。她的双颊冻得艳若红杏，凹陷在颧骨下的小脸很是玲珑，皮肤滑腻，像黄木呈现着缎子般柔和的光泽。绉纱似的头发平直地拢到脑后挽成一个发髻。

"噢，可不是。"这是女主人公的话，她也认为他的负担够重的。

---

① dodge round：闪避。
② jut：突出。
③ apricot：杏。
④ the subdued satiny colour of certain yellow wood：像某种黄木呈现着缎子般柔和的色泽。
⑤ wool chignons：毛织网套。
⑥ the miscellany of small goods：零星小杂物。
⑦ an obliging underling：一位巴结的下属。

drop them by, for me — number seven-hundred-and-eighteen, seventh floor —"

She had not before been inside one of these big flat buildings near where she worked. She lived a bus- and-train-ride away to the West of the city①, but this side of the black townships, in a township for people her tint②. There was a pool with ferns, not plastic, and even a little waterfall pumped electrically over rocks, in the entrance of the building Atlantis③; she didn't wait for the lift marked GOODS but took the one meant for whites and a white woman with one of those sausage-dogs④ on a lead got in with her but did not pay her any attention. The corridors leading to the flats were nicely glassed-in, not draught⑤.

她住在城市西区，得又坐汽车又乘火车的。

甚至还用电提升水，形成了从岩石上泻下的小瀑布。

He wondered if he should give her a twenty-cent piece for her trouble — ten cents would be right for a black; but she said, "Oh no — please, here —" standing outside his open door and awkwardly pushing back at his hand the change from the money he'd given her for the razor-blades. She was smiling, for the first time, in the dignity of refusing a tip. It was difficult to know how to treat these people, in this country; to know what they expected. In spite of her embarrassing refusal of the coin, she stood there, completely unassuming⑥, fists thrust down the pockets of her cheap coat against the cold she'd come in from, rather pretty thin legs neatly aligned⑦, knee to knee, ankle to ankle.

一点也不装腔作势，手深深插在那件用来在屋外御寒的廉价外套的兜里，两腿并立，亭亭玉立，膝对膝，踝对踝。这里写出了姑娘站姿的美丽。

---

① She lived a bus- and- train-ride away to the West of the city. 她住在西城区，得又坐公交又乘火车的。
② her tint：她们那种肤色。
③ Atlantis：传说中沉没于大西洋中的岛。
④ sausage-dogs：猎獾狗，一种狗。
⑤ not draught：一点也不冷飕飕的。
⑥ unassuming：不装腔作势。
⑦ align：对齐，此处指并立。

"Would you like a cup of coffee or something?"

He couldn't very well take her into his study-cum-living-room① and offer her a drink. She followed him to his kitchen, but at the sight of her pulling out the single chair to drink her cup of coffee at the kitchen table, he said, "No — bring it in here —" and led the way into the big room where, among his books and his papers, his files of scientific correspondence② (and the cigar boxes of stamps from the envelopes), his racks of records, his specimens③ of minerals and rocks, he lived alone.

It was no trouble to her; she saved him the trips to the supermarket and brought him his groceries two or three times a week. All he had to do was to leave a list and the key under the doormat, and she would come up in her lunch-hour to collect them, returning to put his supplies in the flat after work. Sometimes he was home and sometimes not. He bought a box of chocolates and left it, with a note, for her to find; and that was acceptable, apparently, as a gratuity④.

她的身体似乎是要掩盖自己的不自在,于是在请她就座的那把椅子里纹丝不动,仿佛是陌生人的衣服被搁放在了一旁,就那么悄悄呆着,只等主人离去时再拿起它。这里写出了姑娘局促不安的心态。

Her eyes went over everything in the flat although her body tried to conceal its sense of being out of place⑤ by remaining as still as possible, holding its contours in the chair offered her as a stranger's coat is set aside and remains exactly as left until the owner takes it up to go. "You collect?"

"Well, these are specimens — connected with my work."

"My brother used to collect. Miniatures. With brandy

---

① study-cum-living-room:书房兼会客室。
② files of scientific correspondence:科学通信的卷宗。
③ specimen:样本。
④ gratuity:报偿。
⑤ be out of place:不协调。

and whisky and that, in them. From all over. Different countries."

The second time she watched him grinding① coffee for the cup he had offered her she said, "You always do that? Always when you make coffee?"

"But of course. It is no good, for you. Do I make it too strong?"

"Oh it's just I'm not used to it. We buy it ready — you know, it's in a bottle, you just add a bit to the milk or water."

He laughed, instructive: "That's not coffee, that's a synthetic flavouring②. In my country we drink only real coffee, fresh, from the beans — you smell how good it is as it's being ground?"

She was stopped by the caretaker and asked what she wanted in the building? Heavy with the bona fide of groceries③ clutched to her body, she said she was working at number 718, on the seventh floor. The caretaker did not tell her not to use the whites' lift; after all, she was not black; her family was very light-skinned.

There was the item "grey button for trousers" on one of his shopping lists. She said as she unpacked the supermarket career, "Give me the pants④, so long, then," and sat on his sofa that was always gritty with fragments of pipe tobacco⑤, sewing in and out through the four holes of the button with firm, fluent movements of the right hand, gestures supplying the articulacy⑥

右手平稳顺畅地将针线从扣子的四个小孔中推进拉出，动作比她平时说话可流利多啦。写出了姑娘钉扣子的熟练程度。

---

① grind: 研磨。
② synthetic flavouring: 合成的味道。
③ bona fide of groceries: 货真价实的货物。
④ pant: 裤子。
⑤ gritty with fragments of pipe tobacco: 沾着碎烟丝末。
⑥ articulacy: 口齿清楚的说话能力。

161

她的小脸削成了瓜子形，眼睛专注地垂下来，柔软的双唇几乎闭上。这是冯·雷恩斯多夫博士眼中美丽的她。

missing from her talk. She had a little yokel's, peasant's①（he thought of it）gap between her two front teeth when she smiled that he didn't much like, but, face ellipsed to three-quarter angle, eyes cast down in concentration with soft lips almost closed, this didn't matter. He said, watching her sew, "You're a good gril"; and touched her.

She remade the bed every late afternoon when they left it and she dressed again before she were home. After a week there was a day when late afternoon became evening, and they were still in the bed.

"Can't you stay the night?"

"My mother," she said.

"phone her. Make an excuse." He was a foreigner. He had been in the country five years, but he didn't understand that people don't usually have telephones in their houses, where she lived. She got up to dress. He didn't want that tender body to go out in the night cold and kept hindering her with the interruption of his hands; saying nothing. Before she put on her coat, when the body had already disappeared, he spoke, "But you must make some arrangement."

"Oh my mother!" Her face opened to fear and vacancy② he could not read.

He was not entirely convinced the woman would think of her daughter as some pure and unsullied virgin③... "Why?"

The girl said, "She'll be scared. She'll be scared we get caught."

"Don't tell her anything Say I'm employing you." In this country he was working in now them were generally

---

① yokel's, peasant's：乡下佬式的、农民式的。

② vacancy：失神。

③ pure and unsullied virgin：纯洁无瑕的处女。

rooms on the roofs of flat buildings for tenants' servants.

She said: "That's what I told the caretaker."

She ground flesh coffee beans every time he wanted a cup while he was working at night. She never attempted to cook anything until she had watched in silence while he did it the way he liked, and she learned to reproduce exactly the simple dishes he preferred. She handled his piece of rock and stone, at first admiring the colours — "It'd make a beautiful ring or necklace, ay." Then he showed her the striations①, the formation of each piece, and explained what each was, and how, in the long life of the earth, it had been formed. He named the mineral it yielded②, and what that was used for. He worked at his papers, writing, every night, so it did not matter that they could not go out together to public places. On Sundays she got into his car in the basement garage and they drove to the country and picnicked away up in the Magaliesberg③, where there was no one. He read or poked about among the rocks④; they climbed together, to the mountain pools. He taught her to swim. She had never seen the sea. She squealed and shrieked in the water⑤, showing the gap between her teeth, as — it crossed his mind — she must do when among her own people. Occasionally he had to go out to dinner at the houses of colleagues from the mining company; she sewed and listened to the radio in the flat and he found her in the bed, warm and already asleep, by the time he came in. He made his way into her body without speaking; she

他看到她在水里又嚎又叫，露出牙齿间的豁缝，联想到她就像在自己人中一定会做的那样。

---

① striations：条纹。
② the mineral it yielded：这种矿石可以提炼出的矿物质。
③ Magaliesberg：马加利斯堡，地名。
④ poked about among the rocks：在石岩中摸来摸去。
⑤ She squealed and shrieked in the water：她在水中又是嚎又是叫的。

163

她仿佛看到了宽敞的大厅里灯火辉煌，人们翩翩起舞，有如剧装的电影中那样，手牵着手，庄重典雅。她看到他的装扮产生的联想。

made him welcome without a word. Once he put on evening dress for a dinner at his country's consulate①; watching him brush one or two fallen hairs from the shoulders of the dark jacket that sat so well on him②, she saw a huge room, all chandeliers③ and people dancing some dance from a costume film④— stately, hand-to-hand. She supposed he was going to fetch, in her place in the car, a partner for the evening. They never kissed when either left the flat; he said, suddenly, kindly, pausing as he picked up cigarettes and keys, "Don't be lonely." And added, "Wouldn't you like to visit your family sometimes, when I have to go out?"

He had told her he was going home to his mother in the forests and mountains of his country near the Italian border (he showed her on the map) after Christmas. She had not told him how her mother, not knowing there was any other variety, assumed he was a medical doctor, so she had talked to her about the doctor's children and the doctor's wife who was a very kind lady, glad to have someone who could help out in the surgery as well as the flat.

She remarked wonderingly on his ability to work until midnight or later, after a day at work. She was so tired when she came home from her cash register at the supermarket that once dinner was eaten she could scarcely keep awake⑤. He explained in a way she could understand that while the work she did was repetitive, undemanding of any real response from her intelligence, requiring little

---

① consulate：领事馆。
② the dark jacket that sat so well on him：笔挺的黑上衣。
③ chandelier：吊灯。
④ costume film：古装片。
⑤ scarcely keep awake：困得眼睛都快睁不开了。

mental or physical effort and therefore unrewarding，his work was his greatest interest，it taxed his mental capacities to their limit，exercised all his concentration，and rewarded him constantly as much with the excitement of a problem presented as with the satisfaction of a problem solved. He said later，putting away his papers，speaking out of a silence："Have you done other kinds of work?" She said，"I was in a clothing factory before. Sportbeau shirts①；you know? But the pay's better in the shop."

Of course. Being a conscientious newspaper-reader in every country he lived in，he was aware that it was only recently that the retail② consumer trade in this one had been allowed to employ coloureds as shop assistants；even punching a cash register represented advancement. With the continuing shortage of semi-skilled whites a girl like this might be able to edge a little farther into the white-collar category. He began to teach her to type. He was aware that her English was poor，even though，as a foreigner，in his ears her pronunciation did not offend，nor categorize her as it would in those of someone of his education whose mother tongue was English. He corrected her grammatical mistakes but missed the less obvious ones because of his own sometimes exotic English usage — she continued to use the singular pronoun "it" when what was required was the plural "they." Because he was a foreigner (although so clever，as she saw) she was less inhibited③ than she might have been by the words she knew she misspelled in her typing. While she sat at the typewriter she thought how one day she would type notes for him，as

使他最大限度地集中精神，发挥自己的思维能力，并不断地给他带来提出问题时的兴奋和解决问题时的满足。写出了他对自己工作的热情。

也不像同样受过高等教育但母语是英语的人那样一下子把她打入另册。

---

① Sportbeau shirts："健儿"牌衬衣。
② retail：零售。
③ less inhibited：不那么压抑沮丧。

well as making coffee the way he liked it, and taking him inside her body without saying anything, and sitting (even if only through the empty streets of quiet Sundays①) beside him in his car, like a wife.

On a summer night near Christmas — he had already bought and hidden a slightly showy but nevertheless good watch② he thought she would like — there was a knocking at the door that brought her out of the bathroom and him to his feet, at his work-table. No one ever came to the flat at night; he had no friends intimate enough to drop in without warning. The summons was an imperious③ banging that did not pause and clearly would not stop until the door was opened.

这敲门声来势汹汹,接连不断。暗示下文将出现紧急的情况。

She stood in the open bathroom doorway gazing at him across the passage into the living-room; her bare feet and shoulders were free of a big bath-towel. She said nothing, did not even whisper. The flat seemed to shake with the strong unhurried blows.

He made as if to go to the door, at last, but now she ran and clutched him by both arms. She shook her head wildly; her lips drew back but her teeth were clenched④, she didn't speak. She pulled him into the bedroom, snatched some clothes from the clean laundry laid out on the bed, and got into the wall-cupboard, thrusting the key at his hand. Although his arms and calves felt weakly cold he was horrified, distastefully embarrassed at the sight of her pressed back crouching there under his suits and coat; it was horrible and ridiculous. Come out! he whispered. No! Come out! She hissed: Where? Where can I go?

虽然他胳膊腿肚都冷丝丝地发软,看到她躲在他的西装和大衣下面一个劲地后缩,仍然觉得不成体统,丢人现眼,令人难堪;这太骇人听闻,太荒唐滑稽了。

---

① through the empty streets of quiet Sundays:在寂静的星期天驶过空旷无人的街道。
② a slightly showy but nevertheless good watch:有点花哨但也确实不错的手表。
③ imperious:专横的。
④ her lips drew back but her teeth were clenched:嘴唇抿着但牙齿紧合。

Never mind: Get out of there!

He put out his hand to grasp her. At bay, she said with all the force of her terrible whisper, baring the gap in her teeth: I'll throw myself out the window.

She forced the key into his hand like the handle of a knife. He closed the door on her face and drove the key home in the lock, then dropped it among coins in his trouser pocket.

He unspotted the chain that was looped across① the flat door. He turned the serrated knob of the Yale lock②. The three policemen, two in plain clothes③, stood there without impatience although they had been banging on the door for several minutes. The big dark one with an elaborate mustache held out in a hand wearing a plaited gilt ring④ some sort of identity card.

Dr. von Leinsdorf said quietly, the blood coming strangely back to legs and arms, "What is it?"

The sergeant⑤ told him they knew there was a coloured girl in the flat. They had had information: "I been watching this flat three months, I know."

"I am alone here." Dr. von Leinsdorf did not raise his voice.

"I know, I know who is here. Come —" And the sergeant and his two assistants went into the living-room, the kitchen, the bathroom (the sergeant picked up a bottle of after-shave cologne⑥, seemed to study the French label), and the bedroom. The assistants removed the clean laundry that was laid upon the bed and then

---

① looped across: 加固。
② the serrated knob of the Yale lock: 耶鲁牌门上的齿状纽。
③ in plain clothes: 身穿便衣。
④ a plaited gilt ring: 一只拧花镀金戒指。
⑤ sergeant: 警官。
⑥ a bottle of after-shave cologne: 一瓶刮脸后用的古龙水。

turned back the bedding, carrying the sheets over to be examined by the sergeant under the lamp. They talked to one another in Afrikaans①, which the Doctor did not understand. The sergeant himself looked under the bed, and lifted the long curtains at the window. The wall-cupboard was of the kind that has no knobs; he saw that it was locked and began to ask in Afrikaans, then politely changed to English, "Give us the key."

Dr. von Leinsdorf said, "I'm sorry, I left it at my office — I always lock and take my keys with me in the mornings."

"It's no good, man, you better give me the key."

He smiled a little, reasonably. "It's on my office desk."

The assistants produced a screwdriver② and he watched while they inserted it where the cupboard doors met, gave it quick, firm but not forceful leverage③. He heard the lock give.

She had been naked, it was true, when they knocked. But now she was wearing a long-sleeved T-shirt with an appliqued butterfly motif④ on one breast, and a pair of jeans. Her feet were still bare; she had managed, by feel, in the dark, to get into some of the clothing she had snatched from the bed, but she had no shoes. She had perhaps been weeping behind the cupboard door (her cheeks looked stained⑤) but now her face was sullen⑥ and she was breathing heavily, her diaphragm⑦ contracting

她沉着脸，喘着粗气，她的膈膜剧烈地舒张收缩，胸脯顶着衬衣。写出了这时她的紧张状态。

① Afrikaans：非洲荷兰语，一种语言。
② screwdriver：螺丝刀。
③ firm but not forceful leverage：稳稳地但并不过于用力。
④ an appliqued butterfly motif：一只绣的蝴蝶图案。
⑤ her cheeks looked stained：她的面颊上有泪痕。
⑥ sullen：阴沉的。
⑦ diaphragm：膈膜。

and expanding exaggeratedly and her breasts pushing against the cloth. It made her appear angry; it might simply have been that she was half-suffocated① in the cupboard and needed oxygen. She did not look at Dr. von Leinsdorf. She would not reply to the sergeant's questions.

They were taken to the police station where they were at once separated and in turn led for examination by the district surgeon. The man's underwear was taken away and examined, as the sheets had been, for signs of his seed. When the girl was undressed, it was discovered that beneath her jeans she was wearing a pair of men's briefs with his name on the neatly-sewn laundry tag②; in her haste, she had taken the wrong garment to her hiding-place.

Now she cried, standing there before the district surgeon in a man's underwear.

He courteously③ pretended not to notice. He handed briefs, jeans, and T-shirt round the door, and motioned her to lie on a white-sheeted high table where he placed her legs apart, resting in stirrups④, and put into her where the other had made his way so warmly a cold hard instrument that expanded wider and wider. Her thighs and knees trembled uncontrollably while the doctor looked into her and touched her deep inside with more hard instruments, carrying wafers of gauze⑤.

When she came out of the examining room back to the charge office, Dr. von Leinsdorf was not there; they

---

① haff-suffocated：憋得半死。
② the neatly-sewn laundry tag：缝得很牢靠的洗衣标签。
③ courteously：有礼貌地。
④ resting in stirrups：放到两只脚蹬上。
⑤ hard instruments, carrying wafers of gauze：带着薄纱布片的冰冷的器具。

must have taken him somewhere else. She spent what was left of the night in a cell, as he must be doing; but early in the morning she was released and taken home to her mother's house in the coloured township by a white man who explained he was the clerk of the lawyer who had been engaged for her by Dr. von Leinsdorf. Dr. von Leins-doff, the clerk said, had also been bailed out① that morning. He did not say when, or if she would see him again.

A statement made by the girl to the police was handed in to Court when she and the man appeared to meet charges of contravening the Immorality Act② in a Johannesburg③ flat on the night of — December, 19—. I lived with the white man in his flat. He had intercourse with me sometimes. He gave me tablets to take to prevent me becoming pregnant.

Interviewed by the Sunday papers, the girl said, "I'm sorry for the sadness brought to my mother." She said she was one of nine children of a female laundry worker. She had left school in Standard Three because there was no money at home for gym clothes or a school blazer④. She had worked as a machinist in a factory and a cashier in a supermarket. Dr. von Leinsdorf taught her to type his notes.

Dr. Franz-Josef von Leinsdorf described as the grandson of a baroness⑤, a cultured man engaged in international mineralogical research, said he accepted social distinctions between people but didn't think they

---

① bailed out: 保释。
② contravening the Immorality Act: 不道德法。
③ Johannesburg: 约翰内斯堡,地名。
④ blazer: (常带有俱乐部、学校、运动队等的颜色或徽章的)夹克。
⑤ Baroness: 女勋爵。

should be legally imposed. "Even in my own country it's difficult for a person from a higher class to marry one from a lower class."

The two accused gave no evidence. They did not greet or speak to each other in Court. The Defence argued that the sergeant's evidence that they had been living together as man and wife was heresay①. (The woman with the dachshund, the caretaker?) The magistrate acquitted them because the State failed to prove carnal intercourse② had taken place on the night of — December, 19—.

The girl's mother was quoted, with photograph, in the Sunday papers: "I won't let my daughter work as a servant for a white man again."

II

The farm children play together when they are small; but once the white children go away to school they soon don't play together any more, even in the holidays. Although most of the black children get some sort of schooling, they drop every year farther behind the grades passed by the white children; the childish vocabulary, the child's exploration of the adventurous possibilities of dam, koppies, mealie lands, and veld — there comes a time when the white children have surpassed these with the vocabulary of boarding-school and the possibilities of inter-school sports matches and the kind of adventures seen at the cinema. This usefully coincides with the age of twelve or thirteen; so that by the time early adolescence is reached③, the black children are making, along with the bodily changes common to all, an easy transition to adult forms of address, beginning to call their old playmates

白人儿童用寄宿学校的词汇取代了稚气的话语,以校内运动比赛和在电影中见到的那类冒险尝试取代了去水坝、玉米地和大草原探查的童年活动。

---

① heresay:纯属捏造。
② carnal intercourse:性交。
③ adolescence is reached:青春期开始。

missus and baasie①— little master.

The trouble was Paulus Eysendyck② did not seem to realize that Thebedi③ was now simply one of the crowd of farm children down at the kraal④, recognizable in his sisters' old clothes. The first Christmas holidays after he had gone to boarding-school he brought home for Thebedi a painted box he had made in his wood-work class. He had to give it to her secretly because he had nothing for the other children at the kraal. And she gave him, before he went back to school, a bracelet she had made of thin brass wire and the grey-and-white beans of the castor-oil crop his father cultivated. (When they used to play together, she was the one who had taught Paulus how to make clay oxen for their toy spans⑤.) There was a craze⑥, even in the platteland towns like the one where he was at school, for boys to wear elephant-hair and other bracelets⑦ beside their watch-straps; his was admired, friends asked him to get similar ones for them. He said the natives made them on his father's farm and he would try.

When he was fifteen, six feet tall, and tramping round at school dances with the girls from the "sister" school in the same town; when he had learnt how to tease and flirt and fondle⑧ quite intimately these girls who were the daughters of prosperous farmers like his father; when he had even met one who, at a wedding he had attended with his parents on a nearby farm, had let him do with

她送给他一条用细铜丝和她爸爸种植的灰白相间的蓖麻籽穿制的手链。这里写出了两个好朋友互送礼物,感情很好。

他学会了如何亲亲密密地和姑娘们开玩笑、献殷勤,并且温存抚爱。这里说出了保勒斯·埃森戴克的变化。

---

① missus and baasie：小姐和少爷。
② Paulus Eysendyck：保勒斯·埃森戴克,人名。
③ Thebedi：赛比蒂,人名。
④ Kraal：土著村。
⑤ make clay oxen for their toy spans：捏泥牛配他们的玩具车辆。
⑥ craze：时尚。
⑦ elephant-hair and other bracelets：鬃编的手镯或别的什么。
⑧ fondle：爱抚。

her in a locked storeroom what people did when they made love — when he was as far from his childhood as all this, he still brought home from a shop in town a red plastic belt and gilt hoop ear-rings① for the black girl, Thebedi. She told her father the missus had given these to her as a reward for some work she had done — it was true she sometimes was called to help out in the farmhouse. She told the girls in the kraal that she had a sweetheart nobody knew about, far away, away on another farm, and they giggled, and teased, and admired her. There was a boy in the Kraal called Njabulo② who said he wished he could have brought her a belt and ear-rings.

她们格格地笑,开玩笑逗她,对她赞美不已。表现了大家对她的羡慕。

When the farmer's son was home for the holidays she wandered far from the kraal and her companions. He went for walks alone. They had not arranged this; it was an urge each followed independently③. He knew it was she, from a long way off. She knew that his dog would not bark at her. Down at the dried-up river-bed where five or six years ago the children had caught a leguaan④ one great day — a creature that combined ideally the size and ferocious aspect of the crocodile with the harmlessness of the lizard⑤— they squatted⑥ side by side on the earth bank. He told her traveler's tales: about school, about the punishments at school, particularly exaggerating both their nature and his indifference to them. He told her about the town of Middle-burg⑦, which she had never seen. She had nothing to tell but she prompted with many

他们童年的一件趣事,他们曾捉住一只大蜥蜴,那家伙真没得挑,看上去像鳄鱼一样庞大凶猛,实际上又如壁虎一般驯善无害。

---

① a red plastic belt and gilt hoop ear-rings：红塑料腰带和镀金大耳环。
② Njabulo：亚布罗,人名。
③ an urge each followed independently：听从一种冲动的指示。
④ leguaan：蜥蜴。
⑤ lizard：壁虎。
⑥ squat：蹲坐。
⑦ Middle-burg：米德尔堡市,地名。

渲染了当时的一种环境，四周的白臭树和好望角柳树的根从被腐蚀的土层中露出，他一边说话，一边把根扯来扯去。

介绍了一个孩子们做游戏的好地方，靠活树支撑着的、被蚂蚁蛀空的老树密如网络，遮掩着那地方，野苜蓿在树间茂密丛生，这儿那儿，间或有仙人掌类的霸王树，表皮塌缩，刺毛挺立，有如老人的脸，干巴巴地活着，等待着下一个雨季。

questions, like any good listener. While he talked he twisted and tugged at the roots of white stinkwood and Cape willow trees[1] that looped out of the eroded earth around them. It had always been a good spot for children's games, down there hidden by the mesh of old, ant-eaten trees held in place by vigorous ones, wild asparagus[2] bushing up between the trunks, and here and there prickly-pear cactus[3] sunken-skinned and bristly, like an old man's face, keeping alive sapless until the next rainy season. She punctured the dry hide of a prickly-pear again and again with a sharp stick while she listened. She laughed a lot at what he told her, sometimes dropping her face on her knees, sharing amusement with the cool shady earth beneath her bare feet[4]. She put on her pair of shoes — white sandals, thickly Blanco-ed[5] against the farm dust — when he was on the farm, but these were taken off and laid aside, at the river-bed.

One summer afternoon when there was water flowing there and it was very hot she waded in as they used to do when they were children, her dress bunched modestly and tucked into the legs of her pants[6]. The schoolgirls he went swimming with at dams or pools on neighbouring farms wore bikinis[7] but the sight of their dazzling bellies and thighs[8] in the sunlight had never made him feel what he felt now, when the girl came up the bank and sat beside him, the drops of water beading off her dark legs

---

① white stinkwood and Cape willow trees：白臭树和好望角柳树。
② wild asparagus：野苜蓿，一种植物。
③ prickly-pear cactus：仙人掌类的霸王树。
④ the cool shady earth beneath her bare feet：赤脚下的阴凉土地。
⑤ thickly Blanco-ed：厚厚的白色。
⑥ her dress bunched modestly and tucked into the legs of her pants：裙子小心卷起掖在裤管处。
⑦ bikinis：比基尼。
⑧ dazzling bellies and thighs：耀眼的腹部和大腿。

the only points of light in the earth-smelling, deep shade. They were not afraid of one another, they had known one another always; he did with her what he had done that time in the storeroom at the wedding, and this time it was so lovely, so lovely, he was surprised ... and she was surprised by it, too — he could see in her dark face that was part of the shade, with her big dark eyes, shiny as soft water, watching him attentively: as she had when they used to huddle over[1] their teams of mud oxen, as she had when he told her about detention[2] weekends at school.

两人的深情对望，他从她的脸上读到她的惊讶，她黑色的面孔是幽暗环境的一部分，她的大大的黑眼睛，像温柔的水一样闪着光，专心致志地望着他。

They went to the river-bed often through those summer holidays. They met just before the light went, as it does quite quickly, and each returned home with the dark — she to her mother's hut, he to the farmhouse — in time for the evening meal. He did not tell her about school or town any more. She did not ask questions any longer. He told her, each time, when they would meet again. Once or twice it was very early in the morning; the lowing of the cows being driven to graze came to them where they lay, dividing them with unspoken recognition of the sound read in their two pairs of eyes, opening so close to each other[3].

He was a popular boy at school. He was in the second, then the first soccer team. The head girl of the "sister" school was said to have a crush on him[4]; he didn't particularly like her, but there was a pretty blonde who put up her long hair into a kind of doughnut with a

---

① huddle over：俯在。
② detention：留堂（处罚学生）。
③ opening so close to each other：四目对望。
④ have a crush on him：对他有意。

black ribbon round it①, whom he took to see films when the schoolboys and girls had a free Saturday afternoon. He had been driving tractors and other farm vehicles since he was ten years old, and as soon as he was eighteen he got a driver's licence and in the holidays, this last year of his school life, he took neighbours' daughters to dances and to the drive-in cinema② that had just opened twenty kilometers from the farm. His sisters were married, by then; his parents often left him in charge of the farm over the weekend while they visited the young wives and grandchildren.

When Thebedi saw the farmer and his wife drive away on a Saturday afternoon, the boot of their Mercedes③ filled with fresh-killed poultry and vegetables from the garden that it was part of her father's work to tend, she knew that she must come not to the river-bed but up to the house. The house was an old one, thick-walled, dark against the heat④. The kitchen was its lively thoroughfare⑤, with servants, food supplies, begging cats and dogs, pots boiling over, washing being damped for ironing, and the big deep-freezer the missus had ordered from town, bearing a crocheted mat and a vase of plastic irises⑥. But the dining-room with the bulging-legged heavy table was shut up in its rich, old smell of soup and tomato sauce. The sitting-room curtains were drawn and the T. V. set silent. The door of the parents' bedroom was locked and the empty rooms where the girls had slept had sheets of plastic spread over the beds. It was in one of

厨房的特点：热闹的通衢大道，里面是众多的仆人、烧滚的油锅、潮湿待熨的衣物，以及太太从城里订购的大冰柜，上面有一条钩织的盖垫和一瓶塑料鸢尾花。

饭厅的特点：摆着餐桌的饭厅是与外部隔绝的，封闭在汤和番茄汁的古老浓郁的气味中。

① a kind of doughnut with a black ribbon round it：挽成圆髻，四周包着黑缎带。
② drive-in cinema：汽车影院。
③ Mercedes：梅赛迪斯牌汽车。
④ thick-walled, dark against the heat：墙厚室幽，能避暑热。
⑤ thoroughfare：大道。
⑥ a crocheted mat and a vase of plastic irises：一条钩织的盖垫和一瓶塑料鸢尾花。

176

these that she and the farmer's son stayed together whole nights — almost: she had to get away before the house servants, who knew her, came in at dawn. There was a risk someone would discover her or traces of her presence if he took her to his own bedroom, although she had looked into it many times when she was helping out in the house and knew well, there, the row of silver cups[①] he had won at school.

When she was eighteen and the farmer's son nineteen and working with his father on the farm before entering a veterinary college[②], the young man Njabulo asked her father for her. Njabulo's parents met with hers and the money he was to pay in place of the cows it is customary to give a prospective bride's parents was settled upon. He had no cows to offer; he was a labourer on the Eysendyck farm[③], like her father. A bright youngster; old Eysendyck had taught him brick-laying and was using him for odd jobs[④] in construction, around the place. She did not tell the farmer's son that her parents had arranged for her to marry. She did not tell him, either, before he left for his first term at the veterinary college, that she thought she was going to have a baby. Two months after her marriage to Njabulo, she gave birth to a daughter. There was no disgrace in that; among her people it is customary for a young man to make sure, before marriage, that the chosen girl is not barren, and Njabulo made love to her then. But the infant was very light and did not quickly grow darker as most African babies do. Already at birth there was on its head a quantity of

赛比蒂女儿出生的特征：她出生时头上就有不少平直纤细的浅色胎毛，就像大草原上一些草籽的细绒，她睁开眼，那尚不能调节瞳孔的眼睛灰里透黄。

① the row of silver cups：一排银奖杯。
② veterinary college：兽医学院。
③ Eysendyck farm：埃森戴克家。
④ odd jobs：修修建建的营生。

177

straight, fine floss, like that which carries the seeds of certain weeds in the veld. The unfocused eyes it opened were grey flecked with yellow. Njabulo was the matt, opaque coffee-grounds colour① that has always been called black; the colour of Thebedi's legs on which beaded water looked oyster-shell blue②, the same colour as Thebedi's face, where the black eyes, with their interested gaze and clear whites③, were so dominant.

Njabulo made no complaint. Out of his farm labourer's earnings he bought from the Indian store a cellophane-windowed pack④ containing a pink plastic bath, six napkins, a card of safety pins, a knitted jacket, cap and bootees, a dress, and a tin of Johnson's Baby Powder⑤, for Thebedi's baby.

When it was two weeks old Paulus Eysendyck arrived home from the veterinary college for the holidays. He drank a glass of fresh, still-warm milk in the childhood familiarity of⑥ his mother's kitchen and heard her discussing with the old house-servant where they could get a reliable substitute to help out⑦ now that the girl Thebedi had had a baby. For the first time since he was a small boy he came right into the kraal. It was eleven o'clock in the morning. The men were at work in the lands. He looked about him, urgently; the women turned away, each not wanting to be the one approached to point out where Thebedi lived. Thebedi appeared, coming slowly from the

他四下里看看，很焦急。

---

① opaque coffee-grounds colour：半透明的暗咖啡渣色。
② oyster-shell blue：贝壳蓝。
③ interested gaze and clear whites：神情专注，黑白分明。
④ a cellophane-windowed pack：一块透明的玻璃纸。
⑤ Johnson's Baby Powder：强生牌婴儿爽身粉。
⑥ in the childhood familiarity of：从小熟悉的。
⑦ a reliable substitute to help out：一个可靠并能替换的帮手。

hut Njabulo had built in white man's style, with a tin chimney, and a proper window with glass panes set in straight as walls made of unfired bricks would allow. She greeted him with hands brought together and a token movement representing the respectful bob① with which she was accustomed to acknowledge she was in the presence of his father or mother. He lowered his head under the doorway of her home and went in. He said, "I want to see. Show me."

She had taken the bundle off her back before she came out into the light to face him. She moved between the iron bedstead made up with Njabulo's checked blankets and the small wooden table where the pink plastic bath stood among food and kitchen pots, and picked up the bundle from the snugly-blanketed grocer's box② where it lay. The infant was asleep; she revealed the closed, pale, plump tiny face, with a bubble of spit at the corner of the mouth, the spidery pink hands stirring. She took off the woollen cap and the straight fine hair flew up after it in static electricity③, showing gilded strands here and there. He said nothing. She was watching him as she had done when they were little, and the gang of children had trodden down a crop in their games or trangressed in some other way④ for which he, as the farmer's son, the white one among them, must intercede with the farmer, she disturbed the sleeping face by scratching or tickling gently at a cheek with one finger, and slowly the eyes opened, saw nothing, were still asleep, and then, awake, no longer narrowed, looked out at them, grey with yellowish

赛比蒂家的房子构造：亚布罗仿照白人房子修造的，有铁皮烟囱，玻璃窗尽可能周正地安装在用未经烧制的砖砌成的窗框里，像模像样的。

赛比蒂抱起孩子的过程：她从铺着亚布罗的花格毯的铁床和上面堆放着食物、铁锅以及那只浴盆的小桌之间走过，从一只舒舒服服地铺着毯子的杂货箱里捧起襁褓中的孩子。

婴儿可爱的状态：他睡着，露出闭着眼的、胖胖的浅肤色的小脸，嘴边处吐出些泡沫，纤纤小粉手摆动着。她取下婴孩的毛帽子，平柔的细发由于静电的作用纷纷飞起，这里那里现出一缕缕的金色。

---

① the respectful bob：尊敬的鞠躬。
② the snugly-blanketed grocer's box：铺着毯子的杂货箱。
③ static electricity：静电。
④ trangressed in some other way：捅了别的什么娄子。

flecks①，his own hazel eyes.

He struggled for a moment with a grimace of tears, anger, and self-pity. She could not put out her hand to him. He said, "You haven't been near the house with it?"

She shook her head.

"Never?"

Again she shook her head.

"Don't take it out. Stay inside. Can't you take it away somewhere. You must give it to someone —"

She moved to the door with him.

He said, "I'll see what I will do. I don't know." And then he said: "I feel like killing myself."

Her eyes began to glow②, to thicken with tears. For a moment there was the feeling between them that used to come when they were alone down at the river-bed.

He walked out.

Two days later, when his mother and father had left the farm for the day, he appeared again. The women were away on the lands, weeding, as they were employed to do as casual labour in the summer; only the very old remained, propped up③ on the ground outside the huts in the flies and the sun Thebedi did not ask him in. The child had not been well; it had diarrhoea④. He asked where its food was. She said, "The milk comes from me." He went into Njabulo's house, where the child lay; she did not follow but stayed outside the door and watched without⑤ seeing an old crone who had lost her mind, talking to herself, talking to the fowls who ignored her.

---

① grey with yellowish flecks：灰色中闪着微黄的光点。
② glow：发红。
③ propped up：东倒西歪地。
④ diarrhoea：拉肚子。
⑤ watched without：视而不见的。

She thought she heard small grunts from the hut, the kind of infant grunt that indicates a full stomach, a deep sleep. After a time, long or short she did not know, he came out and walked away with plodding stride① (his father's gait) out of sight, towards his father's house.

The baby was not fed during the night and although she kept telling Njabulo it was sleeping, he saw for himself in the morning that it was dead. He comforted her with words and caresses. She did not cry but simply sat, staring at the door. Her hands were cold as dead chickens' feet to his touch.

Njabulo buried the little baby where farm workers were buried, in the place in the veld the farmer had given them. Some of the mounds had been left to weather away unmarked, others were covered with stones and a few had fallen wooden crosses. He was going to make a cross but before it was finished the police came and dug up the grave and took away the dead baby: someone — one of the other labourers? their women? — had reported that the baby was almost white, that, strong and healthy, it had died suddenly after a visit by the farmer's son. Pathological tests② on the infant corpse showed intestinal③ damage not always consistent with death by natural causes.

Thebedi went for the first time to the country town where Paulus had been to school, to give evidence at the preparatory examination④ into the charge of murder brought against him. She cried hysterically in the witness

---

① walked away with plodding stride: 步履沉重的。
② Pathological tests: 病理检查。
③ intestinal: 肠的。
④ the preparatory examination: 预审。

box①, saying yes, yes (the gilt hoop ear-rings swung in her ears), she saw the accused pouring liquid into the baby's mouth. She said he had threatened to shoot her if she told anyone.

More than a year went by before, in that same town, the case was brought to trial. She came to Court with a new-born baby on her back. She wore gilt hoop ear-rings; she was calm; she said she had not seen what the white man did in the house.

Paulus Eysendyck said he had visited the hut but had not poisoned the child.

The Defence did not contest that there had been a love relationship between the accused and the girl, or that intercourse had taken place, but submitted there was no proof that the child was the accused's.

The judge told the accused there was strong suspicion against him but not enough proof that he had committed the crime. The Court could not accept the girl's evidence because it was clear she had committed perjury② either at this trial or at the preparatory examination. There was the suggestion in the mind of the Court that she might be an accomplice in the crime③; but, again, insufficient proof.

The judge commended the honourable behaviour of the husband (sitting in court in a brown-and-yellow-quartered golf cap④ bought for Sundays) who had not rejected his wife and had "even provided clothes for the unfortunate infant out of his slender means⑤."

The verdict⑥ on the accused was "not guilty".

① in the witness box: 证人席。
② perjury: 伪证。
③ an accomplice in the crime: 杀婴的同谋犯。
④ brown-and-yellow-quartered golf cap: 棕黄相间的四分格高尔夫球帽。
⑤ slender means: 微薄的收入。
⑥ verdict: (陪审团的)裁决。

The young white man refused to accept the congratulations of press and public and left the Court with his mother's raincoat shielding his face from photographers. His father said to the press, "I will try and carry on as best I can to hold up my head in the district."

Interviewed by the Sunday papers, who spelled her name in a variety of ways, the black girl, speaking in her own language, was quoted beneath her photograph: "It was a thing of our childhood, we don't see each other anymore."

【思考题】

1. 冯·雷恩斯多夫博士是个怎样的科学家？营业员姑娘和他产生了短暂的爱情。你认为他们最终分开的原因是什么？

2. 故事反映了冯·雷恩斯多夫博士暂居的国家有着怎样的社会文化背景？反映了怎样的传统社会习俗？

3. 第二个短篇中婴儿的真正死因是什么？谁是真正的凶手？

4. 两个短篇中的姑娘有哪些相似之处？说明了什么社会问题？

Debbie and Julie

黛比和朱莉

多丽丝·莱辛

【导读】

多丽丝·莱辛(Doris Lessing, 1919—2013),当代英国杰出的作家。她作为一名"女性经验的史诗作者","以其怀疑的态度、激情和远见,清楚地剖析了一个分裂的文化"从而赢得了 2007 年度诺贝尔文学奖。

莱辛 1919 年 10 月 22 日出生于波斯(即现在的伊朗),父母均为英国人。莱辛自幼随父母过着漂泊动荡的生活。1925 年跟随父母搬到英国在非洲的殖民地南罗得西亚(现属津巴布韦)生活,在那里度过了大部分童年和青年时光。由于生活动荡,加之眼疾,莱辛并未受过多少正规的学校教育,十二三岁时就离开了学校;十六岁便外出打工谋生,先后做过电话接线员、保姆、速记员等工作。1949 年,在经历了两次失败的婚姻之后,莱辛携幼子移居英国。从此,她开始了专业作家的写作生涯。

莱辛早期的作品很多取材于她早年在南部非洲的经历。1951 年莱辛的处女作《野草在歌唱》(*The Grass Is Singing*)出版,小说因深刻揭露了非洲殖民地的种族压迫和种族矛盾而引起强烈反响,莱辛从此在文坛崭露头角。1962 年莱辛发表了小说《金色笔记》(*The Golden Notebook*),该作品被公认为是莱辛的代表作。《金色笔记》因其对女性独立意识及生存困境的真实描写而受到各国女权主义者的青睐,被奉为"女权主义者的《圣经》"。

20 世纪 70 年代末 80 年代初,莱辛的创作风格从关注社会现实的主流文学创作转向非主流的科幻小说创作。从 1979 年开始,她以一年一部小说的速度,连续推出五部"太空小说"系列:《南船座中的老人星:档案》(*Canopus in Argos*,1979—1983),包括《关于沦为殖民地的五号行星:什卡斯塔》(*Shikasta*,1979)、《第三、四、五区域间的联姻》(*The Marriage Between Zones Three*,*Four*,*and Five*,1980)、《天狼星人的试验》(*The Sirian Experiments*,1981)、《八号行星代表的产生》(*The Making of Representatives for Planets*,1982)和《有关伏尔英帝国多情人的文件》(*Documents Relating to the Sentimental Agents in the Volen Empire*,1983)。

除了"太空小说"系列，莱辛还陆续发表了《善良的恐怖分子》（*The Good Terrorist*，1985）、《第五个孩子》（*The Fifth Child*，1988）等短篇小说，在题材和创作手法上，又回到莱辛一贯擅长的现实主义风格。1996 年莱辛又推出了长篇小说《又来了，爱情》（*Love，Again*，1996），讲述了一个惊世骇俗的老年女性的爱情故事。1999 年，莱辛推出了长篇小说《玛拉和丹恩历险记》（*Mara and Dann：An Adventure*，1999），讲述了一个发生在几千年后的探险故事；2000 年，发表了《第五个小孩》的续集《本，在这个世上》（*Ben，in the World*）；2002 年、2003 年，两部关注当代社会和女性问题的小说《最甜的梦》（*The Sweetest Dream*）和《祖母们》（*The Grandmothers*）发表。2007 年的《裂缝》（*The Cleft*）是对历史的某种重构。

自 1950 年步入文坛至今，莱辛凭借自己的艺术天分和不懈的努力，已先后发表了五十多部风格独特，内容深邃的长、中篇以及短篇小说集，两部自传，大量的诗歌、剧本、散文、文论及纪实性文学作品，堪称英国文坛的"常青树"。而莱辛的作品，无论是涉及现实世界，还是虚幻的太空世界，无论是聚焦于女性个体生命体验，还是社会政治热点问题的思考，都体现出一种强烈的道德责任感和社会担当意识。

莱辛的代表作《金色笔记》是一部百科全书式的作品，不仅真实再现了 20 世纪 60 年代西方女性的生存困境，更以史诗般的笔触描绘了"二战"之后整个英国社会生活的时代面貌。小说的主人公安娜是一个离异的女作家。五本笔记中的黑色笔记写的是作家安娜在非洲的经历，其中许多内容涉及了殖民主义、种族主义问题；红色笔记写安娜的政治生活，记录了她对斯大林主义从憧憬到幻灭的思想过程；黄色笔记是安娜根据自身的生活经历所创作的一个爱情故事，题为"第三者的影子"；蓝色笔记是安娜的日记，记录了她精神危机的轨迹，其中相当大的篇幅是一些从《快讯》《政治家》等报纸上直接剪下来的时事新闻报道。出于对崩溃和混乱的恐惧，安娜同时在这四本笔记上写作。当她能面对生活中的混乱时，便结束了这四本笔记，开始在一本新的笔记（《金色笔记》）里记下她的一切，对人生进行总结。这五本笔记中还包括安娜未完成的一些短篇小说的片断、故事梗概、提纲，以及安娜粘贴在笔记上的新闻剪报。这让《金色笔记》看似是一些凌乱、无序的素材的胡乱堆砌，使人无法卒读。《金色笔记》似乎没有连贯的故事情节，也没有传统小说的开端、发展、高潮、结局的叙述模式。但它既有当时时代图景的广阔呈现，又有对人类生存状态的执着探求；既涉及政治、社会和民族方面的问题，又涉及心理、种族、女性等问题，从而实现了莱辛写作此书的意图，即"要写一本全面描写整个时代的精神状况和道德气候的书"。

短篇小说《黛比和朱莉》以心理刻画见长，故事情节取材于真实事件，内容并不复杂。朱莉一直是个乖女孩，但不幸在学校被一个男生强奸怀孕，朱莉不敢告诉对她冷漠、不闻不问的父母,知道父母了解真相后只会把她赶出家门。朱莉选择离家出走,令她感到无比温暖的是碰到了黛比,黛比请她住到自己的房子里,像亲姐姐一样无微不至地照顾关心她,让朱莉对生活充满了憧憬和渴望。朱莉快要临产时黛比正好不在身边,朱莉选了一个隐蔽之处生下了女儿,整个生产过程只有一条野狗相伴。朱莉把女儿放在一个电话亭里,亲眼看到她被救护车带走后回到了家中,她打算完成学业后离开父母,把女儿领养回来,勇敢地肩负起自己的使命,过与黛比一样独立自强的生活。

  小说将女性心理刻画得惟妙惟肖,真实再现了朱莉在整个事情过程中的痛苦挣扎、渴望温暖友爱的心理特征,表现了莱辛典型的女性主义观。而通过小说揭示的父母与子女的隔阂问题深刻暴露了英国当代社会的家庭危机。

Debbie and Julie

  The fat girl in the sky-blue coat again took herself to the mirror. She could not keep away from it. Why did the others not comment on her scarlet cheeks, just like when she got measles①, and the way her hair was stuck down with② sweat? But they didn't notice her; she thought they did not see her. This was because of Debbie who protected her, so they got nothing out of noticing her.

  She knew it was cold outside, for she had opened a window to check. Inside this flat it was, she believed, warm, but the heating in the block was erratic③, particularly in bad weather, and then the electric fires were brought out and Debbie swore and complained and said she was going to move. But Julie knew Debbie would not move. She could not: she had fought for this flat to be hers, and people (men) from everywhere — "from all over the world," as Julie would proudly say to herself — knew Debbie was here. And besides, Julie was going to need to think of Debbie here, when she herself got home:

---

① measles:麻疹,风疹。
② be stucked down with:被……卡住。
③ erratic:古怪的,反常的。

remember the bright rackety place where people came and went, some of them frightening, but none threatening her, Julie, because Debbie looked after her.

She was so wet she was afraid she would start squelching①. What if the wet came through the coat? Back she went to the bathroom and took off the coat. The dress — Debbie's, like the once smart coat — was now orange instead of yellow, because it was soaked. Julie knew there would be a lot of water at some point, because the paperback② Debbie had bought her said so, but she didn't know if she was simply sweating. In the book everything was so tidy and regular, and she had checked the stages she must expect a dozen times. But now she stood surrounded by jars of bath salts③ and lotions④ on the shelf that went all around the bathroom, and felt cold water springing from her forehead, hot water running down her legs. She seemed to have pains everywhere, but could not match what she felt with the book.

On went the blue coat again. It was luckily still loose on her, for Debbie was a big girl, and she was small. Back she went to the long mirror in Debbie's room, and what she saw on her face, a look of distracted pain, made her decide it was time to leave. She longed for Debbie, who might after all just turn up. She could not bear to go without seeing her... she had promised! But she had to, now, at once, and she wrote on a piece of paper she had kept ready just in case. "I am going now. Thanks for everything. Thank you, thank you, thank you. All my love, Julie." Then her home address. She stuck this letter

这是朱莉感激黛比对她的爱与呵护。

① squenlch：发出吧唧声（和水摩擦的声音）。
② paperback：平装书，平装本。
③ bath salts：浴盐。
④ lotion：洗液。

in a sober① white envelope into the frame of Debbie's mirror and went into the living room, where a lot of people were lolling② about watching the TV. No, not really a lot, four people crammed③ the little room. No one even looked at her. Then the man she was afraid of, and who had tried to "get" her, took in the fact that she stood there, enormous and smiling foolishly in her blue coat, and gave her the look she always got from him, which said he didn't know why Debbie bothered with her but didn't care. He was a sharp clever man, handsome she supposed, in a flashy Arab way. He was from Lebanon, and she must make allowances because there was a war there. Sitting beside him on the sofa was the girl who took the drugs around for him. She was smart and clever, like him, but blonde shiny and she looked like a model for cheap clothes. A model was what she said she was, but Julie knew she wasn't. And there were two girls Julie had never seen before, and she supposed they were innocents, as she had been. They looked all giggly④ and anxious to please, and they were waiting. For Debbie?

Julie went quietly through the room to the landing outside and stood watching for the lift. She checked her carrier bag, ready for a month now, stuffed⑤ under her bed. In it was a torch⑥, pieces of string wrapped in a piece of plastic, two pairs of knickers⑦, a cardigan⑧, a thick towel with an old blouse of Debbie's cut open to lie

---

① sober：素净的。
② loll：懒洋洋地躺着。
③ cram：塞入，填入，塞满。
④ giggly：傻笑的。
⑤ stuff：塞入。
⑥ torch：手电筒。
⑦ knickers：（女用）扎口短裤。
⑧ cardigan：开襟羊毛衫。

flat inside it and be soft and satiny and some sanitary pads①. The pads were Debbie's. She bled a lot each month. The lift came but Julie had gone back into the flat, full of trouble and worry She felt ill-prepared②, she did not have enough of something, but what could it be? The way she felt told her nothing, except that what was going to happen would be uncontrollable, and until today she had felt in control, and even confident. From shelves in the bathroom she took, almost at random, some guest towels and stuffed them into the carrier. She told herself she was stealing from Debbie, but knew Debbie wouldn't mind. She never did, would only say, "Just take it, love, if you want it." Then she might laugh and say, "Take what you want and don't pay for it!" Which was her motto③ in life, she claimed on every possible occasion: Julie knew better. Debbie could say this as much as she liked, but what she, Julie, had learned from Debbie was, simply, this: what things cost, the value of everything, and of people, of what you did for them, and what they did for you. When she had first come into this flat, brought by Debbie, who had seen her standing like a dummy④ on the platform at Waterloo at midnight on that first evening she arrived by herself in London, she had been as green⑤ as ... those girls next door, waiting, but not knowing what for. She had been innocent and silly, and what that all boiled down to⑥ was that she hadn't known the price of anything. She hadn't known what had to be paid. This was what she had learned from Debbie,

她第一次到这个小屋是午夜时黛比带她来的,黛比视她站在那儿的样子为滑铁卢平台上的模型,那也是她自己独自到伦敦的第一个晚上,她像楼下那些女孩一样殷切地等待着,但不知道在等待什么。

---

① some sanitary pads: 一些卫生护垫。
② ill-prepared: 准备不足。
③ motto: 座右铭。
④ dummy: 蠢货。
⑤ green: 嫩。
⑥ boil down to: 归结为。

even though Debbie had never allowed her to pay for anything, ever.

From the moment she had been seen on the platform five months ago on a muggy, drizzly① August evening, she had been learning how ignorant she was. For one thing, it was not only Debbie who had seen her; a lot of other people on the lookout in various parts of the station would have moved in on her like sharks② if Debbie hadn't got to her first. Some of these people were baddies③ and some were goodies④, but the kind ones would have sent her straight home.

For the second time she went through the living room and no one looked at her. The Lebanese⑤ was smiling and talking in an elderly-brotherly way to the new girls. Well, they had better watch out for themselves.

For the second time she waited for the lift. She seemed quite wrenched⑥ with pain. Was it worse? Yes, it was.

In the bitter black street that shone with lights from the lamps and the speeding cars she hauled⑦ herself on to a bus. Three stops, and by the time she reached where she wanted, (she knew she had cut it too fine.) She got off in a sleet⑧ shower under a street lamp and saw her blue coat turning dark with wet. Now she was far from being too hot, she was ready to shiver and shake, but could not decide if this was panic. Everything she had planned had

---

① muggy：闷热的，潮湿的；drizzly：下着蒙蒙细雨的。
② shark：鲨鱼。这里形容许多人都群拥地上来看朱莉。
③ baddies：坏蛋，坏人。
④ goodies：好人。
⑤ Lebanese：黎巴嫩人。
⑥ wrench：使感到痛苦。
⑦ haul：拖，曳。
⑧ sleet：雨夹雪。

seemed so easy, one thing after another, but she had not
foreseen that she would stand at a bus stop, afraid to leave
the light there, not knowing what the sensations were that
wrenched her body. Was she hot? Cold? Nauseous①?
Hungry? A good thing the weather was so bad, no one was
about. She walked boldly through the sleet and turned into
a dark and narrow alley② where she hurried, because it
smelled bad and scared her, then out into a yard full of
builders' rubbish and rusty skips③. There was a derelict④
shed at one end. This shed was where she was going,
where she had been only three days before to make sure it
was still there, had not been pulled down, and that she
could get in the door. But now something she had not
foreseen. A large dog stood in the door, a great black
threatening beast, and it was growling⑤. She could see
the gleam of its teeth and eyes. But she knew she had to
get into the shed, and quickly. Again water poured hotly
down her legs. Her head was swim-ruing. Hot knives
carved her back. She found a half brick and flung it at the
wall near the dog, who disappeared into the shed
growling. This was awful ... Julie went into the shed,
shut the door behind her, with difficulty because it
dragged on broken hinges, and switched on the torch. The
dog stood against a wall looking at her, but now she could
see it would not hurt her. Its tail was sweeping about in
the dirt, and it was so thin she could see its ribs⑥ under

---

① nauseous：令人作呕的。
② alley：小巷，胡同。
③ skip：废料桶。
④ derelict：被抛弃了的。
⑤ growl：咆哮，猖猖叫。
⑥ rib：肋骨。

the dirty black shabby① fur. Its eyes were bright and frantic②. It wanted her to be good to it. She said, "It's all right, it's only me," and went to the corner of the shed away from the dog, where she had spread a folded blanket③. The blanket was there, but the dog had been lying on it. She turned the blanket so the clean part inside was on the top. Now, having reached her refuge, she didn't know what to do. She took off her soaking knickers. She put the carrier bag close to the blanket. Afraid someone might see the gleam of light, she switched off the torch, first making sure she knew where it was. She could hear the dog breathing, and the flap-flap of its tail. It was lying down, not far from her. She could smell the wet doggy smell, and she was grateful for that, pleased the dog was there. Now she was in no doubt she had got here just in time, because her whole body was hot and fierce with pain, and she wanted to cry out, but knew she must not. She was groaning, though, and she heard herself:"Debbie, Debbie, Debbie …" All those months Debbie had said, "Don't worry about anything, when the time comes I'll see everything's all right." But Debbie had gone off with the new man to Paris, saying she would be back in a week, but had rung from New York to say, "How are you, honey? I'll be back at the weekend." That was three weeks ago. The "honey" had told Julie this man was different from the others, not only because he was an American: Debbie had never called her anything but Julie, wouldn't have dreamed of changing her behaviour for any man, but this "honey" had not been for Julie, but for the man who was listening. "I don't blame her," Julie

此句描写朱莉遇难时想到了黛比,可见黛比几乎是她的保护神。她的一切等待和希望都在黛比的身上。

① shabby:肮脏的。
② frantic:狂乱的,疯狂的。
③ blanket:地毯。

was muttering① now. "She always said she wanted just one man, not Tom and Dick and Harry." But while Julie was making herself think, I don't blame her, she was groaning, "Oh, Debbie, Debbie, why did you leave me?"

Debbie had left her to cope② on her own, after providing everything from shelter and food and visits to a doctor, to the clothes and the bright blue coat that had hidden her so well no one had known. Debbie and she joked how little people noticed about other people. "You'd better watch your diet," the Lebanese had said. "Don't you let her" — meaning Debbie — "stuff you with food all the time."

Julie was on all fours③ on the blanket, her head between her arms, her fists clenched tight④, and she was crying. The pain was awful, but that wasn't the worst of it. She felt so alone, so lonely. It occurred to her that having her bottom up⑤ in the air was probably not the right thing. She squatted⑥, her back against a cold brick wall, and went on sweating and moaning. She could hear the dog whining⑦, in sympathy, she thought. Water, or was it blood, poured out. She was afraid to switch on the torch to see. She felt the dog sniff at⑧ her face and neck, but it went off again. She could see absolutely nothing, it was so dark. Then she felt a rush, as if her insides were pouring out, and she thought, why didn't the book say there would be all this water all the time? Then she

---

① mutter：咕哝。
② cope：应对。
③ on all fours：趴着。
④ her fist clenched tight：她的拳头握得紧紧的。
⑤ bottom up：底朝上。
⑥ squat：蹲坐。
⑦ whine：哀号。
⑧ sniff at：嗅，闻。

thought，but that's the baby，and put her hand down and under her on the blanket was a wet slippery lump. She felt for the torch and switched it on. The baby was greyish and bloody and its mouth was opening and shutting. Now she was in a panic. Before，she had decided she must wait before cutting the cord①，because the paperback said there was no hurry，but she was desperate② to get the cord cut，in case③ the baby died. She found where the cord came out of the baby，a thick twisted rope of flesh，full of life，hot and pulsing④ in her hand. She found the scissors⑤. She found the string. She cut the birth cord with the scissors，and trembled with fear. Blood everywhere，and the dog had come close and was sitting so near she could touch it. Its eyes were saying，please，please ... It was gulping⑥ and licking its lips，because of all the blood，when it was so hungry.

"You wait a bit，" she said to the poor dog. Now she tied the cord up with the string that had boiled a long time in the saucepan⑦. She was worrying because she was getting something wrong，but couldn't remember what it was. As for⑧ boiling the string，what sense did that make，when you saw the filth⑨ in this shed. Tramps had used it. The dog，other dogs too，probably. For all she knew，other girls had given birth in it. Most sheds were garden sheds，and full of plants in pots，and locked up. She knew，because she had checked so many. Not many

朱莉多次用这本平装书作为她生活的向导，所以每次当她遇到什么事时就会想到那本书上所讲的。

这里写朱莉为自己接生，并成功地解救了自己，但狗已迫不及待地吞噬着她的血；在只有狗的陪伴下，朱莉生下了自己的孩子。

意为流动工，在这体现许多人来过这个小屋，就连狗也来过，可见这儿的肮脏及朱莉当时处境的艰难。

---

① cord：此处指脐带。
② desperate：拼命的。
③ in case：以免。
④ pulsing：脉动。
⑤ scissors：剪刀。
⑥ gulp：吐咽。
⑦ saucepan：有柄小平底锅。
⑧ as for：至于，关于。
⑨ filth：污物，污秽。

places where a girl could give birth to a baby in peace and quiet — or a stray dog① find a dry place out of the rain ... She was getting giggly② and silly, she could feel herself losing control. Meanwhile the baby was lying in a pool of bloody water and was mouthing and pulling its face about, and she ought to be doing something. Surely it ought to be crying? It was so slippery. The paperback didn't say anything about the baby being greasy③ and wet and so slippery she would be afraid to lift it. She pulled out the bundle of towel from the carrier and laid it flat, with the soft pink satin of Debbie's blouse smooth on top. She used both hands to pick the baby up round its middle and felt it squirm④, probably because her hands were so cold. Its wriggling⑤ strength, its warmth, the life she could feel beating there, astonished and pleased her. Unexpectedly she was full of pleasure and pride. The baby's perfectly all right, she thought, looking in the torchlight at hands, feet... what else should she look for? Oh, yes, it was a girl. Was it deformed⑥? The baby had an enormous cunt⑦, a long wrinkled slit⑧. Was that normal? Why didn't the book say?

She folded the baby firmly into the towel, with the bottom of the towel well tucked⑨ in over its feet, and only its face showing. Then she picked it up. It began to roar in short angry spasms⑩. And now the panic began again.

---

① a stray dog：一只流浪的狗。
② giggly：痴笑的。
③ greasy：油滑的。
④ squirm：蠕动。
⑤ wriggling：蠕动的，扭动的。
⑥ deformed：丑的，变形的。
⑦ cunt：女性阴部。
⑧ a long wrinkled slit：一个狭长的带皱纹的口子。
⑨ tuck：盖住。
⑩ spasm：发作。

She had not thought the baby would cry so loudly... someone would come ... what should she do ... but she couldn't leave the shed because there was a thing called the afterbirth①. As she thought this, there was another wet rush, all down her legs, and out plopped② a mass of something that looked like liver with the end of the thick red cord coming out of it.

And now she knew what to do. She raised herself from the squatting position, clutching the baby with one arm and using the other hand to push herself up from the floor. She stood shakily by the bloody mess and moved away a few paces with the baby held high up and close against her. At once the dog crawled forward, giving her a desperate look that said, "Don't get in my way." It ate up the afterbirth in quick gulps. It hopefully licked the bloody blanket, and briefly lifted its muzzle③ to look at her, wagging its long dirty tail. Then it went back to its place and sat with its back to the wall, watching. Meanwhile the baby let out short angry cries and kicked hard in its cocoon of towel. Julie thought, should I just leave the baby here and run for it④? No, the dog ... But as she thought this, the baby stopped and lay quietly looking at her. Well, she wasn't going to look back, she wasn't going to love it.

同时这个婴儿发出了短促愤怒的哭声,使劲地踢着像蚕一样裹着她的毛巾。

She had to leave here, and she was a swamp of blood, water, God only knew what.

She took a cautious look. Blood trickled down⑤ her legs. And she had actually believed a tampon⑥ or two

---

① afterbirth：胎盘。

② plop：砰的一声掉落。

③ muzzle：(狗)等突出的鼻子和口。

④ run for it：匆匆逃离。

⑤ trickle down：滴下,淋下。

⑥ tampoo：棉塞,止血塞。

196

would be enough! She laid the baby down on a clean place on the blanket, keeping an eye on the dog. Its eyes gleamed in the torchlight. She put on a pair of clean knickers and packed in sanitary towels. She tried to tie the guest towels around her waist to make an extra pad, but they were too stiff. Now she picked up the baby which was just like a papoose[1] and looking around with its blurry[2] little eyes. She took up the carrier bag and then the torch. She said to the dog, "Poor dog, I'm sorry." and went out, making sure the door was open for the dog. She switched off the torch, though the ground was rough and had bricks and bits of wood lying about. She could just see: there were lights in windows high up across the street. The sleet still blew down. She was already shivering. And the baby only had the towel around it ... She put the bundle of baby under the flap[3] of the now loose coat and went quickly across the uneven[4] ground to the alley, and even through the bad-smelling place and then along the pavement to a telephone box she had made sure would be conveniently close when she was looking for the shed or somewhere safe. There was no one near the telephone box, no one anywhere around. She put the baby down on the floor and walked towards the brilliant lights of the pub at the conner. She did not look back. The pub was crammed and hot and noisy. Now what she was afraid of was that she might smell so strongly of blood someone would notice. She could hardly make her way to the toilet. There she removed her knickers with the pads of sanitary towels, which were already soaked. She used one

---

① papoose：北美印第安人的婴儿。
② blurry：模糊的。
③ flap：垂下物，前襟的翻褶。
④ uneven：不平坦的，凹凸不平的。

of the guest towels to wash herself down. She went on soaking the towel in hot water and wringing it out①, then wiping herself, watching how the blood at once began trickling② on to the clean white skin of her inner thighs. But she could not stay there for ever, washing. She rubbed③ the same towel, wrung out in hot water, over her sticky④ head. She combed her hair flat. Well, it wouldn't stay flat for long: being naturally curly it would spring back into its own shape soon. Debbie said it was sweet, like a little girl. She filled her knickers with new pads, put the bloody pads into the container, and went out into the pub. Now there was music from the jukebox⑤, pounding away and the beat went straight through her, vibrating⑥ and making her feel sick. She wanted badly to get away from the music, but she bought a shandy⑦, reaching over the shoulders of men arguing about football to get it. Unremarked, she went to stand near a small window that overlooked the telephone box. She could see the bundle, a small pathetic⑧ thing, like folded newspapers or a dropped jersey⑨, on the floor of the box. She had first found the shed, then looked for the telephone box, and then hoped there would be a window somewhere close by, and there was.

She stood by the window for only five minutes or so. Then she saw a young man and a girl go into the telephone box. Through window glass streaked again with sleet, she

---

① wring out：拧干。
② trickle：流，淌，涌。
③ rub：擦，使相擦。
④ sticky：黏的。
⑤ jukebox：在酒吧间、餐饮店等投入硬币就可自动演唱的自动电唱机。
⑥ vibrate：震动。
⑦ shandy：苹果与姜汁的混合饮料。
⑧ pathetic：可怜的。
⑨ jersey：运动衫。

saw the girl pick up the bundle① from the floor, while the young man telephoned. She ought to leave ... she ought not to stand here ... but she stayed, watching, while the noise of the pub beat around her. The ambulance came in no time. Two ambulance men. The girl came out of the telephone box with the bundle, and the young man was behind her. The ambulance men took the bundle, first one, then the other, then handed it back to the girl, who got into the ambulance. The young man stood on the pavement, and the girl inside waved to him, and he got in to go with them. So the baby was safe. It was done. She had done it. As she went out into the sleety rain she saw the ambulance lights vanish, and her heart plunged into② loss and became empty and bitter, in the way she had been determined would not happen. "Debbie," she whispered, the tears running. "Where are you, Debbie?" Not necessarily New York. Or even the States. Canada ... Mexico ... the Costa Brava③ ... South America ... The people coming and going in Debbie's flat were always off somewhere, or just back. Rio ... San Francisco, you name it. And Debbie had said to her, "One day it will be your turn." But now it was Debbie's turn. Why should she ever come back? She wanted to have "just one regular customer." Once she had said, by mistake, "just one man." Julie had heard this, but did not comment. Debbie could be as hard and as jokey as she liked, but she couldn't fool Julie, who knew she was the only person who really understood Debbie.

表现朱莉渴望见到黛比,需要得到她的帮助。

Now Julie was walking to the Underground, as fast as she could. Her legs were shaky, but she felt all right. All

这是朱莉想回家而不能的惨状,她只能待在地铁站那儿。

① bundle：包裹。
② plunge into：陷入。
③ Costa Brava：布拉瓦海岸。

she wanted was to get home. It had been impossible to go home, or even think too much about home where her father (she was sure) would simply throw her out. But now, it was only a question of a few stops on the Underground, and then the train. At the most, an hour and a half.

The Underground train was full of people. They had had a meal after work, or been in a pub. Like Julie! She kept looking at all those faces and thinking, What would you say if you knew? At Waterloo she sat on a benchnear① an old man with a drinker's face, a tramp②. She gave him a pound, but she was thinking of the dog. She did not have to wait long for a train. It was not full. Surely she ought to be tired, or sick or something? Most of all she was hungry. A great plate of steak and eggs, that was what she needed. And Debbie there too, eating opposite her.

朱莉在这又想到了黛比,她无时无刻不在想着黛比。

A plump③ fresh-faced girl in a damp sky-blue coat sat upright among the other home-goers, holding a carrier bag that had on it, written red on black, SUSIE'S STYLES! Her eyes shone. Her young fresh fair hair curled all over her head. She vibrated with confidence, with secrets.

At the station she had to decide between a bus and walking home. Not the bus: on it there'd almost certainly be someone she knew, and perhaps even from her school. She didn't want to be looked at yet. The sleet was now a chilly blowy rain, with the sting④ of ice in it, but it

---

① benchnear:座位附近。
② tramp:流浪汉。
③ plump:肥胖的,丰满的。
④ sting:刺痛,刺伤。

wasn't bad, more of an occasional sharp pattering① coming into her face and invigorating② her. But she was going to arrive home all wet and pathetic, not at all as she had planned.

When she turned into her street, lights showed behind the curtains in all the windows. No one was out. What was she going to do about that coat, wet through, and, worse, hanging on her? Her mother would notice all that space under the coat and wonder. Three doors from home she glanced around to make sure no one was watching, and stripped off③ the coat in one fast movement and dropped it into a dustbin. Even in this half dark, lit with dull gleams from a window, she could see blood-stains on the lining④. And her dress? The yellow dress was limp⑤ and grubby but the cardigan came down low and hid most of it. This was going to be the dangerous part, all right, and only luck would get her through it. She ran up the steps and rang the bell, smiling, while she clutched the carrier bag so it could hide her front, which was still squashy⑥ and fat where the baby had been.

Heavy steps. Her father. The door opened slowly while he fumbled⑦ at locks, and she kept the smile going, and her heart beat, and then he stood in front of her large and black with the light behind him, so that her heart went small and weak... but then he turned so she could see his face and she thought, That can't be him, that can't be my father for he had shrunk and become grey and

---

① patter：急速的轻拍声，啪嗒啪嗒地响。
② invigorating：提神。
③ strip off：脱去。
④ lining：衬里，衣料。
⑤ limp：松软的。
⑥ squashy：压扁的。
⑦ fumble：笨拙地摸索。

ordinary and... what on earth had she been afraid of? She could just hear what Debbie would say about him! Why, he was nothing at all. He called out in a sharp barking① voice, "Anne, Anne, she's here." He was a man waiting for his wife to take command, crying as he went stumbling down the hall. Julie's mother came fast towards her. She was already crying, and that meant she could not see anything much. She put her arms around Julie and sobbed② and said, "Oh, Julie, Julie, why didn't you . . .? But come in, why you're soaked." And she pushed and pulled Julie towards, and then into, the living room, where the old man (which is how Julie was seeing him with her new eyes) sat bowed in his chair, tears running down his face.

"She's all right, Len," said Anne, Julie's mother. She let go of③ her daughter and sat upright in her chair, knees together, feet together, dabbing④ her cheeks under her eyes, and stared at Len with a look that said, there, I told you so.

"Get her a cup of tea, Anne," said Len. And then, to Julie, but without looking at her, looking at his wife in a heavy awful way that told Julie how full of calamity⑤ had been their discussions about her, "Sit down, we aren't going to eat you."

Julie sat on the edge of a chair, but gingerly⑥, because it hurt. It was as if she had been anaesthetized⑦ by urgency, but now she was safe, pains and soreness

---

① bark：咆哮，怒吼。
② sob：哭泣，呜咽。
③ let go of：让走开。
④ dab：轻拍，轻抚。
⑤ calamity：灾难。
⑥ gingerly：小心翼翼地。
⑦ anaesthetize：使麻木。

could make themselves felt. She watched her parents weep①, their bitter faces full of loss. She saw how they sat, each in a chair well apart from the other, not comforting each other, or holding her, or wanting to hold each other, or to hold her.

"Oh, Julie," said her mother, "oh, Julie."

"Mum, can I have a sandwich?"

"Of course you can. We've had our supper. I'll just ..."

Julie smiled, she could not help it, and it was a sour② little smile. She knew that what had been on those plates was exactly calculated, not a pea or a bit of potato left over. The next proper meal (lunch, tomorrow) would already be on a plate ready to cook, with a plastic film over it, in the fridge. Her mother went off to the kitchen, to work out how to feed Julie, and now Julie was alone with her father, and that wasn't good.

"You mustn't think we are going to ask you awkward③ questions," said her father, still not looking at her, and Julie knew that her mother had said, "We mustn't ask her any awkward questions. We must wait for her to tell us."

You bloody well ought to ask some questions, Julie was thinking, noting that already the raucous④ angry irritation her parents always made her feel was back, and strong. And, at the moment, dangerous.

But they had expected her to come back, then? For she had been making things easier for herself by saying, they won't care I'm not there! They probably won't even

朱莉内心复杂地思考着该怎么应对父亲那令人窘迫的问题。

---

① weep：哭泣。
② sour：阴郁的。
③ awkward：困难的，窘迫的。
④ raucous：粗声的。

notice! Now she could see how much they had been grieving① for her. How was she going to get herself out of here up to the bathroom? If she could just have a bath! At this point her mother came back with a cup of tea. Julie took it, drank it down at once, though it was too hot, and handed the cup back. She saw her mother had realized she meant it: she needed to eat, was hungry, could drink six cups of tea one after another. "Would you mind if I had a bath, Mum? I won't take a minute. I fell and the street was all slippery. It was sleeting."

She had already got herself to the door, clutching② the carrier in front of her.

"You didn't hurt yourself?" enquired her father.

"No, I only slipped, I got all muddy."

"You run along③ and have a bath, girl," said her mother. "It'll give me time to boil an egg for sandwiches."

Julie ran upstairs. Quick, quick, she mustn't make a big thing of this bath, mustn't stay in it. Her bedroom was just so, all pretty and pink and her big panda sat on her pillow. She flung off her clothes and waves of a nasty④ sour smell came up at her. She stuffed them all into the carrier and grabbed from the cupboard her pink-flowered dressing gown. What would Debbie have to say about that? she wondered, and wanted to laugh, thinking of Debbie here, sprawling on her bed with the panda. She found childish pyjamas⑤ stuffed into the back of a drawer. What was she going to do for padding? Her knickers showed patches⑥ of blood and that meant the

---

① grieve：悲伤。
② clutch：抓住,握紧。
③ run along：走开。
④ nasty：令人难受的。
⑤ pyjamas：睡衣裤。
⑥ patch：斑块。

pads hadn't been enough. She found some old panties①
and went into the bathroom with them. The bath filled
quickly and there were waves of steam. Careful，she
didn't want to faint，and her head was light. She got in
and submerged her head. Quick quick ... She soaped and
rubbed，getting rid of the birth，the dirty shed，the damp
dog smell，the blood，all that blood. It was still welling②
gently out of her，not much but enough to make her
careful when she dried herself on the fluffy③ pink towels
her mother changed three times a week. She put on her
knickers and packed them with old panties. On went the
pyjamas，the pink dressing gown. She combed her hair.

There. It was all gone. Her breasts，she knew from
the book，would have milk，but she would put on a tight
bra and fill it with cotton wool. She would manage. In
this house，her home，they did not see each other naked.
Her mother hadn't come in for years when she was having
a bath，and she always knocked on the bedroom door. In
Debbie's flat people ran about naked or half dressed and
Debbie might answer the door in her satin camiknickers④，
those great breasts of hers lolling about. Debbie often
came in when Julie was in the bath to sit on the loo⑤ and
chat ... Tears filled Julie's eyes. Oh，no，she certainly
must not cry.

She stuffed the bag with the bloody pads and her dirty
clothes in it under her bed，well to the back. She would
get rid of it all very early in the morning before her
parents woke，which they would，at seven o'clock.

朱莉渴望洗去污
浊，忘却过去的不幸。

以 years 来形容妈
妈在她淋浴的时间里很
久都未来过她。

朱莉妈妈的许久不
来与黛比在她淋浴时的
经常光顾交谈形成了鲜
明的对比，这里朱莉又
想到了黛比。

---

① panty：女裤。
② well：涌出。
③ fluffy：柔毛状的。
④ camiknicker：连裤紧身内衣。
⑤ loo：［口］厕所。

She went down the stairs, a good little girl washed and brushed, ready for the night.

In the living room her parents were silent and apart in their two well separated chairs. They had been crying again. Her father was relieved at what he saw when he cautiously took a look at her (as if it had been too painful to see her before), and he said, "It's good to have you home, Julie." His voice broke.

Her mother said, "I've made you some nice sandwiches."

Four thin slices of white bread had been made into two sandwiches and cut diagonally① across, the yellow of the egg prettily showing, with sprigs② of parsley③ disposed here and there. Hunger sprang in Julie like a tiger, and she ate ravenously④, watching her mother's pitying, embarrassed face. Why, she thinks-I've been short of food! Well, that's a good thing, it'll put her off the scent.

Her mother went off to make more food. Would she boil another egg, perhaps?

"Anything'll do, Mum. Jam ... I'd love some jam on some toast⑤."

She had finished the sandwiches and drunk down the tea long before her mother had returned with a tray⑥, half a loaf of bread, butter, strawberry jam, more tea.

"I don't like to think of you going without food," she said.

"But I didn't, not really," said Julie, remembering all

---

① diagonally: 斜对地。
② sprig: (烹调或装饰用的)带叶小枝。
③ parsley: 香菜。
④ ravenously: 饿极了地。
⑤ toast: 吐司。
⑥ tray: 托盘。

the feasts① she had had with Debbie, the pizzas that arrived all hours of the day and the night from almost next door, the Kentucky chicken, the special steak feeds when Debbie got hungry, which was often. In the little kitchen was a bowl from Morocco kept piled with fruit. "You must get enough vitamins," Debbie kept saying, and brought in more grapes, more apples and pears, let alone fruit Julie had never heard of, like pomegranates② and pawpaws③, which Debbie had learned to like on one of her trips somewhere.

"We aren't going to pester④ you with questions," said her mother.

"I've been with a girl. Her name is Debbie. She was good to me. I've been all right," said Julie, looking at her mother, and then at her father. There, don't ask any more questions.

"A girl?" said her father heavily. He still kept his eyes away from Julie, because when he looked at her the tears started up again.

"Well, I haven't been with a boyfriend," said Julie and could not stop herself from laughing at this ridiculous idea.

They were all laughing with relief, with disbelief... they think I've been off with a boy! What were they imagining? Julie contemplated⑤ the incident in the school cloakroom⑥ with Billy Jayson that so improbably had led to the scene in the shed with the dog. She had joked with Debbie that it would be a virgin birth. "He hardly got it

这是奸污朱莉并使她有身孕的人。

---

① feast：盛宴。
② pomegranate：石榴。
③ pawpaw：木瓜。
④ pester：使烦恼，使为难。
⑤ contemplate：沉思。
⑥ cloakroom：衣帽间。

in," she had said. "I didn't think anything had really happened."

Probably Billy had forgotten all about it. Unless he connected her leaving school and running away from home with that scene in the cloakroom? But why should he? It was four months after they had tussled[1] and shoved[2] and giggled, she saying, no no, and he saying, oh come on, then.

"Are you going back to school?" asked her mother carefully. "The officer came round last week and said you still could. There are two terms left. And you've always been a good girl before this."

"Yes, I'll go back," said Julie. Seven months — she could manage that. She'd be bored, but never mind. And then ... This was the moment she should say something more, explain, make up some lies, for they both sat staring at her, their faces full of what they had been feeling for the long five months she had been gone. She knew she was treating them badly, refusing to say anything. Well, she would, but not now, she was suddenly absolutely exhausted. Full of hot tea and food, she felt herself letting go, letting herself slide[3] ... She began to yawn[4] and could not stop. But they did not suggest she should go to bed, and this was because they simply could not believe they wouldn't get anything more from her.

But there was nothing she could say. She looked at her father, that cautious, greyish, elderly man, sitting heavily in his chair. At her mother, who seemed almost

---

[1] tussle：扭打，争执。
[2] shove：猛推。
[3] slide：滑，滑动。
[4] yawn：打哈欠。

girlish as she sat upright there in her pretty pale blue dress with its nice little collar and the little pearl buttons down the front. Her grey cuffs① were sprightly②, and her blue eyes full of wounded and uncomprehending innocence. Julie thought, I wish I could just snuggle up to③ Mum and she could hold me and I could go to sleep. Surely this must have happened when she was small, but she could not remember it. In this family, they simply did not touch each other.

Full of the clarity of her exhaustion, and because of what she had learned in the last months, she saw her parents and knew that — they cancelled each other out. Debbie would say there was something wrong with their chemistry④. They did not disagree. They never raised their voices, or argued. Each day was a pattern of cups of tea, meals, cups of coffee and biscuits, always at exactly the same times, with bedtime as the goal. They seldom went out. They saw very few people, only each other. It was as if they had switched themselves off.

朱莉父母生活的孤僻及新奇,他们对女儿的关注也是非常特别的。

They had been old when she was born, was that the trouble?

At Debbie's people shouted, kissed, hugged, argued, fought, threatened, wept, and screamed.

There were two bedrooms in that flat. Debbie had given her the little one to herself. She was supposed to make herself scarce when Debbie came in with a man, a new one, but not when Derek was there, Debbie's real boyfriend. Derek joked a lot and ordered Julie about. How about making me a cup of tea, getting me a drink,

---

① cuff：袖口。
② sprightly：活泼的。
③ snuggle up to：依偎着。
④ chemistry：此处指两人之间的关系。

making me some bacon① and eggs, what have you been doing with yourself, why don't you get yourself a new hairdo②, a new dress? He liked Julie, though she did not like him much. She knew he was not good enough for Debbie.

Soon Debbie would get rid of him. As she had the man who once owned the flat and took a percentage of what she earned. But Debbie had found out something bad about him, had put the screws③ on, got the flat for herself, worked for herself. Julie had seen this man just once, and he had given her the creeps④. "My first love," Debbie joked, and laughed loudly when Julie grimaced⑤. Derek did not give her the creeps, he was just nothing! Ordinary. Boring. But the man Debbie had gone to New York with was a TV producer. He was making a series no one had heard about in England, not good enough to sell here, he said. This man was more like it, but Julie thought Debbie would get rid of him too, when something better came up.

All these thoughts, these judgments, so unlike anything ever said or thought in her own home, went on in Julie's mind quite comfortably, though they wouldn't do for herself. Debbie had to be like this, because of her hard life. This included something bad that Debbie had never talked about, it was why she had been so good to Julie. Probably, just like Julie, Debbie had stood very late in a railway station, pregnant, her head full of rubbish about how she would get a job, have the baby, bring it

以火车站比喻黛比的人生旅程。

---

① bacon：熏猪肉，咸肉。
② hairdo：发型。
③ screw：螺丝钉。
④ creeps：毛骨悚然的感觉。
⑤ grimace：愁眉苦脸。

up, find a man who would love her and the baby. Or perhaps it had been something else to do with being pregnant and alone. It was not she, Julie, who had earned five months of Debbie's love and protection, it was pregnant Julie, helpless and alone.

Oh, yes, Debbie was fond of her.

Sometimes she spent the night in Debbie's big bed because Debbie could not bear to sleep alone. She got scared, she said. She could not believe that Julie wasn't frightened of the dark. Debbie always crashed① straight off to sleep, even when she hadn't been drinking. Then Julie cautiously got up on her elbow and bent over sleeping Debbie, to examine her, try and find out ... Debbie was a big handsome girl. Her skin was very white, and she had black shiny straight hair, and she made up her lips to be thin and scarlet and curving, just right for the lashing②, slashing③ tongue behind them. When she was asleep her face was smooth and closed, and her lips were ordinary, quite pathetic Julie thought, and there was wear under her eyes. That face showed nothing of why Debbie said to people coming into the flat who might notice Julie the wrong way, "Lay off, do you hear? Lay off, or I'll ..." And her scarlet lips and her black eyes were nasty, frightening.

But if Debbie woke in the night, she might turn to Julie and draw her into an embrace that told Julie how little she knew about love, about tenderness. Then Julie lay awake, astounded④ at the revelations⑤ this big hot

这里道出了朱莉为什么在困境时一直想着黛比,因为黛比给予了她爱与呵护。

那张脸并未透露黛比对那些或许注意到朱莉有异样的人说话的原因。

---

① crash：躺下睡觉。
② lash：讽刺,严厉地谴责。
③ slash：严厉地批评。
④ astound：使大吃一惊,使惊奇。
⑤ revelation：暴露。

smooth body made, and went on making, even though Debbie was off to sleep again. She never actually "did anything." Julie even waited for "something" to happen. Nothing ever did. Just once Debbie put her hand down to touch the mound① of Julie's stomach, but took it quickly away. Julie lay entangled② with Debbie, and they were like two cats that have finished washing each other and gone to sleep, and Julie knew how terribly she had been deprived③ at home, and how empty and sad her parents were. Suppose she said to her mother now, "Mum, let me come into your bed tonight, I'm scared, I've missed you ..." She could just see her mother's embarrassed, timid face. "But Julie, you're a big girl now."

指朱莉的父亲和母亲。

Anne and Len slept in twin beds stretched out parallel to each other, the night table between them.

There were tears in Julie's eyes, and she did not know it, but then she did and looked quickly at her mother, then her father, for they must not know she would give anything to cry and cry, and be comforted and held ... But they weren't looking at her, only at the television. They had switched it on, without her noticing. Now all three of them sat staring at it.

On the screen a woman announcer smiled the special smile that goes with royalty, animals, and children and said, "At eight o'clock this evening a newly born baby girl was found in a telephone box in Islington. She was warmly wrapped and healthy. She weighed seven pounds and three ounces. The nurses have called her Rosie." Hot waves of jealousy went through Julie when she saw how the nurse smiled down at the little face seen briefly by

---

① mound：这里指胃突起的部分。
② entangle：使缠住。
③ deprive：使不能享受。

Julie in torchlight, and then again through the sleet outside the shed. "The mother is urged to come forward as she might be in need of urgent medical attention."

It was the late news.

Surely they were going to guess? But why should they? It was hard enough for her to believe that she could sit here in her pretty little dressing gown smelling of bath powder, when she had given birth by herself in a dirty shed with only a dog for company. Four hours ago, that was all!

"Why don't we have a dog, Mum?" asked Julie, knowing what she was going to hear.

"But they are such a nuisance①, Julie. And who's going to take it for walks?"

"I will, Mum."

"But you'll have finished school in July, and I don't want the bother of a dog, and I'm sure Len doesn't."

Her father didn't say anything. He leaned forward and turned off the set. The screen went blank.

"I often wonder what Jessie thinks," he remarked, "when she sees something like this on the telly②, I mean."

"Oh, leave it, Len," said Anne warningly.

Julie did not really hear this, but then she did: her ears sprang to life, and she knew something extraordinary was about to happen.

"That's why we were so worried about you," said Julie's father, heavily grief-ridden, reproachful③. "It's easy enough to happen, how were we to know you weren't —"

"Len, we agreed we wouldn't ever —"

朱莉的妈妈意识到朱莉的爸爸注意到了什么,她考虑到朱莉所以警告她的爸爸让他不用去管。

---

① nuisance:令人麻烦讨厌的事。
② telly:电视机。
③ reproachful:责备的。

"What about Auntie Jessie?" asked Julie, trying to take it in. A silence. "Well, what about her, Dad? You can't just leave it like that."

"Len," said Anne wildly.

"Your Auntie Jessie got herself into the family way," said her father, determined to say it, ignoring his wife's face, her distress①. His face was saying, Why should she be spared when she's given us such a bad time? "She wasn't much older than you are now." At last he was looking straight at Julie, full of reproach, and his eyes dripped tears all down his face and on to his tie. "It can happen easy enough, can't it?"

"You mean... but what happened to the baby? Was it born?"

"Your cousin Freda," said Len, still bitter and obstinate②, his accusing③ eyes on his daughter.

"You mean, Freda is ... you mean. Auntie Jessie's mum and dad didn't mind?"

"They minded, all right," said Anne. "I remember all that well enough. They wanted the baby adopted, but Jessie stuck it out and had it, and in the end they came around. I still think they were right and Jessie was wrong. She was only seventeen. She never would say who the father was. She was stuck at home with the baby when she should have been out enjoying herself and learning things. She got married when she was a baby herself."

By now Julie was more or less herself again, though she felt as if she'd been on a roller coaster④. Above all, what she was thinking was, I've got to get it all out of

---

① distress：悲痛，痛苦。
② obstinate：不易克服的。
③ accusing：非难的，谴责的。
④ a roller coaster：过山车，这里指生活的起起落落。

them now, because I know them, they'll clam up① and never talk of it again.

"Didn't Uncle Bob mind?" she asked.

"Not so that he wouldn't marry her, he married her, didn't he, and she had a love child he had to take on," said her father, full of anger and accusations.

"A love child," said Julie derisively②, unable to stop herself. But her parents didn't notice.

"That's what they call it, I believe," said her father, all heavy and sarcastic③. "Well, that's what can happen, Julie, and you've always been such a sensible girl and that made it worse." And now, unbelievably, this father of hers, whom she had so feared she ran away from home, sat sobbing, covering his face with his hands.

Her mother was weeping, her eyes bright, her cheeks red.

In a moment Julie would be bawling④ too.

"I'm going to bed," she said, getting up. "Oh, I'm sorry Mum, I'm sorry, Dad, I'm sorry ..."

"It's all right, Julie," said her mother.

Julie went out of the room and up the stairs and into her room, walking carefully now, because she was so sore. And she felt numbed⑤ and confused, because of Aunt Jessica and her cousin Freda. Why, she, Julie, could have ... she could be sitting here now, with her baby Rosie, they wouldn't have thrown her out.

She didn't know what to think, or to feel ... She felt... she wanted ... "Oh, Debbie," she cried, but

再一次在困惑中想到了黛比,可见朱莉多么渴望黛比的爱与呵护啊!

---

① calm up: 保持沉默。
② derisively: 嘲弄地,愚弄地。
③ sarcastic: 讽刺的,嘲笑的,挖苦的。
④ bawl: 喊叫,咆哮。
⑤ numbed: 麻木的。

silently, tucked into her little bed, her arms around the panda. "Oh, Debbie, what am I to do?"

She thought, in July, when I've finished school, I am going back, I'm going to run away, I'll go to London and get a job, and I can have my baby. For a few minutes she persuaded herself it was not the silly little girl who had run away who said this, but the Debbie-taught girl who knew what things cost. Then she said to herself, stop it, stop it, you know better.

She thought of Aunt Jessie's house. She had always enjoyed that house. It occurred to her now that Debbie's place and Aunt Jessie's had a lot in common — noisy, disturbing, exciting. Which was why her parents did not much like going there. But here, a baby here, Rosie with her long wrinkled cunt here ... Julie was laughing her raucous①, derisive laugh, but it was unhappy because she had understood that Rosie her daughter could not come here, because she, Julie, could not stand it.

I'll take Rosie to Debbie's in London, said Julie, in a final futile② attempt.

But Debbie had taken in pregnant Julie. That was what had been paid.

If Julie brought baby Rosie here, then she would have to stay here. Until she got married. Like Auntie Jessie. Julie thought of Uncle Bob. Now she realized she had always seen him as Auntie Jessie's shadow, not up to much. She had wondered why Auntie Jessie married him. Now she knew.

I've got to get out of here, she thought, I've got to. In July I'll leave. I'll have my O levels. I can get them

朱莉从杰西阿姨那找到与自己相同的遭遇,从而明白了自己人生的去处。

---

① raucous：粗声地吵闹。
② futile：无效的,无意义的,无用的。

easily. I'll work hard and get my five O levels. I'll go to London. I know how things are, now. Look, I've lived in Debbie's flat, and I didn't let myself get hurt by them. I was clever, no one knew I was pregnant, only Debbie. I had Rosie by myself in that shed with only a dog to help me, and then I put Rosie in a safe place and now she's all right, and I've come home, and I've managed it all so well they never even guessed. I'm all right.

With her arms around the panda Julie thought, I can do anything I want to do, I've proved that.

And she drifted off① to sleep.   [1987]

朱莉可以断定,在黛比的呵护和教导下,朱莉可以做任何她想干的。

【思考题】

1. 导致朱莉出走的根本原因是什么?结合其家庭背景进行分析。

2. 朱莉最终选择孤身抚养自己所生的女婴儿说明了什么?

3. 黛比与朱莉的关系体现出莱辛怎样的女性主义观?

---

① drift off: 渐渐离开。

Bliss

幸　福

凯瑟琳·曼斯菲尔德

【导读】

　　凯瑟琳·曼斯菲尔德(Katherine Mansfield，1888—1923)，1888 年 10 月 14 日生于新西兰威灵顿，本名凯瑟琳·包姗普。她的父亲是一位成功的银行家，在威灵顿社交界享有威望。1903 年，她说服父亲同意并前往伦敦学习大提琴。回到威灵顿后不久，她遇到了劳伦斯和弗吉尼亚·沃尔夫，并对文学产生了浓厚的兴趣，立志要成为一名作家。1908 年 7 月，她说服父亲同意她重返伦敦，从此走上文学道路，离开故乡，一去不返。1911 年，她出版了第一本短篇小说集《在德国公寓》，同年，她遇到了文学批评家约翰·米多尔顿·莫里，两人在 1918 年结婚。随后出版的《幸福》和《花园茶会》为其赢得名誉和地位。

　　曼斯菲尔德非常崇拜安东·契诃夫，但是 1918 年她罹患肺结核之后无法继续写作，在她死后出版的《日记》中，可以看出她常常责备自己："看着门槛外一摞摞在那里等着进来的故事，我为什么不让它们进来呢？而它们的位置应该被潜藏在那里等机会的其他东西来取代。"最后，她的病在法国枫丹白露乔治·古德杰夫主办的"人类和谐发展机构"得到治疗，乔治·古德杰夫双管齐下，同时采用精神和物理治疗两种方法。不过，她还是在 34 岁生日后的几个月内去世了。

　　曼斯菲尔德的 48 篇小说一经出版(包括 15 本未完成的)，立刻对文学形式的发展产生了巨大影响。与契诃夫和詹姆斯·乔伊斯一样，她通过简化情节来增强感化力，并将细节戏剧化。

　　她的短篇小说题材多取自亲身经历，主题多为女性的幻灭感、孤独感，以淡化情节、女性视角诗化的语言、印象主义技巧与象征主义的运用高度结合，表现出鲜明的现代主义倾向。她的小说在题材选择上脱离了传统小说的题材形式，而是把平凡人物和琐碎事情写进小说，通过精心选择有意义的细节来刻画人物，揭示主题。细节描写的成功是她的小说取得成功的重要因素之一。曼斯菲尔德的小说更像是对日常生活的记录，仿佛一颗橄榄，酸涩平淡，这需要一种敏锐的眼光来支撑，让人感觉到作家在看似无所事事的、轻松的日常生活中所展示出来的意义。

　　《幸福》是曼斯菲尔德的代表作之一,这部小说的女主人公柏莎是一个生活在梦幻中的少妇,过了而立之年,心头燃烧着幸福的火焰,爱她生活里的一切。当她发现自己的丈夫和她的朋友之间有暧昧关系时,她内心的幸福火焰被冰冷的失望和痛苦浇灭了。在这个美好的春天里,爱唤起了柏莎很少出现的情欲,却被哈里打入了冷宫。开头柏莎是一团烈火,后来是透心凉。这种情节的陡转,也突出了女性情感被摧残的严重性。《幸福》中透出了人物幸福的虚幻性,也透出了作者对两性关系的不信任。

　　曼斯菲尔德关注婚姻关系稳定,笔下却没有幸福的家庭模式。在大多数家庭中,很难说有直接来自男性的压迫、欺凌或暴力,相反,在女性的威慑下,男性失去了自信和权威,如《摩登婚姻》《理想家庭》,男人在家庭中的处境令人想起曼斯菲尔德早期作品中女性的遭遇。

　　曼斯菲尔德自身经历和个性在小说中的充分扩张,传达了对传统女性价值观念的反思和破坏。柏莎清醒后怎么办? 小说结尾,作者的调子是比较沉静的。热心的读者不禁要为柏莎设计两种前途:要么学易卜生笔下的挪拉毅然出走;要么忍辱负重,与哈里继续同床异梦。女人发现自己只是丈夫养的小鸟儿,但发现了又怎么样呢? 在 19 世纪,易卜生的答案是让挪拉出走。而曼斯菲尔德是 20 世纪的作家,她提供的是一条心理解放之途。这正是曼斯菲尔德的独特之处。

Bliss①

Although Bertha Young was thirty she still had moments like this when she wanted to run instead of walk, to take dancing steps on and off the pavement, to bowl a hoop, to throw something up in the air and catch it again, or to stand still and laugh at — nothing — at nothing, simply.

　　通过柏莎的动作,表现了她的活泼开朗和内心的幸福感。

What can you do if you are thirty and, turning the corner of your own street, you are overcome, suddenly by a feeling of bliss — absolute bliss! — as though you'd suddenly swallowed a bright piece of that late afternoon sun and it burned in your bosom, sending out a little

---

① Bliss:幸福。

shower of sparks into every particle①, into every finger and toe?

Oh, is there no way you can express it without being "drunk and disorderly"? How idiotic civilization is! Why be given a body if you have to keep it shut up in a case like a rare, rare fiddle②?

"No, that about the fiddle is not quite what I mean," she thought, running up the steps and feeling in her bag for the key — she'd forgotten it, as usual — and rattling③ the letter-box. "It's not what I mean, because — Thank you, Mary." — she went into the hall. "Is nurse back?"

"Yes, m'm."

"And has the fruit come?"

"Yes, m'm. Everything's come."

"Bring the fruit up to the dining-room, will you? I'll arrange it before I go upstairs."

It was dusky in the dining-room and quite chilly. But all the same Bertha threw off her coat; she could not bear the tight clasp of it another moment, and the cold air fell on her arms.

这里已不单纯是衣服对身体的束缚，而是柏莎真实生活的写照：束缚在婚姻的枷锁里。

But in her bosom there was still that bright glowing place — that shower of little sparks coming from it. It was almost unbearable. She hardly dared to breathe for fear of fanning it higher, and yet she breathed deeply, deeply. She hardly dared to look into the cold mirror — but she did look, and it gave her back a woman, radiant, with smiling, trembling lips, with big, dark eyes and an air of listening, waiting for something ... divine to happen ... that she knew must happen ... infallibly.

Mary brought in the fruit on a tray and with it a glass

---

① particle：微粒，颗粒。
② fiddle：小提琴。
③ rattling：把邮箱摇得哗啦哗啦响。

bowl, and a blue dish, very lovely, with a strange sheen① on it as though it had been dipped in milk.

"Shall I turn on the light, m'm?"

"No, thank you. I can see quite well."

There were tangerines② and apples stained with strawberry pink. Some yellow pears, smooth as silk, some white grapes covered with a silver bloom and a big cluster of purple ones. These last she had bought to tone in with the new dining-room carpet. Yes, that did sound rather far-fetched③ and absurd, but it was really why she had bought them. She had thought in the shop: "I must have some purple ones to bring the carpet up to the table." And it had seemed quite sense at the time.

When she had finished with them and had made two pyramids of these bright round shapes, she stood away from the table to get the effect — and it really was most curious. For the dark table seemed to melt into the dusky light and the glass dish and the blue bowl to float in the air. This, of course, in her present mood, was so incredibly beautiful ... She began to laugh.

"No, no. I'm getting hysterical④." And she seized her bag and coat and ran upstairs to the nursery.

Nurse sat at a low table giving Little B her supper after her bath. The baby had on a white flannel gown and a blue woolen jacket, and her dark, fine hair was brushed up into a funny little peak. She looked up when she saw her mother and began to jump.

"Now, my lovely, eat it up like a good girl," said

---

① sheen: 光泽。
② tangerine: 蜜橘。
③ far-fetched: 牵强的。
④ hysterical: 情绪异常激动的,歇斯底里的。

nurse, setting her lips in a way that Bertha knew, and that meant she had come into the nursery at another wrong moment.

"Has she been good, Nanny?"

"She's been a little sweet all the afternoon," whispered Nanny. "We went to the park and I sat down on a chair and took her out of the pram① and a big dog came along and put its head on my knee and she clutched its ear, tugged② it. Oh, you should have seen her."

柏莎作为母亲,却不能亲自抚养自己的孩子,写出了母亲与孩子之间的陌生与疏离感。

Bertha wanted to ask if it wasn't rather dangerous to let her clutch at a strange dog's ear. But she did not dare to. She stood watching them, her hands by her side, like the poor little girl in front of the rich girl with the doll.

The baby looked up at her again, stared, and then smiled so charmingly that Bertha couldn't help crying: "Oh, Nanny, do let me finish giving her supper while you put the bath things away."

"Well, m'm, she oughtn't to be changed hands while she's eating," said Nanny, still whispering. "It unsettles her; it's very likely to upset her."

How absurd it was. Why has a baby if it has to be kept — not in a case like a rare, rare fiddle— but in another woman's arms?

此处出现了第一个意象——小提琴,写出了维多利亚时代理想女性的生存状态:从小就像一把珍稀的小提琴那样被禁锢在关闭的盒子里。

"Oh, I must!" said she.

Very offended, Nanny handed her over.

"Now, don't excite her after her supper. You know you do, m'm. And I have such a time with her after!"

Thank heaven! Nanny went out of the room with the bath towels.

"Now I've got you to myself, my little precious," said

---

① pram:婴儿车。
② tug:拖,拽。

Bertha, as the baby leaned against her.

She ate delightfully, holding up her lips for the spoon and then waving her hands. Sometimes she wouldn't let the spoon go; and sometimes, just as Bertha had filled it, she waved it away to the four winds.

When the soup was finished Bertha turned round to the fire. "You're nice — you're very nice!" said she, kissing her warm baby. "I'm fond of you. I like you."

And indeed, she loved Little B so much — her neck as she bent forward, her exquisite toes as they shone transparent① in the firelight — that all her feeling of bliss came back again, and again she didn't know how to express it — what to do with it.

"You're wanted on the telephone," said Nanny, coming back in triumph and seizing her Little B.

Down she flew. It was Harry.

"Oh, is that you, Ber? Look here. I'll be late. I'll take a taxi and come along as quickly as I can, but get dinner put back ten minutes — will you? All right?"

"Yes, perfectly. Oh, Harry!"

"Yes?"

What had she to say? She'd nothing to say. She only wanted to get in touch with him for a moment. She couldn't absurdly cry:"Hasn't it been a divine day②!"

"What is it?" rapped out the little voice.

"Nothing. *Entendu*③," said Bertha, and hung up the receiver, thinking how much more than idiotic civilization was.

意犹未尽,却又不知道说什么,夫妻之间心理距离拉大。

---

①　transparent：透明的。
②　Hasn't it been a divine day! 今儿个是多美好的一天啊!
③　*Entendu*：(法语)好了。

They had people coming to dinner. The Norman Knights — a very sound couple — he was about to start a theatre, and she was awfully keen on interior decoration①, a young man, Eddie Warren, who had just published a little book of poems and whom everybody was asking to dine, and a "find" of Bertha's called Pearl Fulton. What Miss Fulton did, Bertha didn't know. They had met at the club and Bertha had fallen in love with her, as she always did fall in love with beautiful women who had something strange about them.

The provoking② thing was that, though they had been about together and met a number of times and really talked, Bertha couldn't make her out. Up to a certain point Miss Fulton was rarely, wonderfully frank, but the certain point was there, and beyond that she would not go.

Was there anything beyond it? Harry said "No." Voted her dullish③, and "cold like all blonde women, with a touch, perhaps, of anaemia④ of the brain." But Bertha wouldn't agree with him; not yet, at any rate.

"No, the way she has of sitting with her head a little on one side, and smiling, has something behind it, Harry, and I must find out what that something is."

"Most likely it's a good stomach," answered Harry.

He made a point of catching Bertha's heels with replies of that kind ... "liver frozen, my dear girl," or "pure flatulence⑤," or "kidney disease⑥," ... and so on. For some strange reason Bertha liked this, and almost

---

① interior decoration：内部装修。
② provoking：令人恼怒的。
③ dullish：迟钝的。
④ anaemia：贫血症。
⑤ pure flatulence：肠胃气胀。
⑥ kidney disease：肾脏疾病。

admired it in him very much.

She went into the drawing-room and lighted the fire; then, picking up the cushions, one by one, that Mary had disposed so carefully, she threw them back on to the chairs and the couches. That made all the difference; the room came alive at once. As she was about to throw the last one she surprised herself by suddenly hugging it to her, passionately, passionately. But it did not put out the fire in her bosom. Oh, on the contrary!

The windows of the drawing-room opened on to a balcony overlooking the garden. At the far end, against the wall, there was a tall, slender pear tree in fullest, richest bloom; it stood perfect, as though becalmed against the jade-green sky. Bertha couldn't help feeling, even from this distance, that it had not a single bud or a faded petal. Down below, in the garden beds, the red and yellow tulips, heavy with flowers, seemed to lean upon the dusk. A grey cat, dragging its belly, crept across the lawn, and a black one, its shadow, trailed after. The sight of them, so intent and so quick, gave Bertha a curious shiver.

"What creepy things cats are!" she stammered, and she turned away from the window and began walking up and down.

How strong the jonquils① smelled in the warm room. Too strong? Oh, no. And yet, as though overcome, she flung down on a couch and pressed her hands to her eyes.

"I'm too happy — too happy!" she murmured.

And she seemed to see on her eyelids the lovely pear tree with its wide open blossoms as a symbol of her own life.

第二个意象——梨树。梨树可以说是小说的中心意象,它在柏莎眼中是自己生命的象征,而梨树是双性同株植物,柏莎的双性恋倾向借梨树巧妙地传达给读者。

"灰猫"象征着柏莎内心不祥的预感,也暗示"幸福"生活的完结。

---

① jonquil: 黄水仙。

Really — really — she had everything. She was young. Harry and she were as much in love as ever, and they got on together splendidly and were really good pals①. She had an adorable baby. They didn't have to worry about money. They had this absolutely satisfactory house and garden. And friends — modern, thrilling friends, writers and painters and poets or people keen on social questions — just the kind of friends they wanted. And then there were books, and there was music, and she had found a wonderful little dressmaker, and they were going abroad in the summer, and their new cook made the most superb omelets②.

"I'm absurd. Absurd!" She sat up; but she felt quite dizzy, quite drunk. It must have been the spring.

Yes, it was the spring. Now she was so tired she could not drag herself upstairs to dress.

A white dress, a string of jade beads, green shoes and stockings. It wasn't intentional. She had thought of this scheme hours before she stood at the drawing-room window.

Her petals rustled softly into the hall, and she kissed Mrs. Norman Knight, who was taking off the most amusing orange coat with a procession of black monkeys round the hem and up the fronts.

"... Why! Why! Why is the middle-class so stodgy③— so utterly without a sense of humor! My dear, it's only by a fluke that I am here at all — Norman being the protective fluke④. For my darling monkeys so upset the

精神生活落后于物质生活，不甘于平凡的生活。

① pal：朋友。
② omelet：鸡蛋卷。
③ stodgy：索然无味的。
④ fluke：侥幸，偶然机会。

train that it rose to a man and simply ate me with its eyes. Didn't laugh — wasn't amused — that I should have loved. No, just stared — and bored me through and through."

"But the cream of it was," said Norman, pressing a large tortoiseshell-rimmed monocle into his eye, "you don't mind me telling this, Face, do you?" (In their home and among their friends they called each other Face and Mug.) "The cream of it was when she, being full fed, turned to the woman beside her and said: 'Haven't you ever seen a monkey before?'"

"Oh, yes!" Mrs. Norman Knight joined in the laughter. "Wasn't that too absolutely creamy?"

And a funnier thing still was that now her coat was off she did look like a very intelligent monkey who had even made that yellow silk dress out of scraped banana skins. And her amber ear-rings: they were like little dangling nuts.

"This is a sad, sad fall!" said Mug, pausing in front of Little B's perambulator①. "When the perambulator comes into the hall —" and he waved the rest of the quotation away.

The bell rang. It was lean, pale Eddie Warren (as usual) in a state of acute distress.

"It is the right house, isn't it?" he pleaded.

"Oh, I think so — I hope so," said Bertha brightly.

"I have had such a dreadful experience with a taxi-man; he was most sinister②. I couldn't get him to stop. The more I knocked and called the faster he went. And in the moonlight this bizarre figure with the flattened head

---

① perambulator：巡逻的人。
② sinister：凶险的，不祥的。

crouching over the lit-tle wheel . . . "

He shuddered, taking off an immense white silk scarf. Bertha noticed that his socks were white, too — most charming.

"But how dreadful!" she cried.

"Yes, it really was," said Eddie, following her into the drawing-room. "I saw myself driving through Eternity in a timeless taxi."

He knew the Norman Knights. In fact, he was going to write a play for N. K. when the theatre scheme came off.

"Well, Warren, how's the play?" said Norman Knight, dropping his monocle① and giving his eye a moment in which to rise to the surface before it was screwed down② again.

And Mrs. Norman Knight: "Oh, Mr. Warren, what happy socks?"

"I am so glad you like them," said he, staring at his feet. "They seem to have got so much whiter since the moon rose." And he turned his lean sorrowful young face to Bertha. "There is a moon, you know."

She wanted to cry: "I am sure there is — often — often!"

He really was a most attractive person. But so was Face, crouched before the fire in her banana skins, and so was Mug, smoking a cigarette and saying as he flicked the ash: "Why doth the bridegroom tarry③?"

"There he is, now."

Bang went the front door open and shut. Harry shouted: "Hallo, you people. Down in five minutes." And

---

① monocle: 单片眼镜。
② screwed down: 压下。
③ tarry: 耽搁，延迟。

they heard him swarm up the stairs. Bertha couldn't help smiling; she knew how he loved doing things at high pressure. What, after all, did an extra five minutes matter? But he would pretend to himself that they mattered beyond measure. And then he would make a great point of coming into the drawing-room, extravagantly① cool and collected.

Harry had such a zest for life. Oh, how she appreciated it in him. And his passion for fighting — for seeking in everything that came up against him another test of his power and of his courage — that, too, she understood. Even when it made him just occasionally, to other people, who didn't know him well, a little ridiculous perhaps ... For there were moments when he rushed into battle where no battle was ... She talked and laughed and positively forgot until he had come in (just as she had imagined) that Pearl Fulton had not turned up.

暗示了哈里的性格。

"I wonder if Miss Fulton has forgotten."

"I expect so," said Harry. "Is she on the phone?"

"Ah! There's a taxi, now." And Bertha smiled with that little air of proprietorship that she always assumed while her women finds were new and mysterious. "She lives in taxis."

"She'll run to fat if she does," said Harry coolly, ringing the bell for dinner. "Frightful danger for blonde women."

"Harry — don't!" warned Bertha, laughing up at him.

Came another tiny moment, while they waited, laughing and talking, just a trifle too much at their ease, a trifle too unaware. And then Miss Fulton, all in silver,

---

① extravagantly: 挥霍无度的。

with a silver fillet① binding her pale blonde hair, came in smiling, her head a little on one side.

"Am I late?"

"No, not at all," said Bertha. "Come along." And she took her arm and they moved into the dining-room.

What was there in the touch of that cool arm that could fan — start blazing — the fire of bliss that Bertha did not know what to do with?

Miss Fulton did not look at her; but then she seldom did look at people directly. Her heavy eyelids lay upon her eyes and the strange half-smile came and went upon her lips as though she lived by listening rather than seeing. But Bertha knew, suddenly, as if the longest, most intimate look had passed between them — as if they had said to each other: "You too?" — that Pearl Fulton, stirring the beautiful red soup in the grey plate, was feeling just what she was feeling.

柏莎的又一次同性恋情结。

And the others? Face and Mug, Eddie and Harry, their spoons rising and falling — dabbing② their lips with their napkins, crumbling bread, fiddling③ with the forks and glasses and talking.

"I met her at the Alpha show — the weirdest little person. She'd not only cut off her hair, but she seemed to have taken a dreadfully good snip off her legs and arms and her neck and her poor little nose as well."

"Isn't she very *liee*④ with Michael Oat?"

"The man who wrote *Love in False Teeth*?"

"He wants to write a play for me. One act. One man. Decides to commit suicide. Gives all the reasons why he

---

① fillet：束发带。
② dab：轻拍。
③ fiddle：不停摆弄。
④ liee：(法语)密切。

230

should and why he shouldn't. And just as he has made up his mind either to do it or not to do it — curtain. Not half a bad idea."

"What's he going to call it — 'Stomach Trouble'?"

"I think I've come across the same idea in a little French review, quite unknown in England."

No, they didn't share it. They were dears — dears — and she loved having them there, at her table, and giving them delicious food and wine. In fact, she longed to tell them how delightful they were, and what a decorative group they made, how they seemed to set one another off and how they reminded her of a play by Tchekof!

Harry was enjoying his dinner. It was part of his — well, not his nature, exactly, and certainly not his pose — his — something or other — to talk about food and to glory in his "shameless passion for the white flash of the lobster" and "the green of pistachio ices①— green and cold like the eyelids of Egyptian dancers."

When he looked up at her and said:"Bertha, this is a very admirable soufflee②!" she almost could have wept with child-like pleasure.

Oh, why did she feel so tender towards the whole world tonight? Everything was good — was right. All that happened seemed to fill again her brimming cup of bliss.

And still, in the back of her mind, there was the pear tree. It would be silver now, in the light of poor dear Eddie's moon, silver as Miss Fulton, who sat there turning a tangerine in her slender fingers that were so pale a light seemed to come from them.

What she simply couldn't make out — what was

写出了柏莎的同性恋情结,她希望富尔顿小姐就是那棵双性同株的梨树。

———————————

① pistachio ices：开心果沙冰。
② soufflee：（德语）蛋奶酥。

miraculous[1]— was how she should have guessed Miss Fulton's mood so exactly and so instantly. For she never doubted for a moment that she was right, and yet what had she to go on? Less than nothing.

"I believe this does happen very, very rarely between women. Never between men," thought Bertha. "But while I am making the coffee in the drawing-room perhaps she will 'give a sign'."

What she meant by that she did not know, and what would happen after that she could not imagine.

While she thought like this she saw herself talking and laughing. She had to talk because of her desire to laugh.

"I must laugh or die."

But when she noticed Face's funny little habit of tucking something down the front of her bodice[2]— as if she kept a tiny, secret hoard of nuts there, too — Bertha had to dig her nails into her hands — so as not to laugh too much.

It was over at last. And: "Come and see my new coffee machine," said Bertha.

"We only have a new coffee machine once a fortnight," said Harry. Face took her arm this time; Miss Fulton bent her head and followed after.

The fire had died down in the drawing-room to a red, flickering "nest of baby phoenixes[3]," said Face.

"Don't turn up the light for a moment. It is so lovely." And down she crouched by the fire again. She was always cold ... "without her little red flannel jacket,

---

① miraculous：奇迹般的。
② bodice：紧身胸衣。
③ phoenix：火凤凰。神话中的鸟，在阿拉伯沙漠中，可活数百年，然后自焚为灰烬而重生。

of course," thought Bertha.

At that moment Miss Fulton "gave the sign."

"Have you a garden?" said the cool, sleepy voice.

This was so exquisite on her part that all Bertha could do was to obey. She crossed the room, pulled the curtains apart, and opened those long windows.

"There!" she breathed.

And the two women stood side by side looking at the slender, flowering tree. Although it was so still it seemed, like the flame of a candle, to stretch up, to point, to quiver in the bright air, to grow taller and taller as they gazed — almost to touch the rim of the round, silver moon.

How long did they stand there? Both, as it were, caught in that circle of unearthly① light, understanding each other perfectly, creatures of another world, and wondering what they were to do in this one with all this blissful treasure that burned in their bosoms and dropped, in silver flowers, from their hair and hands?

Forever — for a moment? And did Miss Fulton murmur:"Yes. Just that." Or did Bertha dream it?

Then the light was snapped on and Face made the coffee and Harry said:"My dear Mrs. Knight, don't ask me about my baby. I never see her. I shan't feel the slightest interest in her until she has a lover," and Mug took his eye out of the conservatory② for a moment and then put it under glass again and Eddie Warren drank his coffee and set down the cup with a face of anguish③ as though he had drunk and seen the spider.

"What I want to do is to give the young men a show.

富尔顿小姐被柏莎对象化了,鲜花盛开的梨树是柏莎的象征,也是富尔顿小姐的象征。

---

① unearthly：怪异的,异常的。
② conservatory：温室,玻璃暖房。
③ anguish：(精神或肉体的)极度痛苦。

I believe London is simply teeming with first-chop, unwritten plays. What I want to say to 'em is: 'Here's the theatre. Fire ahead.'"

"You know, my dear, I am going to decorate a room for the Jacob Nathans. Oh, I am so tempted to do a fried-fish scheme, with the backs of the chairs shaped like frying-pans and lovely chip potatoes embroidered all over the curtains."

"The trouble with our young writing men is that they are still too romantic. You can't put out to sea without being seasick① and wanting a basin. Well, why won't they have the courage of those basins?"

"A dreadful poem about a girl who was violated by a beggar without a nose in a little wood ..."

Miss Fulton sank into the lowest, deepest chair and Harry handed round the cigarettes.

From the way he stood in front of her shaking the silver box and saying abruptly: "Egyptian? Turkish? Virginian? They're all mixed up," Bertha realized that she not only bored him; he really disliked her. And she decided from the way Miss Fulton said: "No, thank you, I won't smoke," that she felt it, too, and was hurt.

"Oh, Harry, don't dislike her. You are quite wrong about her. She's wonderful, wonderful. And, besides, how can you feel so differently about someone who means so much to me. I shall try to tell you when we are in bed tonight what has been happening. What she and I have shared."

At those last words something strange and almost terrifying darted into Bertha's mind. And this something

---

① seasick：晕船的。

blind and smiling whispered to her: "Soon these people will go. The house will be quiet — quiet. The lights will be out. And you and he will be alone together in the dark room — the warm bed . . ."

She jumped up from her chair and ran over to the piano.

"What a pity someone does not play!" she cried. "What a pity somebody does not play."

For the first time in her life Bertha Young desired her husband. Oh, she'd loved him — she'd been in love with him, of course, in every other way, but just not in that way. And equally, of course, she'd understood that he was different. They'd discussed it so often. It had worried her dreadfully at first to find that she was so cold, but after a time it had not seemed to matter. They were so frank with each other — such good pals. That was the best of being modern.

But now — ardently[①]! Ardently! The word ached in her ardent body! Was this what that feeling of bliss had been leading up to? But then, then —

"My dear," said Mrs. Norman Knight, "you know our shame. We are the victims of time and train. We live in Hampstead. It's been so nice."

"I'll come with you into the hall," said Bertha. "I loved having you. But you must not miss the last train. That's so awful, isn't it?"

"Have a whisky, Knight, before you go?" called Harry.

"No, thanks, old chap."

Bertha squeezed his hand for that as she shook it.

"Good night, good-bye," she cried from the top step, feeling that this self of hers was taking leave of them for

为下面的幸福幻灭做铺垫。

---

① ardently：热心地，热烈地。

235

ever.

When she got back into the drawing-room the others were on the move.

"... Then you can come part of the way in my taxi."

"I shall be so thankful not to have to face another drive alone after my dreadful experience."

"You can get a taxi at the rank just at the end of the street. You won't have to walk more than a few yards."

"That's a comfort. I'll go and put on my coat."

Miss Fulton moved towards the hall and Bertha was following when Harry almost pushed past.

"Let me help you."

Bertha knew that he was repenting① his rudeness — she let him go. What a boy he was in some ways — so impulsive — so simple.

And Eddie and she were left by the fire.

"I wonder if you have seen Bilks' new poem called *Table d'Hote*②," said Eddie softly. "It's so wonderful. In the last anthology③. Have you got a copy? I'd so like to show it to you. It begins with an incredibly beautiful line: 'Why Must it Always be Tomato Soup?'"

"Yes," said Bertha. And she moved noiselessly to a table opposite the drawing-room door and Eddie glided noiselessly after her. She picked up the little book and gave it to him; they had not made a sound.

While he looked it up she turned her head towards the hall. And she saw ... Harry with Miss Fulton's coat in his arms and Miss Fulton with her back turned to him and her head bent. He tossed the coat away, put his hands on her

---

① repent：后悔，懊悔。
② *Table d'Hote*：（法语）公司餐。
③ anthology：诗集，文选。

shoulders and turned her violently to him. His lips said："I adore you，" and Miss Fulton laid her moonbeam fingers on his cheeks and smiled her sleepy smile. Harry's nostrils① quivered；his lips curled back in a hideous grin② while he whispered："Tomorrow，" and with her eyelids Miss Fulton said："Yes."

柏莎的幸福感被击得粉碎，全文达到高潮。

"Here it is," said Eddie. "'Why Must it Always be Tomato Soup?' It's so deeply true，don't you feel? Tomato soup is so dreadfully eternal."

"If you prefer," said Harry's voice，very loud，from the hall，"I can phone you a cab to come to the door."

"Oh，no. It's not necessary," said Miss Fulton，and she came up to Bertha and gave her the slender fingers to hold.

"Good-bye. Thank you so much."

"Good-bye," said Bertha.

Miss Fulton held her hand a moment longer.

"Your lovely pear tree!" she murmured.

And then she was gone，with Eddie following，like the black cat following the grey cat.

第三个意象。

"I'll shut up shop," said Harry，extravagantly cool and collected③.

"Your lovely pear tree — pear tree — pear tree!"

Bertha simply ran over to the long windows.

"Oh，what is going to happen now?" she cried.

But the pear tree was as lovely as ever and as full of flower and as still.

【思考题】

1. 作者是如何通过象征手法来对主人公的心理进行描

---

① nostril：鼻孔。
② grin：咧着嘴笑。
③ collected：镇定的。

述的?

    2. 文中的意象是如何反映文章主题的?

    3. 柏莎的性格有什么特点,跟文章主题有什么联系?

    4. 如何解读文章标题?

Kew Gardens

邱 园

弗吉尼亚·伍尔芙

【导读】

弗吉尼亚·伍尔芙（Virginia Woolf，1882—1941），世界知名的小说家、批评家、散文家。也是意识流作家中成就最高的女性，至今仍被认为是 20 世纪现代主义与女性主义的先锋之一。在两次世界大战期间，伍尔芙是伦敦文学界的核心人物，也是布卢姆茨伯里派（Bloomsbury Group）的成员之一，其最著名的小说有《达洛维夫人》（1925）、《到灯塔去》（1927）和《海浪》（1931），女性主义代表散文有《一间自己的房间》（1929）和《三个畿尼》（1938）。

伍尔芙的母亲是社交名媛，父亲是英国著名学者莱斯利·斯蒂芬爵士，知名编辑、批评家，她从小就受父母的指导在自家的书房里接受家庭教育。伍尔芙许多作品与早年的经历有关。她的母亲有三个孩子，继母生有四个，在这样的九口之家，由于年龄差距和性格原因，子女之间经常发生矛盾和冲突，伍尔芙同父异母的两位兄长曾对她和姐姐瓦内萨进行过性侵犯，给她留下了永久的精神创伤。伍尔芙一生多次精神失常，母亲、父亲的相继病逝更成为她难以承受的打击。

1912 年，伍尔芙与新闻记者伦纳德·伍尔芙结婚。丈夫在伍尔芙的文学事业和家庭生活上给予了她很多的照顾和包容，尤其在其患病期间，丈夫对她体贴入微的照顾更让她深受感动，伍尔芙自己也说："要不是为了他的缘故，我早就开枪自杀了。"

然而，1941 年 3 月 28 日，伍尔芙终究还是因为精神上再也无法承受巨大压力写下遗书，投河自杀。

伍尔芙对英语语言的革新良多，在小说中运用意识流的写法，注重人物内心的心理和情绪的变化描写，展现某个人物或某些人物在某个时刻的所思所想、所见所闻，这全然不同于传统现实主义小说中叙述者全知全能、无所不在的"零聚焦"方式。她相信只有当个体及个人意识升华成一个群体的纯粹"瞬间存在"时，存在于表象之下的每日生活的变化和无序才能表现出来。

代表作《达洛维夫人》就是这样一部意识流小说的代表作品。小说讲述了主人公克拉丽莎·达洛维在"一战"后的英国伦敦某一天的生活细节，故事围绕达洛维夫人筹备一个上流社会派对展开。晴朗夏日的早晨,达洛维走在伦敦的街道,为自己晚上的派对采购物品。美好的天气令她想起了自己已逝的青春,以及她年轻时的狂热追随者彼得·沃尔士,同时思索着自己的婚姻是否是一个正确的选择。恰巧沃尔士当天从印度返回伦敦来看望她,更让她思绪不宁。同时,在伦敦的另一角是"一战"退伍军人塞普蒂默斯·史密斯和他的妻子露西娅的生活情景。史密斯患有无名的狂想症,经常在幻觉中看到"一战"中牺牲的好友伊凡。当权威医师决定对他实行强制隔离治疗时,他跳楼自杀。达洛维夫人当晚的派对很成功,名流济济。书中提及的昔日老友悉数到场,可她抽不出身来和他们细聊。她在派对上闻知史密斯自杀的事情,心里暗自佩服这种解脱,认为或许只有这样才能真正保存自己内心纯粹的快乐。小说的每一幕都是对特定人物内心记忆的记载,视角在时空中、主人公的思维和现实之间穿梭。通过对达洛维夫人一天中生活细节的描述来塑造她一生的经历以及"一战"前后的整个英国社会。从女性主义的角度来考察,女主人翁克拉丽莎的角色揭示的是"一战"后的英国女性在家中扮演的"家庭天使"这样的角色,她们受着性别和经济的双重压迫,同时也在自己的小天地中寻找着对社会生活及个人命运的参与和掌控。

《到灯塔去》被誉为作者的准自传体意识流小说,也是现代主义小说创作的里程碑。小说以"到灯塔去"为贯穿全书的中心线索,写了拉姆齐一家和几位客人在第一次世界大战前后的生活经历。小说分为三个部分,分别是"窗户""时光流逝"和"灯塔"。故事一开始,拉姆齐一家和借宿的客人过着安稳的生活,其间儿子詹姆斯提出想去灯塔,由于天气不好而一直未能如愿。后来,"一战"爆发,太太去世,拉姆齐一家历经沧桑。战后,拉姆齐先生携带儿女乘舟出海,终于到达灯塔。而坐在岸边画画的莉丽·布里斯科(曾是拉姆齐家的客人之一)也正好在拉姆齐一家到达灯塔的时候,在瞬间的感悟中,向画幅中央落下一笔,终于画出了萦绕心中多年的幻象,从而超越自己,成为一名真正的艺术家。

小说并没有跌宕起伏的情节,有些读者对此提出了批评,认为情节太少,人物面貌不清晰。对于这些批评,伍尔芙给出了自己的答案——"让我们考察一下一个普通人在普通的一天中的内心活动吧。心灵接纳了成千上万个印象——琐屑的、奇异的、倏忽即逝的或者用锋利的钢刀深深铭刻在心头的印象。它们来自四面八方,犹如不计其数的原子在不停地簇射;当这些原子坠落下来,构成了星期一或星期二的生活,其侧重点就和往昔有所不同;重要的瞬间不在于此而在于彼。因此,如果作家是个自由人而不是奴隶,如果他能随心所欲而不是墨守成规,如果他能够以个人的感受而不是以因袭的传统作为他作品的依据,那么就不会有约定俗成的那种情节、喜剧、悲剧、爱情的欢乐或灾难,而且也许不会有一粒纽扣是用庞德街的裁缝所惯用的那种方式钉上去的"(《论现代小说》)。《到灯塔去》延续了现代小说家,如詹姆斯·乔伊斯等小说创作的传统,在故事中相比于人物的心理反思来说,情节总是排在第二位的,这必然会造成读者对小说理解的困难。小说里的对白非常少,大部分都是在描写主人公的思考和观察。

伍尔芙一直在小说中寻找外部世界与内心世界的连接点,情节只是一个必要的框架,不必复杂,如果太多反而是阻碍。正如埃·奥尔巴赫(Erich Auerbach)所说,"在弗吉尼亚·伍尔芙手中,外部事件实际上已经丧失了它们统帅一切的地位,它们是用来释放并解释内部事件的"。(《摹仿——西方文学中所描绘的现实》)

本书选取的短篇意识流小说《邱园》也几乎没有所谓的故事情节,只有炎热夏日伦敦郊区皇家植物园——邱园里四组游人的几个描写片断,集中记叙了他们的感觉、情绪、心理活动,中间穿插着对邱园中景物看似随意、实则精心安排的描绘。

作者以小说标题中的"邱园"作为故事发生的地点,用邱园中的花坛做中心来展开对整篇故事的叙述。在这样一个天地中,自然界中的植物、昆虫、色彩、光线、声音等不断地被呈现。故事不再局限于小说家常见的人的世界,叙述的视角在人与自然物甚至机器之间来回穿梭,一会儿是娇嫩而坚挺的花朵,一会儿是向着目的地努力爬动的蜗牛,一会儿是光线照射下事物呈现出的瑰丽色彩,甚至包含了一些没有生命的物体比如汽车、飞机,他们似乎也和园中的行人、动植物一般在阳光的照耀下,释放着自己鲜活的生命。

总的说来,《邱园》中有关人的部分叙述的是一系列的日常琐事,通过人物内心独白的刻画,表现人物之间微妙复杂的关系。而通过对不同叙事视角的把握表现自然背景与人以外的生物,也是作者关注的一个焦点,并与人的世界形成鲜明的对照。所有的事件都以邱园和花坛为舞台,景物的描写、人物的对话片断与内心独白是交错在一起的,小说包涵了丰富的意象,以其洗练简约的风格为评论家所赞赏。

Kew Gardens[①]

From the oval-shaped flower-bed there rose perhaps a hundred stalks spreading into heart-shaped or tongue-shaped leaves half way up[②] and unfurling at the tip red or blue or yellow petals marked with spots of colour[③] raised

作者用人体的器官来比喻叶子的形状,自然而然地拉近人与自然界的关系。植物是有生命的。

---

① Kew Gardens:邱园,位于伦敦郊区的皇家植物园。
② a hundred stalks spreading into heart-shaped or tongue-shaped leaves half way up:花梗从半腰伸展出团团绿叶。
③ spots of colour:五颜六色的斑点。

诗人的景物描写犹如画家的作品,似乎是用画笔在画布上细细勾勒。光线、层次的处理生动而轻盈。

upon the surface; and from the red, blue or yellow gloom of the throat emerged a straight bar①, rough with gold dust② and slightly clubbed at the end. The petals were voluminous③ enough to be stirred by the summer breeze, and when they moved, the red, blue and yellow lights passed one over the other, staining an inch of the brown earth beneath with a spot of the most intricate colour. The light fell either upon the smooth, grey back of a pebble, or, the shell of a snail with its brown, circular veins④, or falling into a raindrop, it expanded with such intensity of red, blue and yellow the thin walls of water that one expected them to burst and disappear. Instead, the drop was left in a second silver grey once more, and the light now settled upon the flesh of a leaf, revealing the branching thread of fibre beneath the surface⑤, and again it moved on and spread its illumination in the vast green spaces beneath the dome⑥ of the heart-shaped and tongue-shaped leaves. Then the breeze stirred rather more briskly overhead and the colour was flashed into⑦ the air above, into the eyes of the men and women who walk in Kew Gardens in July.

将人物的行走与蝴蝶作比,再次拉近了人与自然的距离。

The figures of these men and women straggled past the flower-bed with a curiously irregular movement not unlike that of the white and blue butterflies who crossed the turf in zig-zag flights from bed to bed. The man was about six inches in front of the woman, strolling

---

① a straight bar:挺直的花柱。
② gold dust:此处指金色的花粉。
③ voluminous:肥大的。形容花瓣张得很开。
④ brown, circular veins:蜗牛壳棕色的螺旋纹。
⑤ the branching thread of fibre beneath the surface:叶子表皮下的叶脉。
⑥ dome:圆屋顶。像圆屋顶一样的叶片。
⑦ flash into:一闪而入。

carelessly, while she bore on① with greater purpose, only turning her head now and then to see that the children were not too far behind. The man kept this distance in front of the woman purposely, though perhaps unconsciously, for he wished to go on with his thoughts.

"Fifteen years ago I came here with Lily," he thought. "We sat somewhere over there by a lake and I begged her to marry me all through the hot afternoon. How the dragonfly kept circling round us: how clearly I see the dragonfly and her shoe with the square silver buckle at the toe. All the time I spoke I saw her shoe and when it moved impatiently I knew without looking up what she was going to say: the whole of her seemed to be in her shoe. And my love, my desire, were in the dragonfly; for some reason I thought that if it settled there, on that leaf, the broad one with the red flower in the middle of it, if the dragonfly settled on the leaf she would say 'Yes' at once. But the dragonfly went round and round: it never settled anywhere — of course not, happily not, or I shouldn't be walking here with Eleanor and the children — Tell me, Eleanor. D'you ever think of the past?"

"Why do you ask, Simon?"

"Because I've been thinking of the past. I've been thinking of Lily, the woman I might have married . . . . Well, why are you silent? Do you mind my thinking of the past?"

"Why should I mind, Simon? Doesn't one always think of the past, in a garden with men and women lying under the trees? Aren't they one's past, all that remains of it, those men and women, those ghosts lying under the

One 指代"我们自己",妻子和丈夫,以及所有活着的人。

---

① bear on: 受到……的影响,在这里指妻子受到了孩子的影响,走路时不时张望。

trees, ... one's happiness, one's reality?"

"For me, a square silver shoe buckle and a dragonfly —"

"For me, a kiss. Imagine six little girls sitting before their easels① twenty years ago, down by the side of a lake, painting the water-lilies, the first red water-lilies I'd ever seen. And suddenly a kiss, there on the back of my neck. And my hand shook all the afternoon so that I couldn't paint. I took out my watch and marked the hour when I would allow myself to think of the kiss for five minutes only — it was so precious — the kiss of an old grey-haired woman with a wart② on her nose, the mother of all my kisses all my life. Come, Caroline, come, Hubert."

They walked on the past the flower-bed, now walking four abreast③, and soon diminished in size among the trees and looked half transparent as the sunlight and shade swam over their backs in large trembling irregular patches④.

In the oval flower bed the snail, whose shell had been stained red, blue, and yellow for the space of two minutes or so, now appeared to be moving very slightly in its shell, and next began to labour over⑤ the crumbs of loose earth which broke away and rolled down as it passed over them. It appeared to have a definite goal in front of it, differing in this respect from the singular high stepping angular⑥ green insect who attempted to cross in front of it, and waited for a second with its antennae⑦ trembling as if in deliberation, and then stepped off as rapidly and

在花园中，丈夫回忆起了十五年前向一个叫莉莉的女孩求婚的情形。而妻子回忆的是二十年前一个轻轻的吻。

从老太太的吻开始，妻子才真正懂得了吻的意义。

space 在这里指时间。

---

① easel：画架。
② wart：疣。
③ abreast：并列，并排。
④ large trembling irregular patches：摇摆不定的，大块斑驳的碎影。
⑤ labour over：费力地爬。
⑥ angular：有尖角的。
⑦ antennae：触角。

strangely in the opposite direction. Brown cliffs with deep green lakes in the hollows, flat, blade-like trees that waved from root to tip, round boulders of grey stone, vast crumpled surfaces of a thin crackling texture — all these objects lay across the snail's progress between one stalk and another to his goal. Before he had decided whether to circumvent① the arched tent of a dead leaf or to breast② it there came past the bed the feet of other human beings.

This time they were both men. The younger of the two wore an expression of perhaps unnatural calm; he raised his eyes and fixed them very steadily in front of him while his companion spoke, and directly his companion had done speaking he looked on the ground again and sometimes opened his lips only after a long pause and sometimes did not open them at all. The elder man had a curiously uneven and shaky method of walking③, jerking his hand forward and throwing up his head abruptly, rather in the manner of an impatient carriage horse tired of waiting outside a house; but in the man these gestures were irresolute and pointless. He talked almost incessantly; he smiled to himself and again began to talk, as if the smile had been an answer. He was talking about spirits — the spirits of the dead, who, according to him, were even now telling him all sorts of odd things about their experiences in Heaven.

"Heaven was known to the ancients as Thessaly④, William, and now, with this war, the spirit matter is rolling between the hills like thunder." He paused, seemed to listen, smiled, jerked his head and

---

① circumvent: 绕道。
② breast: 此处指登到叶片顶上。
③ a curiously uneven and shaky method of walking: 走起路来高一脚低一脚,不平稳。
④ Thessaly: 地名,古希腊城市。

continued：—

"You have a small electric battery and a piece of rubber to insulate the wire-isolate? -insulate?①— well, we'll skip the details, no good going into details that wouldn't be understood — and in short the little machine stands in any convenient position by the head of the bed, we will say, on a neat mahogany stand②. All arrangements being properly fixed by workmen under my direction, the widow applies her ear and summons the spirit by sign as agreed. Women! Widows! Women in black③—"

Here he seemed to have caught sight of a woman's dress in the distance, which in the shade looked a purple black. He took off his hat, placed his hand upon his heart, and hurried towards her muttering and gesticulating feverishly. But William caught him by the sleeve and touched a flower with the tip of his walking-stick in order to divert the old man's attention. After looking at it for a moment in some confusion the old man bent his ear to it and seemed to answer a voice speaking from it, for he began talking about the forests of Uruguay④ which he had visited hundreds of years ago in company with the most beautiful young woman in Europe. He could be heard murmuring about forests of Uruguay blanketed with⑤ the wax petals of tropical roses, nightingales, sea beaches, mermaids⑥, and women drowned at sea, as he suffered himself to be moved on by William, upon whose face the look of stoical⑦ patience grew slowly deeper and deeper.

年轻人威廉脸上冷漠的表情越来越严峻，他已经听不下去年长者的唠叨，推着他往前走。

---

① isolate? -insulate? 是叫隔电呀还是叫绝缘呀？
② mahogany stand：桃红木小茶几。
③ Women in black：戴孝的女人。
④ Uruguay：乌拉圭（拉丁美洲国家）。
⑤ blanketed with：布满，覆盖。
⑥ mermaid：美人鱼。
⑦ stoical：坚忍的。

Following his steps so closely as to be slightly puzzled by his gestures came two elderly women of the lower middle class, one stout and ponderous①, the other rosy cheeked and nimble. Like most people of their station they were frankly fascinated by any signs of eccentricity betokening② a disordered brain, especially in the well-to-do③; but they were too far off to be certain whether the gestures were merely eccentric or genuinely mad. After they had scrutinised④ the old man's back in silence for a moment and given each other a queer, sly look, they went on energetically piecing together their very complicated dialogue:

第三对出现在花圃边的是两个中年妇女。她们的对话内容杂糅凌乱，叫人难以琢磨。

"Nell, Bert, Lot, Cess, Phil, Pa, he says, I says, she says, I says, I says, I says —"

"My Bert, Sis, Bill, Grandad, the old man, sugar,

Sugar, flour, kippers, greens,

Sugar, sugar, sugar."

The ponderous woman looked through the pattern of falling words at the flowers standing cool, firm, and upright in the earth, with a curious expression. She saw them as a sleeper waking from a heavy sleep sees a brass candlestick reflecting the light in an unfamiliar way, and closes his eyes and opens them, and seeing the brass candlestick again, finally starts broad awake⑤ and stares at the candlestick with all his powers. So the heavy woman came to a standstill opposite the oval-shaped flower bed, and ceased even to pretend to listen to what the other woman was saying. She stood there letting the

falling 形容话语如雨点一般洒落，本段倒数第二句也用到了这个词。

大个子女人完全沉醉在花朵的绮丽姿态中，甚至身体也跟着摇动起来，对朋友的话充耳不闻。

① one stout and ponderous：一个粗壮臃肿。
② betoken：预示，表示。
③ well-to-do：有钱人。
④ scrutinise：详细检查。
⑤ broad awake：完全醒了。

words fall over her, swaying the top part of her body slowly backwards and forwards, looking at the flowers. Then she suggested that they should find a seat and have their tea.

The snail had now considered every possible method of reaching his goal without going round the dead leaf or climbing over it. Let alone① the effort needed for climbing a leaf, he was doubtful whether the thin texture which vibrated with such an alarming crackle when touched even by the tip of his horns would bear his weight; and this determined him finally to creep beneath it, for there was a point where the leaf curved high enough from the ground to admit him. He had just inserted his head in the opening and was taking stock② of the high brown roof and was getting used to the cool brown light when two other people came past outside on the turf. This time they were both young, a young man and a young woman. They were both in the prime of youth③, or even in that season which precedes④ the prime of youth, the season before the smooth pink folds of the flower have burst their gummy case⑤, when the wings of the butterfly, though fully grown, are motionless in the sun.

在这里,作者将最后出场的一对年轻人比作含苞待放的花朵和尚未展翅的彩蝶。

"Lucky it isn't Friday," he observed.

"Why? D'you believe in luck?"

反问句,意为"你也相信运气?"

"They make you pay sixpence on Friday."

"What's sixpence anyway? Isn't it worth sixpence?"

"What's 'it' — what do you mean by 'it'?"

---

① Let alone：且不说。
② take stock：此处指考量,评估。
③ in the prime of youth：正值青春妙龄。
④ precede：在……之前,还不到。
⑤ the smooth pink folds of the flower have burst their gummy case：粉红娇嫩的蓓蕾含苞欲放。

"O, anything — I mean — you know what I mean."

Long pauses came between each of these remarks; they were uttered in toneless and monotonous voices. The couple stood still on the edge of the flower bed, and together pressed the end of her parasol① deep down into the soft earth. The action and the fact that his hand rested on the top of hers expressed their feelings in a strange way, as these short insignificant words also expressed something, words with short wings for their heavy body of meaning, inadequate to carry them far and thus alighting awkwardly upon the very common objects that surrounded them, and were to their inexperienced touch so massive; but who knows (so they thought as they pressed the parasol into the earth) what precipices② aren't concealed in them, or what slopes of ice don't shine in the sun on the other side? Who knows? Who has ever seen this before? Even when she wondered what sort of tea they gave you at Kew, he felt that something loomed up③ behind her words, and stood vast and solid behind them; and the mist very slowly rose and uncovered-O, Heavens, what were those shapes? — little white tables, and waitresses who looked first at her and then at him; and there was a bill that he would pay with a real two shilling piece, and it was real, all real, he assured himself, fingering the coin in his pocket, real to everyone except to him and to her; even to him it began to seem real; and then-but it was too exciting to stand and think any longer, and he pulled the parasol out of the earth with a jerk and was impatient to find the place where one had tea with other people, like other people.

将情侣之间的对话比作短小的翅膀，承载不了话语间传达的情感的力量，充分揭示了情侣对于彼此情绪的敏感体察。

---

① parasol：遮阳伞。
② precipice：峭壁。
③ loom up：隐隐呈现。

"Come along, Trissie; it's time we had our tea."

"Wherever *does* one have one's tea?" she asked with the oddest thrill of excitement in her voice, looking vaguely round and letting herself be drawn on down the grass path, trailing her parasol, turning her head this way and that way, forgetting her tea, wishing to go down there and then down there, remembering orchids① and crane② among wild flowers, a Chinese pagoda③ and a crimson crested bird④; but he bore her on.

文章的结尾，这一对对从花圃前走过的人，在炙热的阳光下，似乎都与自然融为一体，色彩斑斓。之前的纷繁思绪都化作快乐的色彩，跳跃起来。

Thus one couple after another with much the same irregular and aimless movement passed the flower-bed and were enveloped in layer after layer of green blue vapour⑤, in which at first their bodies had substance and a dash of colour, but later both substance and colour dissolved in the green-blue atmosphere. How hot it was! So hot that even the thrush chose to hop, like a mechanical bird, in the shadow of the flowers, with long pauses between one movement and the next; instead of rambling vaguely the white butterflies danced one above another, making with their white shifting flakes the outline of a shattered marble column⑥ above the tallest flowers; the glass roofs of the palm house shone as if a whole market full of shiny green umbrellas had opened in the sun; and in the drone of the aeroplane⑦ the voice of the summer sky murmured its fierce soul. Yellow and black, pink and snow white, shapes of all these colours, men, women, and children were spotted for a second

---

① orchid：兰花。
② crane：仙鹤。
③ pagoda：塔。
④ crimson crested bird：红冠鸟。
⑤ layer after layer of green blue vapour：层层叠叠苍翠的雾霭。
⑥ the outline of a shattered marble column：勾勒出摇摇欲坠的白色大理石廊柱残垣般的轮廓。
⑦ in the drone of the aeroplane：飞机的嗡嗡声。

upon the horizon, and then, seeing the breadth of yellow that lay upon the grass, they wavered and sought shade beneath the trees, dissolving like drops of water in the yellow and green atmosphere, staining it faintly with red and blue. It seemed as if all gross and heavy bodies had sunk down in the heat motionless and lay huddled upon the ground, but their voices went wavering from them as if they were flames lolling from the thick waxen bodies of candles. Voices. Yes, voices. Wordless voices, breaking the silence suddenly with such depth of contentment, such passion of desire, or, in the voices of children, such freshness of surprise; breaking the silence? But there was no silence; all the time the motor omnibuses were turning their wheels and changing their gear; like a vast nest of Chinese boxes① all of wrought steel② turning ceaselessly one within another the city murmured; on the top of which the voices cried aloud and the petals of myriads of flowers flashed their colours into the air.

【思考题】

1. 本文自然景物描写的音乐美和画面美是如何体现出来的?

2. 文中作者的视角从人物到植物之间反复切换,这对主题的展示有什么意义?

3. 比较伍尔芙和乔伊斯这两位意识流小说大师的短篇小说的创作风格。

---

① Chinese boxes:中国套盒,指大盒子套一串小盒子的玩具。
② wrought steel:锻钢。

The Yellow Wallpaper

黄色墙纸

夏洛特·帕金·吉尔曼

【导读】

夏洛特·帕金·吉尔曼(Charlotte Perkins Gilman，1860—1935)，生于美国康涅狄格州哈特福德。在她幼年时期，父亲抛弃了母亲。此后，家里几乎一贫如洗。尽管童年惨淡，但是吉尔曼仍成为美国首位女权主义运动的主要理论家和活动家。吉尔曼这种对于社会公平和女性平权的信念和决心来源于长辈。例如，她的姨婆就是《汤姆叔叔的小屋》的作者哈莉叶·毕秋·斯托(Harriet Beecher Stowe)——她曾大力呼吁废除黑奴制度。

1884 年，吉尔曼嫁给了查尔斯·华特·史德森(Charles Walter Stetson)。史德森是个典型的美国男人，他对妻子的写作抱负不以为然。他们的女儿出生后，吉尔曼越来越觉得在这种职业抱负和家庭生活之间不能取得平衡，渐渐患上抑郁症。1888 年，她毅然带着女儿离开了丈夫，只身前往加州独立生活，靠写作维生。1900 年，吉尔曼与乔治·修顿·吉尔曼(George Houghton Gilman)再婚，直到 34 年后过世，乔治始终全力支持妻子的改革运动。1935 年夏洛特罹患乳癌，末期时决定服毒自杀，并且声明：在面对可怕漫长的死亡时，个人应有选择死亡的基本权利。

她一生写作不计其数，著名的作品有：被妇女运动视为“圣经”的《女人与经济》(Women and Economics，1898)和《关于小孩》(Concerning Children，1900)、《人类工程》(Human Work，1904)、《男人创造的世界》(Man-Made World，1911)、《他的宗教和她的》(His Religion and Hers，1923)等。其中《女人与经济》被认为是美国妇女运动早期最重要的巨作之一。1909 年到 1917 年，吉尔曼出版了自己主编的杂志《先驱者》(The Forerunner)，她在由她主办的报刊中经常鼓励妇女应该“接受教育、经济独立且不依附男人”。

今天，吉尔曼最为著名的作品要数她的短篇小说《黄色壁纸》。《黄色壁纸》第一次发表于 1892 年，基于作者自身的经历和遭遇改写而成。生下女儿以后，吉尔曼的身体和精神状况每况愈下，于是求助于费城的名医西拉斯·威尔·米切尔(Silas Weir Mitchell)。米切尔让她多吃多睡，尽量减少“外界刺激”，尽量待在家里，沉浸在“家庭生活”里面。还劝她放弃写作，尽量多休息，且每天不要超过两个小时的精神思考活动。可是她的病情并没有好转,相反还越来越严重,差点接近疯狂的边缘。后来她放弃了医生的建议,却慢慢痊愈。这便是这部小说的灵感来源。

小说以女主人公患有抑郁症,身为内科医生的丈夫将她带往乡下的一所豪宅接受"休息疗法"这样一个开端进行叙述。她的丈夫认为意志上的锻炼有助于恢复精神衰弱,而禁止女主人公思考和写作。在这座哥特式的古老建筑里,铁床是被固定住的,而窗户也加了保护木栅,女主人每天所能面对的就是黄色的壁纸。这座孤寂的房子让她的精神日渐紊乱,对黄色的墙纸产生幻觉,觉得这些可怕的图案背后藏着一个可怕的疯女人。最终,女主人公走向彻底的疯狂,她扯碎了壁纸,坚信自己放出了禁锢在壁纸中的女人,并令其得到了自由。这篇小说向我们展示了在男权主导的社会里女性的悲惨命运,并且提出了女性要挣脱桎梏,寻求解放这样的隐喻。

The Yellow Wallpaper

1

It is very seldom that mere ordinary people like John and myself secure ancestral① halls for the summer.

A colonial mansion②, a hereditary estate, I would say a haunted house and reach the height of romantic felicity③—but that would be asking too much of fate!

Still I will proudly declare that there is something queer about it.

Else, why should it be let so cheaply? And why have stood so long untenanted?

John laughs at me, of course, but one expects that.

John is practical in the extreme. He has no patience with faith, an intense horror of superstition④, and he scoffs openly at any talk of things not to be felt and seen and put down in figures.

John is a physician, and perhaps — (I would not say

她的丈夫就是一个典型的极端现实派,是当时男权主导下的社会里男性的代表。

---

① ancestral:祖先的,祖传的。
② mansion:豪宅。
③ felicity:幸福。
④ superstition:迷信。

it to a living soul, of course, but this is dead paper and a great relief to my mind) — perhaps that is one reason I do not get well faster.

You see, he does not believe I am sick! And what can one do?

If a physician of high standing, and one's own husband, assures friends and relatives that there is really nothing the matter with one but temporary nervous depression — a slight hysterical[①] tendency — what is one to do?

My brother is also a physician, and also of high standing, and he says the same thing.

So I take phosphates or phosphites[②]— whichever it is — and tonics, and air and exercise, and journeys, and am absolutely forbidden to "work" until I am well again.

Personally, I disagree with their ideas.

Personally, I believe that congenial[③] work, with excitement and change, would do me good.

But what is one to do?

I did write for a while in spite of them; but it does exhaust me a good deal — having to be so sly about it, or else meet with heavy opposition.

I sometimes fancy that in my condition, if I had less opposition and more society and stimulus — but John says the very worst thing I can do is to think about my condition, and I confess it always makes me feel bad.

So I will let it alone and talk about the house.

The most beautiful place! It is quite alone, standing well back from the road, quite three miles from the village. It makes me think of English places that you read

女主人公的内科医生丈夫不相信她是病态的,在不征求妻子意见的情况下将她送往这个哥特式建筑静养,与世隔绝。这句轻轻的"我又能怎么办呢"道尽了她深深的无奈,以及对丈夫的嘲弄。

与上文的"我又能怎么办呢"相呼应,指出了她精神崩溃的另一个原因,丈夫禁止她思考和写作,她剩下的只能是胡思乱想。为下文中她将注意力集中在黄色的墙纸埋下伏笔。

---

① hysterical：歇斯底里。
② phosphites：磷酸盐。
③ congenial：宜人的。

about, for there are hedges and walls and gates that lock, and lots of separate little houses for the gardeners and people.

There is a delicious garden! I never saw such a garden — large and shady, full of box-bordered paths, and lined with long grape-covered arbors① with seats under them.

There were greenhouses, but they are all broken now.

There was some legal trouble, I believe, something about the heirs and co-heirs; anyhow, the place has been empty for years.

That spoils my ghostliness, I am afraid, but I don't care — there is something strange about the house — I can feel it.

I even said so to John one moonlight evening, but he said what I felt was a draught, and shut the window.

I get unreasonably angry with John sometimes. I'm sure I never used to be so sensitive. I think it is due to this nervous condition.

But John says if I feel so I shall neglect proper self-control; so I take pains to control myself — before him, at least, and that makes me very tired.

I don't like our room a bit. I wanted one downstairs that opened onto the piazza② and had roses all over the window, and such pretty old-fashioned chintz③ hangings! But john would not hear of it.

He said there was only one window and not room for two beds, and no near room for him if he took another.

He is very careful and loving, and hardly lets me stir without special direction.

铁栏杆、厚石墙、铁栅大门、铁锁以及荒废的花房,这些将女主人公彻底地与外界隔绝,就像深处在一个孤寂的囚笼。可是作者用极美的地方、甜美的花园来形容,这反衬出作者的孤苦,也让人深深地理解她走向崩溃的原因。

---

① arbors:凉亭。
② piazza:走廊。
③ chintz:印花棉布。

255

I have a schedule prescription for each hour in the day; he takes all care from me, and so I feel basely ungrateful not to value it more.

He said he came here solely on my account, that I was to have perfect rest and all the air I could get. "Your exercise depends on your strength, my dear," said he, "and your food somewhat on your appetite; but air you can absorb all the time." So we took the nursery at the top of the house.

It is a big, airy room, the whole floor nearly, with windows that look all ways, and air and sunshine galore①. It was nursery first, and then playroom and gymnasium, I should judge, for the windows are barred for little children, and there are rings and things in the wails.

The paint and paper look as if a boys' school had used it. It is stripped off — the paper — in great patches all around the head of my bed, about as far as I can reach, and in a great place on the other side of the room low down. I never saw a worse paper in my life.

One of those sprawling, flamboyant② patterns committing every artistic sin.

It is dull enough to confuse the eye in following, pronounced enough constantly to irritate and provoke study, and when you follow the lame uncertain curves for a little distance they suddenly commit suicide — plunge off at outrageous angles, destroy themselves in unheard-of contradictions.

The color is repellent③, almost revolting: a smouldering④ unclean yellow, strangely faded by the slow-turning

---

① galore：丰富地。
② flamboyant：华丽的。
③ repellent：排斥的。
④ smouldering：焦油一样的。

sunlight. It is a dull yet lurid orange in some places, a sickly sulphur tint in others.

No wonder the children hated it! I should hate it myself if I had to live in this room long.

There comes John, and I must put this away — he hates to have me write a word.

2

We have been here two weeks, and I haven't felt like writing before, since that first day.

I am sitting by the window now, up in this atrocious① nursery and there is nothing to hinder my writing as much as I please, save lack of strength.

John is away all day, and even some nights when his cases are serious.

I am glad my case is not serious!

But these nervous troubles are dreadfully depressing.

John does not know how much I really suffer. He knows there is no reason to suffer, and that satisfies him.

Of course it is only nervousness. It does weigh on me so not to do my duty in any way!

I meant to be such a help to John, such a real rest and comfort, and here I am a comparative burden already!

Nobody would believe what an effort it is to do what little I am able — to dress and entertain, and order things.

It is fortunate Mary is so good with the baby. Such a dear baby!

And yet I cannot be with him, it makes me so nervous.

I suppose John never was nervous in his life. He laughs at me so about this wallpaper!

女主人公第一次对墙纸进行详细的描述，她称那些墙纸上的图案是艺术中的犯罪。它又是让人反胃的、肮脏的染着疾病的黄色。给人一种狂躁不安的感觉，此时她对墙纸有深深的憎恨。

---

① atrocious：凶恶的。

At first he meant to repaper the room, but afterward he said that I was letting it get the better of me, and that nothing was worse for a nervous patient than to give way to such fancies.

He said that after the wallpaper was changed it would be the heavy bedstead, and then the barred windows, and then that gate at the head of the stairs, and so on.

"You know the place is doing you good," he said, "and really, dear, I don't care to renovate① the house just for a three months' rental."

"Then do let us go downstairs," I said. "There are such pretty rooms there."

Then he took me in his arms and called me a blessed little goose, and said he would go down cellar, if I wished, and have it whitewashed into the bargain.

But he is right enough about the beds and windows and things.

It is as airy and comfortable a room as anyone need wish, and, of course, I would not be so silly as to make him uncomfortable just for a whim.

I'm really getting quite fond of the big room, all but that horrid paper.

Out of one window I can see the garden — those mysterious deep-shaded arbors, the riotous old-fashioned flowers, and bushes and gnarly② trees.

Out of another I get a lovely view of the bay and a little private wharf belonging to the estate. There is a beautiful shaded lane that runs down there from the house. I always fancy I see people walking in these numerous paths and arbors, but John has cautioned me not

继续强调她丈夫是一个极端现实派，完全没考虑到妻子的需要和感受。

小傻鹅是约翰对她的称呼，约翰总是用这种和小孩子说话类似的词语来称呼她，看护她，完全将她看成没有任何主见、没有任何行为能力的孩子。

---

① renovate：刷新，修复。
② gnarly：粗糙的。

to give way to fancy in the least. He says that with my imaginative power and habit of story-making, a nervous weakness like mine is sure to lead to all manner of excited fancies, and that I ought to use my will and good sense to check the tendency. So I try.

I think sometimes that if I were only well enough to write a little it would relieve the press of ideas and rest me.

But I find I get pretty tired when I try.

It is so discouraging not to have any advice and companionship about my work. When I get really well, John says we will ask Cousin Henry and Julia down for a long visit; but he says he would as soon put fireworks in my pillow-case as to let me have those stimulating people about now.

I wish I could get well faster.

But I must not think about that. This paper looks to me, if it knew what a vicious influence it had!

There is a recurrent spot where the pattern lolls like a broken neck and two bulbous① eyes stare at you upside down.

I get positively angry with the impertinence② of it and the everlastingness. Up and down and sideways they crawl, and those absurd unblinking eyes are everywhere. There is one place where two breadths didn't match, and the eyes go all up and down the line, one a little higher than the other.

I never saw so much expression in an inanimate③ thing before, and we all know how much expression they have! I used to lie awake as a child and get more

墙纸中的图案渐渐
在她的脑中成形,她把
她想象成一个割裂的脖
子和两只眼球的形象。

---

① bulbous：球状的。
② impertinence：无礼。
③ inanimate：死气沉沉的。

entertainment and terror out of blank walls and plain furniture than most children could find in a toy-store.

I remember what a kindly wink the knobs① of our big old bureau used to have, and there was one chair that always seemed like a strong friend.

I used to feel that if any of the other things looked too fierce I could always hop into that chair and be safe.

The furniture in this room is no worse than inharmonious, however, for we had to bring it all from downstairs. I suppose when this was used as a playroom they had to take the nursery things out, and no wonder! I never saw such ravages as the children have made here.

The wallpaper, as I said before, is torn off in spots, and it sticketh closer than a brother — they must have had perseverance as well as hatred.

Then the floor is scratched and gouged② and splintered, the plaster itself is dug out here and there, and this great heavy bed, which is all we found in the room, looks as if it had been through the wars.

But I don't mind it a bit — only the paper.

There comes John's sister. Such a dear girl as she is, and so careful of me! I must not let her find me writing.

强调女主人公的孤独无助,她丈夫的妹妹不能理解她,帮助她,反而和她的丈夫一起监视她。

She is a perfect and enthusiastic③ housekeeper, and hopes for no better profession. I verily believe she thinks it is the writing which made me sick!

But I can write when she is out, and see her a long way off from these windows.

There is one that commands the road, a lovely shaded winding road; and one that just looks off over the

① knobs:(门,抽屉等的)球形捏手。
② gouged:用圆凿子削除。
③ enthusiastic:热心的,热情的。

country. A lovely country, too, full of great elms① and velvet meadows.

This wallpaper has a kind of sub-pattern in a different shade, a particularly irritating one, for you can only see it in certain lights, and not clearly then.

But in the places where it isn't faded and where the sun is just so — I can see a strange, provoking②, formless sort of figure that seems to skulk③ about behind that silly and conspicuous front design.

There's sister on the stairs!

3

Well, the Fourth of July is over! The people are all gone, and I am tired out. John thought it might do me good to see a little company so we just had mother and Nellie and the children down for a week.

7 月 4 日,是美国的国庆节。

Of course I didn't do a thing. Jennie sees to everything now.

But it tired me all the same.

John says if I don't pick up faster he shall send me to Weir Mitchell 1 in the fall.

But I don't want to go there at all. I had a friend who was in his hands once, and she says he is just like John and my brother, only more so!

Besides, it is such an undertaking to go so far.

I don't feel as if it was worthwhile to turn my hand over for anything, and I'm getting dreadfully fretful④ and querulous⑤.

说明她的病情加重了。

I cry at nothing, and cry most of the time.

①　elms：榆树。
②　provoking：虚幻的。
③　skulk：隐藏。
④　fretful：愤怒。
⑤　querulous：爱发牢骚。

Of course I don't when John is here, or anybody else, but when I am alone.

And I am alone a good deal just now. John is kept in town very often by serious cases, and Jennie is good and lets me alone when I want her to.

So I walk a little in the garden or down that lovely lane, sit on the porch under the roses, and lie down up here a good deal.

I'm getting really fond of the room in spite of the wallpaper perhaps because of the wallpaper.

It dwells in my mind so!

I lie here on this great immovable bed — it is nailed down, I believe — and follow that pattern about by the hour. It is as good as gymnastics, I assure you. I start, we'll say at the bottom, down in the corner over there where it has not been touched, and I determine for the thousandth time that I will follow that pointless pattern to some sort of a conclusion.

I know a little of the principle of design, and I know this thing was not arranged on any laws of radiation, or alternation, or repetition①, or symmetry②, or anything else that I ever heard of.

It is repeated, of course, by the breadths③, but not otherwise.

Looked at in one way each breadth stands alone; the bloated curves and flourishes — a kind of "debased Romanesque" with delirium tremens go waddling up and down in isolated columns of fatuity.

But, on the other hand, they connect diagonally④,

> 她仍然不喜欢那些壁纸，但是她所能做的事就是观察这些壁纸。

---

① repetition：重复,循环。
② symmetry：对称。
③ breadths：宽度。
④ diagonally：对角地。

and the sprawling outlines run off in great slanting waves of optic horror, like a lot of wallowing sea-weeds in full chase.

The whole thing goes horizontally, too, at least it seems so, and I exhaust myself trying to distinguish the order of its going in that direction.

They have used a horizontal breadth for a frieze, and that adds wonderfully to the confusion.

There is one end of the room where it is almost intact, and there, when the cross-lights fade and the low sun shines directly upon it, I can almost fancy radiation after all — the interminable grotesque① seems to form around a common center and rush off in headlong plunges of equal distraction.

It makes me tired to follow it. I will take a nap, I guess.

I don't know why I should write this.

I don't want to.

I don't feel able.

And I know John would think it absurd. But I must say what I feel and think in some way — it is such a relief!

But the effort is getting to be greater than the relief.

Half the time now I am awfully lazy, and lie down ever so much. John says I mustn't lose my strength, and has me take cod liver oil and lots of tonics② and things, to say nothing of ale and wines and rare meat.

Dear John! He loves me very dearly, and hates to have me sick. I tried to have a real earnest reasonable talk with him the other day, and tell him how I wish he would

---

① grotesque：奇形怪状的人（或物、图案等）。
② tonics：滋补品。

她满心的挣扎,想方设法离开这座古屋,到表哥家做客。

let me go and make a visit to Cousin Henry and Julia.

But he said I wasn't able to go, nor able to stand it after I got there; and I did not make out a very good case for myself, for I was crying before I had finished.

It is getting to be a great effort for me to think straight. Just this nervous weakness, I suppose.

And dear John gathered me up in his arms, and just carried me upstairs and laid me on the bed, and sat by me and read to me till it tired my head.

He said I was his darling and his comfort and all he had, and that I must take care of myself for his sake, and keep well.

He says no one but myself can help me out of it, that I must use my will and self-control and not let any silly① fancies run away with me.

There's one comfort the baby is well and happy, and does not have to occupy this nursery with the horrid wallpaper.

If we had not used it, that blessed child would have! What a fortunate② escape! Why, I wouldn't have a child of mine, an impressionable③ little thing, live in such a room for worlds.

女主人公为了维持家庭,为了丈夫和孩子,甘愿牺牲自己的利益,放弃自己的需求,听从丈夫的安排。如此反复地处在挣扎与矛盾中使得她困住了自己,找不到出路,得不到解放,最终走向了自我分裂,成为一个真正的、严重的精神病人。

I never thought of it before, but it is lucky that John kept me here after all; I can stand it so much easier than a baby, you see.

Of course I never mention it to them any more — I am too wise — but I keep watch for it all the same.

There are things in the wallpaper that nobody knows about but me, or ever will.

Behind that outside pattern the dim shapes get clearer

---

① silly: 傻的,愚蠢的。
② fortunate: 幸运的。
③ impressionable: 易受影响的。

every day.

It is always the same shape, only very numerous.

And it is like a woman stooping down and creeping about behind that pattern. I don't like it a bit. I wonder — I begin to think — I wish John would take me away from here!

It is so hard to talk with John about my case, because he is so wise, and because he loves me so.

But I tried it last night.

It was moonlight. The moon shines in all around just as the sun does.

I hate to see it sometimes, it creeps so slowly, and always comes in by one window or another.

John was asleep and I hated to waken him, so I kept still and watched the moonlight on that undulating[①] wallpaper till I felt creepy.

The faint figure behind seemed to shake the pattern, just as if she wanted to get out.

I got up softly and went to feel and see if the paper did move, and when I came back John was awake.

"What is it, little girl?" he said. "Don't go walking about like that — you'll get cold."

I thought it was a good time to talk, so I told him that I really was not gaining here, and that I wished he would take me away.

"Why, darling!" said he, "Our lease will be up in three weeks, and I can't see how to leave before."

"The repairs are not done at home, and I cannot possibly leave town just now. Of course, if you were in any danger, I could and would, but you really are better,

---

① undulating: 敏感的。

dear, whether you can see it or not. I am a doctor, dear, and I know. You are gaining flesh and color, your appetite is better, I feel really much easier about you."

"I don't weigh a bit more," said I, "nor as much; and my appetite may be better in the evening when you are here but it is worse in the morning when you are away!"

"Bless her little heart!" said he with a big hug. "She shall be as sick as she pleases! But now let's improve the shining hours by going to sleep, and talk about it in the morning!"

"And you won't go away?" I asked gloomily.

"Why, how can I, dear? It is only three weeks more and then we will take a nice little trip for a few days while Jennie is getting the house ready. Really dear, you are better!"

"Better in body perhaps —" I began, and stopped short, for he sat up straight and looked at me with such a stem, reproachful① look that I could not say another word.

男人的简单动作却让她不得不住口——在男权主义压制下，女性连表达自己的权利都没有。

"My darling," said he, "I beg you, for my sake and for our child's sake, as well as for your own, that you will never for one instant let that idea enter your mind! There is nothing so dangerous, so fascinating, to a temperament like yours. It is a false and foolish fancy. Can you trust me as a physician when I tell you so?"

So of course I said no more on that score, and we went to sleep before long. He thought I was asleep first, but I wasn't, and lay there for hours trying to decide whether that front pattern and the back pattern really did move together or separately.

女主人公的无奈及妥协。

4

On a pattern like this, by daylight, there is a lack of

---

① reproachful：责备的。

sequence，a defiance① of law，that is a constant irritant to a normal mind.

The color is hideous② enough，and unreliable enough，and infuriating③ enough，but the pattern is torturing.

You think you have mastered it，but just as you get well under way in following，it turns a back-somersault④ and there you are. It slaps you in the face，knocks you down，and tramples upon you. It is like a bad dream.

The outside pattern is a florid arabesque，reminding one of a fungus. If you can imagine a toadstool in joints，an interminable string of toadstools，budding and sprouting in endless convolutions⑤— why，that is something like it.

That is，sometimes!

There is one marked peculiarity⑥ about this paper，a thing nobody seems to notice but myself，and that is that it changes as the light changes.

When the sun shoots in through the east window — I always watch for that first long，straight ray-it changes so quickly that I never can quite believe it.

That is why I watch it always.

By moonlight — the moon shines in all night when there is a moon — I wouldn't know it was the same paper.

At night in any kind of light，in twilight，candlelight，lamplight，and worst of all by moonlight，it becomes bars! The outside pattern，I mean，and the woman behind it is as plain as can be.

在她看来，白天就是男性和他们主宰的社会，而夜晚和月光才属于她。

---

① defiance：挑衅。
② hideous：骇人听闻的，可怕的。
③ infuriating：令人发怒的。
④ back-somersault：翻筋斗。
⑤ convolutions：回旋，盘旋，卷绕。
⑥ peculiarity：特性，怪癖。

墙纸里的女人实际上是在暗示女主人公本人以及整个男性主导下的广大女性。

I didn't realize for a long time what the thing was that showed behind, that dim sub-pattern, but now I am quite sure it is a woman.

By daylight she is subdued①, quiet. I fancy it is the pattern that keeps her so still. It is so puzzling. It keeps me quiet by the hour.

I lie down ever so much now. John says it is good for me, and to sleep all can.

Indeed he started the habit by making me lie down for an hour after each meal.

It is a very bad habit, I am convinced, for you see, I don't sleep.

And that cultivates deceit, for I don't tell them I'm awake — oh, no!

The fact is I am getting a little afraid of John.

He seems very queer② sometimes, and even Jennie has an inexplicable③ look.

It strikes me occasionally, just as a scientific hypothesis, that perhaps it is the paper!

I have watched John when he did not know I was looking, and come into the room suddenly on the most innocent excuses, and I've caught him several times looking at the paper! And Jennie too. I caught Jennie with her hand on it once.

She didn't know I was in the room, and when I asked her in a quiet, a very quiet voice, with the most restrained manner possible, what she was doing with the paper, she turned around as if she had been caught stealing, and looked quite angry — asked me why I should frighten her so!

① be subdued：被抑制的，柔和的。
② queer：古怪的。
③ inexplicable：目光游离。

Then she said that the paper stained everything it touched, that she had found yellow smooches① on all my clothes and John's and she wished we would be more careful!

Did not that sound innocent? But I know she was studying that pattern, and I am determined that nobody shall find it out but myself!

5

Life is very much more exciting now than it used to be. You see, I have something more to expect, to look forward to, to watch. I really do eat better, and am more quiet than I was.

John is so pleased to see me improve! He laughed a little the other day, and said I seemed to be flourishing in spite of my wallpaper.

I turned it off with a laugh. I had no intention of telling him it was because of the wallpaper — he would make fun of me. He might even want to take me away.

I don't want to leave now until I have found it out. There is a week more, and I think that will be enough.

6

I'm feeling ever so much better! I don't sleep much at night, for it is so interesting to watch developments; but I sleep a good deal during the daytime.

In the daytime it is tiresome and perplexing②.

There are always new shoots on the fungus③, and new shades of yellow all over it. I cannot keep count of them, though I have tried conscientiously④.

It is the strangest yellow, that wallpapers! It makes

女主人公对待墙纸态度的转变——从厌恶害怕到兴奋和期待。

① smooches：污渍。
② perplexing：困惑。
③ fungus：菌类，蘑菇。
④ conscientiously：良心上地。

me think of all the yellow things I ever saw — not beautiful ones like buttercups, but old, foul①, bad yellow things.

But there is something else about that paper — the smell! I noticed it the moment we came into the room, but with so much air and sun it was not bad. Now we have had a week of fog and rain, and whether the windows are open or not, the smell is here.

It creeps all over the house.

I find it hovering in the dining-room, skulking in the parlor②, hiding in the hall, lying in wait for me on the stairs.

It gets into ray hair.

Even when I go to ride, if I turn my head suddenly and surprise it — there is that smell!

Such a peculiar odor, too! I have spent hours in trying to analyze it, to find what it smelled like.

It is not bad — at first — and very gentle, but quite the subtlest, most enduring odor I ever met.

In this damp weather it is awful. I wake up in the night and find it hanging over me.

It used to disturb me at first. I thought seriously of burning the house to reach the smell.

But now I am used to it. The only thing I can think of that it is like is the color of the paper! A yellow smell.

There is a very funny mark on this wall, low down, near the mopboard. A streak that runs round the room. It goes behind every piece of furniture, except the bed, a long, straight, even smooch, as if it had been rubbed over and over.

墙纸的形态变成了一种气味缭绕在她的四周,让她想急切地冲破这种充斥在四周的压迫感,预示着女主人公慢慢走向崩溃。

① foul：污秽的，肮脏的。
② parlor：客厅。

I wonder how it was done and who did it, and what they did it for. Round and round and round — round and round and round — it makes me dizzy①!

7

I really have discovered something at last.

Through watching so much at night, when it changes so, I have finally found out.

The front pattern does move- and no wonder! The woman behind shakes it!

Sometimes I think there are a great many women behind, and sometimes only one, and she crawls② around fast, and her crawling shakes it all over.

Then in the very bright spots she keeps still, and in the very shady③ spots she just takes hold of the bars and shakes them hard.

And she is all the time trying to climb through. But nobody could climb through that pattern — it strangles so; I think that is Why it has so many heads.

They get through and then the pattern strangles them off and turns them upside down, and makes their eyes white!

象征着在男性主导的社会里女性所受到的压制和禁锢。

If those heads were covered or taken off it would not be half so bad.

8

I think that woman gets out in the daytime!

And I'll tell you why — privately — I've seen her!

I can see her out of every one of my windows!

It is the same woman, I know, for she is always creeping, and most women do not creep by daylight.

I see her in that long shaded lane, creeping up and

---

① dizzy：头晕目眩的，眼花的。
② crawls：爬行，蠕动。
③ shady：阴暗的。

down. I see her in those dark grape arbors①, creeping all round the garden.

I see her on that long road under the trees, creeping along, and when a carriage comes she hides under the blackberry vines.

I don't blame her a bit. It must be very humiliating② to be caught creeping by daylight!

I always lock the door when I creep by daylight. I can't do it at night, for I know John would suspect something at once.

And John is so queer now that I don't want to irritate③ him. I wish he would take another room! Besides, I don't want anybody to get that woman out at night but myself.

I often wonder if I could see her out of all the windows at once.

But, turn as fast as I can, I can only see out of one at one time.

And though I always see her, she may be able to creep faster than I can turn! I have watched her sometimes away off in the open country, creeping as fast as a cloud shadow in a wind.

9

If only that top pattern could be gotten off from the under one! I mean to try it, little by little.

I have found out another funny thing, but I shan't tell it this time! It does not do to trust people too much.

There are only two more days to get this paper off, and I believe John is beginning to notice. I don't like the look in his eyes.

---

① arbors：凉亭。
② humiliating：羞辱性的。
③ irritate：激怒。

And I heard him ask Jennie a lot of professional questions about me. She had a very good report to give.

She said I slept a good deal in the daytime.

John knows I don't sleep very well at night, for all I'm so quiet!

He asked me all sorts of questions too, and pretended to be very loving and kind.

As if I couldn't see through him!

Still, I don't wonder he acts so, sleeping under this paper for three months.

It only interests me, but I feel sure John and Jennie are affected by it.

10

Hurrah! This is the last day, but it is enough. John is to stay in town over night, and won't be out until this evening.

Jennie wanted to sleep with me — the sly thing; but I told her I should undoubtedly rest better for a night all alone.

That was clever, for really I wasn't alone a bit! As soon as it was moonlight and that poor thing began to crawl and shake the pattern, I got up and ran to help her.

I pulled and she shook. I shook and she pulled, and before morning we had peeled off① yards of that paper.

A strip about as high as my head and half around the room.

And then when the sun came and that awful pattern began to laugh at me, I declared I would finish it today!

We go away tomorrow, and they are moving all my furniture down again to leave things as they were before.

Jennie looked at the wall in amazement, but I told her merrily② that I did it out of pure spite at the vicious③

女主人公对丈夫产生不信任感,从开始的迷茫到现在的有所隐瞒,昭示了女性的觉醒。

---

① peeled off: 剥,削,剥落。
② merrily: 愉快地,高兴地。
③ vicious: 不道德的,恶意的。

273

thing.

She laughed and said she wouldn't mind doing it herself, but I must not get tired.

How she betrayed① herself that time!

But I am here, and no person touches this paper but me — not *alive*!

She tried to get me out of the room — it was too patent! But I said it was so quiet and empty and clean now that I believed I would lie down again and sleep all I could, and not to wake me even for dinner — I would call when I woke.

So now she is gone, and the servants are gone, and the things are gone, and there is nothing left but that great bedstead nailed down, with the canvas mattress we found on it.

We shall sleep downstairs tonight, and take the boat home tomorrow.

I quite enjoy the room, now it is bare again.

How those children did tear about here!

This bedstead is fairly gnawed②!

But I must get to work.

I have locked the door and thrown the key down into the front path.

I don't want to go out, and I don't want to have anybody come in, till John comes.

I want to astonish him.

I've got a rope up here that even Jennie did not find. If that woman does get out, and tries to get away, I can tie her!

But I forgot I could not reach far without anything to

---

① betrayed：出卖，背叛。
② gnawed：折磨人的。

stand on!

This bed will *not move*!

I tried to lift and push it until I was lame, and then I got so angry I bit off a little piece at one corner — but it hurt my teeth.

Then I peeled off all the paper I could reach standing on the floor. It sticks horribly and the pattern just enjoys it! All those strangled heads and bulbous eyes and waddling① fungus growths just shriek② with derision③!

I am getting angry enough to do something desperate. To jump out of the window would be admirable exercise, but the bars are too strong even to try.

Besides I wouldn't do it. Of course not. I know well enough that a step like that is improper and might be misconstrued④.

I don't like to look out of the windows even — there are so many of those creeping women, and they creep so fast.

I wonder if they all come out of that wallpaper as I did!

女主人公最终走向自我分裂，将自己视为墙纸里受压制的女人之一。

But I am securely fastened now by my well-hidden rope — you don't get me out in the road there!

I suppose I shall have to get back behind the pattern when it comes night, and that is hard!

It is so pleasant to be out in this great room and creep around as I please!

女主人公冲破种种禁锢而获得自由，让她欣喜不已。

I don't want to go outside. I won't, even if Jennie asks me to.

For outside you have to creep on the ground, and everything is green instead of yellow.

① waddling：蹒跚的。
② shriek：尖叫。
③ derision：嘲笑。
④ misconstrued：误解。

But here I can creep smoothly on the floor, and my shoulder, just fits in that long smooch around the wall, so I cannot lose my way.

Why, there's John at the door!

It is no use, young man, you can't open it!

How he does call and pound!

Now he's crying to Jennie for an axe.

It would be a shame to break down that beautiful door!

"John, dear!" said I in the gentlest voice. "The key is down by the front steps, under a plantain① leaf!"

That silenced him for a few moments.

Then he said, very quietly indeed, "Open the door, my darling!"

"I can't," said I. "The key is down by the front door under a plantain leaf!" And then I said it again, several times, very gently and slowly, and said it so often that he had to go and see, and he got it of course, and came in. He stopped short by the door.

"What is the matter?" he cried, "For God's sake, what are you doing?"

I kept on creeping just the same, but I looked at him over my shoulder.

"I've got out at last," said I, "in spite of you and Jane. And I've pulled off most of the paper, so you can't put me back?"

表明了作者对实现男女平等的渴望与自信。

Now why should that man have fainted②? But he did, and right across my path by the wall, so that I had to creep over him every time!　　　　　　　　　　[1892]

约翰的晕倒象征着男性统治下的父权社会的崩溃和瓦解。

① plantain：车前草。
② fainted：晕倒。

【思考题】

1. 壁纸的象征意义是什么？是什么导致了女主人公对壁纸态度的转变？

2. 壁纸上的图案引起了女主人公的恐惧,在你看来,这种恐惧源于哪些方面？

3. 这篇文章以第一人称的口吻进行叙事,作者如此安排的用意何在？

4. 文章中出现了大量的心理描写,你认为这对于主题的揭示有何帮助？

5. 纵观全文,究竟是什么导致了女主人公的疾病？

6. 作者对结尾的设计有什么特别含义？

Young Goodman Brown

小伙子布朗

纳撒尼尔·霍桑

【导读】

纳撒尼尔·霍桑(Nathaniel Hawthorne，1804—1864)，美国小说家，是美国 19 世纪影响最大的浪漫主义小说家和心理小说家。霍桑 1804 年 7 月 4 日出生于马萨诸塞州塞勒姆镇一个没落的世家。霍桑的父亲是一名船长，在他 4 岁时去世。1821 年霍桑在亲戚资助下进入博多因学院，同学中有诗人朗费罗(Henry Wadsworth Longfellow)与后来当选为总统的皮尔斯等。1825 年霍桑大学毕业，回到塞勒姆镇，从事写作。他曾匿名发表长篇小说《范肖》(*Fanshawe*，1828)和几十个短篇作品，陆续出版短篇小说集《古宅青苔》(*Moses from an Old Manse*，1843)、《雪影》(*The Snow-Image*，1851)等，逐渐得到重视和好评。

霍桑的短篇小说大多取材于新英格兰(包括美国现在东北部的康涅狄格州、马萨诸塞州、新罕布什尔州、罗得岛和弗蒙特州一带地区)的历史或现实生活，着重探讨人性和人的命运等问题。著名的短篇小说《小伙子布朗》(*Young Goodman Brown*，1835)、《教长的黑纱》(*The Minister's Black Veil*，1836)揭露人人皆有的隐秘的罪恶，表达了人性是恶的和人是孤独的等观点。另一些小说如《拉伯西尼医生的女儿》(*Rappaccini's Daughter*，1844)，反映了他对科学和理性的怀疑，以及他反对过激和偏执的思想。《通天的铁路》(*The Celestial Railroad*，1843)则指出技术的进步丰富了人的物质享受，却败坏了人的精神。有少数作品表达了霍桑的理想，如《玉石雕像》(*The Marble Faun*，1860)。另外有些故事记叙了新英格兰殖民地人民的抗英斗争，但往往带有浓厚的宗教气氛和神秘色彩。

1836 年和 1846 年霍桑曾两度在海关任职，1841 年曾参加超验主义者创办的布鲁克农场。他于 1842 年结婚，在康科德村居住，结识了作家爱默生(Ralph Waldo Emerson)、梭罗(Henry David Thoreau)等人。1848 年由于政见与当局不同，霍桑失去海关的职务，便致力于创作活动，写出了他最重要的长篇小说《红字》(*The Scarlet Letter*，1850)。这部作品以殖民地时期新英格兰生活为背景，描写一个受不合理的婚姻束缚的少妇犯了被加尔文教派所严禁的通奸罪而被示众，暴露了当时政教合一体制统治下殖民地社会中的某些黑暗。小说的角色是，经过长期赎罪而在精神上自新的少妇海斯特·白兰,受到信仰和良心的责备而终于坦白承认了罪过的狄姆斯台尔牧师,以及满怀复仇心理以致完全丧失人性的白兰的丈夫罗杰。小说层层深入地探究有关罪恶和人性的各种道德、哲理问题,情节以监狱和玫瑰花开场,以墓地结束,充满丰富的象征意义。

《红字》发表后获得巨大成功,霍桑继而创作了不少作品。其中《带有七个尖角阁的房子》(*The House of the Seven Gables*, 1851)描写品恩钦家族的祖先谋财害命而使后代遭到报应的故事,说明财富是祸患,而"一代人的罪孽要殃及子孙"。这部小说也反映了资本主义发展初期的血腥掠夺。另一部小说《福谷传奇》(*The Blithedale Romance*, 1852)以布鲁克农场生活为题材,表达了作者对这种社会改良尝试的失望心情以及对狂热改革者的厌恶。

皮尔斯当选为美国总统后,霍桑于1853年被任命为驻英国利物浦的领事。1857年后,霍桑侨居意大利,创作了另一部讨论善恶问题的长篇小说《玉石雕像》。1860年霍桑返回美国,在康科德定居,坚持写作。1864年5月19日去世,身后留下4部未完成的长篇小说。

霍桑是一个思想上充满矛盾的作家,新英格兰的清教主义传统对他影响很深。一方面他反抗这个传统,抨击宗教狂热和狭隘、虚伪的宗教信条;另一方面他又受这个传统的束缚,以加尔文教派的善恶观念来认识社会和整个世界。作家赫尔曼·梅尔维尔曾指出,他的作品中渗透着"加尔文教派的'人性本质'和'原罪'的观念"。霍桑思想保守,对生产的发展和技术进步抱有抵触情绪,对社会改革持怀疑态度,对当时蓬勃开展的废奴运动不很理解。这些在他的作品中都有所流露。在艺术上他独具一格,擅长心理描写,善于揭示人物的内心冲突。他把自己的小说称为"心理罗曼史"。他潜心挖掘隐藏在事物背后的不易觉察的意义,作品想象丰富,结构严谨。

霍桑的祖辈之中有人曾参与清教徒迫害异端的事件,为著名的1692年"塞勒姆驱巫案"的3名法官之一。这段历史对霍桑的思想产生了深刻的影响,这里所选用的《小伙子布朗》便以此为背景,因此这篇小说具有相当的真实性。16至17世纪,欧洲进入一个"焚烧女巫"的时期;而与此同时,当时清教徒的生活又十分严格,清教徒奉行严苛的道德准绳和行为规范,使得他们的感情和躯体备受压抑。到了17世纪末叶,攻击女巫的情形达到高潮。1692年,被殖民化不久的北美塞勒姆村里,一群小女孩突然出现怪异行为,她们哭泣,说感到难受并四肢着地爬行,其中一人称她受到了女巫的威胁,还有一位是基督教牧师的女儿。在讯问她们时,女孩子们指责巴巴多斯的一个女奴、一个丑陋的老妇人和一个妓女,说她们施用妖术和"魔术"把戏来吸引和诱惑她们。这件事发生后不久,便刮起了审判、绞刑和火刑的旋风。高峰时,被捕者达到了200人之多。所有这一切都发生在美国马萨诸塞州州长宣布大赦之前,当时就连殖民当局的高层都处于危险之中。

Young Goodman Brown

Young Goodman① Brown came forth at sunset into the street at Salem② village; but put his head back, after crossing the threshold③, to exchange a parting kiss④ with his young wife. And Faith⑤, as the wife was aptly⑥ named, thrust⑦ her own pretty head into the street, letting the wind play with the pink ribbons⑧ of her cap while she called to Goodman Brown.

作者用词简洁地介绍了布朗新婚妻子的可爱和美丽,凸显了布朗和妻子分别时的依依不舍。同时也引人入胜,到底布朗在深夜出门去做什么呢?

"Dearest heart," whispered she, softly and rather sadly, when her lips were close to his ear, "prithee⑨ put off⑩ your journey until sunrise and sleep in your own bed to-night. A lone woman is troubled with such dreams and such thoughts that she's afeared of herself sometimes⑪. Pray tarry⑫ with me this night, dear husband, of all nights in the year."

"My love and my Faith," replied young Goodman Brown, "of all nights in the year, this one night must I tarry away from thee⑬. My journey, as thou⑭ callest it,

---

① Goodman:即 good man,好人的意思。原注:专用来称呼体面、富裕的公民,并不涉及家族关系。
② Salem:现在为美国马萨诸塞州东北部的一处海港。
③ threshold:门槛。
④ parting kiss:吻别,临别吻。
⑤ Faith:费丝,英语名。在英语中有"忠诚"之意。
⑥ aptly:适当地,恰当地。
⑦ thrust:自己向前挤。
⑧ ribbon:装饰带,丝带。
⑨ prithee:[古]请。
⑩ put off:推迟。
⑪ A lone woman is troubled with such dreams and such thoughts that she's afeared of herself sometimes. 孤单的女人会做些可怕的梦,生些吓人的念头,有时候连自己都害怕。
⑫ tarry:逗留。
⑬ thee:你,thou 的宾格。
⑭ thou:你,用作第二人称单数动词的主格。

forth and back again, must needs be done 'twixt① now and sunrise. What, my sweet, pretty wife, dost thou doubt me already, and we but② three months married?"

"Then God bless you!" said Faith, with the pink ribbons, "and may you find all well when you come back."

"Amen!" cried Goodman Brown. "Say thy prayers, dear Faith, and go to bed at dusk③, and no harm will come to thee."

So they parted; and the young man pursued his way until, being about to turn the corner by the meeting-house④, he looked back and saw the head of Faith still peeping⑤ after him with a melancholy air, in spite of her pink ribbons.

"Poor little Faith!" thought he, for his heart smote⑥ him. "What a wretch⑦ am I to have her on such an errand⑧! She talks of dreams, too. Methought⑨ as she spoke there was trouble in her face, as if a dream had warned her what work is to be done to-night. But no, no! 't would kill her to think it. Well, she's a blessed angel on earth, and after this one night I'll cling to her skirts and follow her to heaven."

With this excellent resolve for the future, Goodman Brown felt himself justified in making more haste⑩ on his

这是布朗的心理活动,表现了他内心的矛盾。

这一段描写了布朗行走的道路,渲染了森林中的神秘氛围。

① twixt:[诗]在……之间。
② but:副词,只,仅仅。
③ dusk:黄昏,傍晚。
④ meeting-house:指基督教教友会的礼拜堂。
⑤ peep:偷看。
⑥ smote:smite 的过去式,重击。
⑦ wretch:无耻之徒。
⑧ errand:差事。
⑨ methinks:[古](无人称动词),据我看来,我以为。
⑩ haste:匆忙。

present evil purpose. He had taken a dreary① road, darkened by all the gloomiest trees of forest, which barely stood aside to let the narrow path creep② through, and closed immediately behind. It was all as lonely as could be; and there is this peculiarity③ in such a solitude, that the traveler knows not who may be conceale by the innumerable trunks and the thick boughs④ overhead; so that with lonely foot steps he may yet be passing through an unseen multitude⑤.

"There may be a devilish Indian behind every tree," said Goodman Brown to himself; and he glanced fearfully behind him as he added, "What if the devil himself should be at my very elbow⑥!"

His head being turned back, he passed a crook⑦ of the road, and, looking forward again, beheld⑧ the figure of a man, in grave and decent attire⑨, seated at the foot of an old tree. He arose at Goodman Brown's approach and walked onward side by side with him.

"You are late, Goodman Brown," said he. "The clock of the Old South was striking as I came through Boston, and that is full fifteen minutes agone⑩."

"Faith kept me back a while," replied the young man, with a tremor⑪ in his voice, caused by the sudden appearance of his companion, though not wholly

---

① dreary：沉闷的。
② creep：蔓延，延伸。
③ peculiarity：特质。
④ bough：大树枝。
⑤ multitude：人群。
⑥ What if the devil himself should be at my very elbow! 要是魔鬼出现在我的身边该怎么办！
⑦ crook：拐弯处。
⑧ behold：看。
⑨ attire：服装。
⑩ agone：以前地。
⑪ tremor：颤抖。

unexpected.

It was now deep dusk in the forest, and deepest in that part of it where these two were journeying. As nearly as could be discerned①, the second traveler was about fifty years old, apparently in the same rank of life as Goodman Brown, and bearing a considerable resemblance② to him, though perhaps more in expression than features. Still they might have been taken for③ father and son. And yet, though the elder person was simply clad④ as the younger, and as simple in manner too, he had an indescribable air of one who knew the world, and who would not have felt abashed⑤ at the governor's dinner table or in King William's⑥ court, were it possible that his affairs should call him thither. But the only thing about him that could be fixed upon as remarkable was his staff, which bore the likeness of a great black snake, so curiously wrought⑦ that it might almost be seen to twist and wriggle⑧ itself like a living serpent⑨. This, of course, must have been an ocular⑩ deception, assisted by the uncertain light.

"Come, Goodman Brown," cried his fellow-traveller, "this is a dull pace for the beginning of a journey. Take my staff, if you are so soon weary."

"Friend," said the other, exchanging his slow pace

显然,布朗和此人是熟悉的。

这里介绍了和布朗同行之人的特征。

这里详细描写了神秘人物的手杖上的毒蛇,凸显了神秘的氛围和不祥的预兆。

① discern:分辨。
② resemblance:相似,相像。
③ take for:误认为。
④ clad:穿着。
⑤ abashed:不安的,窘迫的。
⑥ King William:指英国国王威廉三世(1689—1702)。
⑦ wrought:锻造的。
⑧ wriggle:蜿蜒,扭动。
⑨ serpent:大蛇。
⑩ ocular:视觉的。

283

for a full stop, "having kept covenant① by meeting thee here, it is my purpose now to return whence② I came. I have scruples③ touching the matter thou wot'st of."

"Sayest④ thou so?" replied he of the serpent, smiling apart. "Let us walk on, nevertheless, reasoning as we go; and if I convince thee not thou shalt⑤ turn back. We are but a little way in the forest yet."

"Too far! Too far!" exclaimed the Goodman, unconsciously resuming his walk. "My father never went into the woods on such an errand, nor his father before him. We have been a race of honest men and good Christians since the days of the martyrs⑥; and shall I be the first of the name of Brown that ever took his path and kept —"

"Such company, thou wouldst⑦ say," observed the elder person, interpreting his pause. " Well said, Goodman Brown! I have been as well acquainted with your family as with ever a one among the Puritans; and that's no trifle to say. I helped your grandfather, the constable⑧, when he lashed⑨ the Quaker⑩ woman so smartly⑪ through the streets of Salem; and it was I that brought your father a pitch-pine knot, kindled at my own

① covenant：契约，盟约。
② whence：从何处来。
③ scruple：踌躇，犹豫。
④ sayest：say 的第二人称单数现在式。
⑤ shalt：shall 的第二人称单数现在式。
⑥ martyr：殉教者。
⑦ wouldst：would 的第二人称单数过去式。
⑧ constable：治安官。
⑨ lash：鞭打。
⑩ Quaker：贵格会，为基督教一个教派，又名"教友派"。该英文词词根 quake(音"贵格")意为"颤抖"。据说该教派创始人乔治·福克斯(George Fox)嘱其信徒："在圣谕面前颤抖吧"("Tremble at the word of the lord!")，故被人称为贵格派。
⑪ smartly：刺痛地，火辣辣地。

hearth①, to set fire to an Indian village, in King Philip's war②. They were my good friends, both; and many a pleasant walk have we had along this path, and returned merrily after midnight. I would fain③ be friends with you for their sake."

"If it be as thou sayest," replied Goodman Brown, "I marvel they never spoke of these matters; or, verily, I marvel not, seeing that the least rumor of the sort would have driven them from New England④. We are a people of prayer, and good works to boot, and abide no such wickedness."

"Wickedness or not," said the traveller with the twisted staff, "I have a very general acquaintance here in New England. The deacons⑤ of many a church have drunk the communion wine⑥ with me; the selectmen⑦ of divers⑧ towns make me their chairman; and a majority of the Great and General Court are firm supporters of my interest. The governor and I, too — But these are state secrets."

"Can this be so?" cried Goodman Brown, with a state of amazement at his undisturbed companion. "Howbeit⑨, I have nothing to do with the governor and council; they have their own ways, and are no rule for a simple husbandman like me. But, were I to go on with thee, how

> 与布朗一起的长者（其实是魔鬼）揭露了布朗祖父和父亲的罪恶，他们都曾与他为友。下面谈话进一步揭示州里大大小小的官员都曾有过类似罪恶行径。

> 布朗惊异于听到的罪恶，开始犹豫是否要继续此次森林之行。

---

① it was I that brought your father a pitch-pine knot, kindled at my own hearth：是我递给他的松脂火把，还是在我家炉子上点燃的。
② King Philip's war：菲利普王是印第安人万帕诺诺部落的酋长。清教徒殖民地的扩张使他大为惊慌，于是在 1675 年出动反抗入侵者。经过多次粗暴冷酷的厮杀之后，菲利普败下阵来，遭到追捕，被杀害。
③ fain：乐意地，欣然地。
④ New England：指美国现在东北部的康涅狄格州、缅因州、马萨诸塞州、新罕布什尔州、罗得岛和费蒙特州一带地区。
⑤ deacon：执事。
⑥ communion wine：圣餐酒。
⑦ selectman：行政委员。
⑧ divers：好几个。
⑨ howbeit：不过。

should I meet the eye of that good old man, our minister, at Salem village? Oh, his voice would make me tremble both Sabbath① day and lecture day."

Thus far the elder traveller had listened with due gravity; but now burst into a fit of irrepressible mirth②, shaking himself so violently that his snake-like staff actually seemed to wriggle in sympathy.

"Ha! ha! ha!" shouted he again and again; then composing himself, "Well, go on, Goodman Brown, go on; but, prithee, don't kill me with laughing."

"Well, then, to end the matter at once," said Goodman Brown, considerably nettled③, "there is my wife, Faith. It would break her dear little heart; and I'd rather break my own."

"Nay, if that be the case," answered the other, "e'en go thy ways, Goodman Brown. I would not for twenty old women like the one hobbling④ before us that Faith should come to any harm."

As he spoke he pointed his staff at a female figure on the path, in whom Goodman Brown recognized a very pious⑤ and exemplary⑥ dame⑦, who had taught him his catechism⑧ in youth, and was still his moral and spiritual adviser, jointly with the minister and Deacon Gookin.

"A marvel, truly that Goody Cloyse⑨ should be so far in the wilderness at nightfall," said he. "But with your

---

① Sabbath：安息日。
② mirth：[书]欢乐。
③ nettled：恼火的。
④ hobbling：蹒跚。
⑤ pious：虔诚的。
⑥ exemplary：杰出的，值得效仿的。
⑦ dame：夫人。
⑧ catechism：教义问答。
⑨ Goody Cloyse：克洛伊斯，和下文出现的卡里尔一样，也在 1692 年因为行使巫术而被判罪。霍桑的一位祖先是判处她死刑的那个法庭的法官。

leave, friend, I shall take a cut① through that woods until we have left this Christian woman behind. Being a stranger to you, she might ask whom I was consorting with and whither I was going."

"Be it so②," said his fellow-traveller. "Betake you to the woods, and let me keep the path."

Accordingly the young man turned aside, but took care to watch his companion, who advanced softly along the road until he had come within a staff's length of the old dame. She, meanwhile, was making the best of her way, with singular speed for so aged a woman, and mumbling some indistinct words, a prayer, doubtless, as she went. The traveller put forth his staff and touched her withered③ neck with what seemed the serpent's tail.

"The devil!" screamed the pious old lady.

"Then Goody Cloyse knows her old friend?" observed the traveller, confronting her and leaning on his writhing④ stick.

"Ah, forsooth⑤, and is it your worship indeed?" cried the good dame. "Yea, truly is it, and in the very image of my old gossip, Goodman Brown, the grandfather of the silly fellow that now is. But — would your worship believe it? my broomstick⑥ hath strangely disappeared, stolen, as I suspect, by that unhanged witch, Goody Cory, and that, too, when I was all anointed⑦

---

① cut: (shortcut 的省略)近道,捷径。
② Be it so: 就这样吧,好吧。
③ withered: 枯萎的。
④ writhing: 扭动。
⑤ forsooth: 的确。
⑥ broomstick: (童话故事中女巫常骑于空中的带柄的)扫帚。西方民间传说中,女巫总是乘一柄长条帚在空中飞行。故事中的老太婆也系女巫。
⑦ anoint: 施以涂油礼。

287

with the juice of smallage①, and cinquefoil②, and wolf's bane③—"

"Mingled with fine wheat and the fat of a new-born babe," said the shape of old Goodman Brown.

"Ah, your worship knows the recipe," cried the old lady, cackling④ aloud. "So, as I was saying, being all ready for the meeting, and no horse to ride on, I made up my mind to foot it; for they tell me there is a nice young man to be taken into communion to-night. But now your good worship will lend me your arm, and we shall be there in a twinkling⑤."

"That can hardly be," answered her friend. "I may not spare you my arm, Goody Cloyse; but here is my staff, if you will."

So saying, he threw it down at her feet, where, perhaps, it assumed life, being one of the rods which its owner had formerly lent to the Egyptian magi⑥. Of this fact, however, Goodman Brown could not take cognizance⑦. He had cast up his eyes in astonishment, and looking down again, beheld neither Goody Cloyse nor the serpentine staff, but his fellow-traveller alone, who waited for him as calmly as if nothing had happened.

"That old woman taught me my catechism," said the young man; and there was a world of meaning in this simple comment⑧.

布朗看到的是幻觉,其实他是在面对心中的罪恶。

---

① smallage:块根芹。
② cinquefoil:洋莓属的一种。
③ wolf's bane:附子草。
④ cackling:咯咯笑。
⑤ twinkling:转瞬间。
⑥ magi:暗示亚伦之杖的故事,当摩西的哥哥亚伦把他的杖丢在法老面前时,杖就变作蛇。法老的博士看到这情形,也把自己的杖丢下(根据霍桑的故事,这些杖是由撒旦提供的),那些杖也显示出了同样的魔力。见《旧约·出埃及记》第七章。
⑦ cognizance:认识,审理,认定。
⑧ there was a world of meaning in this simple comment:简简单单一句话,意味深长。

They continued to walk onward, while the elder traveller exhorted① his companion to make good speed and persevere② in the path, discoursing so aptly that his arguments seemed rather to spring up in the bosom③ of his auditor④ than to be suggested by himself. As they went, he plucked⑤ a branch of maple to serve for a walking stick, and began to strip⑥ it of the twigs⑦ and little boughs, which were wet with evening dew. The moment his fingers touched them they became strangely withered and dried up as with a week's sunshine. Thus the pair proceeded, at a good free pace, until suddenly, in a gloomy hollow of the road, Goodman Brown sat himself down on the stump⑧ of a tree and refused to go any farther.

"Friend," he said, stubbornly⑨, "my mind is made up. Not another step will I budge⑩ on this errand. What if a wretched old woman do choose to go to the devil when I thought she was going to heaven! Is that any reason why I should quit my dear Faith and go after her?"

"You will think better of this by and by," said his acquaintance, composedly⑪. "Sit here and rest yourself a while; and when you feel like moving again, there is my staff to help you along."

Without more words, he threw his companion the

魔鬼诱惑布朗走向邪恶,"似乎他说的话是出自听者的内心",说明人的心灵深处本来就有邪恶。而布朗还在犹豫是否要继续森林之行。

---

① exhort：劝诫，忠告。
② persevere：坚持。
③ bosom：内心。
④ auditor：旁听者。
⑤ pluck：折断。
⑥ strip：剥去。
⑦ twig：细枝。
⑧ stump：树墩。
⑨ stubbornly：倔强地。
⑩ budge：(使)稍微移动。
⑪ composedly：从容地。

maple stick, and was as speedily out of sight as if he had vanished into the deepening gloom. The young man sat a few moments by the roadside, applauding himself greatly, and thinking with how clear a conscience① he should meet the minister in his morning walk, nor shrink from the eye of good old Deacon Gookin. And what calm sleep would be his that very night, which was to have been spent so wickedly, but so purely and sweetly now, in the arms of Faith! Amidst these pleasant and praiseworthy meditations②, Goodman Brown heard the tramp③ of horsed along the road, and deemed it advisable to conceal himself within the verge of the forest, conscious of the guilty purpose that had brought him thither, though now so happily turned from it.

布朗正为罪恶目的感到内疚，想象自己即将回头而感到欣慰。

On came the hoof-tramps and the voices of the riders, two grave old voices, conversing soberly as they draw near. These mingled sounds appeared to pass along the road, within a few yards of the young man's hiding-place; but, owing doubtless to the depth of the gloom at that particular spot, neither the travelers nor their steeds④ were visible. Though their figures brushed the small boughs by the wayside, it could not be seen that they intercepted, even for a moment, the faint gleam from the strip of bright sky athwart⑤ which they must have passed. Goodman Brown alternately⑥ crouched⑦ and stood on tiptoe, pulling aside the branches and thrusting forth his head as far as he durst without discerning so much as a

---

① conscience：良心。
② meditation：沉思，冥想。
③ tramp：沉重的脚步声。
④ steed：坐骑。
⑤ athwart：斜地横过。
⑥ alternately：交替地。
⑦ crouch：蜷缩。

shadow. It vexed① him the more, because he could have sworn, were such a thing possible, that he recognized the voices of the minister and Deacon Gookin, jogging along quietly, as they were wont② to do, when bound to some ordination③ or ecclesiastical④ council. While yet within hearing, one of the riders stopped to pluck a switch.

"Of the two, reverend⑤ sir," said the voice like the deacon's, "I had rather miss an ordination dinner than to-night's meeting. They tell me that some of our community are to be here from Falmouth and beyond, and others from Connecticut and Rhode Island, besides several of the Indian powwows⑥, who, after their fashion, know almost as much deviltry as the best of us. Moreover, there is a goodly young woman to be taken into communion."

"Mighty well, Deacon Gookin!" replied the solemn old tones of the minister. "Spur up⑦, or we shall be late. Nothing can be done, you know, until I get on the ground."

The hoofs clattered again; and the voices, talking so strangely in the empty air, passed on through the forest, where no church had ever been gathered or solitary Christian prayed. Whither, then, could these holy men be journeying so deep into the heathen⑧ wilderness? Young Goodman Brown caught hold of a tree for support, being ready to sink down on the ground, faint and overburdened with there really was a heaven above him. Yet there was

---

① vex：焦躁。
② wont：惯于，常常。
③ ordination：神职授任。
④ ecclesiastical：教会的。
⑤ reverend：对牧师或神父的尊称。
⑥ powwow：巫师。
⑦ spur up：策马前行。
⑧ heathen：异教徒。

布朗看到牧师等神职人员也来参加魔鬼的聚会，他不禁开始怀疑"头顶是否有个天国"。不过，他仍然想抵抗魔鬼，不愿屈服。

村里的人，包括众多的村民，甚至费斯，都来参加魔鬼的聚会，说明了所谓的"魔鬼"或者"邪恶"其实存在于每个人的内心。

the blue arch①, and the stars brightening in it.

"With heaven above and Faith below, I will get stand firm against the devil!" cried Goodman Brown.

While he still gazed upward into the deep arch of the firmament② and had lifted his hands to pray, a cloud, though no wind was stirring, hurried across the zenith③ and hid the brightening stars. The blue sky was still visible, except directly overhead, where this black mass of cloud was sweeping swiftly northward. Aloft④ in the air, as if from the depths of the cloud, came a confused and doubtful sound of voices. Once the listener fancied that he could distinguish the accents of towns-people of his own, men and women, both pious and ungodly⑤, many of whom he had met at the communion table, and had seen others rioting⑥ at the tavern⑦. The next moment, so indistinct were the sounds, he doubted whether he had heard aught⑧ but the murmur of the old forest, whispering without a wind. Then came a stronger swell⑨ of those familiar tones, heard daily in the sunshine at Salem village, but never until now from a cloud of night. There was one voice, of a young woman, uttering lamentations⑩, yet with an uncertain sorrow, and entreating for some favor, which, perhaps, it would grieve her to obtain; and all the unseen multitude, both saints and sinners, seemed to encourage her onward.

① arch：苍穹。
② firmament：天空。
③ zenith：顶点。
④ aloft：在高处的。
⑤ ungodly：不虔诚的。
⑥ rioting：骚乱。
⑦ tavern：酒馆。
⑧ aught：任何事。
⑨ swell：声音渐强。
⑩ lamentations：耶利米哀歌，这里指的纵声恸哭。

"Faith!" shouted Goodman Brown, in a voice of agony desperation; and the echoes of the forest mocked him, crying, "Faith! Faith!" as if bewildered wretches were seeking her all through the wilderness.

The cry of grief, rage, and terror was yet piercing the night, when the unhappy husband held his breath for a response. There was a scram①, drowned immediately in a louder murmur of voice, fading into far-off laughter, as the dark cloud swept away, leaving the clear and silent sky above Goodman Brown. But something fluttered② lightly down through the air and caught on the branch of a tree. The young man seized it, and beheld a pink ribbon.

"My Faith is gone!" cried he after one stupefied③ moment. "There is no good on earth; and sin is but a name. Come, devil! for to thee is this world given."

And, maddened with despair, so that he laughed loud and long, did Goodman Brown grasp his staff and set forth again, at such a rate that he seemed to fly along the forest path rather than to walk or run. The road grew wilder and drearier and more faintly traced, and vanished at length, leaving him in the heart of the dark wilderness, still rushing onward with the instinct that guides mortal man to evil. The whole forest was peopled with frightful sounds: the creaking of the trees, the howling of wild beasts, and the yell of Indians; while sometimes the wind tolled like a distant church bell, and sometimes gave a broad roar around the traveller, as if all Nature were laughing him to scorn. But he was himself the chief horror of the scene, and shrank not from its other horrors.

"Ha! ha! ha!" roared Goodman Brown when the

粉红色缎带从空中飘落下来,象征布朗一直坚信纯洁的妻子费丝的堕落,也直接促使彻底绝望的他进入森林,与魔鬼同流。

---

① scram:紧急刹车。
② flutter:飘动。
③ stupefied:愣的。

wind laughed at him. "Let us hear which will laugh loudest. Think not to frighten me with your deviltry! Come witch, come wizard①, come Indian powwow, come devil himself, and here comes Goodman Brown. You may as well fear him as he fear you."

In truth, all through the haunted forest there could be nothing more frightful than the figure of Goodman Brown. On he flew among the black pines, brandishing② his staff with frenzied③ gestures, now giving vent to an inspiration of horrid blasphemy④, and now shouting forth such laughter as set all the echoes of the forest laughing like demons around him. The fiend⑤ in his own shape is less hideous than when he rages in the breast of man. Thus sped the demoniac⑥ on his course, until, quivering among the trees, he saw a red light before him, as when the felled trunks and branches of a clearing have been set on fire, and throw up their lurid blaze against the sky, at the hour of midnight. He paused, in a lull⑦ of the tempest that had driven him onward, and heard the swell of what seemed a hymn⑧, rolling solemnly from a distance with the weight of many voices. He knew the tune; it was a familiar one in the choir of the village meeting-house. The verse died heavily away, and was lengthened by a chorus, not of human voices, but of all the sounds of the benighted wilderness pealing in awful harmony together. Goodman Brown cried out, and his cry was lost to his own

布朗"不时地从心中发出亵渎神灵的咒骂",而在愤怒中"狰狞的面目比魔鬼的样子还要可怕"。表明他心中的邪恶也是存在的。

---

① wizard：男巫师。
② brandish：挥舞。
③ frenzied：狂热的，狂乱的。
④ blasphemy：亵渎。
⑤ fiend：恶魔。
⑥ demoniac：着魔的人。
⑦ lull：间歇。
⑧ hymn：赞美诗，圣歌。

ear by its unison with the cry of the desert.

In the interval of silence, he stole forward, until the light glared full upon his eyes. At one extremity of an open space, hemmed① in by the dark wall of the forest, arose a rock, bearing some rude, natural resemblance either to an alter or a pulpit, and surrounded by four blazing pines, their tops aflame, their stems untouched, like candles at an evening meeting. The mass of foliage② that had overgrown the summit of the rock was all on fire, blazing high into the night and fitfully③ illuminating the whole field. Each pendent twig and leafy festoon④ was in a blaze. As the red light arose and fell, a numerous congregation alternately shone forth, then disappeared in shadow, and again grew, as it were, out of the darkness, peopling the heart of the solitary woods at once. ⑤

"A grave and dark-clad company." quoth⑥ Goodman Brown.

In truth they were such. Among them, quivering to and fro between gloom and splendor, appeared faced that would be seen next day at the council board of the province, and others which, Sabbath after Sabbath, looked devoutly heavenward, and benignantly over the crowded pews, from the holiest pulpits in the land⑦.

布朗发现在魔鬼聚会的人群中根本没有什么好坏之分：淫妇与贞洁的少女欢谈，罪人与圣徒并肩，好人与坏人畅言，甚至还有给家乡的森林带来极大恐惧的印第安巫师。

---

① hem：包围。
② foliage：树叶。
③ fitfully：断断续续地。
④ festoon：花环。
⑤ As the red light arose and fell, a numerous congregation alternately shone forth, then disappeared in shadow, and again grew, as it were, out of the darkness, peopling the heart of the solitary woods at once：随着红光一起一落，数不清的会众时而被照亮，时而消失于暗影，时而又从黑幕中冒出头，荒凉山林的深处一时人影憧憧。
⑥ quoth：[古]说，用在第一人称和第三人称的过去式。
⑦ Among them, quivering to and fro between gloom and splendor, appeared faced that would be seen next day at the council board of the province, and others which, Sabbath after Sabbath, looked devoutly heavenward, and benignantly over the crowded pews, from the holiest pulpits in the land. 明暗之间交替显现出一些翌日将在州议会上露面的人物。另一些人则个个安息日都立在本地的圣坛上，虔诚地仰望天堂，慈祥地俯视拥挤的会众。

Some affirm that the lady of the governor was there. At least there were high dames well known to her, and wives of honored husbands, and widows, a great multitude, and ancient maidens, all of excellent repute, and fair young girls, who trembled lest their mothers should espy① them. Either the sudden gleams of light flashing over the obscure field bedazzled Goodman Brown, or he recognized a score of the church members of Salem village famous for their especial sanctity. Good old Deacon Gookin had arrived, and waited at the skirts of that venerable② saint, his revered pastor. But, irreverently consorting with these grave, reputable, and pious people, these elders of the church, these chaste③ dames and dewy virgins, there were men of dissolute④ lives and women of spotted fame, wretches given over to all mean and filthy vice, and suspected even of horrid crimes. It was strange to see that the good shrank not from the wicked, nor were the sinners abashed by the saints. Scattered also among their pale-faced enemies were the Indian priests, or powwows, who had often scared their native forest with more hideous incantations⑤ than any known to English witchcraft.

"But where is Faith?" thought Goodman Brown; and, as hope came into his heart, he trembled.

作者用表演动作、声音等细节描写了魔鬼集会的情景,并与宗教仪式中的赞美诗进行了对比。

Another verse of the hymn arose, a slow and mournful strain, such as the pious love, but joined to words which expressed all that our nature can conceive of sin, and darkly hinted at far more. Unfathomable⑥ to

---

① espy:看到。
② venerable:庄严的。
③ chaste:贞节的。
④ dissolute:放荡的。
⑤ incantations:咒语。
⑥ unfathomable:深不可测的,难解的。

mere mortals is the lore of fiends. Verse after verse was sung; and still the chorus of the desert swelled between like the deepest tone of a mighty organ; and with the final peal of that dreadful anthem there came a sound, as if the roaring wind, the rushing streams, the howling beasts, and every other voice of the unconcerted wilderness were mingling and according with the voice of guilty man in homage① to the prince of all. The four blazing pines threw up a loftier② flame and obscurely discovered shapes and visages of horror on the smoke wreaths above the impious assembly. At the same moment the fire on the rock shot redly forth and formed a flowing arch above its base, where now appeared a figure. With reverence be it spoken, the figure born no slight similitude, both in garb③ and manner, to some grave divine of the New England churches.

"Bring forth the converts!④" cried a voice that echoed through the field and rolled into the forest.

At the word, Goodman Brown stepped forth from the shadow of the tree and approached the congregation, with whom he felt a loathful brotherhood by the sympathy of all that was wicked in his heart. He could have well-nigh⑤ sworn that the shape of his own dead father beckoned⑥ him to advance, looking downward from a smoke wreath, while a woman, with dim features of despair, threw out her hand to warn him back. Was it his mother? But he had no power to retreat one step, nor to resist, even in thought, when the minister and good old Deacon Gookin

布朗在魔鬼的聚会中看到了他一生敬重的父亲、母亲,以及他最亲爱的妻子——他的一生信仰之所在。

① homage:敬意。
② loftier:崇高的。
③ garb:[正]装束。
④ Bring forth the converts! 带上皈依者!
⑤ well-nigh:几乎。
⑥ beckon:召唤。

seized his arms and led him to the blazing rock. Thither came also the slender form of a veiled female, led between Goody Cloyse, that pious teacher of the catechism, and Martha Carrier, who had received the devil's promise to be queen of hell. A rampant[①] hag was she! And there stood the proselytes, beneath the canopy[②] of fire.

"Welcome, my children," said the dark figure, "to the communion of your race! Ye have found, thus young your nature and your destiny. My children, look behind you!"

They turned; and flashing forth, as it were, in a sheet of flame, the fiend worshippers were seen; the smile of welcome gleamed darkly on every visage.

魔鬼就像布道一样讲述他的教义,"整个世界就是一个罪恶之地","每个人心中所包藏的罪恶隐秘"。

"There," resumed the sable[③] form, "are all whom ye have reverenced from youth. Ye deemed them holier than yourselves and shrank from your own sin, contrasting it with their lives of righteousness and prayerful aspirations heavenward. Yet here are they all in my worshipping assembly. This night it shall be granted you to know their secret deeds: how hoary[④]-bearded elders of the church have whispered wanton[⑤] words to the young maids of their households; how many a woman, eager for widows' weeds, has given her husband a drink at bedtime and let him sleep his last sleep in her bosom; how beardless youths have made haste to inherit fathers' wealth; and how fair damsels — blush not, sweet ones — have dug little graves in the garden, and bidden me, the sole guest, to an infant's funeral. By the sympathy of your human

① rampant：骄横跋扈的。
② canopy：天篷。
③ sable：黑暗的。
④ hoary：灰白的。
⑤ wanton：淫荡的。

hearts for sin ye shall scent out all the places — whether in church, bedchamber①, street, field, or forest — where crime has been committed, and shall exult② to behold the whole earth one stain③ of guilt, one mighty blood spot. Far more than this! It shall be yours to penetrate, in every bosom, the deep mystery of sin, the fountain of all wicked arts, and which inexhaustibly④ supplies more evil impulses than human power — than my power at its utmost — can make manifest in deeds. And now, my children, look upon each other."

They did so; and, by the blaze of the hell-kindled torches, the wretched man beheld his Faith, and the wife her husband, trembling before that unhallowed altar.

"Lo, there ye stand, my children," said the figure, in a deep and solemn tone, almost sad with its despairing awfulness, as if his once angelic nature could yet mourn for our miserable race. "Depending upon one another's hearts, ye had still hoped that virtue were not all a dream. Now are ye undeceived! Evil is the nature of mankind. Evil must be your only happiness. Welcome again, my children, to the communion of your race."

"Welcome!" repeated the fiend worshippers, in one cry of despair and triumph.

魔鬼的崇拜者们因为新人的加入而感到胜利,又因为意识到"人心本恶"而感到绝望。

And there they stood, the only pair, as it seemed, who were yet hesitating on the verge of wickedness in this dark world. A basin was hallowed, naturally, in the rock. Did it contain water, reddened by the lurid⑤ light? or was it blood? or, perchance⑥, a liquid flame? Herein did the

---

① bedchamber：卧室。
② exult：狂喜。
③ stain：污点。
④ inexhaustibly：无穷无尽的。
⑤ lurid：亮得古怪的。
⑥ perchance：偶然。

299

shape of evil dip his hand and prepare to lay the mark of baptism① upon their foreheads that they might be partakers of the mystery of sin, more conscious of the secret guilt of others, both in deed and thought, than they could now be of their own. The husband cast one look at his pale wife, and Faith at him. What polluted wretches would the next glance show them to each other, shuddering alike at what they disclosed and what they saw!

"Faith! Faith!" cried the husband, "look up to heaven, and resist the wicked one."

Whether Faith obeyed he knew not. Hardly had he spoken when he found himself amid calm night and solitude, listening to a roar of the wind which died heavily away through the forest. He staggered against the rock, and felt it chill and damp; while a hanging twig, that had been all on fire, besprinkled② his cheek with the coldest dew.

参加过魔鬼的夜晚聚会,见识到各种人的邪恶,第二天清晨,布朗彻底地改变了,对这个世界充满了绝望。

The next morning young Goodman Brown came slowly into the street of Salem village, staring around him like a bewildered man. The good old minister was talking a walk along the graveyard to get an appetite for breakfast and meditate his sermon, and bestowed③ a blessing, as he passed, on Goodman Brown. He shrank from the venerable saint as if to avoid an anathema④. Old Deacon Gookin was at demotic⑤ worship, and the holy words of his prayer were heard through the open window, "What God doth the wizard pray to?" quoth Goodman Brown. Goody Cloyse, that excellent old Christian, stood in the

---

① baptism: 洗礼。
② besprinkle: 布满,洒。
③ bestowed: 赐予。
④ anathema: 诅咒。
⑤ demotic: 通俗的。

early sunshine at her own lattice①, catechizing② a little girl who had brought her a pint of morning's milk. Goodman Brown snatched away the child as from the grasp of the fiend himself. Turning the corner by the meeting-house, he spied the head of Faith, with the pink ribbons, gazing anxiously forth, and bursting into such joy at sight of him that she skipped along the street and almost kiss her husband before the whole village. But Goodman Brown looked sternly and sadly into her face, and passed on without a greeting.

Had Goodman Brown fallen asleep in the forest and only dreamed a wild dream of a witch-meeting?

Be it so if you will. But, alas! it was a dream of evil omen③ for young Goodman Brown. A stern, a sad, a darkly meditative, a distrustful if not a desperate man did he become from the night of that tearful dream. On the Sabbath day, when the congregation were singing a holy psalm④, he could not listen because an anthem of sin rushed loudly upon his ear and drowned all the blessed strain. When the minister spoke from the pulpit with power and fervid⑤ eloquence, and, with his hand on the open Bible, of the scared truths of our religion, and of saint-like lives and triumphant deaths, and of future bliss or misery unutterable, then did Goodman Brown turn pale, dreading lest⑥ the roof should thunder down upon the gray blasphemer and his hearers. Often, awaking suddenly at midnight, he shrank from the bosom of Faith; and at morning or eventide, when the family knelt down

---

① lattice: 格子窗户。
② catechize: 问答式讲授。
③ omen: 预兆。
④ psalm: 圣歌。
⑤ fervid: 充满激情的。
⑥ lest: 担心。

从那天晚上之后，布朗成了一个严厉、悲伤和疑心病重的人，直到临终时刻还是忧郁、沮丧的。

at prayer, he scowled① and muttered to himself, and gazed sternly at his wife, and turned away. And when he had lived long, and was borne to his grave a hoary corpse, followed by Faith, an aged woman, and children and grandchildren, a goodly procession, besides neighbors not a few, they carved no hopeful verse upon his tombstone②, for his dying hour was gloom.

【思考题】

1. 小说主人公小伙子布朗是一个怎样的人物？请结合他的森林之行及其最后的结局谈谈。

2. 小说最典型的艺术特色是什么？具体表现在哪几个方面？

3. 小说表达作家霍桑怎样的道德善恶观？

---

① scowl：皱着眉毛。
② tombstone：墓碑。

Four Meetings

四次会见

亨利·詹姆斯

【导读】

　　亨利·詹姆斯(Henry James，1843—1916)，是小说艺术的巨匠，在英美文学史上占有举足轻重的地位。他开创了心理分析小说的先河，被誉为"西方现代心理分析小说的开拓者"。他的小说构思精巧，情节缜密，且富于独特的叙述视角，常常能为读者展现出一个"仿佛是迷宫般的普通人的内心世界"。在兰登书屋(Random House)1996 年评选的 "20 世纪百部最佳英文小说"中，他一个人就占了三部作品。

　　詹姆斯于 1843 年 4 月 15 日出生在纽约市的一个上等知识分子家庭。父亲老亨利·詹姆斯是一位著名的学者，哥哥威廉·詹姆斯(William James)是知名的哲学家和心理学家。很小的时候，詹姆斯和兄长就被父亲送往欧洲接受教育，掌握多种语言。1862 年詹姆斯考入哈佛大学法学院。1869 年游历了英国、法国和意大利等国后，决定离开美国，移居欧洲。1875 至 1876 年住在巴黎，结识了屠格涅夫、左拉、都德等作家。两年后迁居伦敦。1904 至 1905 年曾回美国，1915 年因不满美国在第一次世界大战初期的"中立"态度而加入英国籍。

　　幼年时，他的背部受了伤，这使得他离开了社交圈，转而成为一名旁观美国和欧洲上层生活的内省式作家。他的主要作品是小说，此外还有一些文学传记、评论、剧本和游记。他的小说常着眼于美国人和欧洲人之间的交往问题，物质与精神之间的矛盾、艺术家的孤独、成人的罪恶、善良的和丑陋的人性，以及后期的唯美主义倾向——这表明作家对描述个人道德品质的兴趣，体现了一种浓厚的人文主义倾向。在书中，他赞美纯朴宽厚的品德，将个人品质和他人利益作为衡量角色的重要标准。

　　詹姆斯从 1864 年起开始文学创作。在他的代表作中，长篇小说有《贵妇的画像》《一个美国人》等。中短篇小说有《黛丝·米勒》《螺丝在旋紧》等。另外，他还写了很多有见地的评论文章，涉及英、美、法等国作家，如乔治·艾略特(George Eliot)、斯蒂文森(Robert Louis Stevenson)、爱默生(Ralph Waldo Emerson)、巴尔扎克、乔治·桑以及屠格涅夫等。有自传三种流传于世：《童年及其他》《作为儿子与兄弟》和《中年》。

　　《四次会见》是亨利·詹姆斯早期的短篇名作,它围绕着卡罗琳·斯潘塞小姐去欧洲旅行一事逐层展开,情节简单,丝丝入扣。但作品的可读性在于它向读者提供了一个没有任何外来干预的故事。文中描写了年轻美国的"天真"与古老欧洲的"世故"的冲突,反映了去欧洲的美国人之间的差别,揭示了表面的和实际的欧洲之间的矛盾。

　　整个故事由四个场景,即四次会见构成,它们层层推进,不蔓不枝,形成一种有头有尾的发展,各部分匀称而又各自有重点。第一个场景是大约 17 年前,在美国北维罗那的一个小型茶会上,"我"见到了"并不十分美丽但娇小奇妙,惹人喜爱"的卡罗琳·斯潘塞小姐。她一个人坐在那儿,带着"拘谨的、掩饰的渴望"。当"我"给她讲解在欧洲拍的照片,介绍外国的风土景色时,"她看上去很是高兴,实则非常激动"。那时的她一无所有,仅仅靠教书维持生计。谈及去欧洲旅行,她说"我在存钱,已经存了起来,我还总是不断添上一点","不去我是会发疯的","我朝思暮想的就是这个问题"。她梦想到古欧洲去,并且认定她在那边的亲戚会照顾她。这样,一个善良、单纯、诚实、美丽且富有想象力的卡罗琳·斯潘塞便栩栩如生地跃然纸上。第二个场景发生在三年后的一天,在法国勒阿弗尔海港一家咖啡店门前的圆桌边,"我"碰巧看到了卡罗琳·斯潘塞小姐。她还是像以前那样端庄、美丽,不显老。她独自坐着,"她观察、她辨认、她赞叹、她紧张得令人感动,她注意地看着街上从我们面前经过的一切事物"。她的新鲜感、她那梦想终于实现的高兴劲儿,都使她显得妩媚。她是那样单纯、善良,上岸才半个小时就把自己的"一点点钱"交到她堂兄手里。第三个场景仍在勒阿弗尔海港,同一天日暮时分,"我"拜访了住在小客栈里的斯潘塞小姐。她一个人坐在那里,样子十分痛苦。原来她在为她的堂兄——那个在斯潘塞小姐眼里"聪明、和气、年轻的"美术学生和他那所谓的妻子——一个冒牌的"伯爵夫人"而难过。斯潘塞说,"他很傻,这个可怜的人完全依靠我的仁爱和帮助了",除了自己的回程路费,她把所有的钱都给了她的堂兄。这可怜的姑娘在到达她朝思暮想的欧洲之后,只待了将近十三个小时就又登上了返程。而她的堂兄靠花言巧语,吃着用她的钱买的水果、饭菜,无半点羞愧,无丝毫愧疚,反而是那样自得惬意。斯潘塞与她堂兄的品格,孰上孰下,不判自明。第四个场景是在又隔了五年后的美国。这一次,在她那寓优雅于简朴之中的住所,"我"又见到了斯潘塞小姐,"她声音颤抖",看起来"疲倦又衰弱","像是老了十岁"。当谈到去欧洲旅行的事时,她绝望地说了句,"永远不去了"。同时,"我"还见到了斯潘塞堂兄的妻子——那个冒牌的"伯爵夫人",一个肥壮的中年女人。在她那张肥胖苍白的面孔上,一双小而盯人的眼睛和斯潘塞堂兄的如出一辙,还故作姿态地向陌生人卖弄风情。在陷于不幸,生活没有出路时,她从欧洲来到美国,靠斯潘塞生活;

她不劳而获,却还让斯潘塞小姐"像侍女一样站在一旁","像仆人一样侍奉她"。她像沉重的十字架一样让斯潘塞小姐背在身上,毁了她的一生。

《四次会见》的全文,是用第一人称叙事方法写成的。"我"在《四次会见》中虽然并非主角,但一切都是透过"我"的眼睛来观察的。这种叙事角度给人一种真实、直接的感觉,拉近了角色与读者的距离。詹姆斯的文风,也与同时代的其他作家迥然不同,他喜欢用艰深文雅的大词、成语和外来词,其语言风格独树一帜,不同凡响。在表达上,他力求委婉描述,而不是直接剖白。而这种设计实则是为主题服务的。比如结构曲折的长句,在描述人物多角度的思维过程和复杂的心理状态时有独到的作用。在詹姆斯看来,艺术的真实与人生的真实是同一回事。因此,他笔下的人物寻求人生意义的过程,也就是作家艺术创作的过程。

Four Meetings

I saw her but four times, though I remember them vividly; she made her impression on me. I thought her very pretty and very interesting — a touching specimen① of a type with which I had had other and perhaps less charming associations. I'm sorry to hear of her death, and yet when I think of it why *should* I be? The last time I saw her she was certainly not —! But it will be of interest to take our meetings in order.

I

The first was in the country, at a small tea-party, one snowy night of some seventeen years ago. My friend Latouche, going to spend Christmas with his mother, had insisted on my company, and the good lady had given in our honour the entertainment of which I speak. To me it was really full of savour② — it had all the right marks: I had never been in the depths of New England at that season. It had been snowing all day and the drifts were knee-high. I wondered how the ladies had made their way

题目可以译为"四次会见"或"四次会面",指"我"和斯潘塞小姐四次会见的场景。

全文的叙述都以第一人称的视角展开。

"我"第一次见到斯潘塞小姐时的场景。

---

① specimen:标本,样本。
② savour:味道,情趣,趣味。

to the house; but I inferred that just those general rigours rendered any assembly offering the attraction of two gentlemen from New York worth a desperate effort.

Mrs. Latouche in the course of the evening asked me if I "didn't want to" show the photographs to some of the young ladies. The photographs were in a couple of great portfolios①, and had been brought home by her son, who, like myself, was lately returned from Europe. I looked round and was struck with the fact that most of the young ladies were provided with an object of interest more absorbing than the most vivid sun-picture. But there was a person alone near the mantel-shelf who looked round the room with a small vague smile, a discreet②, a disguised yearning③, which seemed somehow at odds with her isolation. I looked at her a moment and then chose. "I should like to show them to that young lady."

"Oh yes," said Mrs. Latouche, "she's just the person. She doesn't care for flirting — I'll speak to her." I replied that if she didn't care for flirting she wasn't perhaps just the person; but Mrs. Latouche had already, with a few steps, appealed to her participation. "She's delighted," my hostess came back to report; "and she's just the person — so quiet and so bright." And she told me the young lady was by name Miss Caroline Spencer — with which she introduced me.

Miss Caroline Spencer was not quite a beauty, but was none the less, in her small odd way, formed to please. Close upon thirty, by every presumption, she was made almost like a little girl and had the complexion of a child. She had also the prettiest head, on which her hair was

此处虽着墨不多，却以精当的选词和描写，刻画了人物神态。

这段细致入微的外貌描写，向读者展示了一个并不非常美丽，却可爱迷人的斯潘塞小姐。

① portfolio：影集，文件夹。
② discreet：谨慎的，审慎的。
③ yearning：渴望。

arranged as nearly as possible like the hair of a Greek
bust, though indeed it was to be doubted if she had ever
seen a Greek bust. She was "artistic," I suspected, so far
as the polar influences of North Verona could allow for
such yearnings or could minister to them. Her eyes were
perhaps just too round and too inveterately① surprised,
but her lips had a certain mild decision and her teeth,
when she showed them, were charming. About her neck
she wore what ladies call, I believe, a "ruche②" fastened
with a very small pin of pink coral, and in her hand she
carried a fan made of plaited straw and adorned with pink
ribbon. She wore a scanty black silk dress. She spoke with
slow soft neatness, even without smiles showing the
prettiness of her teeth, and she seemed extremely pleased,
in fact quite fluttered, at the prospect of my
demonstrations. These went forward very smoothly after I
had moved the portfolios out of their corner and placed a
couple of chairs near a lamp. The photographs were
usually things I knew — large views of Switzerland, Italy
and Spain, landscapes, reproductions③ of famous
buildings, pictures and statues. I said what I could for
them, and my companion, looking at them as I held them
up, sat perfectly still, her straw fan raised to her under-lip
and gently, yet, as I could feel, almost excitedly, rubbing
it. Occasionally, as I laid one of the pictures down, she
said without confidence, which would have been too
much: "Have you seen that place?" I usually answered that
I had seen it several times — I had been a great traveller,
though I was somehow particularly admonished not to

"我"向斯潘塞小姐
展示旅行中拍的照片,
介绍外国的风土景色。

---

① inveterately: 积习的,根深蒂固的。
② ruche: 褶带,褶饰。
③ reproductions: 复制,此处指翻印的照片。

swagger①— and then I felt her look at me askance② for a
moment with her pretty eyes. I had asked her at the outset
whether she had been to Europe; to this she had answered
"No, no, no" — almost as much below her breath as if the
image of such an event scarce, for solemnity, brooked
phrasing. But after that, though she never took her eyes
off the pictures, she said so little that I feared she was at
last bored. Accordingly when we had finished one
portfolio I offered, if she desired it, to desist. I rather
guessed the exhibition really held her, but her reticence③
puzzled me and I wanted to make her speak. I turned
round to judge better and then saw a faint flush in each of
her cheeks. She kept waving her little fan to and fro.
Instead of looking at me she fixed her eyes on the
remainder of the collection, which leaned, in its
receptacle, against the table.

"Won't you show me that?" she quavered④, drawing
the long breath of a person launched and afloat but
conscious of rocking a little.

"With pleasure," I answered, "if you're really not
tired."

"Oh I'm not tired a bit. I'm just fascinated." With
which as I took up the other portfolio she laid her hand on
it, rubbing it softly. "And have you been here too?"

On my opening the portfolio it appeared I had indeed
been there. One of the first photographs was a large view
of the Castle of Chillon by the Lake of Geneva. ⑤"Here,"
I said, "I've been many a time. Isn't it beautiful?" And I

① swagger：吹嘘。
② askance：斜视,横眼看。
③ reticence：缄默。
④ quaver：用颤声说。
⑤ the Castle of Chillon by the Lake of Geneva："西庸"古堡,坐落在瑞士日内瓦湖边,是世界有名的建筑。

pointed to the perfect reflexion of the rugged rocks and pointed towers① in the clear still water. She didn't say "Oh enchanting②!" and push it away to see the next picture. She looked a while and then asked if it weren't where Bonnivard, about whom Byron③ wrote, had been confined. I assented, trying to quote Byron's verses, but not quite bringing it off.

She fanned herself a moment and then repeated the lines correctly, in a soft flat voice but with charming conviction. By the time she had finished, she was nevertheless blushing. I complimented her and assured her she was perfectly equipped for visiting Switzerland and Italy. She looked at me askance again, to see if I might be serious, and I added that if she wished to recognize Byron's descriptions she must go abroad speedily — Europe was getting sadly dis-Byronised④. "How soon must I go?" she thereupon enquired.

"Oh I'll give you ten years."

"Well, I guess I can go in *that* time," she answered as if measuring her words.

"Then you'll enjoy it immensely," I said; "you'll find it of the highest interest." Just then I came upon a photograph of some nook⑤ in a foreign city which I had been very fond of and which recalled tender memories. I discoursed (as I suppose) with considerable spirit; my companion sat listening breathless.

"Have you been *very* long over there?" she asked some time after I had ceased.

1816 年，拜伦曾来此居住，完成了《恰尔德·哈罗德游记》第3章。描写旅居比利时和瑞士的见闻与感受。

为后文的交代做铺垫。

话语间，斯潘塞小姐流露出了对欧洲旅行的向往之情。

---

① the rugged rocks and pointed towers：陡峭的岩石和尖塔。
② enchanting：迷人的，讨人喜欢的。
③ Byron：拜伦（1788—1824），英国诗人。
④ Europe was getting sadly dis-Byronised：欧洲有关拜伦的遗迹已经日益凋零。
⑤ nook：角落。

"Well, it mounts up, put all the times together."

"And have you travelled everywhere?"

"I've travelled a good deal. I'm very fond of it and happily have been able."

Again she turned on me her slow shy scrutiny. "Do you know the foreign languages?"

"After a fashion.①"

"Is it hard to speak them?"

"I don't imagine you'd find it so," I gallantly② answered.

两人谈论着巴黎的
剧院,一问一答间,斯潘
塞小姐难掩其神往
之情。

"Oh I shouldn't want to speak — I should only want to listen." Then on a pause she added: "They say the French theatre's so beautiful."

"Ah the best in the world."

"Did you go there very often?"

"When I was first in Paris I went every night."

"Every night!" And she opened her clear eyes very wide. "That to me is" — and her expression hovered③— "as if you tell me a fairy-tale." A few minutes later she put to me: "And which country do you prefer?"

"There's one I love beyond any. I think you'd do the same."

Her gaze rested as on a di revelation and then she breathed "Italy?"

"Italy," I answered softly too; and for a moment we communed over④ it. She looked as pretty as if instead of showing her photographs I had been making love to her. To increase the resemblance she turned off blushing. It made a pause which she broke at last by saying: "That's

---

① after a fashion: 勉强,不是很好。
② gallantly: 勇敢地,殷勤地。
③ hover: 彷徨,犹豫。
④ commune over: 交流,交换思想和感受。

the place which — in particular — I thought of going to. ”

“Oh that’s the place — that’s the place!” I laughed.

She looked at two or three more views in silence. “They say it’s not very dear. ” “As some other countries? Well，one gets back there one’s money. That’s not the least of the charms. ”

“But it’s *all* very expensive，isn’t it?”

“Europe，you mean?”

“Going there and travelling. That has been the trouble. I’ve very little money. I teach，you know，” said Miss Caroline Spencer.

“Oh of course one must have money，” I allowed; “but one can manage with a moderate amount judiciously① spent. ”

斯潘塞小姐靠教书为生，因而欧洲旅行对她来说会是一笔不小的开支。

“I think I should manage. I’ve saved and saved up，and I’m always adding a little to it. It’s all for that. ” She paused a moment，and then went on with suppressed eagerness，as if telling me the story were a rare，but possibly an impure satisfaction. “You see it hasn’t been only the money — it has been everything. Everything has acted against it. I’ve waited and waited. It has been my castle in the air. I’m almost afraid to talk about it. Two or three times it has come a little nearer，and then I’ve talked about it and it has melted away. I’ve talked about it too much，” she said hypocritically② — for I saw such talk was now a small tremulous ecstasy③. “There’s a lady who’s a great friend of mine — she doesn’t want to go，but I’m always at her about it. I think I must tire her dreadfully. She told me just the other day she didn’t know what would become of me. She guessed I’d go crazy if I

为了实现欧洲旅行的梦想，她已经在一点一点地存钱了，为下文情节的发展埋下了伏笔。

斯潘塞小姐的欧洲旅行之梦在旁人看来近乎痴狂，但我们也可借此窥见她单纯、梦幻的性格特征。

① judiciously：明智而审慎地。
② hypocritically：心口不一地。
③ tremulous ecstasy：令人不安的狂喜。

didn't sail, and yet certainly I'd go crazy if I did."

"Well," I laughed, "you haven't sailed up to now — so I suppose you *are* crazy."

She took everything with the same seriousness. "Well, I guess I must be. It seems as if I couldn't think of anything else — and I don't require photographs to work me up! I'm always right *on* it. It kills any interest in things nearer home — things I ought to attend to. That's a kind of craziness."

"Well then the cure for it's just to go," I smiled — "I mean the cure for this kind. Of course you may have the other kind worse," I added — "the kind you get over there."

"Well, I've a faith that I'll go *some* time all right!" she quite elatedly cried. "I've a relative right there on the spot," she went on, "and I guess he'll know how to control me." I expressed the hope that he would, and I forget whether we turned over more photographs; but when I asked her if she had always lived just where I found her, "Oh no sir," she quite eagerly replied; "I've spent twenty-two months and a half in Boston." I met it with the inevitable joke that in this case foreign lands might prove a disappointment to her, but I quite failed to alarm her. "I know more about them than you might think" — her earnestness resisted even that. "I mean by reading — for I've really read considerable. In fact I guess I've prepared my mind about as much as you *can* — in advance. I've not only read Byron — I've read histories and guide-books and articles and lots of things. I know I shall rave about everything."

"'Everything' is saying much, but I understand your case," I returned. "You've the great American disease, and you've got it 'bad' — the appetite, morbid① and monstrous, for colour and form, for the picturesque and the romantic at any price. I don't know whether we come into the world with it — with the germs implanted② and antecedent③ to experience; rather perhaps we catch it early, almost before developed consciousness — we *feel*, as we look about, that we're going (to save our souls, or at least our senses) to be thrown back on it hard. We're like travellers in the desert — deprived of water and subject to the terrible mirage④, the torment of illusion, of the thirst-fever. They hear the plash of fountains, they see green gardens and orchards that are hundreds of miles away. So we with OUR thirst — except that with us it's MORE wonderful; we have before us the beautiful old things we've never seen at all, and when we do at last see them — if we're lucky! — we simply recognise them. What experience does is merely to confirm and consecrate our confident dream."

She listened with her rounded eyes. "The way you express it's too lovely, and I'm sure it will be just like that. I've dreamt of everything — I'll know it all!"

"I'm afraid," I pretended for harmless comedy, "that you've wasted a great deal of time."

"Oh yes, that has been my great wickedness⑤!" The people about us had begun to scatter; they were taking their leave. She got up and put out her hand to me, timidly, but as if quite shining and throbbing⑥.

"I'm going back there — one HAS to," I said as I

"我"在此向她阐释，在某种层面上，旅行其实并不是那么浪漫的一件趣事，常常是需要付出一些代价的。此处对接下来她的遭遇可谓埋下了一个精彩的伏笔。

斯潘塞小姐涉世不深、单纯热情的性格让她无法放弃对欧洲旅行越来越强烈的渴望。

"我"在此不经意地冷幽默了一下，鼓励她早日启程。

---

① morbid：病态的。
② implant：植入的。
③ antecedent：先行的。
④ mirage：海市蜃楼。
⑤ wickedness：邪恶。
⑥ throbbing：悸动的。

斯潘塞小姐的单纯和活力给"我"留下了很好的印象。

shook hands with her. "I shall look out for you."

Yes, she fairly glittered with her fever of excited faith. "Well, I'll tell you if I'm disappointed." And she left me, fluttering all expressively her little straw fan.

II

三年后,第二个场景展开了。

A few months after this I crossed the sea eastward again and some three years elapsed. I had been living in Paris and, toward the end of October, went from that city to the Havre, to meet a pair of relatives who had written me they were about to arrive there. On reaching the Havre I found the steamer already docked — I was two or three hours late. I repaired directly to the hotel, where my travellers were duly established. My sister had gone to bed, exhausted and disabled by her voyage; she was the unsteadiest of sailors and her sufferings on this occasion had been extreme. She desired for the moment undisturbed rest and was able to see me but five minutes — long enough for us to agree to stop over, restoratively, till the morrow. My brother-in-law, anxious about his wife, was unwilling to leave her room; but she insisted on my taking him a walk for aid to recovery of his spirits and his land-legs.

半明半暗、景色宜人的秋日里,"我"和家人走在海港边的街道上,不期然地,与斯潘塞小姐重逢了。

The early autumn day was warm and charming, and our stroll① through the bright-coloured busy streets of the old French seaport beguiling② enough. We walked along the sunny noisy quays③ and then turned into a wide pleasant street which lay half in sun and half in shade — a French provincial street that resembled an old water-colour drawing: tall grey steep-roofed red-gabled many-

---

① stroll: 散步,闲逛。
② beguiling: 迷人的。
③ quay: 码头。

storied houses; green shutters on windows and old scroll-work① above them; flower-pots in balconies and white-capped women in doorways. We walked in the shade; all this stretched away on the sunny side of the vista and made a picture. We looked at it as we passed along; then suddenly my companion stopped — pressing my arm and staring. I followed his gaze and saw that we had paused just before reaching a cafe where, under an awning②, several tables and chairs were disposed upon the pavement. The windows were open behind; half a dozen plants in tubs were ranged beside the door; the pavement was besprinkled with③ clean bran. It was a dear little quiet old-world cafe; inside, in the comparative dusk, I saw a stout handsome woman, who had pink ribbons in her cap, perched up with a mirror behind her back and smiling at some one placed out of sight. This, to be exact, I noted afterwards; what I first observed was a lady seated alone, outside, at one of the little marble-topped tables. My brother-in-law had stopped to look at her. Something had been put before her, but she only leaned back, motionless and with her hands folded, looking down the street and away from us. I saw her but in diminished profile; nevertheless I was sure I knew on the spot that we must already have met.

这一场景中, 对环境、人物的静态描写可谓不动声色而又精当传神。

"The little lady of the steamer!" my companion cried.

"Was she on your steamer?" I asked with interest.

"From morning till night. She was never sick. She used to sit perpetually④ at the side of the vessel with her

此等痴迷的神态, 的确符合斯潘塞小姐的风格。

---

① scroll-work: 涡型装饰。
② awning: 遮阳棚。
③ besprinkle with: 洒满, 布满。
④ perpetually: 长久地, 持续地。

hands crossed that way, looking at the eastward horizon."

"And are you going to speak to her?"

"I don't know her. I never made acquaintance with her. I wasn't in form to make up to ladies. But I used to watch her and — I don't know why — to be interested in her. She's a dear little Yankee woman. I've an idea she's a school-mistress taking a holiday — for which her scholars have made up a purse."

这段描写，意在暗示斯潘塞小姐气质不凡、令人着迷。

She had now turned her face a little more into profile, looking at the steep grey house-fronts opposite. On this I decided. "I shall speak to her myself."

"I wouldn't — she's very shy," said my brother-in-law.

"My dear fellow, I know her. I once showed her photographs at a tea-party." With which I went up to her, making her, as she turned to look at me, leave me in no doubt of her identity. Miss Caroline Spencer had achieved her dream. But she was less quick to recognise me and showed a slight bewilderment①. I pushed a chair to the table and sat down. "Well," I said, "I hope you're not disappointed!"

两人不期而遇，可是斯潘塞小姐看起来有些狼狈。个中缘由，在后文中会有交代。

She stared, blushing a little — then gave a small jump and placed me. "It was you who showed me the photographs — at North Verona."

"Yes, it was I. This happens very charmingly, for isn't it quite for me to give you a formal reception here — the official welcome? I talked to you so much about Europe."

"You didn't say too much. I'm so intensely happy!" she declared.

---

① bewilderment: 困惑。

Very happy indeed she looked. There was no sign of her being older; she was as gravely, decently, demurely pretty as before. If she had struck me then as a thin-stemmed mild-hued flower of Puritanism① it may be imagined whether in her present situation this clear bloom was less appealing. Beside her an old gentleman was drinking absinthe②; behind her the dame de comptoir③ in the pink ribbons called "Alcibiade, Alcibiade!" to the long-aproned waiter④. I explained to Miss Spencer that the gentleman with me had lately been her shipmate, and my brother-in-law came up and was introduced to her. But she looked at him as if she had never so much as seen him, and I remembered he had told me her eyes were always fixed on the eastward horizon. She had evidently not noticed him, and, still timidly smiling, made no attempt whatever to pretend the contrary. I staid with her on the little terrace of the cafe while he went back to the hotel and to his wife. I remarked to my friend that this meeting of ours at the first hour of her landing partook, among all chances, of the miraculous, but that I was delighted to be there and receive her first impressions.

"Oh I can't tell you," she said — "I feel so much in a dream. I've been sitting here an hour and I don't want to move. Everything's so delicious and romantic. I don't know whether the coffee has gone to my head — it's *so* unlike the coffee of my dead past."

"Really," I made answer, "if you're so pleased with this poor prosaic⑤ Havre you'll have no admiration left

此时,斯潘塞小姐的严肃、端庄、美丽还没有被岁月侵蚀。

① a thin-stemmed mild-hued flower of Puritanism:一朵枝颈纤细、色彩柔和的清教主义之花。
② absinthe:苦艾酒。
③ dame de comptoir:(法语)柜台小姐。
④ long-aproned waiter:穿着长围裙的招待。
⑤ prosaic:平淡的。

317

for better things. Don't spend your appreciation all the first day — remember it's your intellectual letter of credit. Remember all the beautiful places and things that are waiting for you. Remember that lovely Italy we talked about."

"I'm not afraid of running short," she said gaily, still looking at the opposite houses. "I could sit here all day — just saying to myself that here I am at last. It's so dark and strange — so old and different."

眼中与想象中的欧洲差别之大,让她感慨良多。

"By the way then," I asked, "how come you to be encamped in this odd place? Haven't you gone to one of the inns?" For I was half-amused, half-alarmed at the good conscience with which this delicately pretty woman had stationed herself in conspicuous① isolation on the edge of the sidewalk.

"My cousin brought me here and — a little while ago — left me," she returned. "You know I told you I had a relation over here. He's still here — a real cousin. Well," she pursued with unclouded candour②, "he met me at the steamer this morning."

It was absurd — and the case moreover none of my business; but I felt somehow disconcerted. "It was hardly worth his while to meet you if he was to desert you so soon."

围绕钱的去向展开的对话,寥寥数笔,斯潘塞小姐的率真跃然纸上。

"Oh he has only left me for half an hour," said Caroline Spencer. "He has gone to get my money."

I continued to wonder. "Where *is* your money?"

She appeared seldom to laugh, but she laughed for the joy of this. "It makes me feel very fine to tell you! It's in circular notes③."

---

① conspicuous：明显的,显眼的。
② candour：正直,坦率。
③ circular note：［经］旅行支票。

"And where are your circular notes?"

"In my cousin's pocket."

This statement was uttered with such clearness of candour that — I can hardly say why — it gave me a sensible chill. I couldn't at all at the moment have justified my lapse from ease, for I knew nothing of Miss Spencer's cousin. Since he stood in that relation to her — dear respectable little person — the presumption was in his favour. But I found myself wincing at the thought that half an hour after her landing her scanty funds should have passed into his hands. "Is he to travel with you?" I asked.

"Only as far as Paris. He's an art-student in Paris — I've always thought that so splendid. I wrote to him that I was coming, but I never expected him to come off to the ship. I supposed he'd only just meet me at the train in Paris. It's very kind of him. But he *is*," said Caroline Spencer, "very kind — and very bright."

I felt at once a strange eagerness to see this bright kind cousin who was an art-student. "He's gone to the banker's?" I enquired.

"Yes, to the banker's. He took me to an hotel — such a queer quaint cunning little place, with a court in the middle and a gallery all round, and a lovely landlady in such a beautifully fluted cap and such a perfectly fitting dress! After a while we came out to walk to the banker's, for I hadn't any French money. But I was very dizzy from the motion of the vessel and I thought I had better sit down. He found this place for me here — then he went off to the banker's himself. I'm to wait here till he comes back."

Her story was wholly lucid and my impression

perfectly wanton①, but it passed through my mind that the gentleman would never come back. I settled myself in a chair beside my friend and determined to await the event. She was lost in the vision and the imagination of everything near us and about us — she observed, she recognised and admired, with a touching intensity. She noticed everything that was brought before us by the movement of the street — the peculiarities of costume, the shapes of vehicles, the big Norman horses, the fat priests, the shaven poodles②. We talked of these things, and there was something charming in her freshness of perception and the way her book-nourished fancy sallied forth for the revel.

"And when your cousin comes back what are you going to do?" I went on.

For this she had, a little oddly, to think. "We don't quite know."

"When do you go to Paris? If you go by the four o'clock train I may have the pleasure of making the journey with you."

"I don't think we shall do that." So far she was prepared. "My cousin thinks I had better stay here a few days."

"Oh!" said I — and for five minutes had nothing to add. I was wondering what our absentee was, in vulgar parlance, "up to."③ I looked up and down the street, but saw nothing that looked like a bright and kind American art-student. At last I took the liberty of observing that the Havre was hardly a place to choose as one of the aesthetic stations of a European tour. It was a place of convenience,

"我"在此处总结道,斯潘塞小姐那被书本培养的幻想得以实现,这让她对一切新鲜事物都倍感好奇。

---

① wanton：荒唐的。
② the shaven poodle：修剪过毛发的狮子狗。
③ in vulgar parlance, "up to."：说句粗鲁的话,"搞什么鬼"。

nothing more; a place of transit, through which transit should be rapid. I recommended her to go to Paris by the afternoon train and meanwhile to amuse herself by driving to the ancient fortress at the mouth of the harbour — that remarkable circular structure which bore the name of Francis the First and figured a sort of small Castle of Saint Angelo①. (I might really have foreknown that it was to be demolished②.)

She listened with much interest — then for a moment looked grave. "My cousin told me that when he returned he should have something particular to say to me, and that we could do nothing or decide nothing till I should have heard it. But I'll make him tell me right off, and then we'll go to the ancient fortress. Francis the First, did you say? Why, that's lovely. There's no hurry to get to Paris; there's plenty of time."

她此时言必称"my cousin",明显已经被他哄骗得晕头转向。

She smiled with her softly severe little lips as she spoke those last words, yet, looking at her with a purpose, I made out in her eyes, I thought, a tiny gleam of apprehension. "Don't tell me," I said, "that this wretched man's going to give you bad news!"

She coloured as if convicted of a hidden perversity, but she was soaring too high to drop③. "Well, I guess it's a *little* bad, but I don't believe it's *very* bad. At any rate④ I must listen to it."

I usurped an unscrupulous⑤ authority. "Look here; you didn't come to Europe to listen — you came to *see*!" But now I was sure her cousin would come back; since he

---

① Castle of Saint Angelo: (拉丁语)圣天使古堡,位于罗马西北角梵蒂冈城对面的一座堡垒建筑。

② demolish: 拆毁,推倒。

③ She coloured as if convicted of a hidden perversity, but she was soaring too high to drop. 她脸上泛起红晕,好像心里藏着什么不可告人的事情,不过又觉得她已经振翅高飞,不会跌落下来。

④ at any rate: 无论如何,至少。

⑤ unscrupulous: 肆无忌惮的。

had something disagreeable to say to her he'd infallibly①
turn up. We sat a while longer and I asked her about her
plans of travel. She had them on her fingers' ends and told
over the names as solemnly as a daughter of another faith
might have told over the beads of a rosary②: from Paris to
Dijon③ and to Avignon④, from Avignon to Marseilles⑤
and the Cornice road; thence to Genoa⑥, to Spezia⑦, to
Pisa⑧, to Florence, to Rome. It apparently had never
occurred to her that there could be the least incommodity
in her travelling alone; and since she was unprovided with
a companion I of course civilly abstained from disturbing
her sense of security.

At last her cousin came back. I saw him turn toward
us out of a side-street, and from the moment my eyes
rested on him I knew he could but be the bright, if not the
kind, American art-student. He wore a slouch⑨ hat and a
rusty black velvet jacket, such as I had often encountered
in the Rue Bonaparte⑩. His shirt-collar displayed a
stretch of throat that at a distance wasn't strikingly
statuesque. He was tall and lean, he had red hair and
freckles. These items I had time to take in while he
approached the cafe, staring at me with natural surprise
from under his romantic brim. When he came up to us I
immediately introduced myself as an old acquaintance of
Miss Spencer's, a character she serenely permitted me to

① infallibly：绝对无误地。
② rosary：念珠。
③ Dijon：第戎，法国东部城市。
④ Avignon：亚维农，法国城市。
⑤ Marseilles：马赛，法国城市。
⑥ Genoa：热那亚，意大利城市。
⑦ Spezia：斯培西亚，意大利西北部港市。
⑧ Pisa：比萨，意大利城市。
⑨ slouch：帽檐耷拉着的。
⑩ Rue Bonaparte：拿破仑街。

claim. He looked at me hard with a pair of small sharp eyes, then he gave me a solemn wave, in the "European" fashion, of his rather rusty sombrero①.

"You weren't on the ship?" he asked.

"No, I wasn't on the ship. I've been in Europe these several years."

He bowed once more, portentously②, and motioned me to be seated again. I sat down, but only for the purpose of observing him an instant — I saw it was time I should return to my sister. Miss Spencer's European protector was, by my measure, a very queer quantity. Nature hadn't shaped him for a Raphaelesque or Byronic attire③, and his velvet doublet and exhibited though not columnar throat weren't in harmony with his facial attributes. His hair was cropped close to his head; his ears were large and ill-adjusted to the same. He had a lackadaisical④ carriage and a sentimental droop which were peculiarly at variance with his keen conscious strange-coloured eyes — of a brown that was almost red. Perhaps I was prejudiced, but I thought his eyes too shifty. He said nothing for some time; he leaned his hands on his stick and looked up and down the street. Then at last, slowly lifting the stick and pointing with it, "That's a very nice bit," he dropped with a certain flatness. He had his head to one side — he narrowed his ugly lids. I followed the direction of his stick; the object it indicated was a red cloth hung out of an old window. "Nice bit of colour," he continued; and without moving his head transferred his half-closed gaze to me. "Compose well.

对斯潘塞小姐堂兄的描写,使读者对他长相不善、装腔作势的特征一目了然。

---

① sombrero：墨西哥阔边帽。
② portentously：严肃地。
③ Raphaelesque or Byronic attire：拉斐尔或者拜伦的服饰。
④ lackadaisical：无精打采的。

Fine old tone. Make a nice thing." He spoke in a charmless vulgar voice.

"I see you've a great deal of eye," I replied. "Your cousin tells me you're studying art." He looked at me in the same way, without answering, and I went on with deliberate urbanity: "I suppose you're at the studio of one of those great men." Still on this he continued to fix me, and then he named one of the greatest of that day; which led me to ask him if he liked his master.

"Do you understand French?" he returned.

"Some kinds."

He kept his little eyes on me; with which he remarked: "Je suis fou de la peinture!"①

"Oh I understand that kind!" I replied. Our companion laid her hand on his arm with a small pleased and fluttered movement; it was delightful to be among people who were on such easy terms with foreign tongues. I got up to take leave and asked her where, in Paris, I might have the honour of waiting on her. To what hotel would she go?

She turned to her cousin enquiringly and he favoured me again with his little languid leer②. "Do you know the Hotel des Princes?"

"I know where it is."

"Well, that's the shop."

"I congratulate you," I said to Miss Spencer. "I believe it's the best inn in the world; but, in case I should still have a moment to call on you here, where are you lodged?"

"Oh it's such a pretty name," she returned gleefully.

---

① Je suis fou de la peinture!: (法语) 我超喜欢绘画。
② leer: 斜眼看。

"A la Belle Normande."①

"I guess I know my way round!" her kinsman② threw in; and as I left them he gave me with his swaggering head-cover a great flourish that was like the wave of a banner over a conquered field.

III

My relative, as it proved, was not sufficiently restored to leave the place by the afternoon train; so that as the autumn dusk began to fall I found myself at liberty to call at the establishment named to me by my friends. I must confess that I had spent much of the interval in wondering what the disagreeable thing was that the less attractive of these had been telling the other. The auberge③ of the Belle Normande proved an hostelry in a shady by-street, where it gave me satisfaction to think Miss Spencer must have encountered local colour in abundance. There was a crooked little court, where much of the hospitality of the house was carried on; there was a staircase climbing to bedrooms on the outer side of the wall; there was a small trickling fountain with a stucco statuette④ set in the midst of it; there was a little boy in a white cap and apron cleaning copper vessels at a conspicuous kitchen door; there was a chattering landlady, neatly laced, arranging apricots⑤ and grapes into an artistic pyramid upon a pink plate. I looked about, and on a green bench outside of an open door labelled Salle-a-Manger, I distinguished Caroline Spencer. No sooner had I looked at her than I was sure something had

此处，她堂兄向"我"道别时，挥舞破帽子的场景读来滑稽可笑。

原来，斯潘塞小姐居住的旅馆只是个简陋的小客栈。

---

① A la Belle Normande：(法语)在美丽的诺曼底。
② kinsman：男亲戚。
③ auberge：(法语)小旅馆。
④ stucco statuette：灰泥小雕像。
⑤ apricot：杏子。

happened since the morning. Supported by the back of her bench, with her hands clasped in her lap, she kept her eyes on the other side of the court where the landlady manipulated the apricots.

But I saw that, poor dear, she wasn't thinking of apricots or even of landladies. She was staring absently, thoughtfully; on a nearer view I could have certified she had been crying. I had seated myself beside her before she was aware; then, when she had done so, she simply turned round without surprise and showed me her sad face. Something very bad indeed had happened; she was completely changed, and I immediately charged her with it. "Your cousin has been giving you bad news. You've had a horrid time."

For a moment she said nothing, and I supposed her afraid to speak lest her tears should again rise. Then it came to me that even in the few hours since my leaving her she had shed them all — which made her now intensely, stoically① composed. "My poor cousin has been having one," she replied at last. "He has had great worries. His news was bad." Then after a dismally conscious wait: "He was in dreadful want of money."

"In want of yours, you mean?"

"Of any he could get — honourably of course. Mine *is* all — well, that's available."

Ah it was as if I had been sure from the first! "And he has taken it from you?"

Again she hung fire, but her face meanwhile was pleading. "I gave him what I had."

I recall the accent of those words as the most angelic human sound I had ever listened to — which is exactly

原来，她伤心、痛苦的模样，却是为了那个骗子堂兄而难过。

"我"是最清醒的旁观者，早已预料到她会接二连三地上当受骗。

① stoically：坚忍地。

why I jumped up almost with a sense of personal outrage①. "Gracious goodness, madam, do you call that his getting it 'honourably'?"

I had gone too far — she coloured to her eyes. "We won't speak of it."

"We *must* speak of it," I declared as I dropped beside her again. "I'm your friend — upon my word I'm your protector; it seems to me you need one. What's the matter with this extraordinary person?"

She was perfectly able to say. "He's just badly in debt."

"No doubt he is! But what's the special propriety of your — in such tearing haste! — paying for that?"

"Well, he has told me all his story. I *feel* for him so much."

"So do I, if you come to that! But I hope," I roundly added, "he'll give you straight back your money."

As to this she was prompt. "Certainly he will — as soon as ever he can."

"And when the deuce will that be?②"

Her lucidity③ maintained itself. "When he has finished his great picture."

It took me full in the face. "My dear young lady, damn his great picture! Where is this voracious④ man?"

It was as if she must let me feel a moment that I did push her! — though indeed, as appeared, he was just where he'd naturally be. "He's having his dinner."

I turned about and looked through the open door into

斯潘塞小姐的遭遇让"我"愤怒,决心要帮她讨回公道。

---

① outrage:义愤,愤慨。
② And when the deuce will that be? 那到底是什么时候?
③ lucidity:清醒的神志。
④ voracious:贪婪的。

此处，"我"对这位堂兄的轻蔑、不屑之情不言自明。

the salle-a-manger①. There, sure enough, alone at the end of a long table, was the object of my friend's compassion — the bright, the kind young art-student. He was dining too attentively to notice me at first, but in the act of setting down a well-emptied wine-glass he caught sight of my air of observation. He paused in his repast and, with his head on one side and his meagre② jaws slowly moving, fixedly returned my gaze. Then the landlady came brushing lightly by with her pyramid of apricots.

"And that nice little plate of fruit is for him?" I wailed.

斯潘塞小姐对堂兄的忠诚丝毫不减。在这样的场景中，"我"的恼怒和不安令人感同身受。

Miss Spencer glanced at it tenderly. "They seem to arrange everything so nicely!" she simply sighed.

I felt helpless and irritated. "Come now, really," I said; "do you think it right, do you think it decent, that that long strong fellow should collar your funds?" She looked away from me — I was evidently giving her pain. The case was hopeless; the long strong fellow had "interested" her.

"Pardon me if I speak of him so unceremoniously③," I said. "But you're really too generous, and he hasn't, clearly, the rudiments of delicacy④. He made his debts himself — he ought to pay them himself."

"He has been foolish," she obstinately said — "of course I know that. He has told me everything. We had a long talk this morning — the poor fellow threw himself on my charity. He has signed notes to a large amount."

"The more fool he!"

---

① salle-a-manger：餐厅。
② meagre：瘦的。
③ unceremoniously：随便地，不礼貌地。
④ the rudiments of delicacy：基本的体谅。

"He's in real distress① — and it's not only himself. It's his poor young wife."

"Ah he has a poor young wife?"

"I didn't know — but he made a clean breast of② it. He married two years since — secretly."

"Why secretly?"

My informant③ took precautions④ as if she feared listeners. Then with low impressiveness: "She was a Countess⑤!"

"Are you very sure of that?"

"She has written me the most beautiful letter."

"Asking you — whom she has never seen — for money?"

"Asking me for confidence and sympathy" — Miss Spencer spoke now with spirit. "She has been cruelly treated by her family — in consequence of what she has done for him. My cousin has told me every particular, and she appeals to me in her own lovely way in the letter, which I've here in my pocket. It's such a wonderful old-world romance," said my prodigious⑥ friend. "She was a beautiful young widow — her first husband was a Count, tremendously high-born, but really most wicked, with whom she hadn't been happy and whose death had left her ruined after he had deceived her in all sorts of ways. My poor cousin, meeting her in that situation and perhaps a little too recklessly pitying her and charmed with her, found her, don't you see?" — Caroline's appeal on this head was amazing! — "but too ready to trust a better man

这个冒牌的伯爵夫人,是日后斯潘塞小姐的另一个沉重的包袱。

仅凭漂亮的字迹,她便轻信于人,这种单纯、善良的品格令她再度受骗。

---

① distress: 忧虑,不幸。
② make a clean breast of: 坦白讲出来。
③ informant: 线人,情报者(此处指斯潘塞小姐)。
④ precaution: 带警惕之心。
⑤ Countess: 伯爵夫人。
⑥ prodigious: 惊人的。

after all she had been through. Only when her 'people,' as he says — and I do like the word! — understood she WOULD have him, poor gifted young American art-student though he simply was, because she just adored him, her great-aunt, the old Marquise, from whom she had expectations of wealth which she could yet sacrifice for her love, utterly cast her off and wouldn't so much as speak to her, much less to *him*, in their dreadful haughtiness and pride. They *can* be haughty over here, it seems," she ineffably① developed — "there's no mistake about that! It's like something in some famous old book. The family, my cousin's wife's," she by this time almost complacently② wound up, "are of the oldest Provencal noblesse."

I listened half-bewildered. The poor woman positively found it so interesting to be swindled③ by a flower of that stock — if stock or flower or solitary grain of truth was really concerned in the matter — as practically to have lost the sense of what the forfeiture④ of her hoard meant for her. "My dear young lady," I groaned, "you don't want to be stripped of every dollar for such a rigmarole⑤!"

她的经历读来令人揪心,可她自己依旧一无所知。高明的写作技巧表现在这一强烈的对比之中。

She asserted, at this, her dignity — much as a small pink shorn lamb might have done. "It isn't a rigmarole, and I shan't be stripped. I shan't live any worse than I *have* lived, don't you see? And I'll come back before long to stay with them. The Countess — he still gives her, he says, her title, as they do to noble widows, that is, to

---

① ineffably：难以言喻地。
② complacently：自满地,满足地。
③ swindle：诈骗。
④ forfeiture：(财产、名誉等)丧失。
⑤ rigmarole：连篇的鬼话。

'dowagers,'① don't you know? in England — insists on a visit from me SOME time. So I guess for *that* I can start afresh — and meanwhile I'll have recovered my money."

It was all too heart-breaking. "You're going home then at once?"

I felt the faint tremor of voice she heroically tried to stifle. "I've nothing left for a tour."

"You gave it *all* up?"

"I've kept enough to take me back."

I uttered, I think, a positive howl, and at this juncture the hero of the situation, the happy proprietor of my little friend's sacred savings and of the infatuated grande dame② just sketched for me, reappeared with the clear consciousness of a repast bravely earned and consistently enjoyed. He stood on the threshold an instant, extracting the stone from a plump apricot he had fondly retained; then he put the apricot into his mouth and, while he let it gratefully dissolve there, stood looking at us with his long legs apart and his hands thrust into the pockets of his velvet coat. My companion got up, giving him a thin glance that I caught in its passage and which expressed at once resignation and fascination — the last dregs③ of her sacrifice and with it an anguish of upliftedness. Ugly vulgar pretentious dishonest as I thought him, and destitute④ of every grace of plausibility⑤, he had yet appealed successfully to her eager and tender imagination. I was deeply disgusted, but I had no warrant to interfere, and at any rate felt that it

---

① dowager：伯爵未亡人。
② grande dame：迷人的夫人。
③ dregs：残渣。
④ destitute：赤贫的，缺乏的。
⑤ plausibility：似乎有道理。

would be vain. He waved his hand meanwhile with a breadth of appreciation. "Nice old court. Nice mellow old place. Nice crooked old staircase. Several pretty things."

Decidedly I couldn't stand it, and without responding I gave my hand to my friend. She looked at me an instant with her little white face and rounded eyes, and as she showed her pretty teeth I suppose she meant to smile. "Don't be sorry for me," she sublimely[1] pleaded; "I'm very sure I shall see something of this dear old Europe yet."

I refused however to take literal leave of her — I should find a moment to come back next morning. Her awful kinsman, who had put on his sombrero again, flourished it off at me by way of a bow — on which I hurried away.

On the morrow early I did return, and in the court of the inn met the landlady, more loosely laced than in the evening. On my asking for Miss Spencer, "Partie[2], monsieur[3]," the good woman said. "She went away last night at ten o'clock, with her — her — not her husband, eh? — in fine her Monsieur. They went down to the American ship." I turned off — I felt the tears in my eyes. The poor girl had been some thirteen hours in Europe.

IV

I myself, more fortunate, continued to sacrifice to opportunity as I myself met it. During this period — of some five years — I lost my friend Latouche, who died of a malarious[4] fever during a tour in the Levant. One of the

她堂兄又一次拿起破帽子和"我"道别，这副伪君子的嘴脸让"我"不想多看。

这可怜的姑娘在她朝思暮想的欧洲只呆了匆匆 13 个小时，"我"的同情与泪水委婉且令人动容。

---

① sublimely：高尚地。
② Partie：(法语)走了，离开了。
③ monsieur：(法语)先生。
④ malarious：疟疾。

first things I did on my return to America was to go up to North Verona on a consolatory① visit to his poor mother. I found her in deep affliction and sat with her the whole of the morning that followed my arrival — I had come in late at night — listening to her tearful descant② and singing the praises of my friend. We talked of nothing else, and our conversation ended only with the arrival of a quick little woman who drove herself up to the door in a "carry-all" and whom I saw toss the reins to the horse's back with the briskness of a startled sleeper throwing off the bedclothes③. She jumped out of the carry-all and she jumped into the room. She proved to be the minister's wife and the great town-gossip, and she had evidently, in the latter capacity, a choice morsel to communicate. I was as sure of this as I was that poor Mrs. Latouche was not absolutely too bereaved to listen to her. It seemed to me discreet to retire, and I described myself as anxious for a walk before dinner.

"And by the way," I added, "if you'll tell me where my old friend Miss Spencer lives I think I'll call on her."

The minister's wife immediately responded. Miss Spencer lived in the fourth house beyond the Baptist church; the Baptist church was the one on the right, with that queer green thing over the door; they called it a portico④, but it looked more like an old-fashioned bedstead⑤ swung in the air. "Yes, do look up poor Caroline," Mrs. Latouche further enjoined. "It will refresh her to see a strange face."

---

① consolatory：安慰的，慰藉的。
② descant：详述。
③ toss the reins to the horse's back with the briskness of a startled sleeper throwing off the bedclothes：把缰绳甩到马背上，就像被惊起的睡眠者把床单甩开那样利落。
④ portico：有圆柱的门廊。
⑤ bedstead：床架。

"I should think she had had enough of strange faces!" cried the minister's wife.

"To see，I mean，a charming visitor" — Mrs. Latouche amended her phrase.

"I should think she had had enough of charming visitors!" her companion returned. "But *you* don't mean to stay ten years," she added with significant eyes on me.

"Has she a visitor of that sort?" I asked in my ignorance.

"You'll make out the sort!" said the minister's wife. "She's easily seen；she generally sits in the front yard. Only take care what you say to her，and be very sure you're polite."

"Ah she's so sensitive?"

The minister's wife jumped up and dropped me a curtsey — a most sarcastic① curtsey②. "That's what she is，if you please. 'Madame la Comtesse！③'"

And pronouncing these titular④ words with the most scathing accent，the little woman seemed fairly to laugh in the face of the lady they designated. I stood staring，wondering，remembering.

"Oh I shall be very polite!" I cried；and，grasping my hat and stick，I went on my way.

I found Miss Spencer's residence without difficulty. The Baptist church was easily identified，and the small dwelling near it，of a rusty white，with a large central chimney-stack and a Virginia creeper，seemed naturally and properly the abode of a withdrawn old maid with a taste for striking effects inexpensively obtained. As I

字字推敲、句句斟酌的语言，简洁而明了地交代了斯潘塞小姐在美国住所的情形。

---

① sarcastic：嘲笑的，挖苦的。
② curtsey：(妇女行的)屈膝礼。
③ Madame la Comtesse：(法语)伯爵夫人。
④ titular：头衔的。

approached I slackened① my pace, for I had heard that some one was always sitting in the front yard, and I wished to reconnoitre②. I looked cautiously over the low white fence that separated the small garden-space from the unpaved street, but I descried nothing in the shape of a Comtesse. A small straight path led up to the crooked door-step, on either side of which was a little grass-plot fringed with currant-bushes. In the middle of the grass, right and left, was a large quince-tree, full of antiquity and contortions, and beneath one of the quince-trees were placed a small table and a couple of light chairs. On the table lay a piece of unfinished embroidery③ and two or three books in bright-coloured paper covers. I went in at the gate and paused halfway along the path, scanning the place for some further token of its occupant, before whom — I could hardly have said why — I hesitated abruptly to present myself. Then I saw the poor little house to be of the shabbiest and felt a sudden doubt of my right to penetrate, since curiosity had been my motive and curiosity here failed of confidence. While I demurred a figure appeared in the open doorway and stood there looking at me. I immediately recognised Miss Spencer, but she faced me as if we had never met. Gently, but gravely and timidly, I advanced to the door-step, where I spoke with an attempt at friendly banter.

"I waited for you over there to come back, but you never came."

"Waited where, sir?" she quavered, her innocent eyes rounding themselves as of old. She was much older; she looked tired and wasted.

岁月的侵蚀，让她看起来疲倦而衰老。给这个角色的悲剧色彩又新添了一笔。

---

① slacken：放缓。
② reconnoitre：侦查，探看。
③ embroidery：刺绣。

"Well," I said, "I waited at the old French port."

She stared harder, then recognised me, smiling, flushing, clasping her two hands together. "I remember you now — I remember that day." But she stood there, neither coming out nor asking me to come in. She was embarrassed.

I too felt a little awkward while I poked at the path with my stick. "I kept looking out for you year after year."

"You mean in Europe?" she ruefully[①] breathed.

"In Europe of course! Here apparently you're easy enough to find."

She leaned her hand against the unpainted door-post and her head fell a little to one side. She looked at me thus without speaking, and I caught the expression visible in women's eyes when tears are rising. Suddenly she stepped out on the cracked slab of stone before her threshold and closed the door. Then her strained smile prevailed and I saw her teeth were as pretty as ever. But there had been tears too. "Have you been there ever since?" she lowered her voice to ask.

"Until three weeks ago. And you — you never came back?"

Still shining at me as she could, she put her hand behind her and reopened the door. "I'm not very polite," she said. "Won't you come in?"

"I'm afraid I incommode[②] you."

"Oh no!" — she wouldn't hear of it now. And she pushed back the door with a sign that I should enter.

I followed her in. She led the way to a small room on

此次重逢,不免物是人非。大段的描写中,有结构复杂的长句,有文雅雕琢的用语,更有细腻深邃的心理描写,引领着人们更好地理解场景,进入角色。

---

① ruefully:悲伤地。
② incommode:打扰。

the left of the narrow hall, which I supposed to be her parlour, though it was at the back of the house, and we passed the closed door of another apartment which apparently enjoyed a view of the quince-trees. This one looked out upon a small wood-shed and two clucking① hens. But I thought it pretty until I saw its elegance to be of the most frugal kind②; after which, presently, I thought it prettier still, for I had never seen faded chintz③ and old mezzotint engravings④, framed in varnished autumn leaves, disposed with so touching a grace. Miss Spencer sat down on a very small section of the sofa, her hands tightly clasped in her lap. She looked ten years older, and I needn't now have felt called to insist on the facts of her person. But I still thought them interesting, and at any rate I was moved by them. She was peculiarly agitated. I tried to appear not to notice it; but suddenly, in the most inconsequent fashion — it was an irresistible echo of our concentrated passage in the old French port — I said to her: "I do incommode you. Again you're in distress."

She raised her two hands to her face and for a moment kept it buried in them. Then taking them away, "It's because you remind me," she said.

"I remind you, you mean, of that miserable day at the Havre?"

She wonderfully shook her head. "It wasn't miserable. It was delightful."

Ah was it? my manner of receiving this must have commented. "I never was so shocked as when, on going

---

① clucking: 咯咯叫。
② its elegance to be of the most frugal kind: 简朴的优雅。
③ faded chintz: 褪色的印花棉布。
④ old mezzotint engravings: 旧铜板版画。

back to your inn the next morning, I found you had wretchedly retreated."

She waited an instant, after which she said: "Please let us not speak of that."

"Did you come straight back here?" I nevertheless went on.

"I was back here just thirty days after my first start."

"And here you've remained ever since?"

"Every minute of the time."

I took it in; I didn't know what to say, and what I presently said had almost the sound of mockery①. "When then are you going to make that tour?" It might be practically aggressive; but there was something that irritated me in her depths of resignation②, and I wished to extort from her some expression of impatience.

动作描写为最后的坚定表态做铺垫，张弛有度的节奏有深刻的美学内涵。

She attached her eyes a moment to a small sunspot on the carpet; then she got up and lowered the window-blind a little to obliterate③ it. I waited, watching her with interest — as if she had still something more to give me. Well, presently, in answer to my last question, she gave it. "Never!"

"I hope at least your cousin repaid you that money," I said.

她那施惠于人的善良美德依旧不减当年风采。

At this again she looked away from me. "I don't care for it now."

"You don't care for your money?"

"For ever going to Europe."

"Do you mean you wouldn't go if you could?"

"I can't — I can't," said Caroline Spencer. "It's all over. Everything's different. I never think of it."

---

① mockery：嘲笑。
② resignation：顺从。
③ obliterate：抹去，遮住。

"The scoundrel① never repaid you then!" I cried.

"Please, please —!" she began.

But she had stopped — she was looking toward the door. There had been a rustle and a sound of steps in the hall.

I also looked toward the door, which was open and now admitted another person — a lady who paused just within the threshold. Behind her came a young man. The lady looked at me with a good deal of fixedness — long enough for me to rise to a vivid impression of herself. Then she turned to Caroline Spencer and, with a smile and a strong foreign accent, "Pardon, ma chere!② I didn't know you had company," she said. "The gentleman came in so quietly." With which she again gave me the benefit of her attention. She was very strange, yet I was at once sure I had seen her before. Afterwards I rather put it that I had only seen ladies remarkably like her. But I had seen them very far away from North Verona, and it was the oddest of all things to meet one of them in that frame. To what quite other scene did the sight of her transport me? To some dusky landing before a shabby Parisian quatrieme — to an open door revealing a greasy ante-chamber and to Madame leaning over the banisters③ while she holds a faded wrapper together and bawls down to the portress to bring up her coffee. My friend's guest was a very large lady, of middle age, with a plump dead-white face and hair drawn back a la chinoise④. She had a small penetrating eye and what is called in French le sourire

① scoundrel：无赖。
② Pardon，ma chere！：（法语）对不起，亲爱的！
③ banister：栏杆。
④ a la chinoise：（法语）中式的。

agreable①. She wore an old pink cashmere dressing-gown covered with white embroideries, and, like the figure in my momentary vision, she confined it in front with a bare and rounded arm and a plump and deeply-dimpled hand.

"It's only to spick about my cafe," she said to her hostess with her sourire agreable. "I should like it served in the garden under the leetle tree."

The young man behind her had now stepped into the room, where he also stood revealed, though with rather less of a challenge. He was a gentleman of few inches but a vague importance, perhaps the leading man of the world of North Verona. He had a small pointed nose and a small pointed chin; also, as I observed, the most diminutive feet② and a manner of no point at all. He looked at me foolishly and with his mouth open.

"You shall have your coffee," said Miss Spencer as if an army of cooks had been engaged in the preparation of it.

"C'est bien!③" said her massive inmate. "Find your bouk" — and this personage turned to the gaping youth.

He gaped now at each quarter of the room. "My grammar, d'ye mean?"④

The large lady however could but face her friend's visitor while persistently engaged with a certain laxity in the flow of her wrapper. "Find your bouk⑤," she more absently repeated.

"My poetry, d'ye mean?" said the young man who also couldn't take his eyes off me.

---

① le sourire agreable: (法语)令人舒服的微笑。
② diminutive feet: 小脚。
③ C'est bien!: (法语)太好了!
④ My grammar, d'ye mean?: (法语)你是说我的语法吗?
⑤ bouk: 形容发音不准,应该是 book。

"Never mind your bouk" — his companion reconsidered. "To-day we'll just talk. We'll make some conversation. But we mustn't interrupt Mademoiselle's①. Come, come" — and she moved off a step. "Under the leetle tree," she added for the benefit of Mademoiselle. After which she gave me a thin salutation, jerked a measured "Monsieur!" and swept away again with her swain following.

I looked at Miss Spencer, whose eyes never moved from the carpet, and I spoke, I fear, without grace. "Who in the world's that?"

"The Comtesse — that WAS: my cousine as they call it in French."

"And who's the young man?"

"The Countess's pupil, Mr. Mixter." This description of the tie uniting the two persons who had just quitted us must certainly have upset my gravity; for I recall the marked increase of my friend's own as she continued to explain. "She gives lessons in French and music, the simpler sorts —"

"The simpler sorts of French?" I fear I broke in.

But she was still impenetrable②, and in fact had now an intonation that put me vulgarly in the wrong. "She has had the worst reverses — with no one to look to. She's prepared for any exertion — and she takes her misfortunes with gaiety③."

"Ah well," I returned — no doubt a little ruefully, "that's all I myself am pretending to do. If she's determined to be a burden to nobody, nothing could be more right and proper."

---

① Mademoiselle：(法语)小姐。
② impenetrable：不可理解的。
③ gaiety：欢乐，快乐。

拖上伯爵夫人这个沉重的负担,斯潘塞小姐任劳任怨地担当了女仆的角色。这样的安排看似不可理喻却又在情理之中。

My hostess looked vaguely, though I thought quite wearily enough, about: she met this proposition in no other way. "I must go and get the coffee," she simply said.

"Has the lady many pupils?" I none the less persisted.

"She has only Mr. Mixter. She gives him all her time." It might have set me off again, but something in my whole impression of my friend's sensibility urged me to keep strictly decent. "He pays very well," she at all events inscrutably① went on. "He's not very bright — as a pupil; but he's very rich and he's very kind. He has a buggy②— with a back, and he takes the Countess to drive."

"For good long spells I hope," I couldn't help interjecting③— even at the cost of her so taking it that she had still to avoid my eyes. "Well, the country's beautiful for miles," I went on. And then as she was turning away: "You're going for the Countess's coffee?"

"If you'll excuse me a few moments."

"Is there no one else to do it?"

She seemed to wonder who there should be. "I keep no servants."

"Then can't I help?" After which, as she but looked at me, I bettered it. "Can't she wait on herself?"

Miss Spencer had a slow headshake — as if that too had been a strange idea. "She isn't used to *manual* labour."

The discrimination was a treat, but I cultivated decorum. "I see — and you *are*." But at the same time I couldn't abjure curiosity. "Before you go, at any rate, please tell me this: who *is* this wonderful lady?"

---

① inscrutably：费解地,高深莫测地。
② buggy：轻型马车。
③ interject：插话。

"I told you just who in France — that extraordinary day. She's the wife of my cousin, whom you saw there."

"The lady disowned by her family in consequence of her marriage?"

"Yes; they've never seen her again. They've completely broken with her."

"And where's her husband?"

"My poor cousin's dead."

I pulled up①, but only a moment. "And where's your money?"

The poor thing flinched②— I kept her on the rack. "I don't know," she woefully③ said.

I scarce know what it didn't prompt me to — but I went step by step. "On her husband's death this lady at once came to you?"

在"我"层层追问下,斯潘塞小姐这几年来的不幸遭遇一件一件地浮出水面。

It was as if she had had too often to describe it. "Yes, she arrived one day."

"How long ago?"

"Two years and four months."

"And has been here ever since?"

"Ever since."

I took it all in. "And how does she like it?"

"Well, not *very* much," said Miss Spencer divinely.

That too I took in. "And how do *you* —?"

She laid her face in her two hands an instant as she had done ten minutes before. Then, quickly, she went to get the Countess's coffee.

她多次以双手捂面的动作,昭示着一种难以忍受而又不得不忍的心境。

Left alone in the little parlour④ I found myself divided between the perfection of my disgust and a

---

① pull up：停了下来。
② flinch：退缩。
③ woefully：悲伤地。
④ parlour：客厅。

contrary wish to see, to learn more. At the end of a few minutes the young man in attendance on the lady in question reappeared as for a fresh gape at me. He was inordinately grave — to be dressed in such parti-coloured flannels; and he produced with no great confidence on his own side the message with which he had been charged. "She wants to know if you won't come right out."

为下文"我"识破假伯爵夫人的嘴脸埋下了伏笔。

"Who wants to know?"

"The Countess. That French lady."

"She has asked you to bring me?"

"Yes sir," said the young man feebly — for I may claim to have surpassed him in stature and weight.

I went out with him, and we found his instructress seated under one of the small quince-trees in front of the house; where she was engaged in drawing a fine needle with a very fat hand through a piece of embroidery not remarkable for freshness. She pointed graciously to the chair beside her and I sat down. Mr. Mixter glanced about him and then accommodated himself on the grass at her feet; whence① he gazed upward more gapingly than ever and as if convinced that between us something wonderful would now occur.

"I'm sure you spick② French," said the Countess, whose eyes were singularly protuberant③ as she played over me her agreeable smile.

"I do, madam — tant bien que mal,"④ I replied, I fear, more dryly.

"Ah voila!"⑤ she cried as with delight. "I knew it as

---

① whence：从何处，从哪里。
② spick：讽刺发音不准确，应该为 speak。
③ protuberant：突出的，隆起的。
④ tant bien que mal：(法语)马马虎虎。
⑤ Voila!：(法语)那就是了!

soon as I looked at you. You've been in my poor dear country."

"A considerable time."

"You love it then, mon pays de France①?"

"Oh it's an old affection." But I wasn't exuberant.

"And you know Paris well?"

"Yes, sans me vanter②, madam, I think I really do." And with a certain conscious purpose I let my eyes meet her own.

She presently, hereupon, moved her own and glanced down at Mr. Mixter. "What are we talking about?" she demanded of her attentive pupil.

He pulled his knees up, plucked at the grass, stared, blushed a little. "You're talking French," said Mr. Mixter.

"La belle decouverte!③" mocked the Countess. "It's going on ten months," she explained to me, "since I took him in hand. Don't put yourself out not to say he's la betise meme④," she added in fine style. "He won't in the least understand you."

A moment's consideration of Mr. Mixter, awkwardly sporting at our feet, quite assured me that he wouldn't. "I hope your other pupils do you more honour," I then remarked to my entertainer.

"I have no others. They don't know what French — or what anything else — is in this place; they don't want to know. You may therefore imagine the pleasure it is to me to meet a person who speaks it like yourself." I could but reply that my own pleasure wasn't less, and she

---

① mon pays de France：(法语)我的祖国—法国。
② sans me vanter：(法语)不是我吹牛。
③ La belle decouverte!：(法语)多伟大的发现!
④ la betise meme：(法语)愚蠢本身。

continued to draw the stitches① through her embroidery with an elegant curl of her little finger. Every few moments she put her eyes, near-sightedly, closer to her work — this as if for elegance too. She inspired me with no more confidence than her late husband, if husband he was, had done, years before, on the occasion with which this one so detestably matched: she was coarse, common, affected, dishonest — no more a Countess than I was a Caliph②. She had an assurance — based clearly on experience; but this couldn't have been the experience of "race." Whatever it was indeed it did now, in a yearning fashion, flare out of her. "Talk to me of Paris, mon beau Paris③ that I'd give my eyes to see. The very name of it me fait languir④. How long since you were there?"

"A couple of months ago."

"Vous avez de la chance!⑤ Tell me something about it. What were they doing? Oh for an hour of the Boulevard!"

"They were doing about what they're always doing — amusing themselves a good deal."

"At the theatres, hein?⑥" sighed the Countess.

"At the cafes-concerts? sous ce beau ciel⑦— at the little tables before the doors? Quelle existence!⑧ You know I'm a Parisienne⑨, monsieur," she added, "to my finger-tips."

"Miss Spencer was mistaken then," I ventured to

作者的贬讽之意在此不言而喻。

伯爵夫人的做作矫情、虚伪殷勤和"我"的漫不经心、草草应付形成了鲜明对比。

---

① stitches：缝线。
② Caliph：回主教。
③ mon beau Paris：(法语)美丽的巴黎。
④ me fait languir：(法语)使我憔悴。
⑤ Vous avez de la chance：(法语)你真幸运。
⑥ hein：(法语)怎么样?
⑦ sous ce beau ciel：(法语)在这蓝色的天空下。
⑧ Quelle existence!：(法语)多美丽的地方啊!
⑨ Parisienne：(法语)巴黎人。

return, "in telling me you're a Provencale①. "

She stared a moment, then put her nose to her embroidery, which struck me as having acquired even while we sat a dingier and more desultory air. "Ah I'm a Provencale by birth, but a Parisienne by — inclination②. " After which she pursued: "And by the saddest events of my life — as well as by some of the happiest, helas!③"

"In other words by a varied experience!" I now at last smiled.

She questioned me over it with her hard little salient eyes. "Oh experience! — I could talk of that, no doubt, if I wished. On en a de toutes les sortes④— and I never dreamed that mine, for example, would ever have THIS in store for me. " And she indicated with her large bare elbow and with a jerk of her head all surrounding objects: the little white house, the pair of quince-trees, the rickety paling⑤, even the rapt⑥ Mr. Mixter.

I took them all bravely in. "Ah if you mean you're decidedly in exile —!"

"You may imagine what it is. These two years of my epreuve — elles m'en ont donnees, des heures, des heures!⑦ One gets used to things" — and she raised her shoulders to the highest shrug ever accomplished at North Verona; "so that I sometimes think I've got used to this. But there are some things that are always beginning again. For example my coffee."

I so far again lent myself. "Do you always have

---

① Provencale: 普罗旺斯人。
② inclination: 爱好。
③ helas: (法语)感叹词,表遗憾。
④ On en a de toutes les sortes: (法语)人们各有各的命运。
⑤ rickety paling: 摇摇晃晃的篱笆。
⑥ rapt: 全神贯注的。
⑦ elles m'en ont donnees, des heures, des heures: (法语)这是多么漫长的时间呀!

coffee at this hour?"

Her eyebrows went up as high as her shoulders had done. "At what hour would you propose to me to have it? I must have my little cup after breakfast."

"Ah you breakfast at this hour?"

"At mid-day — comme cela se fait①. Here they breakfast at a quarter past seven. That 'quarter past' is charming!"

"But you were telling me about your coffee," I observed sympathetically.

"My cousine can't believe in it; she can't understand it. "C'est une fille charmante②, but that little cup of black coffee with a drop of 'fine③,' served at this hour — they exceed her comprehension. So I have to break the ice each day, and it takes the coffee the time you see to arrive. And when it does arrive, monsieur —! If I don't press it on *you* — though monsieur here sometimes joins me! — it's because you've drunk it on the Boulevard."

I resented extremely so critical a view of my poor friend's exertions, but I said nothing at all — the only way to be sure of my civility. I dropped my eyes on Mr. Mixter, who, sitting cross-legged and nursing his knees, watched my companion's foreign graces with an interest that familiarity had apparently done little to restrict. She became aware, naturally, of my mystified view of him and faced the question with all her boldness. "He adores me, you know," she murmured with her nose again in her tapestry — "he dreams of becoming mon amoureux④.

简单的一个反问，点出了伯爵夫人好吃懒做、拖累他人的丑陋嘴脸。

---

① comme cela se fait：(法语)像人们做的那样。
② C'est une fille charmante：(法语)她是个迷人的姑娘。
③ fine：白兰地。
④ mon amoureux：(法语)他梦想成为我的情人。

Yes，il me fait une cour acharnee①— such as you see him. That's what we've come to. He has read some French novel — it took him six months. But ever since that he has thought himself a hero and me — such as I am，monsieur — je ne sais quelle devergondee!②"

Mr. Mixter may have inferred that he was to that extent the object of our reference；but of the manner in which he was handled he must have had small suspicion — preoccupied as he was，as to my companion，with the ecstasy of contemplation③. Our hostess moreover at this moment came out of the house，bearing a coffee-pot and three cups on a neat little tray. I took from her eyes，as she approached us，a brief but intense appeal — the mute expression，as I felt，conveyed in the hardest little look she had yet addressed me，of her longing to know what，as a man of the world in general and of the French world in particular，I thought of these allied forces now so encamped on the stricken field of her life. I could only "act" however，as they said at North Verona，quite impenetrably — only make no answering sign. I couldn't intimate，much less could I frankly utter，my inward sense of the Countess's probable past，with its measure of her virtue，value and accomplishments，and of the limits of the consideration to which she could properly pretend. I couldn't give my friend a hint of how I myself personally "saw" her interesting pensioner — whether as the runaway wife of a too-jealous hair-dresser or of a too-morose pastry-cook，say；whether as a very small bourgeoise，in

这一连串的诙谐妙语，读来令人忍俊不禁。

---

① il me fait une cour acharnee：（法语）他疯狂地追求我。
② je ne sais quelle devergondee：（法语）我不知道把我当成多么无耻的女人。
③ contemplation：沉思，思考。

fine①, who had vitiated② her case beyond patching up, or even as some character, of the nomadic sort, less edifying still. I couldn't let in, by the jog of a shutter, as it were, a hard informing ray and then, washing my hands of the business, turn my back for ever. I could on the contrary but save the situation, my own at least, for the moment, by pulling myself together with a master hand and appearing to ignore everything but that the dreadful person between us *was* a "grande dame." This effort was possible indeed but as a retreat in good order and with all the forms of courtesy. If I couldn't speak, still less could I stay, and I think I must, in spite of everything, have turned black with disgust to see Caroline Spencer stand there like a waiting-maid. I therefore won't answer for the shade of success that may have attended my saying to the Countess, on my feet and as to leave her: "You expect to remain some time in these parages③?"

What passed between us, as from face to face, while she looked up at me, *that* at least our companion may have caught, that at least may have sown, for the after-time, some seed of revelation. The Countess repeated her terrible shrug. "Who knows? I don't see my way —! It isn't an existence, but when one's in misery —! Chere belle④," she added as an appeal to Miss Spencer, "you've gone and forgotten the 'fine'!"

I detained that lady as, after considering a moment in silence the small array, she was about to turn off in quest of this article. I held out my hand in silence — I had to

---

① in fine: 总而言之。
② vitiate: 损害。
③ parage: (法语)地方。
④ Chere belle: (法语)亲爱的美人。

go. Her wan① set little face, severely mild and with the question of a moment before now quite cold in it, spoke of extreme fatigue, but also of something else strange and conceived — whether a desperate patience still, or at last some other desperation, being more than I can say. What was clearest on the whole was that she was glad I was going. Mr. Mixter had risen to his feet and was pouring out the Countess's coffee. As I went back past the Baptist church I could feel how right my poor friend had been in her conviction at the other, the still intenser, the now historic crisis, that she should still see something of that dear old Europe.

【思考题】

1. 你认为,小说为何要命名为"四次会见"?

2. 小说中的主要人物各自有何性格特征? 斯潘塞小姐为何会屡次被人欺骗?

3. 每次会见当中,斯潘塞小姐对欧洲的印象分别是怎样的? 这一印象的改变是由什么原因引起的?

4. "我"这个角色的设置,对于故事情节的推动起到了什么作用?

---

① wan:苍白的,无血色的。

A Summer's Reading

暑假阅读计划

伯纳德·马拉默德

【导读】

伯纳德·马拉默德(Bernard Malamud, 1914—1986),是当代美国犹太作家中重要的一位,与索尔·贝娄(Saul Bellow)等人一样,执教高等学府,故也有"高知"作家之称,他常常以一个犹太人特殊的视角关注人类"大我"的命运和个人"小我"的道德精神风貌。

马拉默德于1914年生于纽约的布鲁克林,父母均是俄国的移民。他们家靠经营一间小小的杂货店艰难度日,马拉默德从小就生活在狭窄的柜台后面。沉闷而闭塞的环境几乎让他感到窒息,童年时代所有的乐趣,便是躲在那里读一些破旧的书籍,但这也给他打下了良好的文字基础。1936年,马拉默德毕业于纽约城市大学(CUNY),接着又进入哥伦比亚大学攻读英语硕士学位。他第一部小说《天才》(*Natural*)1952年发表时,已经38岁,可以说他是一个大器晚成的作家。他真正的成名作是1957年出版的《伙计》(*Assistant*)(又译《店员》),使他在文坛上崭露头角。紧接着第二年,他又出版了短篇小说集《魔桶》(*The Magic Barrel*),以其传神的笔触描绘了众多犹太贫民艰辛的生活状态以及他们的情感风貌,形成了他以小见大,深入开掘道德主题的"马拉默德式小说"的风格,备受读者的赞赏。

马拉默德是一个著述颇丰的作家,写作非常认真,故几乎每一篇作品都受到重视。20世纪60年代以后的主要作品如《装配工》(*The Fixer*, 1966)、《杜宾的生活》(*Dubin's Lives*, 1979)都曾引起反响,前者不仅为他再次获得了全美图书奖,而且还被改编成电影,取名《我无罪》(又译《基辅怨》),风靡西方。

《伙计》作为马拉默德的代表作,最能反映作者的道德观和犹太人的生活观。主人公莫里斯·鲍伯是一个年逾花甲的杂货店业主,他几十年辛辛苦苦的劳作,换来的只是一贫如洗的生活状况。正当他处于穷愁潦倒,整日唉声叹气的时候,几名蒙面的歹徒闯进了店铺,抢走了他仅有的一点现金并砸伤了他的头部。这雪上加霜的抢劫行为使他家里乱作一团,难以支撑,此时有一位青年主动出来帮助他照料铺子。莫里斯接受了这个叫弗兰克的青年,殊不知他就是入室抢劫的罪犯之一,因为良心发现,为赎罪而受雇于此。在莫里斯精神的感召下,弗兰克从一个罪人几经反复逐步走向新生。当莫里斯最后因扫雪患肺炎去世之后,弗兰克毅然挑起了抚养莫里斯妻女的重任,还像旧主人一样,用一颗金子般的心照料着诸多的穷人顾客。他受苦,但为了别人,他有了人生的目标。

这部小说打动了许多读者。马拉默德为人们塑造了一个现代社会的道德英雄和他的追随者。作家相信,人类感情的交流和道德上的净化是生活价值的中心,其意义是远远超过物质追求的。

马拉默德的短篇小说同样精彩。本书选用的《暑假阅读计划》,就能见出其卓尔不凡的手笔。

《暑假阅读计划》以心理刻画见长。内容十分简单,16岁的"邻家男孩"乔治因不堪忍受学业压力,一时冲动下辍学在家,终日无所事事,晃来晃去,虽然打过几份工,但均未做久。他白天躲在家里,晚上出去走走,坐在街心花园里做他的白日梦。有一天在回家的路上,偶然遇见邻居的大叔凯坦扎拉问起他近日的情况,羞于直言无业在家,乔治撒谎说在家进修,暑假准备读完百本书。凯坦扎拉听后肃然起敬,褒扬有加,不久邻里街坊都知道乔治的"上进"举动并对他笑脸相迎。为此,乔治很得意了一番。但事实上,他压根儿就没有读过一本正经的书。为避免尴尬,他害怕再次遇到那位关心他的凯坦扎拉,但不巧的是他们还是碰上了。尽管乔治再次支吾应对了追问,但巨大的心理压力和邻居、家里的反应都使他难以招架,最后他去了图书馆,开始了真正的读书"充电"。

这篇小说成功的地方,在于刻画了一个心理不成熟,苦于学业而又敏感、虚荣、懒散无奈、不敢正视现实的青年形象。这是一个特殊的人物,但又是成千上万个"失意青年"的代表。这样的人物以及他们的生活遭遇,不仅美国社会有,相信其他社会也不乏其人,故小说精确而深入的描写,自然会引起读者的共鸣。

马拉默德的另一个短篇《魔桶》体现了马拉默德写作上的娴熟与构思的巧妙,它已经成为美国文科学生的必读经典,其隽永之笔令人久久回味。

这是一个略带幽默又不失睿智的人生故事。主人公列奥是一个前途光明的研究犹太教法典的博士,为了在神职工作中更具亲和力,他已经到了必须定亲娶亲的时日。于是,他找到了一个叫萨尔兹曼的专业媒人为己作伐。萨尔兹曼乃此行老手,初次见到这位年轻人,便有了好感。他在自己的"魔术桶"一般的盒子里找到几份登记婚介的卡片给列奥。这几位姑娘虽然各有长处,但也有"致命伤":不是年龄太大,就是残疾跛足之类。看到列奥失望的样子,萨尔兹曼答应改天再提供新的资讯和姑娘们的玉照。接下来的介绍也不顺利,列奥自感在这方面灰心丧气。但有一天,一位漂亮姑娘的照片在萨尔兹曼的资料袋中落到地上。列奥顿时眼睛一亮,一种不可捉摸的直觉告诉他这就是他所想娶的另一半。而萨尔兹曼却故作惊慌,仓皇而走,列奥好不容易追到这位媒人家中,萨尔兹曼告诉他这就是他那个该死的女儿的照片,一个已经堕落了的姑娘,根本配不上他。但列奥并不在乎她的以往,他恳求萨尔兹曼把他的女儿介绍给他,因为他已经认定她是自己的终身所爱。一个春天的晚上,萨尔兹曼在街头的另一边看到列奥欢快地与自己的女儿约会,他不禁得意地吟起了犹太教的经文。

萨尔兹曼这种"瞒天过海,暗渡陈仓,以售其奸"的做媒手段看上去狡猾欺诈,但实际上不乏爱人及爱女之心。他真诚地希望列奥,这位犹太教法典的研究者,能够在生活上和道德精神上救赎他那已经偏离了犹太人道德法规的女儿。他这种善良的滑头和精明并不惹人讨厌。

这篇小说最大的艺术特色也和萨尔兹曼婚姻介绍的手段一样先藏后露,读者必须看完小说才能体味出这位犹太媒人的障眼法,识破他小小的计谋并为他的成功而感到欣慰。而老头对列奥的心理把握以及装腔作势的样子,更使读者会心地感受到马拉默德幽默、清新的文风和深入人心的探索。

题目"暑期阅读"也可译为"暑期阅读计划"或"暑期充电计划"。

开门见山几句话已写出了邻家男孩乔治的窘境。

A SUMMER'S READING

George Stoyonovich was a neighborhood boy who had quit high school on an impulse when he was sixteen, run out of patience①, and though he was ashamed every time he went looking for a job, when people asked him if he had finished and he had to say no, he never went back to school. This summer was a hard time for jobs and he had none. Having so much time on his hands②, George thought of going summer school, but the kids in his classes would be too young. He also considered registering in a night high school, only he didn't like the idea of the teachers always telling him what to do. He felt they had not respected him. The result was he stayed off③ the streets and in his room most of the day. He was close to twenty and had needs with the neighborhood girls, but no money to spend, and he couldn't get more than an

---

① run out of patience:失去耐心,忍受不了。
② Having so much time on his hands:他有大把时间。
③ stay off:远离。

occasional few cents because his father was poor, and his sister Sophie, who resembled George, a tall bony girl of twenty-three, earned very little and what she had she kept for herself. Their mother was dead, and Sophie had to take care of the house.

Very early in the morning George's father got up to go to work in a fish market. Sophie left about eight for her long ride in the subway to a cafeteria in the Bronx. George had his coffee by himself, then hung around[①] in the house. When the house, a five-room railroad flat above a butcher store[②], got on his nerves[③] he cleaned it up — mopped the floor with a wet mop and put things away. But most of the time he sat in his room. In the afternoons he listened to the ball game. Otherwise he had a couple of old copies of the *World Almanac*[④] he had bought long ago, and he liked to read in them and also the magazines and newspapers that Sophie brought home, that had been left on the tables in the cafeteria[⑤]. They were mostly picture magazines about movie stars and sports figures, also usually the *News* and *Mirror*[⑥]. Sophie herself read whatever fell into her hands, although she sometimes read good books.

She once asked George what he did in his room all day and he said he read a lot too.

"Of what besides what I bring home? Do you ever read any worthwhile books?"

"Some," George answered, although he really didn't.

作者很少用浓墨重彩的形容词，但写出了乔治家的清寒。用他父亲每天一早就得赶往鱼市干活和姐姐得乘地铁到很远一家自助餐馆工作，点出他们家有五间房，却是"狭窄简陋的房间"，又在肉铺之上。

乔治听球赛广播，看书报杂志中电影明星或者体育明星之类，其耳濡目染可见一斑。而这些东西都是在餐馆里人家丢弃的消遣读物。

① hang around: 闲荡，踱步。
② butcher store: 肉铺。
③ get on his nerves: 使人心烦或易怒，此处指除非房间内（乱七八糟）难以忍受。
④ *World Almanac*:《世界年鉴》。
⑤ Sophie brought home, that had been left on the tables in the cafeteria: 索菲亚带家的那些顾客丢在餐馆里的杂志、报纸。
⑥ *News* and *Mirror*:《新闻报》和《镜报》。

He had tried to read a book or two that Sophie had in the house but found he was in no mood① for them. Lately he couldn't stand made-up stories, they got on his nerves. He wished he had some hobby to work at it? — as a kid he was good in carpentry②, but mostly he did his walking after the hot sun had gone down and it was cooler in the streets.

在闷热的夏夜,人们在大街上纳凉的场景。可见出当时的社会环境。

In the evening after supper George left the house and wandered in the neighborhood. During the sultry③ days some of the storekeepers and their wives sat in chairs on the thick, broken sidewalks④ in front of their shops, fanning themselves, and George walked past them and the guys hanging out⑤ on the candy store corner. A couple of them he had known his whole life, but nobody recognized each other. He had no place special to go, but generally, saving it till the last, he left the neighborhood and walked for blocks till he came to a darkly lit little park with benches and trees and an iron railing⑥, giving it a feeling of privacy. He sat on a bench here, watching the leafy trees and the flowers blooming on the inside of the railing, thinking of a better life for himself. He thought of the jobs he had had since he had quit school — delivery boy, stock, clerk, runner, latterly working in a factory — and he was dissatisfied with all of them. He felt he would someday like to have a good job and live in a private house with a porch⑦, on a street with trees. He wanted to have

在夜色中,他游游荡荡,那里仿佛是他私人的小花园,他坐在那儿做起了白日梦……一番想入非非之后,飘然回到了他那又闷热又乏味的街区。这里用词精当、传神。

① in no mood:没心思,没情绪。
② carpentry:木匠业。
③ sultry:湿热难耐的。
④ sidewalk:人行道。
⑤ hang out:闲逛。
⑥ railing:栏杆。
⑦ porch:门廊。

some dough① in his pocket to buy things with, and a girl to go with, so as not to be so lonely, especially on Saturday nights. He wanted people to like and respect him. He thought about these things often but mostly when he was alone at night. Around midnight he got up and drifted back to his hot and stony② neighborhood.

One time while on his walk, George met Mr. Cattanzara coming home very late from work. He wondered if he was drunk but then could tell he wasn't. Mr. Cattanzara, stocky③, bald-headed man who worked in a change booth on an IRT station④, lived on the hot weather; he sat on his stoop⑤ in an undershirt⑥, reading the *New York Times* on the light of the shoemaker's window. He read it from the first page to the last, then went up to sleep. And all the time he was reading the paper, his wife, a fat woman with a white face, leaned out of the window, gazing into the street, her thick white arms folded under her loose breast, on the window ledge.

那个把《纽约时报》从头看到尾的凯坦扎拉先生在乔治的眼中既和善又特别。

Once in a while Mr. Cattanzara came home drunk, but it was a quiet drunk. He never made any trouble, only walked stiffly up the street and slowly climbed the stairs into the hall. Though drunk, he looked the same as always, except for his tight walk, the quietness, and that his eyes were wet⑦. George liked Mr. Cattanzara because he remembered him giving him nickels to buy lemon ice with when he was a squirt⑧. Mr. Cattanzara was a

寥寥数笔刻画了一个手臂粗壮、乳房松弛的白白胖胖的女人形象。

---

① dough：钱。
② stony：无情的，冷漠的。
③ stocky：粗短而结实的。
④ who worked in a change booth on an IRT station：高架地铁站的零钱兑换员。
⑤ stoop：门阶。
⑥ undershirt：汗衫。
⑦ except for his tight walk, the quietness, and that his eyes were wet：除了步履蹒跚、略显沉默和眼睛湿润之外。
⑧ squirt：小鬼，小孩子。

different type than those in the neighborhood. He asked different questions than the others when he met you, and he seemed to know what went on in all the newspapers. He read them, as his fat sick wife watched from the window.

"What are you doing with yourself this summer, George?" Mr. Cattanzara asked. "I see you walkin' around at nights."

George felt embarrassed. "I like to walk."

"What are you doin' in the day now?"

"Nothing much just right now. I'm waiting for a job." Since it shamed him to admit he wasn't working, George said, "I'm staying home — but I'm reading a lot to pick up① my education."

Mr. Cattanzara looked interested. He mopped his hot face with a red handkerchief.

"What are you readin'?"

George hesitated, then said, "I got a list of books in the library once, and now I'm gonna read them this summer." He felt strange and a little unhappy saying this, but he wanted Mr. Cattanzara to respect him.

"How many books are there on it?"

"I never counted them. Maybe around a hundred."

Mr. Cattanzara whistled② through his teeth.

"I figure③ if I did that," George went in earnestly④, "it would help me in my education. I don't mean the kind they give you in high school. I went to know different things than they learn there, if you know what I mean."

凯坦扎拉确实有些特别,他醉后的样子以及与人聊的话题都不一样。

乔治一副迟疑的样子。

---

① pick up: 继续。
② whistle: 嘘声,口哨。
③ figure: 认为。
④ earnestly: 认真地。

The change maker① nodded. "Still and all②, one hundred books is a pretty big load for one summer."

"It might take longer."

"After you're finished with some, maybe you and I can shoot the breeze③ about them?" said Mr. Cattanzara.

Mr. Cattanzara went home and George continued on his walk. After that, though he had the urge to, George did nothing different from usual. He still took his walks at night, ending up in the little park. But one evening the shoemaker on the next block stopped George to say he was a good boy, and George figured that Mr. Cattanzara had told him all about the books he was reading. From the shoemaker it must have gone down the street, because George saw a couple of people smiling kindly at him, though nobody spoke to him personally. He felt a little better around the neighborhood and liked it more, though not so much he would want to live in it forever. He had never exactly disliked the people in it, yet he had never liked them very much either. It was the fault of the neighborhood. To his surprise, George found out that his father and Sophie knew about his reading too. His father was too shy to say anything about it — he was never much of a talker in his whole life — but Sophie was softer to George, and she showed him in other ways she was proud of him.

As the summer went on George felt in a good mood about thing. He cleaned the house every day, as a favor to Sophie, and he enjoyed the ball games more. Sophie gave him a buck④ a week allowance, and though it still wasn't

乔治看到街坊邻居的笑脸，知道自己的"读书计划"已经广为人知。他很喜欢这种感觉，虽然他还是和过去一样，什么书都没读。

乔治很惊讶地发现：他的父亲和姐姐也一样感到欣喜和骄傲。

---

① change maker：零钱兑换员，此处有双关意思，既指零钱兑换员，也指改变命运的人。
② Still and all：不过，尽管如此。
③ shoot the breeze：聊聊。
④ buck：一元钱（美俚）。

尽管每周只有一块
钱的零花钱,他用得很
舒心。

每天晚上他都能感
觉到人们对他的敬意,
心情特别好。

乔治对凯坦扎拉先
生撒谎后,内心充满
矛盾。

enough and he had to use it carefully, it was a helluva① lot better than just having two bits now and then. What he bought with money — cigarettes mostly, an occasional beer or movie ticket — he got a big kick out of②. Life wasn't so bad if you knew how to appreciate it. Occasionally he bought a paperback book③ from the newsstand④, but he never got around to reading it, though he was glad to have a couple of books in his room. But he read thoroughly Sophie's magazines and newspapers. And at night it was the most enjoyable time, because when he passed the storekeepers sitting outside their stores, he could fell they regarded him highly. He walked erect, and though he did not say much to them, or they to him, he could feel approval on all sides⑤. A couple of nights he felt so good that he skipped the park at the end of the evening. He just wandered in the neighborhood, where people had known him from the time he was a kid playing punchball⑥ whenever there was a game of it going; he wandered there, then came home and got undressed for bed, feeling fine.

For a few weeks he had talked only once with Mr. Cattanzara, and though the change maker had said nothing more about the books, asked no questions, his silence made George a little uneasy. For a while George didn't pass in front of Mr. Cattanzara's house anymore, until one night, forgetting himself, he approached it from a different direction than he usually did when he did. It was already past midnight. The street, except for one or

① helluva:可观的,大量的。
② get a big kick out of:感到很满足,感到很愉快。
③ paperback book:平装书,廉价书。
④ newsstand:报摊。
⑤ he could feel approval on all sides:他能感受到来自各方的赞许。
⑥ punchball:弹珠游戏。

two people, was deserted, and George was surprised when he saw Mr. Cattanzara still reading his newspaper by the light of the street lamp overhead. His impulse was to stop at the stoop and talk to him. He wasn't sure what he wanted to say, though he felt the words would come when he began to talk; but the more he thought about it, the more the idea scared him, and he decided he'd better not. He even considered beating it home by another street, but he was too near Mr. Cattanzara, and the change maker might see him as he ran, and get annoyed. So George unobtrusively① crossed the street, trying to make it seem as if he had to look in a store window on the other side, which he did, and then went on, uncomfortable at what he was doing. He feared Mr. Cattanzara would glance up from his paper and call him a dirty rat② for walking on the other side of the street, but all he did was sit there, sweating through his undershirt, his bald head shining in the dim light as he read his *Times*, and upstairs his fat wife leaned out of the window, seeming to read the paper along with him. George thought she would spy him and yell out to Mr. Cattanzara, but she never moved her eyes off her husband.

George made up his mind to stay away③ from the change maker until he had got some of his softback books read, but when he started them and saw they were mostly story books, he lost his interest and didn't bother to finish them. He lost his interest in reading other things too. Sophie's magazines and newspapers went unread. She saw them piling up on a chair in his room and asked why he was no longer looking at them, and George told her it was

此时乔治非但读不进去好书，连那些报纸杂志也无心翻看，心情更加烦躁无聊了。描写在步步深入。

---

① unobtrusively：悄悄地。
② dirty rat：无耻之徒。
③ stay away：避开。

because of all the other reading he had to do. Sophie said she had guessed that was it. So for most of the day, George had the radio on, turning to music when he was sick of the human voice. He kept the house fairly neat, and Sophie said nothing on the days when he neglected it. She was still kind and gave him his extra buck, though things weren't so good for him as they had been before.

But they were good enough, considering①. Also his night walks invariably picked him up, no matter how had the day was. Then one night George saw Mr. Cattanzara coming down the street toward him. George was about turn and run but he recognized from Mr. Cattanzara's walk that he was drunk, and if so, probably he would not even bother to notice him. So George kept on walking straight ahead until he came abreast of② Mr. Cattanzara and though he felt wound up enough to pop into the sky③, he was not surprised when Mr. Cattanzara passed him without a word, walking slowly, his face and body stiff. George drew a breath in relief at his narrow escape④, when he heard his name called, and there stood Mr. Cattanzara at his elbow, smelling like the inside of a beer barrel. His eyes were sad as he gazed at George, and George felt so intensely uncomfortable he was tempted to shove⑤ the drunk aside and continue on his walk.

But he couldn't act that way to him, and, besides, Mr. Cattanzara took a nickel out of his pants⑥ pocket and handed it to him.

"Go buy yourself a lemon ice, Georgie."

乔治遇上醉酒的凯坦扎拉先生,彼此展开了戏剧性的对话。乔治感到对方的咄咄逼人,显示了此时他内心的虚弱。

---

① considering：从各方面考虑。
② come abreast of：并肩而过。
③ felt wound up enough to pop into the sky：紧张得不敢喘气。
④ George drew a breath in relief at his narrow escape：乔治庆幸自己狭路逃生而长舒一口气。
⑤ shove：推开。
⑥ pants：裤子。

"It's not that time anymore, Mr. Cattanzara," George said, "I am a big guy now."

"No, you ain't," said Mr. Cattanzara, to which George made no reply he could think of.

"How are all your books comin' along now?" Mr. Cattanzara asked. Though he tried to stand steady, he swayed① a little.

"Fine, I guess," said George, feeling the red crawling up his face②.

"You ain't sure?" The change maker smiled slyly, a way George had never seen him smile.

"Sure, I'm sure. They're fine."

Though his head swayed in little arcs, Mr. Cattanzara's eyes were steady. He had small blue eyes which could hurt if you looked at them too long.

"George," he said, "name me one book on that list that you read this summer, and I will drink to your health."

"I don't want anybody drinking to me."

George knew he looked passable on the outside, but inside he was crumbling apart. ③

Unable to reply, he shut his eyes, but when — years later — he opened them, he saw that Mr. Cattanzara had, out of pity, gone away④, but in his ears he still heard the words he had said when he left: "George, don't do what I did."

The next night he was afraid to leave his room, and

凯坦扎拉一句"不要走我的老路",震撼了乔治。第二天乔治再也不出门了。

---

① sway：摇晃。

② the red crawling up his face：感到脸涨得通红。

③ he looked passable on the outside, but inside he was crumbling apart：意即乔治自知表面上还佯装镇静,骨子里已全无自信。

④ Unable to reply, he shut his eyes, but when — years later — he opened them, he saw that Mr. Cattanzara had, out of pity, gone away：他无言以对,闭上眼睛,似乎已过去了好多年,他再张开眼睛时,谢天谢地,凯坦扎拉先生已经走了。

though Sophie argued with him he wouldn't open the door.

"What are you doing in there?" she asked.

"Nothing."

"Aren't you reading?"

"No."

She was silent a minute, then asked, "Where do you keep the books you read? I never see any in your room outside of a few cheap trashy ones."

He wouldn't tell her.

"In that case you're not worth a buck of my hard-earned money. Why should I break my back for you①? Go on out, you bum②, and get a job."

乔治一星期闭门不出。父亲、姐姐求他,他都不为所动。

He stayed in his room for almost a week, except to sneak into③ the kitchen when nobody was home. Sophie railed at④ him, then begged him to come out, and his old father wept, but George wouldn't budge⑤, though the weather was terrible and his small room stifling⑥. He found it very hard to breathe, each breath was like drawing a flame into his lungs.

相当形象地描写出了乔治的狼狈相。

One night, unable to stand the heat anymore, he burst into the street at one A.M., a shadow of himself. He hoped to sneak to the park without being seen, but there were people all over the block, wilted and listless⑦, waiting for a breeze. George lowered his eyes and walked, in disgrace, away from them, but before long he discovered they were still friendly to him. He figured Mr.

---

① Why should I break my back for you? 为什么我要为你卖命?
② bum:懒虫。
③ sneak into:偷偷溜进。
④ rail at:责骂。
⑤ but George wouldn't budge:但乔治不为所动。
⑥ stifling:窒息的。
⑦ wilted and listless:萎蔫无精打采的样子。

Cattanzara hadn't told on① him. Maybe when he woke up out of his drunk the next morning, he had forgotten all about meeting George. George felt his confidence slowly come back to him.

一场虚惊之后,他发现街坊邻居并未识破他的谎言,于是,自信和尊严又渐回心头。

That some night a man on a street corner asked him if it was true that he had finished reading so many books, and George admitted he had. The man said it was a wonderful thing for a boy his age to read so much.

"Yeah," George said, but he felt relieved. He hoped nobody would mention the books anymore, and then, after a couple of days, he accidentally met Mr. Cattanzara again, he didn't, though George had the idea he was the one who had started the rumor that he had finished all the books.

One evening in the fall, George ran out of his house to the library, where he hadn't been in years. There were books all over the place, wherever he looked, and though he was struggling to control an inward trembling, he easily counted off② a hundred, then sat down at a table to read.

一个秋天的晚上,乔治来到久未涉足的图书馆,开始了他真正的读书计划。结局既在情理之中,又在意料之外。

【思考题】

1. 乔治是个什么样的青年,他身上体现出怎样的特点?

2. 从小说中我们能够感受到美国的犹太社区较为特殊的环境和普通犹太人的社会观等,这些对小说中人物有何影响?

3. 什么是马拉默德式的风格?

---

① tell on:告发。
② count off:挑出。

The Grave

坟

凯瑟琳·安·波特

【导读】

  凯瑟琳·安·波特(Katherine Anne Porter，1890—1980)，当代美国女作家中杰出的一位。因为她生于南方的德克萨斯州，故一般文学史把她列入南方作家，而事实上，无论从她的个人经历还是写作范围来看，她都远远超越了这个界限。

  波特1890年生于德州的印第安港湾，故乡的印象成了她日后许多小说的背景。她从小丧母，接受的是修道院的教育，但她是一个倔强的女孩和不听话的学生。她少女时代的大部分时间是在新奥尔良度过的，16岁那年她与一个南太平洋铁路局的职工一起私奔，从此改信天主教，但三年后便离了婚。从那时起她先后在纽约、墨西哥城、巴黎、路易斯安那、加利福尼亚及华盛顿等多处居住过，行迹漂泊，四海为家。

  波特很早就开始了笔耕生涯，20岁出头就已经在芝加哥为一家电影公司写稿，1922年她发表了第一篇小说，从此走上了文学创作的道路。波特的主要作品有《开花的犹太树和其他故事》(*Flowering Judas and Other Stories*，1930)、《中午酒》(*Noon Wine*，1937)、《灰白色的马，苍白的骑士》(*Pale Horse，Pale Rider*，1939)、《斜塔及其他故事》(*Leaning Tower and Other Stories*，1944)和一部长篇小说《愚人船》(*Ship of Fools*，1962)。1965年出版的《故事选集》(*Collected Stories*)使她获得了国家图书奖和普利策奖。

  《愚人船》是波特唯一的一部长篇小说，是一部道德寓言和社会批评式的小说。这部小说一经出版，立即引起社会的强烈反响。

  《愚人船》写一艘叫"维拉"号的法国客轮从墨西哥的维拉克鲁兹驶往德国的不来梅。"维拉"在拉丁语中是"真理"的意思。在这艘"维拉"号28天的旅程中，作者以既超脱于这艘代表世界的船，同时又以乘客的双重身份来审视一个微观世界中人们的生活。她自称是其中的一位，但在小说中未曾露面。这种手法，能让读者很容易地感受到我们都是芸芸众生中的一个角色，船上人物的言行活动常常使我们产生同一的感想，同时会激起我们对自身及周围世界的观察与思考。从作者的题词及情节安排中，我们可以看出波特转弯抹角的主题思想，这艘满载了人类化身的客轮出发去寻找"真理与幸福",却发现人类缺少自己的安身之处,也没有精神的故乡,并且连前景也虚幻黯淡。

波特称这部小说只是描写"一个有关好人共谋犯罪的故事,并无恶意,只是与生俱来的罪恶"。这部小说的价值与意义在于以象征的手法,启发人们去探索人类本质的某些方面,它不可能也无须提出解决的方法和答案。从这个角度看,《愚人船》确实是一部达到了相当深度并取得了极大成功的小说。

波特是以短篇小说蜚声美国文坛的,她的小说一向以精巧的构思、细腻的文笔和隽永的内涵给人以深刻的印象。《坟》是波特短篇小说力作,它自问世以来,深受评论界的好评。

《坟》这篇小说的情节极为简单,没有传统小说中那种大起大落的矛盾冲突,而更像一个描写儿童心理的故事。小说中的两个孩子——12岁的保罗和9岁的米兰达,在一个已经迁葬的墓地寻找着宝藏。他们感受到死亡的恐惧,同时在他们眼中,墓地又是一个神秘所在,相信一定能遇上某些值得冒险的奇遇,墓地因此成了他们戏耍的乐园了。两人挎着猎枪到别处寻找野兔、鸽子或者任何其他可能碰上的小动物。保罗猎到了一只母兔,当他剖开母兔后,一堆小兔崽子便暴露在他们面前。小米兰达并不显得害怕,反而略显得有些激动,心中充满了对这些不可思议的小生灵的怜悯、惊奇。20年后一个极其偶然的场合,这桩陈年往事出其不意地从深深埋藏的地方蹦出来,此时米兰达早已饱经风霜,目睹过无数死亡,当她猛然间意识到自己当年的戕害行为时,不由得毛骨悚然,死亡使她深感生之宝贵。

波特的小说给人最大的感受就是蕴含着无限的寓意。《坟》也不例外,它暗喻人从幼年的纯真到成年懂事的过程,而探宝也就是探寻知识。小说中墓地的废弃容易使人联想到作者家族几次迁居的家道中落,以及美国南方家族强烈的家庭观念和南方人的思想感情。米兰达从拾到的戒指中发现了作为女性的天性,保罗枪杀一只怀孕的母兔使米兰达思考令人困惑的生死问题等。

The Grave (1944)

The grandfather, dead for more than thirty years, had been twice disturbed in his long repose① by the constancy and possessiveness of his widow. She removed his bones first to Louisiana and then to Texas, as if she

① long repose:长眠,安息。

367

had set out to① find her own burial place, knowing well she would never return to the places she had left. In Texas she set up a small cemetery in a corner of her first farm, and as the family connection grew, and oddments of relations came over from Kentucky to settle, it contained at last about twenty graves. After the grandmother's death, part of her land was to be sold for the benefit of certain of her children, and the cemetery happened to lie in the part set aside② for sale. It was necessary to take up the bodies and bury them again in the family plot③ in the big new public cemetery, where Grandmother had been recently buried. At long last④ her husband was to lie beside her for eternity, as she had planned.

以上段落介绍祖父及家族墓地的变迁经历,暗示家道中落。

The family cemetery had been a pleasant small neglected garden of tangled rose bushes and ragged cedar trees and cypress⑤, the simple flat stones rising out of uncropped sweet-smelling wild grass⑥. The graves were lying open and empty one burning day when Miranda and her brother Paul, who often went together to hunt rabbits and doves, propped their twenty-two Winchester rifles⑦ carefully against the rail fence⑧, climbed over and explored among the graves. She was nine years old and he was twelve.

以上文字是墓地周围的环境介绍,并引出两个小主人公。

---

① set out to:着手于,开始准备。
② set aside:留出,预留下来。
③ family plot:家族的小块土地。
④ at long last:终于。
⑤ small neglected garden of tangled rose bushes and ragged cedar trees and cypress:一个被遗忘的小型花园,密布着杂乱的玫瑰花丛和参差不齐的雪松与水杉树。
⑥ the simple flat stones rising out of uncropped sweet-smelling wild grass:平滑的岩石从散发着甜蜜气味的野草丛中露出来。
⑦ propped their twenty-two Winchester rifles:架着他们的点22温彻斯特来复枪。Winchester rifles:温彻斯特来复枪是专指在美国制造的温切斯特连发武器公司的步枪。温彻斯特,已经成为杠杆式枪械的代名词,在20世纪的美国非常有名,此枪在西进运动中发挥了巨大作用。
⑧ rail fence:铁道围栏。

They peered into① the pits all shaped alike with such purposeful accuracy, and looking at each other with pleased adventurous eyes, they said in solemn tones②: "These were graves!" trying by words to shape a special, suitable emotion in their minds, but they felt nothing except an agreeable thrill of wonder③: they were seeing a new sight, doing something they had not done before. In them both there was also a small disappointment at the entire commonplaceness of the actual spectacle④. Even if it had once contained a coffin for years upon years, when the coffin was gone a grave was just a hole in the ground. Miranda leaped into the pit⑤ that had held her grandfather's bones. Scratching around⑥ aimlessly and pleasurably, as any young animal, she scooped up a lump of earth⑦ and weighed it in her palm⑧. It had a pleasantly sweet, corrupt smell, being mixed with cedar needles⑨ and small leaves, and as the crumbs⑩ fell apart, she saw a silver dove no larger than a hazel nut⑪, with spread wings and a neat fan-shaped tail⑫. The breast had a deep round hollow in it. Turning it up to the fierce sunlight, she saw that the inside of the hollow was cut in little whorls⑬. She

---

① peered into：盯着。
② in solemn tones：郑重其事的语气。
③ they felt nothing except an agreeable thrill of wonder：他们除了探险所带来的激动和兴奋外，什么都感觉不到。
④ a small disappointment at the entire commonplaceness of the actual spectacle：对于这些实际景致的普通样感到有点失望。
⑤ leaped into the pit：跳进墓穴。
⑥ scratching around：没有目标地东挖西挖。
⑦ scooped up a lump of earth：挖出一小块土。
⑧ weighed it in her palm：在手中掂量。
⑨ cedar needles：雪松针叶。
⑩ crumbs：碎屑。
⑪ hazel nut：榛子。
⑫ neat fan-shaped tail：整齐的扇形尾巴。
⑬ whorls：涡型螺纹。

scrambled out①, over the pile of loose earth that had fallen back into one end of the grave, calling to Paul that she had found something, he must guess what .... His head appeared smiling over the rim of another grave②. He waved a closed hand at her:"I've got something too!" They ran to compare treasures, making a game of it, so many guesses each, all wrong, and a final show-down with opened palms③. Paul had found a thin wide gold ring carved with intricate flowers and leaves④. Miranda was smitten at sight of the ring⑤ and wished to have it. Paul seemed more impressed by the dove. They made a trade, with some little bickering⑥. After he had got the dove in his hand, Paul said, "Don't you know what this is? This is a screw head⑦ for a coffin! ... I'll bet nobody else in the world has one like this!"

以上文字描写在墓地里,保罗找到了一枚金戒指,米兰达找到了一只银鸽子,他们俩交换了各自的战利品。

Miranda glanced at it without covetousness⑧. She had the gold ring on her thumb; it fitted perfectly. "Maybe we ought to go now," she said, "maybe one of the niggers'll see us and tell somebody." They knew the land had been sold, the cemetery was no longer theirs, and they felt like trespassers⑨. They climbed back over the fence, slung their rifles loosely under their arms⑩— they had been shooting at targets with various kinds of firearms since they were seven years old — and set out to look for the

---

① scrambled out:爬出去。
② His head appeared smiling over the rim of another grave:他从另一个坟墓边上探出头来,微笑着。
③ so many guesses each, all wrong, and a final show-down with opened palms:猜了很多遍都错了,最后打开手展示。
④ carved with intricate flowers and leaves:刻有精细繁复花纹的花和叶。
⑤ smitten at sight of the ring:一看到戒指就被迷住了。
⑥ bickering:争吵。
⑦ screw head:螺钉头。
⑧ glanced at it without covetousness:不感兴趣地瞟了一眼。
⑨ trespassers:入侵者。
⑩ slung their rifles loosely under their arms:把来复枪松松垮垮地悬在手臂上。

rabbits and doves or whatever small game might happen along①. On these expeditions Miranda always followed at Paul's heels along the path②, obeying instructions about handling her gun when going through fences; learning how to stand it up properly so it would not slip and fire unexpectedly③; how to wait her time for a shot and not just bang away in the air without looking④, spoiling shots for Paul, who really could hit things if given a chance. Now and then, in her excitement at seeing birds whizz up⑤ suddenly before her face, or a rabbit leap across her very toes⑥, she lost her head⑦, and almost without sighting she flung her rifle up and pulled the trigger. She hardly ever hit any sort of mark. She had no proper sense of hunting at all⑧. Her brother would be often completely disgusted with her. "You don't care whether you get your bird or not," he said. "That's no way to hunt." Miranda could not understand his indignation⑨. She had seen him smash his hat⑩ and yell with fury⑪ when he had missed his aim. "What I like about shooting," said Miranda, with exasperating inconsequence⑫, "is pulling the trigger and hearing the noise."

"Then, by golly⑬," said Paul, "whyn't you go back

---

① happen along: 偶然,碰巧出现。
② followed at Paul's heels along the path: 沿着小路紧跟在保罗的后面。
③ fire unexpectedly: 走火。
④ bang away in the air without looking: 盲目地在空中不断乱射。
⑤ whizz up: 飕飕掠过。
⑥ leap across her very toes: 就在双脚间跳过。
⑦ lost her head: 慌了神。
⑧ She hardly ever hit any sort of mark. She had no proper sense of hunting at all: 她没有击中任何东西的迹象,她根本没有打猎的感觉。
⑨ indignation: 气愤。
⑩ smash his hat: 摔了他的帽子。
⑪ yell with fury: 愤怒地大叫。
⑫ exasperating inconsequence: 逻辑混乱的气话。
⑬ by golly: 天哪。

to the range① and shoot at tin cans?"

"I'd just as soon," said Miranda, "only like this, we walk around more."

"Well, you just stay behind and stop spoiling my shots," said Paul, who, when he made a kill, wanted to be certain he had made it. Miranda, who alone brought down a bird once in twenty rounds, always claimed as her own any game they got when they fired at the same moment. It was tiresome and unfair and her brother was sick of it.

"Now, the first dove we see, or the first rabbit, is mine," he told her. "And the next will be yours. Remember that and don't get smarty②."

"What about snakes?" asked Miranda idly. "Can I have the first snake?"

Waving her thumb gently and watching her gold ring glitter③, Miranda lost interest in shooting. She was wearing her summer roughing outfit④: dark blue overalls⑤, a light blue shirt, a hired-man's straw hat⑥, and rough brown sandals. Her brother had the same outfit except his was a sober hickory-nut color⑦. Ordinarily Miranda preferred her overalls to any other dress, though it was making rather a scandal in the countryside, for the year was 1903, and in the back country⑧ the law of female decorum⑨ had teeth⑩ in it. Her father had been criticized

米兰达与哥哥保罗以往打猎时的争执,凸显本次两人面对猎物的默契。

米兰达戴上戒指后觉得自己寒碜的衣服很不协调,想起村里老妪对自己的品评和父亲节衣缩食给自己念书的情形。不标准的英语表明她和周围人受教育低。

---

① range：靶场。
② get smarty：自作聪明。
③ glitter：闪闪发光。
④ outfit：一套服装。
⑤ overall：罩衫。
⑥ hired-man's straw hat：雇工草帽。
⑦ sober hickory-nut color：朴素的胡桃木色。
⑧ in the back country：在穷乡僻壤。
⑨ law of female decorum：端庄典雅的女性礼仪。
⑩ had teeth：有重大影响。

for letting his girls dress like boys and go careering around
astride barebacked horses①. It was said the motherless
family was running down②, with the grandmother no
longer there to hold it together. Miranda knew this,
though she could not say how. She had met along the road
old women of the kind who smoked corncob pipes③, who
had treated her grandmother with most sincere respect.
They slanted their gummy old eyes side-ways at④ the
granddaughter and said, "Ain't you ashamed of yoself,
Missy? It's aginst the Scriptures⑤ to dress like that. Whut
yo Pappy thinkin about?" Miranda, with her powerful
social sense, which was like a fine set of antennae
radiating from every pore of her skin⑥, would feel
ashamed because she knew well it was rude and ill-bred⑦
to shock anybody, even bad-tempered old crones, though
she had faith in her father's judgment and was perfectly
comfortable in the clothes. Her father had said, "They're
just what you need, and they'll save your dresses for
school . . . ." This sounded quite simple and natural to her.
She had been brought up in rigorous economy⑧.
Wastefulness was vulgar. It was also a sin⑨. These were
truths; she had heard them repeated many times and never
once disputed.

Now the ring, shining with the serene purity of fine

---

① astride barebacked horses: 骑无鞍马。
② running down: 垮掉。
③ corncob pipes: 麦秆烟。
④ slanted their gummy old eyes side-ways at: 斜着昏花的老眼看。
⑤ Scriptures: 圣经经文。
⑥ with her powerful social sense, which was like a fine set of antennae radiating from every pore of her skin: 强烈的传统意识(淑女情结)，像动物的触须一样从她每一个毛孔中渗透出来。
⑦ ill-bred: 没有教养的。
⑧ brought up in rigorous economy: 成长于不宽裕的环境中。
⑨ Wastefulness was vulgar. It was also a sin. 浪费是可耻的。并且是一桩罪过。

gold on her rather grubby① thumb, turned her feelings against her overalls and sockless feet, toes sticking through the thick brown leather straps. She wanted to go back to the farm house, take a good cold bath, dust herself with plenty of her sister's violet talcum powder②— provided she was not present to object③, of course — put on the thinnest, most becoming dress she owned, with a big sash④, and sit in a wicker chair⑤ under the trees .... These things were not all she wanted, of course; she had vague stirrings of desire for luxury and a grand way of living which could not take precise form in her imagination⑥, being founded on a family legend of past wealth and leisure. But these immediate comforts were what she could have, and she wanted them at once. She lagged rather far behind⑦ Paul, and once she thought of just turning back without a word and going home. She stopped, thinking that Paul would never do that to her, and so she would have to tell him. When a rabbit leaped, she let Paul have it without dispute⑧. He killed it with one shot.

打死的母兔被保罗像以往那样剥皮,但他们意外发现这只母兔怀孕了。

When she came up with him, he was already kneeling, examining the wound, the rabbit trailing from his hands⑨. "Right through the head," he said complacently⑩, as if he had aimed for it. He took out his

① grubby:肮脏的。
② violet talcum powder:紫罗兰色的爽身粉。
③ provided she was not present to object:假装她没有遭到诟病。
④ big sash:大绶带。
⑤ wicker chair:藤椅。
⑥ take precise form in her imagination:在她的想象中具体成形。
⑦ lagged rather far behind:远远落后于。
⑧ without dispute:毫无争议地,没有争执地。
⑨ trailing from his hands:用手倒着提(兔子)。
⑩ complacently:洋洋得意,心满意足。

sharp, competent Bowie knife[①] and started to skin the body[②]. He did it very cleanly and quickly. Uncle Jimbilly knew how to prepare the skins[③] so that Miranda always had fur coats for her dolls, for though she never cared much for her dolls she liked seeing them in fur coats. The children knelt facing each other over the dead animal. Miranda watched admiringly while her brother stripped the skin away as if he were taking off a glove. The flayed flesh emerged dark scarlet, sleek, firm[④]; Miranda with thumb and finger felt the long fine muscles with the silvery flat strips binding them to the joints[⑤]. Brother lifted the oddly bloated belly[⑥]. "Look," he said, in a low, amazed voice. "It was going to have young ones."

Very carefully he slit the thin flesh from the center ribs to the flanks, and a scarlet bag[⑦] appeared. He slit again and pulled the bag open, and there lay a bundle of tiny rabbits, each wrapped in a thin scarlet veil[⑧]. The brother pulled these off and there they were, dark grey, their sleek wet down lying in minute even ripples[⑨], over pink skin, like a baby's head just washed; their unbelievably small delicate ears folded close, their little blind faces almost featureless.

Miranda said, "Oh, I want to see," under her breath. She looked and looked — excited but not frightened, for

米兰达一直以来对被打死猎物所抱有的心情：惊奇、怜爱，但这次的感受大不一样，她因为一个小生命即将诞生却被扼杀在母胎中而感到一种触动灵魂的震撼和悲悯。

---

① Bowie knife：鲍伊猎刀，单刃猎刀。
② skin the body：剥皮。
③ prepare the skins：处理皮毛。
④ The flayed flesh emerged dark scarlet, sleek, firm：剥开的肉呈现出暗深红色，光滑、结实。
⑤ with thumb and finger felt the long fine muscles with the silvery flat strips binding them to the joints：用拇指和食指触碰那些靠着银白色的筋连接着关节的平滑肌肉。
⑥ lifted the oddly bloated belly：提起胀得鼓鼓的肚子。
⑦ scarlet bag：猩红色的袋状物。
⑧ wrapped in a thin scarlet veil：裹在细小的猩红的胎膜中。
⑨ their sleek wet down lying in minute even ripples：他们湿漉漉地躺着，几分钟之内还能蠕动。

she was accustomed to the sight of animals killed in hunting — filled with pity and astonishment and a kind of shocked delight in the wonderful little creatures for their own sakes①, they were so pretty. She touched one of them ever so carefully. "Ah, there's blood running over② them," she said, and began to tremble without knowing why. Yet she wanted most deeply to see and to know. Having seen, she felt at once as if she had known all along. The very memory of her former ignorance faded, she had always known just this. No one had ever told her anything outright③, she had been rather unobservant④ of the animal life around her because she was so accustomed to animals. They seemed simply disorderly and unaccountably rude in their habits, but altogether natural and not very interesting. Her brother had spoken as if he had known about everything all along. He may have seen all this before. He had never said a word to her, but she knew now a part at least of what he knew. She understood a little of the secret, formless intuitions⑤ in her own mind and body, which had been clearing up, taking form, so gradually and so steadily she had not realized that she was learning what she had to know. Paul said cautiously, as if he were talking about something forbidden: "They were just about ready to be born." His voice dropped on the last word⑥. "I know," said Miranda, "like kittens. I know, like babies." She was quietly and terribly agitated⑦, standing again with her rifle under her arm, looking down

哥哥保罗同样震撼,他们将胎盘连同仔兔放回母兔腹中,小心埋葬,并相约永守这个秘密。

---

① for their own sakes:为了自己(享乐)的缘故。
② running over:流着血。
③ outright:彻底地。
④ unobservant:不善于观察的。
⑤ formless intuitions:无形的直觉。
⑥ dropped on the last word:重音落在后一个字上。
⑦ terribly agitated:非常不安。

at the bloody heap①. "I don't want the skin," she said, "I won't have it." Paul buried the young rabbits again in their mother's body, wrapped the skin around her, carried her to a clump of sage bushes②, and hid her away. He came out again at once and said to Miranda, with an eager friendliness, a confidential tone quite unusual in him, as if he were taking her into an important secret on equal terms: "Listen now. Now you listen to me, and don't ever forget. Don't you ever tell a living soul that you saw this. Don't tell a soul. Don't tell Dad because I'll get into trouble. He'll say I'm leading you into things you ought not to do. He's always saying that. So now don't you go and forget and blab out③ sometime the way you're always doing .... Now, that's a secret. Don't you tell."

Miranda never told, she did not even wish to tell anybody. She thought about the whole worrisome affair④ with confused unhappiness for a few days. Then it sank quietly into her mind and was heaped over by accumulated thousands of impressions⑤, for nearly twenty years. One day she was picking her path among the puddles and crushed refuse of a market street in a strange city of a strange country, when, without warning, in totality, plain and clear in its true colors as if she looked through a frame upon a scene that had not stirred nor changed since the moment it happened, the episode of the far-off day⑥ leaped from its burial place before her mind's eye. She

---

① bloody heap：血糊糊的那一堆。
② a clump of sage bushes：一丛鼠尾草。
③ blab out：泄露。
④ worrisome affair：令人不安的事件。
⑤ Then it sank quietly into her mind and was heaped over by accumulated thousands of impressions：这件事悄悄地沉入她的心底,同千万种感觉一样被堆积起来。
⑥ the episode of the far-off day：遥远往昔的片段。

was so reasonlessly horrified she halted suddenly staring①, the scene before her eyes dimmed by the vision back of them. An Indian vendor② had held up before her a tray of dyed-sugar sweets③, shaped like all kinds of small creatures: birds, baby chicks, baby rabbits, lambs, baby pigs. They were in gay colors and smelled of vanilla④, maybe .... It was a very hot day and the smell in the market, with its piles of raw flesh and wilting flowers⑤, was like the mingled sweetness and corruption⑥ she had smelled that other day in the empty cemetery at home: the day she had remembered vaguely⑦ always until now as the time she and her brother had found treasure in the opened graves. Instantly upon this thought the dreadful⑧ vision faded, and she saw clearly her brother, whose childhood face she had forgotten, standing again in the blazing sunshine⑨, again twelve years old, a pleased sober smile in his eyes, turning the silver dove over and over in his hands.

【思考题】

1. 小说中的男女主人公是怎样的人物？
2. 小说题目"坟"有多重指涉意义，请仔细分析。
3. 小说表达了波特怎样独特的美国南方怀旧意识？

---

① She was so reasonlessly horrified she halted suddenly staring：无来由的恐惧袭上心头，她突然停下，凝视前方。
② vendor：小贩。
③ a tray of dyed-sugar sweets：一托盘染色的糖果。
④ They were in gay colors and smelled of vanilla：它们有着鲜艳的颜色，散发出香草的味道。
⑤ wilting flowers：正在枯萎的花朵。
⑥ mingled sweetness and corruption：混合着腐败和香甜的味道。
⑦ remembered vaguely：依稀记得。
⑧ dreadful：可怕的。
⑨ in the blazing sunshine：在耀眼的阳光下。

The Spinoza of Market Street

市场街的斯宾诺莎

艾萨克·巴什维斯·辛格

【导读】

艾萨克·巴什维斯·辛格(Issac Bashevis Singer，1904—1991)，20 世纪美国著名的犹太作家，他的创作一直受到国际文学批评界的关注，并于 1978 年获得了诺贝尔文学奖。

辛格 1904 年生于波兰附近拉兹明的一个贫穷的犹太家庭。他在 1935 年移居美国之前曾在华沙培养拉比的犹太教的经院读过书，对于犹太教的宗教观念和民俗民风非常熟悉，并成为他日后创作的文化背景。辛格深受他的哥哥，著名的意第绪语作家伊斯雷尔·约瑟夫·辛格的影响，摆脱了狭隘的宗教观念的束缚并走上了文学的道路。初到纽约，辛格不得不为生计而奔波。二战后，他开始用意第绪语为《犹太人前进日报》(*Jewish Daily Forward*)写稿。他的第一部小说《莫斯卡特一家》(*The Family Moskat*，1950)以及短篇小说《傻瓜吉姆佩尔》(*Gimpel the Fool*，1957，由著名小说家索尔贝娄(Saul Bellow)译成英文，以下时间都是指英文版)等一批故事相继出版，博得了读者和文学评论界的好评与赞誉。1960 年发表的《卢布林的魔术师》(*The Magician of Lublin*)是其小说中最受欢迎的一部。

辛格小说的背景往往是世纪之交的波兰，一个东正教占主导地位的社会。40 年的辛勤耕耘，他一共写出了 13 部长篇小说、12 篇短篇小说集、4 个剧本、3 本回忆录以及 13 种儿童故事集等。在辛格的所有作品中，他一直探索着犹太人的生活，他们的过去与未来。

辛格的长篇小说大致分为两类。一类以《莫斯卡特一家》、《庄园》(*The Manor*，1967)、《农庄》(*The Estate*，1969)等为代表作，描写波兰犹太人在现代社会中分崩离析的历史过程；另一类如《撒旦在戈雷》(*Satan in Goray*，1955)、《卡夫卡的朋友》(*A Friend of Kafka*，1970)、《仇敌，一个爱情故事》(*Enemies: A Love Story*，1972)等，大都写灾难深重及传统枷锁下的犹太人的生活场景，还时时夹杂了鬼怪精灵的故事。

长篇小说《卢布林的魔术师》是辛格最负盛名的一部作品。故事发生在 19 世纪末沙俄统治下的波兰。主人公雅夏是一个以表演魔术、杂技为职业的犹太人，出生在卢布林一个笃信犹太教的穷苦商人家庭，自幼失去父母，只在犹太小学念过几年书。长大后,他凭着自己的聪明和勤学苦练精神,成了一个技艺超群的魔术师。但他在生活上丧失理智,放纵情欲,不惜拿自己的血汗钱换取片刻欢愉。他对妻子不忠,同时与几个女人有染:助手玛格达是他公开的情妇,雅夏出钱供养玛格达一家;小偷弃妇泽特尔也与雅夏暗中勾搭,雅夏在她身上挥霍了大量钱物;此外,雅夏还疯狂地爱上了在华沙结识的教授遗孀埃米莉亚,并陷入情网不可自拔。为了达到与埃米莉亚结婚的目的,雅夏决定与妻子离婚,放弃犹太教,改信天主教。为了能拿出埃米莉亚要求的婚后定居国外的一大笔钱,他不惜铤而走险,入室偷窃,但以失败受伤而告终。一个才华横溢的魔术师就这样葬送了大好前程。小说的结尾是雅夏在与外界隔绝的小屋苦修赎罪。

《卢布林的魔术师》所揭示的主题,是人们的行为在道德伦理意义上的矛盾,而这种揭示是通过雅夏·梅休尔这个犹太魔术师的生活经历来体现的。辛格的视线超越了人类的大浩劫,醉心于人类内心善恶力量的交锋以及对人类道德状态的探索。

辛格自己认为短篇小说是他的强项,《傻瓜吉姆佩尔》中的主人公成了西方社会中家喻户晓的倒霉蛋的典型,《市场街的斯宾诺莎》含义深刻又充满了机智与幽默。

《市场街的斯宾诺莎》里的菲谢尔森是一个专心研究哲学,高度强调精神生活的老鳏夫、老博士。这个居住在华沙市场街阁楼里的犹太人,总是手里拿着斯宾诺莎的一本《伦理学》在研究,生活陷入多重困境中,卧病不起、生命垂危。幸好邻居女黑人多比发现了他。在多比的精心料理下,菲谢尔森身体好转,两人产生了感情。最终,菲谢尔森博士和老处女多比走入婚姻殿堂,开始尝到人生乐趣,宿疾痊愈。

辛格的作品体现了他对整个犹太民族宗教、伦理、历史等深刻的思考,在某种程度上,也是对全人类普遍境遇的思考。在这篇小说中,菲谢尔森一开始对斯宾诺莎《伦理学》在能否理性地追求幸福和快乐上的理解充满了矛盾。最后,他接受了世俗中合理的快乐,从而主动、理性而又能动地改造了自己犹太宗教伦理观,找到了自己心中的迦南:一个理性地信仰犹太宗教伦理的地方。

The Spinoza of Market Street

Translated by Martha Glicklich and Cecil Hemley

I

Dr. Nahum Fischelson paced back and forth in his garret[①] room in Market Street, Warsaw[②]. Dr. Fischelson

---

① garret:阁楼。
② Warsaw:华沙(波兰首都)。

was a short, hunched① man with a grayish beard, and was quite bald except for a few wisps② of hair remaining at the nape③ of the neck. His nose was as crooked④ as a beak⑤ and his eyes were large, dark, and fluttering like those of some huge bird. It was a hot summer evening, but Dr. Fischelson wore a black coat which reached to his knees, and he had on a stiff collar and a bow tie. From the door he paced slowly to the dormer⑥ window set high in the slanting room and back again. One had to mount several steps to look out. A candle in a brass⑦ holder was burning on the table and a variety of insects buzzed⑧ around the flame. Now and again one of the creatures would fly too close to the fire and sear⑨ its wings, or one would ignite and glow on the wick⑩ for an instant. At such moments Dr. Fischelson grimaced⑪. His wrinkled face would twitch and beneath his disheveled⑫ moustache he would bite his lips. Finally he took a handkerchief from his pocket and waved it at the insects.

"Away from there, fools and imbeciles⑬," he scolded. "You won't get warm here; you'll only burn yourself."

The insects scattered but a second later returned and once more circled the trembling flame. Dr. Fischelson

上下文交代主人公
菲谢尔森博士体貌年
龄、居住陋室以及对待
一切的不同态度。

① hunched：驼背的。
② wisp：一缕。
③ nape：后颈。
④ crooked：弯曲的。
⑤ beak：鹰钩嘴。
⑥ dormer：屋顶窗。
⑦ brass：黄铜。
⑧ buzz：发出嗡嗡声。
⑨ sear：烧焦。
⑩ wick：灯芯。
⑪ grimace：做鬼脸。
⑫ disheveled：蓬乱的。
⑬ imbecile：（口）白痴。

wiped the sweat from his wrinkled forehead and sighed, "Like men they desire nothing but the pleasure of the moment."

On the table lay an open book written in Latin, and on its broad-margined pages were notes and comments printed in small letters by Dr. Fischelson. The book was Spinoza's *Ethics*① and Dr. Fischelson had been studying it for the last thirty years. He knew every proposition, every proof, every corollary②, every note by heart. When he wanted to find a particular passage, he generally opened to the place immediately without having to search for it. But, nevertheless, he continued to study the Ethics for hours every day with a magnifying glass in his bony hand, murmuring and nodding his head in agreement. The truth was that the more Dr. Fischelson studied, the more puzzling sentences, unclear passages, and cryptic③ remarks he found. Each sentence contained hints unfathomed④ by any of the students of Spinoza. Actually the philosopher had anticipated all of the criticisms of pure reason made by Kant⑤ and his followers. Dr. Fischelson was writing a commentary on the Ethics. He had drawers full of notes and drafts, but it didn't seem that he would ever be able to complete his work.

The stomach ailment⑥ which had plagued him for years was growing worse from day to day. Now he would

菲谢尔森博士花费 30 多年潜心研究斯宾诺莎的《伦理学》,这是造成他现状的原因。

菲谢尔森博士观念中有的是上帝的无限和灵魂的不朽,可现实生活的窘迫和身体的疾病却无情地反映出与思想相悖的痛苦和死亡的威胁。

---

① Spinoza's *Ethics*:斯宾诺莎(Spinoza, 1632—1677),荷兰唯物主义哲学家,祖先为犹太人,认为自然界的一切都是必然的,"实体"有无数的属性,给自己的哲学体系披上了泛神论外衣。《伦理学》(1662—1675)是他的重要遗著。

② corollary:推论。

③ cryptic:含义模糊的。

④ unfathomed:尚未理解的。

⑤ Kant:伊曼努尔·康德(Immanuel Kant,1724—1804),德国思想家、哲学家、天文学家、星云说的创立者之一、德国古典哲学的创始人。他被认为是对现代欧洲最具影响力的思想家之一,也是启蒙运动的主要思想家。

⑥ ailment:疾病(尤其指慢性病)。

get pains in his stomach after only a few mouthfuls of oatmeals①. "God in Heaven, it's difficult, very difficult," he would say to himself using the same intonation as had his father, the late Rabbi of Tishevitz②. "It's very, very hard."

Dr. Fischelson was not afraid of dying. To begin with, he was no longer a young man. Secondly, it is stated in the fourth part of the *Ethics* that "a free man thinks of nothing less than of death and his wisdom is a meditation③ not of death, but of life." Thirdly, it is also said that "the human mind cannot be absolutely destroyed with the human body but there is some part of it that remains eternal." And yet Dr. Fischelson's ulcer④ (or perhaps it was a cancer) continued to bother him. His tongue was always coated⑤. He belched⑥ frequently and emitted⑦ a different foul-smelling gas each time. He suffered from heartburn and cramps⑧. At times he felt like vomiting⑨ and at other times he was hungry for garlic, onions, and fried foods. He had long ago discarded the medicines prescribed for him by the doctors and had sought his own remedies. He found it beneficial to take grated radish⑩ after meals and lie on his bed, belly down, with his head hanging over the side. But these home remedies offered only temporary relief. Some of the doctors he consulted

---

① oatmeals: 麦片粥。
② Rabbi of Tishevitz: 已故的蒂歇维支拉比。拉比,希伯来文 rabbi 的音译,原意"吾主""夫子",是犹太教中的教士,他既主持宗教仪式,又执掌犹太人的法律,同时教学和从事精神治疗。
③ meditation: 沉思。
④ ulcer: 溃疡。
⑤ coated: 此处指舌苔厚。
⑥ belch: 打嗝。
⑦ emit: 吐出。
⑧ cramps: 痉挛。
⑨ vomit: 呕吐。
⑩ radish: 磨碎的萝卜丝。

insisted there was nothing the matter with him. "It's just nerves," they told him. "You could live to be a hundred."

But on this particular hot summer night, Dr. Fischelson felt his strength ebbing. His knees were shaky, his pulse weak. He sat down to read and his vision blurred①. The letters on the page turned from green to gold. The lines became waved and jumped over each other, leaving white gaps as if the text had disappeared in some mysterious way.

The heat was unbearable, flowing down directly from the tin roof; Dr. Fischelson felt he was inside of an oven. Several times he climbed the four steps to the window and thrust his head out into the cool of the evening breeze. He would remain in that position for so long his knees would become wobbly②. "Oh it's a fine breeze," he would murmur, "really delightful," and he would recall that according to Spinoza, morality and happiness were identical, and that the most moral deed a man could perform was to indulge in some pleasure which was not contrary to reason.

斯宾诺莎的哲学思想："道德和幸福是同一性的，一个人最符合道德的行为，就是尽情享受并不违反理性的乐事。"

II

Dr. Fischelson, standing on the top step at the window and looking out, could see into two worlds. Above him were the heavens, thickly strewn with③ stars. Dr. Fischelson had never seriously studied astronomy but he could differentiate between the planets, those bodies which like the earth, revolve around the sun, and the fixed stars, themselves distant suns, whose light reaches us a hundred or even a thousand years later. He recognized

① blur：模糊。
② wobbly：不稳，颤抖。
③ strewn with：布满。

the constellations① which mark the path of the earth in space and that nebulous sash, the Milky Way②. Dr. Fischelson owned a small telescope he had bought in Switzerland where he had studied and he particularly enjoyed looking at the moon through it. He could clearly make out on the moon's surface the volcanoes bathed in sunlight and the dark, shadowy craters③. He never wearied of gazing at these cracks and crevasses④. To him they seemed both near and distant, both substantial and insubstantial. Now and then he would see a shooting star trace a wide arc across the sky and disappear, leaving a fiery trail behind it. Dr. Fischelson would know then that a meteorite⑤ had reached our atmosphere, and perhaps some unburned fragment of it had fallen into the ocean or had landed in the desert or perhaps even in some inhabited region. Slowly the stars which had appeared from behind Dr. Fischelson's roof rose until they were shining above the house across the street. Yes, when Dr. Fischelson looked up into the heavens, he became aware of that infinite extension which is, according to Spinoza, one of God's attributes. It comforted Dr. Fischelson to think that although he was only a weak, puny⑥ man, a changing mode of the absolutely infinite substance, he was nevertheless a part of the cosmos, made of the same matter as the celestial⑦ bodies; to the extent that he was a part of the Godhead, he knew he could not be destroyed. In such moments, Dr. Fischelson experienced the Amor

---

① constellations: 星座。
② nebulous sash, the Milky Way: 星云状的衣带——银河。
③ crater: 火山口。
④ crevasse: 裂缝。
⑤ meteorite: 陨星。
⑥ puny: 弱小的。
⑦ celestial: 神的。

菲谢尔森博士举目苍穹，感受到了星体背后的无限、永恒和神性，他体味到了理性之爱。

Dei Intellectualis① which is, according to the philosopher of Amsterdam②, the highest perfection of the mind. Dr. Fischelson breathed deeply, lifted his head as high as his stiff collar permitted and actually felt he was whirling in company with the earth, the sun, the stars of the Milky Way, and the infinite host of galaxies③ known only to infinite thought. His legs became light and weightless and he grasped the window frame with both hands as if afraid he would lose his footing and fly out into eternity.

When Dr. Fischelson tired of observing the sky, his glance dropped to Market Street below. He could see a long strip extending from Yanash's market to Iron Street with the gas lamps lining it merged into a string of fiery dots. Smoke was issuing from the chimneys on the black, tin roofs; the bakers were heating their ovens, and here and there sparks mingled with the black smoke. The street never looked so noisy and crowded as on a summer evening. Thieves, prostitutes, gamblers, and fences④ loafed in the square which looked from above like a pretzel⑤ covered with poppy⑥ seeds. The young men laughed coarsely and the girls shrieked. A peddler⑦ with a keg⑧ of lemonade on his back pierced the general din⑨ with his intermittent cries. A watermelon vendor⑩ shouted in a savage voice, and the long knife which he used for cutting the fruit dripped with the blood-like juice.

---

① the Amor Dei Intellectualis：(拉丁文)理性之爱。
② the philosopher of Amsterdam：即斯宾诺莎。
③ galaxies：星系。
④ fence：买卖赃物者。
⑤ pretzel：椒盐煎饼。
⑥ poppy：罂粟。
⑦ peddler：不法商贩。
⑧ keg：小桶。
⑨ din：喧闹声。
⑩ vendor：小贩。

Now and again the street became even more agitated①.
Fire engines, their heavy wheels clanging, sped by; they
were drawn by sturdy② black horses which had to be
tightly curbed③ to prevent them from running wild. Next
came an ambulance, its siren④ screaming. Then some
thugs⑤ had a fight among themselves and the police had to
be called. A passerby was robbed and ran about shouting
for help. Some wagons loaded with firewood sought to get
through into the courtyards where the bakeries were
located but the horses could not lift the wheels over the
steep curbs⑥ and the drivers berated⑦ the animals and
lashed them with their whips. Sparks rose from the
clanging hoofs⑧. It was now long after seven, which was
the prescribed closing time for stores, but actually business
had only begun. Customers were led in stealthily⑨ through
back doors. The Russian policemen on the street, having
been paid off, noticed nothing of this. Merchants
continued to hawk their wares, each seeking to outshout
the others.

"Gold, gold, gold," a woman who dealt in
rotten oranges shrieked.

"Sugar, sugar, sugar," croaked a dealer of
overripe plums,

"Heads, heads, heads," a boy who sold fishheads
roared.

---

① agitated：不安的。
② sturdy：强壮的。
③ curb：限制，控制。
④ siren：警报器。
⑤ thug：恶棍。
⑥ curb：此处指路边石。
⑦ berate：训斥。
⑧ clanging hoof：忒忒作响的马蹄。
⑨ stealthily：暗地里。

菲谢尔森博士俯身注视自己生活的市场街,这是一条充满了欲望的肮脏的街道,是一个与他神往的神性世界迥异的世俗世界。

Through the window of a Chassidic① study house across the way, Dr. Fischelson could see boys with long sidelocks swaying over holy volumes, grimacing and studying aloud in singsong voices. Butchers, porters, and fruit dealers were drinking beer in the tavern② below. Vapor drifted from the tavern's open door like steam from a bathhouse, and there was the sound of loud music. Outside of the tavern, streetwalkers snatched at drunken soldiers and at workers on their way home from the factories. Some of the men carried bundles of wood on their shoulders, reminding Dr. Fischelson of the wicked who are condemned to kindle their own fires in Hell Husky record players poured out their raspings through open windows. The liturgy of the high holidays alternated with vulgar vaudeville songs③.

菲谢尔森引用斯宾诺莎的观点:七情六欲从来就不是什么好东西。他们追求的是欢乐,结果得到的只是疾病和监狱、羞辱以及无知带来的苦难。

Dr. Fischelson peered into the halflit bedlam④ and cocked his ears. He knew that the behavior of this rabble was the very antithesis of reason⑤. These people were immersed in the vainest of passions, were drunk with emotions, and, according to Spinoza, emotion was never good. Instead of the pleasure they ran after, all they succeeded in obtaining was disease and prison, shame and the suffering that resulted from ignorance. Even the cats which loitered on the roofs here seemed more savage and passionate than those in other parts of the town. They caterwauled⑥ with the voices of women in labor, and like

---

① Chassidic: 锡德派。
② tavern: 小酒店。
③ The liturgy of the high holidays alternated with vulgar vaudeville songs: 礼拜日的祷告和庸俗的轻松喜剧中的歌曲交替着传过来。
④ bedlam: 疯人院。
⑤ the behavior of this rabble was the very antithesis of reason: 这些胡闹的人的行为跟"理性"正好是对立面。
⑥ caterwaul: 猫求偶的叫声。

demons scampered① up walls and leaped onto eaves② and balconies. One of the toms③ paused at Dr. Fischelson's window and let out a howl which made Dr. Fischelson shudder. The doctor stepped from the window and，picking up a broom, brandished④ it in front of the black beast's glowing，green eyes. "Scat，begone，you ignorant savage！" and he rapped the broom handle against the roof until the tom ran off.

III

When Dr. Fischelson had returned to Warsaw from Zurich⑤ where he had studied philosophy，a great future had been predicted for him. His friends had known that he was writing an important book on Spinoza. A Jewish Polish journal had invited him to be a contributor⑥；he had been a frequent guest at several wealthy households and he had been made head librarian at the Warsaw synagogue⑦. Although even then he had been considered an old bachelor，the matchmakers had proposed several rich girls for him. But Dr. Fischelson had not taken advantage of these opportunities. He had wanted to be as independent as Spinoza himself. And he had been. But because of his heretical ideas he had come into conflict with the rabbi and had had to resign his post as librarian. For years after that，he had supported himself by giving private lessons in Hebrew and German. Then，when he had become sick，the Berlin Jewish community had voted

菲谢尔森的自我封闭是一个渐进的过程，他本可以有很多机会生活得更好，但他想像斯宾诺莎一样，把一切机会都拒绝了。

---

① scamper：快跑。
② eave：屋檐。
③ tom：雄性猫。
④ brandish：威胁地挥动。
⑤ Zurich：苏黎世。
⑥ contributor：这里指撰稿者。
⑦ synagogue：犹太会堂。

him a subsidy of five hundred marks a year①. This had been made possible through the intervention of the famous Dr. Hildesheimer with whom he corresponded about philosophy. In order to get by on② so small a pension, Dr. Fischelson had moved into the attic room and had begun cooking his own meals on a kerosene stove③. He had a cupboard which had many drawers, and each drawer was labelled with the food it contained buckwheat④, rice, barley⑤, onions, carrots, potatoes, mushrooms. Once a week Dr. Fischelson put on his widebrimmed black hat, took a basket in one hand and Spinoza's *Ethics* in the other, and went off to the market for his provisions⑥. While he was waiting to be served, he would open the *Ethics*. The merchants knew him and would motion him to their stalls.

"A fine piece of cheese, Doctor just melts in your mouth."

"Fresh mushrooms, Doctor, straight from the woods."

"Make way for the Doctor, ladies," the butcher would shout. "Please don't block the entrance."

During the early years of his sickness, Dr. Fischelson had still gone in the evening to a cafe which was frequented by Hebrew teachers and other intellectuals. It had been his habit to sit there and play chess while drinking a half a glass of black coffee. Sometimes he would stop at the bookstores on Holy Cross Street where all sorts of old books and magazines could be purchased cheap. On one occasion a former pupil of his had arranged

---

① a subsidy of five hundred marks a year：一年五百马克的津贴。

② get by on：靠……过活。

③ kerosene stove：煤油炉。

④ buckwheat：荞麦。

⑤ barley：大麦。

⑥ provisions：粮食。

to meet him at a restaurant one evening. When Dr. Fischelson arrived, he had been surprised to find a group of friends and admirers who forced him to sit at the head of the table while they made speeches about him. But these were things that had happened long ago. Now people were no longer interested in him. He had isolated himself completely and had become a forgotten man. The events of 1905 when the boys of Market Street had begun to organize strikes, throw bombs at police stations, and shoot strike breakers so that the stores were closed even on weekdays had greatly increased his isolation. He began to despise everything associated with the modern Jew Zionism①, socialism, anarchism②. The young men in question seemed to him nothing but an ignorant rabble intent on destroying society, society without which no reasonable existence was possible. He still read a Hebrew magazine occasionally, but he felt contempt for modern Hebrew which had no roots in the Bible or the Mishnah③. The spelling of Polish words had changed also. Dr. Fischelson concluded that even the so-called spiritual men had abandoned reason and were doing their utmost to pander to the mob④. Now and again he still visited a library and browsed through some of the modern histories of philosophy, but he found that the professors did not understand Spinoza, quoted him incorrectly, attributed their own muddled⑤ ideas to the philosopher. Although Dr. Fischelson was well aware that anger was an emotion unworthy of those who walk the path of reason, he would

---

① Jew Zionism：犹太复国主义。
② anarchism：无政府主义。
③ Mishnah：《米市纳》，犹太教经书。
④ pander to the mob：迎合群众。
⑤ muddled：混乱的。

菲谢尔森已经把自己与外界完全隔绝了，他成了一个被遗忘的人。

become furious, and would quickly close the book and push it from him. "Idiots," he would mutter, "asses, upstarts①." And he would vow never again to look at modern philosophy.

IV

Every three months a special mailman who only delivered money orders brought Dr. Fischelson eighty rubles②. He expected his quarterly allotment③ at the beginning of July but as day after day passed and the tall man with the blond moustache and the shiny buttons did not appear, the Doctor grew anxious. He had scarcely a groshen④ left. Who knows possibly the Berlin community had rescinded⑤ his subsidy; perhaps Dr. Hildesheimer had died, God forbid; the post office might have made a mistake. Every event has its cause, Dr. Fischelson knew. All was determined, all necessary, and a man of reason had no right to worry. Nevertheless, worry invaded his brain, and buzzed about like the flies. If the worst came to the worst, it occurred to him, he could commit suicide, but then he remembered that Spinoza did not approve of suicide and compared those who took their own lives to the insane.

One day when Dr. Fischelson went out to a store to purchase a composition book, he heard people talking about war. In Serbia⑥ somewhere, an Austrian Prince had been shot⑦ and the Austrians had delivered an ultimatum⑧

① upstart：暴发户。
② ruble：卢布。
③ quarterly allotment：季度津贴。
④ groshen：奥地利货币和硬币名，等于 0.01 先令。
⑤ rescind：取消。
⑥ Serbia：塞尔维亚。
⑦ an Austrian Prince had been shot：指 1914 年 6 月 28 日奥匈帝国王位的继承人斐迪南大公爵在塞尔维亚遇刺,这成为第一次世界大战的导火线。
⑧ ultimatum：最后通牒。

to the Serbs. The owner of the store, a young man with a yellow beard and shifty yellow eyes, announced, "We are about to have a small war," and he advised Dr. Fischelson to store up food because in the near future there was likely to be a shortage.

Everything happened so quickly. Dr. Fischelson had not even decided whether it was worthwhile to spend four groshen on a newspaper, and already posters had been hung up announcing mobilization①. Men were to be seen walking on the street with round, metal tags② on their lapels③, a sign that they were being drafted④. They were followed by their crying wives. One Monday when Dr. Fischelson descended to the street to buy some food with his last kopecks⑤, he found the stores closed. The owners and their wives stood outside and explained that merchandise was unobtainable. But certain special customers were pulled to one side and let in through back doors. On the street all was confusion. Policemen with swords unsheathed⑥ could be seen riding on horseback. A large crowd had gathered around the tavern where, at the command of the Tsar⑦, the tavern's stock of whiskey was being poured into the gutter⑧.

Dr. Fischelson went to his old cafe. Perhaps he would find some acquaintances there who would advise him. But he did not come across a single person he knew. He decided, then, to visit the rabbi of the synagogue

---

① mobilization：动员令。
② tag：标牌。
③ lapel：上衣翻领。
④ draft：应征入伍。
⑤ kopeck：俄罗斯小铜板。
⑥ unsheathe：出鞘。
⑦ Tsar：沙皇。
⑧ gutter：阴沟。

where he had once been librarian, but the sexton① with the six-sided skull cap informed him that the rabbi and his family had gone off to the spas. Dr. Fischelson had other old friends in town but he found no one at home. His feet ached from so much walking; black and green spots appeared before his eyes and he felt faint. He stopped and waited for the giddiness② to pass. The passers-by jostled③ him. A dark-eyed high school girl tried to give him a coin. Although the war had just started, soldiers eight abreast were marching in full battle dress the men were covered with dust and were sunburnt. Canteens④ were strapped to their sides and they wore rows of bullets across their chests. The bayonets⑤ on their rifles gleamed with a cold, green light. They sang with mournful voices. Along with the men came cannons, each pulled by eight horses; their blind muzzles⑥ breathed gloomy terror. Dr. Fischelson felt nauseous⑦. His stomach ached; his intestines⑧ seemed about to turn themselves inside out. Cold sweat appeared on his face.

"I'm dying," he thought. "This is the end." Nevertheless, he did manage to drag himself home where he lay down on the iron cot⑨ and remained, panting and gasping. He must have dozed off because he imagined that he was in his home town, Tishvitz. He had a sore throat and his mother was busy wrapping a stocking stuffed with

① sexton：教堂司事。
② giddiness：晕眩。
③ jostle：撞。
④ canteen：军用水壶。
⑤ bayonet：刺刀。
⑥ muzzle：炮口。
⑦ nauseous：恶心的。
⑧ intestine：肠子。
⑨ cot：小床。

hot salt around his neck. He could hear talk going on in the house; something about a candle and about how a frog had bitten him. He wanted to go out into the street but they wouldn't let him because a Catholic procession was passing by. Men in long robes, holding double edged axes in their hands, were intoning① in Latin as they sprinkled holy water. Crosses gleamed; sacred pictures waved in the air. There was an odor of incense and corpses. Suddenly the sky turned a burning red and the whole world started to burn. Bells were ringing; people rushed madly about. Flocks② of birds flew overhead, screeching. Dr. Fischelson awoke with a start. His body was covered with sweat and his throat was now actually sore. He tried to meditate about his extraordinary dream, to find its rational connection with what was happening to him and to comprehend it sub specie etermtatis③, but none of it made sense. "Alas, the brain is a receptacle④ for nonsense," Dr. Fischelson thought. "This earth belongs to the mad."

And he once more closed his eyes; once more he dozed; once more he dreamed.

菲谢尔森在梦中回到了故乡,回到了童年,象征着他的新生。

V

The eternal laws, apparently, had not yet ordained⑤ Dr. Fischelson's end.

There was a door to the left of Dr. Fischelson's attic room which opened off a dark corridor, cluttered⑥ with boxes and baskets, in which the odor of fried onions and laundry soap was always present. Behind this door lived a

---

① intone：吟唱。
② flock：鸟群。
③ sub specie etermtatis：(拉丁文)低于永恒的方式。
④ receptacle：储藏所。
⑤ ordain：命运注定。
⑥ clutter：杂乱地堆放。

spinster① whom the neighbors called Black Dobbe. Dobbe was tall and lean, and as black as a baker's shovel. She had a broken nose and there was a mustache on her upper lip. She spoke with the hoarse voice of a man and she wore men's shoes. For years Black Dobbe had sold breads, rolls, and bagels② which she had bought from the baker at the gate of the house. But one day she and the baker had quarreled and she had moved her business to the market place and now she dealt in what were called "wrinklers"③ which was a synonym④ for cracked eggs. Black Dobbe had no luck with men. Twice she had been engaged to baker's apprentices⑤ but in both instances they had returned the engagement contract to her. Some time afterwards she had received an engagement contract from an old man, a glazier⑥ who claimed that he was divorced, but it had later come to light that he still had a wife. Black Dobbe had a cousin in America, a shoemaker, and repeatedly she boasted⑦ that this cousin was sending her passage, but she remained in Warsaw. She was constantly being teased by the women who would say, "There's no hope for you, Dobbe. You're fated to die an old maid." Dobbe always answered, "I don't intend to be a slave for any man. Let them all rot."

That afternoon Dobbe received a letter from America. Generally she would go to Leizer the Tailor and have him read it to her. However, that day Leizer was out

简单介绍了黑多比：相貌丑陋,生活艰辛,至今未嫁。

---

① spinster：老处女。
② bagel：硬面包卷。
③ wrinklers：“皱皮肤”。
④ synonym：同义词。
⑤ apprentice：学徒工。
⑥ glazier：装玻璃匠。
⑦ boast：自吹自擂。

and so Dobbe thought of Dr. Fischelson whom the other tenants① considered a convert since he never went to prayer. She knocked on the door of the doctor's room but there was no answer. "The heretic② is probably out," Dobbe thought but, nevertheless, she knocked once more, and this time the door moved slightly. She pushed her way in and stood there frightened. Dr. Fischelson lay fully clothed on his bed; his face was as yellow as wax③; his Adam's apple④ stuck out prominently; his beard pointed upward. Dobbe screamed; she was certain that he was dead, but no his body moved. Dobbe picked up a glass which stood on the table, ran into the corridor, filled the glass with water from the faucet⑤, hurried back, and threw the water into the face of the unconscious man. Dr. Fischelson shook his head and opened his eyes.

"What's wrong with you?" Dobbe asked. "Are you sick?"

"Thank you very much. No."

"Have you a family? I'll call them."

"No family," Dr. Fischelson said.

Dobbe wanted to fetch the barber from across the street but Dr. Fischelson signified that he didn't wish the barber's assistance. Since Dobbe was not going to the market that day, no "wrinklers" being available, she decided to do a good deed. She assisted the sick man to get off the bed and smoothed down the blanket. Then she undressed Dr. Fischelson and prepared some soup for him on the kerosene stove. The sun never entered Dobbe's

---

① tenant：租户，房客。
② heretic：异教徒。
③ wax：蜡。
④ Adam's apple：喉结。
⑤ faucet：水龙头。

room, but here squares of sunlight shimmered① on the faded walls. The floor was painted red. Over the bed hung a picture of a man who was wearing a broad frill② around his neck and had long hair. "Such an old fellow and yet he keeps his place so nice and clean," Dobbe thought approvingly. Dr. Fischelson asked for the *Ethics*, and she gave it to him disapprovingly. She was certain it was a gentile prayer book③. Then she began bustling about④, brought in a pail of water, swept the floor. Dr. Fischelson ate; after he had finished, he was much stronger and Dobbe asked him to read her the letter.

He read it slowly, the paper trembling in his hands. It came from New York, from Dobbe's cousin. Once more he wrote that he was about to send her a "really important letter" and a ticket to America. By now, Dobbe knew the story by heart and she helped the old man decipher⑤ her cousin's scrawl⑥. "He's lying," Dobbe said. "He forgot about me a long time ago." In the evening, Dobbe came again. A candle in a brass holder was burning on the chair next to the bed. Reddish shadows trembled on the walls and ceiling. Dr. Fischelson sat propped up⑦ in bed, reading a book. The candle threw a golden light on his forehead which seemed as if cleft in two⑧. A bird had flown in through the window and was perched⑨ on the table. For a moment Dobbe was frightened. This man made her think of witches, of black

① shimmer：闪光。
② frills：皱领。
③ gentile prayer book：这里的异教徒的祈祷书是指非犹太教的祈祷书。
④ bustle about：忙活起来。
⑤ decipher：辨认字迹。
⑥ scrawl：潦草书写。
⑦ prop up：支撑起来。
⑧ cleft in two：一劈为二。
⑨ perch：栖息。

mirrors and corpses wandering around at night and terrifying women. Nevertheless, she took a few steps toward him and inquired, "How are you? Any better?"

"A little, thank you."

"Are you really a convert?" she asked although she wasn't juke sure what the word meant.

"Me, a convert? No, I'm a Jew like any other Jew," Dr. Fischelson answered.

The doctor's assurances made Dobbe feel more at home. She found the bottle of kerosene and lit the stove, and after that she fetched a glass of milk from her room and began cooking kasha①. Dr. Fischelson continued to study the *Ethics*, but that evening he could make no sense of the theorems② and proofs with their many references to axioms③ and definitions and other theorems. With trembling hand he raised the book to his eyes and read, "The idea of each modification④ of the luman body does not involve adequate knowledge of the luman body itself . . . . The idea of the idea of each modiication of the human mind does not involve adequate knowledge of the human mind."

VI

Dr. Fischelson was certain he would die any day now. He made out his will, leaving all of his books and manuscripts to the synagogue library. His clothing and furniture would go to Dobbe since she had taken care of him. But death did not come. Rather his health improved. Dobbe returned to her Business in the market, but she visited the old man several times a day, prepared

菲谢尔森读不进斯宾诺莎的《伦理学》了，暗示了他走向世俗生活的开始。

---

① kasha：麦糊。
② theorem：定理。
③ axiom：公理。
④ modification：变化。

soup for him, left him a glass of tea, and told him news of the war. The Germans had occupied Kalish, Bendin, and Cestechow, and they were marching on Warsaw. People said that on a quiet morning one could hear the rumblings① of the cannon. Dobbe reported that the casualties② were heavy. "They're falling like flies," she said. "What a terrible misfortune for the women."

She couldn't explain why, but the old man's attic room attracted her. She liked to remove the gold-rimmed books from the bookcase, dust them, and then air them on the windowsill③. She would climb the few steps to the window and look out through the telescope. She also enjoyed talking to Dr. Fischelson. He told her about Switzerland where he had studied, of the great cities he had passed through, of the high mountains that were covered with snow even in the summer. His father had been a rabbi, he said, and before he, Dr. Fischelson, had become a student, he had attended a yeshiva④. She asked him how many languages he knew and it turned out that he could speak and write Hebrew, Russian, German, and French, in addition to Yiddish⑤. He also knew Latin. Dobbe was astonished that such an educated man should live in an attic room on Market Street. But what amazed her most of all was that although he had the title "Doctor," he couldn't write prescriptions⑥. "Why don't you become a real doctor?" she would ask him. "I am a doctor," he would answer. "I'm just not a physician." "What kind of a doctor?" "A doctor of philosophy."

---

① rumbling：隆隆声。
② casualties：伤亡情况。
③ windowsill：窗边。
④ yeshiva：犹太经院。
⑤ Yiddish：意第绪语。
⑥ prescription：处方。欧美习惯称医生为"（医学）博士"，因此多比误以为凡是称"博士"的即是医生。

Although she had no idea of what this meant, she felt it must be very important. "Oh my blessed mother," she would say, "where did you get such a brain?"

Then one evening after Dobbe had given him his crackers and his glass of tea with milk, he began questioning her about where she came from, who her parents were, and why she had not married. Dobbe was surprised. No one had ever asked her such questions. She told him her story in a quiet voice and stayed until eleven o'clock. Her father had been a porter① at the kosher butcher shops②. Her mother had plucked chickens in the slaughterhouse. The family had lived in a cellar at No. 19 Market Street. When she had been ten, she had become a maid. The man she had worked for had been a fence who bought stolen goods from thieves on the square. Dobbe had had a brother who had gone into the Russian army and had never returned. Her sister had married a coachman in Praga and had died in childbirth. Dobbe told of the battles between the underworld and the revolutionaries in 1905, of blind Itche and his gang and how they collected protection money from the stores, of the thugs who attacked young boys and girls out on Saturday afternoon strolls if they were not paid money for security. She also spoke of the pimps③ who drove about in carriages and abducted④ women to be sold in Buenos Aires. Dobbe swore that some men had even sought to inveigle⑤ her into a brothel⑥, but that she had run away. She complained of a thousand evils done to her. She had

---

① porter：门房。
② kosher butcher shop：犹太人开的药店。
③ pimp：拉皮条的男子。
④ abduct：诱拐。
⑤ inveilge：哄骗。
⑥ brothel：妓院。

been robbed; her boy friend had been stolen; a competitor had once poured a pint of kerosene into her basket of bagels; her own cousin, the shoemaker, had cheated her out of a hundred rubles before he had left for America. Dr. Fischelson listened to her attentively, asked her questions, shook his head, and grunted.

"Well, do you believe in God?" he finally asked her.

"I don't know," she answered. "Do you?"

"Yes, I believe."

"Then why don't you go to synagogue?" she asked.

"God is everywhere," he replied. "In the synagogue. In the marketplace. In this very room. We ourselves are parts of God."

"Don't say such things," Dobbe said. "You frighten me."

She left the room and Dr. Fischelson was certain she had gone to bed. But he wondered why she had not said "good night." "I probably drove her away with my philosophy," he thought. The very next moment he heard her footsteps. She came in carrying a pile of clothing like a peddler.

"I wanted to show you these," she said. "They're my trousseau①." And she began to spread out, on the chair, dresses woolen, silk, velvet. Taking each dress up in turn, she held it to her body. She gave him an account of every item in her trousseau underwear, shoes, stockings.

"I'm not wasteful," she said. "I'm a saver. I have enough money to go to America."

Then she was silent and her face turned brick-red. She looked at Dr. Fischelson out of the corner of her

_____

① trousseau：嫁妆。

eyes, timidly, inquisitively①. Dr. Fischelson's body suddenly began to shake as if he had the chills. He said, "Very nice, beautiful things." His brow furrowed② and he pulled at his beard with two fingers. A sad smile appeared on his toothless mouth and his large fluttering eyes, gazing into the distance through the attic window, also smiled sadly.

VII

The day that Black Dobbe came to the rabbi's chambers and announced that she was to marry Dr. Fischelson, the rabbi's wife thought she had gone mad. But the news had already reached Leizer the Tailor, and had spread to the bakery, as well as to other shops. There were those who thought that the "old maid" was very lucky; the doctor, they said, had a vast hoard of money③. But there were others who took the view that he was a run-down degenerate④ who would give her syphilis⑤. Although Dr. Fischelson had insisted that the wedding be a small, quiet one, a host of guests assembled in the rabbi's rooms. The baker's apprentices who generally went about barefoot, and in their underwear, with paper bags on the tops of their heads, now put on light-colored suits, straw hats, yellow shoes, gaudy⑥ ties, and they brought with them huge cakes and pans filled with cookies. They had even managed to find a bottle of vodka⑦ although liquor was forbidden in wartime. When

---

① inquisitively: 询问地。
② furrow: 起了皱纹。
③ a vast hoard of money: 一大笔钱财。
④ degenerate: 把身体搞垮的性欲倒错者。
⑤ syphilis: 梅毒。
⑥ gaudy: 绚丽的。
⑦ vodka: 伏特加酒。

the bride and groom① entered the rabbi's chamber, a murmur arose from the crowd. The women could not believe their eyes. The woman that they saw was not the one they had known. Dobbe wore a wide-brimmed hat which was amply adorned with cherries, grapes, and plumes, and the dress that she had on was of white silk and was equipped with a train; on her feet were high-heeled shoes, gold in color, and from her thin neck hung a string of imitation pearls. Nor was this all: her fingers sparkled with rings and glittering stones. Her face was veiled. She looked almost like one of those rich brides who were married in the Vienna Hall②. The bakers' apprentices whistled mockingly. As for Dr. Fischelson, he was wearing his black coat and broadtoed shoes. He was scarcely able to walk; he was leaning on Dobbe. When he saw the crowd from the doorway, he became frightened and began to retreat, but Dobbe's former employer approached him saying, "Come in, come in, bridegroom. Don't be bashful. We are all brethren③ now."

The ceremony proceeded according to the law. The rabbi, in a worn satin gabardine④, wrote the marriage contract and then had the bride and groom touch his handkerchief as a token of agreement; the rabbi wiped the point of the pen on his skullcap⑤. Several porters who had been called from the street to make up the quorum⑥ supported the canopy⑦. Dr. Fischelson put on a white

---

① groom：新郎。
② Vienna Hall：维也纳市政厅。
③ brethren：兄弟。
④ gabardine：华达呢（此处指旧的缎背华达呢外套）。
⑤ skullcap：无檐便帽。
⑥ quorum：凑足人数。
⑦ canopy：华盖。

robe as a reminder of the day of his death and Dobbe walked around him seven times as custom required. The light from the braided candles flickered on the walls. The shadows wavered. Having poured wine into a goblet①, the rabbi chanted the benedictions② in a sad melody. Dobbe uttered only a single cry. As for the other women, they took out their lace handkerchiefs and stood with them in their hands, grimacing. When the baker's boys began to whisper wisecracks③ to each other, the rabbi put a finger to his lips and murmured, "Eh mi oh" as a sign that talking was forbidden. The moment came to slip the wedding ring on the bride's finger, but the bridegroom's hand started to tremble and he had trouble locating Dobbe's index finger. The next thing, according to custom, was the smashing④ of the glass, but though Dr. Fischelson kicked the goblet several times, it remained unbroken. The girls lowered their heads, pinched⑤ each other gleefully, and giggled. Finally one of the apprentices struck the goblet with his heel and it shattered. Even the rabbi could not restrain a smile. After the ceremony the guests drank vodka and ate cookies. Dobbe's former employer came up to Dr. Fischelson and said, "Mazel tov⑥, bridegroom. Your luck should be as good as your wife." "Thank you, thank you," Dr. Fischelson murmured, "but I don't look forward to any luck." He was anxious to return as quickly as possible to his attic room. He felt a pressure in his stomach and his chest ached. His face had become greenish. Dobbe had

---

① goblet：高脚酒杯。
② benedictions：祝福歌曲。
③ wisecrack：俏皮话。
④ smash：弄碎。
⑤ pinch：拧,捏。
⑥ Mazel tov：恭喜,恭喜。

suddenly become angry. She pulled back her veil and called out to the crowd, "What are you laughing at? This isn't a show." And without picking up the cushion-cover in which the gifts were wrapped, she returned with her husband to their rooms on the fifth floor.

Dr. Fischelson lay down on the freshly made bed in his room and began reading the *Ethics*. Dobbe had gone back to her own room. The doctor had explained to her that he was an old man, that he was sick and without strength. He had promised her nothing. Nevertheless she returned wearing a silk nightgown①, slippers with pompoms②, and with her hair hanging down over her shoulders. There was a smile on her face, and she was bashful and hesitant. Dr. Fischelson trembled and the *Ethics* dropped from his hands. The candle went out. Dobbe groped for Dr. Fischelson in the dark and kissed his mouth. "My dear husband," she whispered to him, "Mazel tov."

What happened that night could be called a miracle. If Dr. Fischelson hadn't been convinced that every occurrence is in accordance with the laws of nature, he would have thought that Black Dobbe had bewitched him. Powers long dormant③ awakened in him. Although he had had only a sip of the benediction wine, he was as if intoxicated④. He kissed Dobbe and spoke to her of love. Long forgotten quotations from Klopfstock⑤, Lessing, Goethe, rose to his lips. The pressures and aches stopped. He embraced Dobbe, pressed her to himself, was again a

菲谢尔森和黑多比按照犹太仪式举行了婚礼,暗示着菲谢尔森步入了世俗的生活。

---

① nightgown:睡衣。
② pompom:绒球。
③ dormant:潜伏的。
④ intoxicated:陶醉了。
⑤ Klopfstock:克洛普斯托克(1724—1803),德国诗人,曾与其表妹相恋,著有颂歌,纪念他的爱情。

man as in his youth. Dobbe was faint with delight; crying, she murmured things to him in a Warsaw slang① which he did not understand. Later, Dr. Fischelson slipped off into the deep sleep young men know. He dreamed that he was in Switzerland and that he was climbing mountains running, falling, flying. At dawn he opened his eyes; it seemed to him that someone had blown into his ears. Dobbe was snoring②. Dr. Fischelson quietly got out of bed. In his long nightshirt he approached the window, walked up the steps and looked out in wonder. Market Street was asleep, breathing with a deep stillness. The gas lamps were flickering. The black shutters on the stores were fastened with iron bars. A cool breeze was blowing. Dr. Fischelson looked up at the sky. The black arch was thickly sown with stars there were green, red, yellow, blue stars; there were large ones and small ones, winking③ and steady ones. There were those that were clustered in dense groups and those that were alone. In the higher sphere, apparently, little notice was taken of the fact that a certain Dr. Fischelson had in his declining days married someone called Black Dobbe. Seen from above even the Great War was nothing but a temporary play of the modes④. The myriads of fixed stars continued to travel their destined courses in unbounded space. The comets⑤, planets, satellites, asteroids⑥ kept circling these shining centers. Worlds were born and died in cosmic upheavals. In the chaos of nebulae⑦, primeval matter was

① Warsaw slang: 华沙土语。
② snoring: 打鼾。
③ wink: 眨眼。
④ a temporary play of the modes: 短促的军事游戏。
⑤ comet: 彗星。
⑥ asteroid: 小行星。
⑦ in the chaos of nebulae: 在星际的动乱中。

being formed. Now and again a star tore loose, and swept across the sky, leaving behind it a fiery streak①. It was the month of August when there are showers of meteors②. Yes, the divine substance was extended and had neither beginning nor end; it was absolute, indivisible, eternal, without duration, infinite in its attributes. Its waves and bubbles danced in the universal cauldron③, seething④ with change, following the unbroken chain of causes and effects, and he, Dr. Fischelson, with his unavoidable fate, was part of this. The doctor closed his eyelids and allowed the breeze to cool the sweat on his forehead and stir the hair of his beard. He breathed deeply of the midnight air, supported his shaky hands on the window sill and murmured, "Divine Spinoza, forgive me. I have become a fool."

菲谢尔森在结婚当夜,"在他身上长期沉睡的力量苏醒了",辛格巧妙地讽刺了违反人性的禁欲主义。

【思考题】

1. 斯宾诺莎的伦理学思想对菲谢尔森博士有着怎样的影响?

2. 菲谢尔森的眼中有两个"世界",神性的世界和世俗的世界,他是怎样走向世俗世界的?

3. 谈谈辛格小说的叙事艺术风格。

---

① a fiery streak：一条似火的痕迹。
② showers of meteors：骤雨似的流星,流星雨。
③ cauldron：大锅。
④ seething：沸腾。

Why I Live at the P.O.

我为什么住在邮局

尤多拉·韦尔蒂

【导读】

尤多拉·韦尔蒂(Eudora Welty, 1909—2001),美国著名女作家,在美国当代文学中占有重要的地位。她被誉为短篇小说大师,人们常把她和俄罗斯作家契诃夫(Anton Chekhov)相提并论。

尤多拉·韦尔蒂1909年出生于密西西比州的杰克逊城。父亲是一家保险公司的高级职员,母亲是学校老师。韦尔蒂是家里的老大,在她的下边还有两个弟弟。韦尔蒂的父母很爱读书,所以在韦尔蒂姐弟三个成长的过程中,书籍从来都是他们生活中不可分割的一部分。韦尔蒂在晚年曾在哈佛大学举办系列演讲,回忆她的生活,并据此出版了她的回忆录:《一个作家的开端》。韦尔蒂在回忆录里写道:在她还不识字的时候,她就下决心要读遍天下所有的书了。韦尔蒂是这样想的,也是这样做的。家里的书不够读了,她就去当地的图书馆。后来那所图书馆改建,新图书馆就被命名为尤多拉·韦尔蒂图书馆。20世纪20年代,韦尔蒂先后在密西西比州立女子学院和威斯康星大学读书。1929年,她从威斯康星大学获得学士学位,韦尔蒂的父母又把她送到哥伦比亚大学商学院读了些广告方面的课程。20世纪30年代,韦尔蒂回到老家密西西比,开始为当地的广播电台和报纸撰稿。大萧条期间,韦尔蒂在州政府找了份工作,有机会去密西西比州各地旅行。旅行使韦尔蒂开了眼界,这些美国南方偏远地区普通人家的生活情景,让韦尔蒂深深地着了迷。从十六岁起她就一直住在杰克逊城的那所房子里,直到晚年。她的小说也都是在那所房子里写的,那是她的父亲建造的。韦尔蒂的作品来源于她对美国南方生活细致入微的观察以及她对人性的感受。美国文学巨匠福克纳在1943年读了韦尔蒂的小说后写信给她说:"你写得不错。"直到韦尔蒂去世时,那封信还挂在她卧室的床头。

20世纪40年代是韦尔蒂文学创作的第一个高潮。40年代初,她先后出版了短篇小说集《绿色的帷幕》和《大网》;1946年,韦尔蒂的长篇小说《德尔塔婚礼》出版;1949年,她又出版了短篇小说集《金苹果》。韦尔蒂在70年代初重返文坛,开始了她的文学生涯的第二个高潮。1970年,韦尔蒂出版了小说《失败的战争》;

1972 年,她出版了小说《乐天者的女儿》,并且获得了普利策文学奖。此外,韦尔蒂的作品还获得过美国图书评论家奖、美国图书奖、欧·亨利奖、美国文学艺术金质奖章等美国文学界的重要奖项。这些都足以显示韦尔蒂的作品在美国当代文学中的重要地位。1980 年,当时的美国总统卡特授予韦尔蒂自由勋章,对她进行表彰。1998 年,美国图书馆选编的代表美国文学最高成就的《美国文学巨人作品》系列书籍,收入了韦尔蒂的作品。这打破了过去这套丛书只选已故作家作品的规矩,在美国文学界引起了轰动。这套丛书的出版使韦尔蒂跻身于马克·吐温(Mark Twain)、惠特曼(Walt Whitman)、亨利·沃顿、爱伦·坡(Edgar Allan Poe)、福克纳(William Cuthbert Faulkner)等美国文学巨人之列。

在多年的时间里,文学评论界一直把韦尔蒂列为地方作家,认为她的作品地方色彩浓厚,而且不具有任何政治意义。然而时间使韦尔蒂作品的文学价值逐渐显露了出来。人们正是透过她对美国南方生活的描写认识到了她的作品的普遍意义和价值。文学评论家终于认识到:韦尔蒂描写美国南方生活,正如契诃夫描写俄罗斯生活一样,现实生活不过是给他们提供了具体的、展示他们思想的客观环境。

韦尔蒂对于南方的风俗、人情、社会和人物是极为熟悉的,用她自己谦虚的话说,她"一直在自己的一小块土地上耕耘"。她开始创作的题材大多是关于南方农村地区小城镇上风土迥异的生活,充满了人情的温暖、乡土的气息和穷乡僻壤乡巴佬的真挚之情。韦尔蒂用写实方法来叙述她在南方社会中的所见所闻,以她的独有的才能,给读者描述一幅幅风情画,讲述一个个动人的、朴实的悲喜剧。她注意的是一些普普通通的人物,描写"他们生活的真谛,他们的私人生活,他们对于遥远的过去的回忆,他们在密西西比的童年和他们的梦想"。她清丽的笔调"犹如黄昏时分从鸡舍里飘出来的悠悠之声,撩人心绪",有时却也不乏幽默之感。

在韦尔蒂的早期作品中她描写了大量智力迟钝的人、精神错乱的人、既聋又哑的人。总之,仿佛由于南方的愚昧落后,几乎使人都智力减退,精神失常。小说中既有浸礼会教堂的描写,也有关于乡间学校生活的叙述;既写南方小镇(维克托利镇、勃拉镇、莫尔扎纳镇和奇纳林镇,等等)各种小人物的不幸命运,也写他们生活中的欢乐。她描写了南方守灵和葬礼的仪式,描写了巡回照相师有趣的生活,也描写了在镇乐队伴奏下的欢闹场景。有人被谋杀,有人被倒下的大树压死,有人耽于烈酒,有人疯疯癫癫——在僻远小镇上种种小人物的喜怒哀乐、悲欢离合,像一幅幅寓意深刻的漫画或者写生画呈现在读者的面前。对于韦尔蒂笔下有些人的悲剧,读来令人凄怆,几句安慰同情的话语已毫无意义。而有些人物一直在南方的大平原上追逐着生活,热爱土地,热爱自然,虽然他们的梦幻从未越过乡间的土路。

韦尔蒂是个十分卓越的幽默作家,善于从南方俚俗的闲谈中索取令人发笑的题材和语言。她的早期有名的短篇《我为什么住在邮局》（*Why I Live at the P. O.*，1941）就是南方一个小镇的一场闹剧的写照，令人笑余还觉辛酸。小说的主人公是密西西比全州倒数第二个最小的邮局的邮差。一次，她被激怒之余当着她的古怪的南方同胞的面宣布，她要搬到邮局去住。于是小镇上的人分成两派，一派同情她，支持她；一派反对她，拒绝再到这家邮局去寄任何邮件。韦尔蒂运用南方俚语，使人物和语言妙趣横生。

Why I Live at the P. O.

I was getting along fine with Mama，Papa-Daddy，and Uncle Rondo until my sister Stella-Rondo just separated from her husband and came back home again. Mr. Whitaker! Of course I went with Mr. Whitaker first，when he first appeared here in China Grove①，taking "Pose Yourself" photos，and Stella-Rondo broke us up. Told him I was one-sided. Bigger on one side than the other，which is a deliberate②，calculated falsehood；I'm the same. Stella-Rondo is exactly twelve months to the day younger than I am and for that reason she's spoiled.

She's always had anything in the world she wanted and then she'd throw it away. Papa-Daddy gave her this gorgeous Add-a-Pearl necklace when she was eight years old and she threw it away playing baseball when she was nine，with only two pearls.

So as soon as she got married and moved away from home the first thing she did was separate! From Mr. Whitaker! This photographer with the popeyes③ she said she trusted. Came home from one of those towns up in Illinois and to our complete surprise brought this child of two.

> 文章开始就是"我"的一大段独白，作者利用南方俚语使人物和语言妙趣横生。这段独白写得生动、幽默，并且道出了主要人物。

> 第一段交代了"我"与妹妹的矛盾，自从妹妹搬回来住后，"我"平静的生活被打破了。

> 接下来就历数了妹妹"恶劣"的品性。

---

① Grove：树丛，果园。
② deliberate：有蓄谋的，故意的。
③ popeyes：突出的眼睛。

起初妈妈看到妹妹带回来的孩子很惊讶。

Mama said she like to make her drop dead for a second①. "Here you had this marvelous② blonde child and never so much as wrote your mother a word about it，" says Mama. "I'm thoroughly ashamed of you." But of course she wasn't.

Stella-Rondo just calmly take off this hat, I wish you could see it. She says, "Why, Mama, Shirley-T.'s adopted, I can prove it."

"How?" says Mama, but all I says was, "H'm!" There I was over the hot stove, trying to stretch③ two chickens over five people and a completely unexpected child into the bargain, without one moment's notice.

第一次交锋开始了，从此一发不可收拾。

"What do you mean — 'H'm!'?" says Stella-Rondo, and Mama says, "I heard that, Sister."

I said that oh, I didn't mean a thing, only that whoever Shirley-T. was, she was the spit-image④ of Papa-Daddy if he'd cut off his beard, which of course he'd never do in the world. Papa-Daddy's Mama's papa and sulks⑤.

Stella-Rondo got furious⑥! She said, "Sister, I don't need to tell you you got a lot of nerve and always did have and I'll thank you to make no future reference to my adopted child whatsoever. ⑦"

"Very well," I said. "Very well, very well. Of course I noticed at once she looks like Mr. Whitaker's side too. That frown. She looks like a cross between Mr. Whitaker

① Mama said she like to make her drop dead for a second：妈妈说恨不得叫她倒地死过去一秒钟才好。
② marvelous：妙极了，令人不可思议的。
③ stretch：撕。
④ spit-image：一模一样。
⑤ sulk：此处指板着脸。
⑥ furious：狂怒的。
⑦ I'll thank you to make no future reference to my adopted child whatsoever. 我劳驾您从今以后别再对我抱养的孩子胡加议论。

and Papa-Daddy."

"Well, all I can say is she isn't."

"She looks exactly like Shirley Temple① to me," says Mama, but Shirley-T. just ran away from her.

So the first thing Stella-Rondo did at the table was turn Papa-Daddy against me.

家庭矛盾开始激化，在"我"看来妹妹开始挑拨家人和"我"之间的关系，首先是从祖父开始。

"Papa-Daddy," she says. He was trying to cut up his meat. "Papa-Daddy!" I was taken completely by surprise Papa-Daddy is about a million years old and's got this long-long beard. "Papa-Daddy, Sister says she fails to understand why you don't cut off your beard."

妹妹一句话引起了祖父对"我"的不满。

So Papa-Daddy l-a-y-s② down his knife and fork! He's real rich. Mama says he is, he says he isn't. So he says, "Have I heard correctly? You don't understand why I don't cut off my beard?"

"Why," I says, "Papa-Daddy, of course I understand, I did not say any such of a thing, the idea!"

He says, "Hussy!"

I says, "Papa-Daddy, you know I wouldn't any more want you to cut off your beard than the man in the moon. It was the farthest thing from my mind!③ Stella-Rondo sat there and made that up while she was eating breast of chicken."

But he says, "So the postmistress④ fails to understand why I don't cut off my beard. Which job I got you through my influence with the government. 'Bird's nest' — is that what you call it?"

这里点明了"我"的职业是邮递员。祖父说"我"得到这个工作是因为他的恩惠。

Not that⑤ it isn't the next to smallest P. O. in the

---

① Shirley Temple：秀兰·邓波儿，20 世纪 30 年代好莱坞著名童星。
② l-a-y-s：连字符表示说话时哆哆嗦嗦地。
③ It was the farthest thing from my mind. 我怎么也不会往那儿想。
④ postmistress：女性邮递员。
⑤ not that：倒不是说。

413

entire state of Mississippi.

I says, "Oh, Papa-Daddy," I says, "I didn't say any such of a thing, I never dreamed it was a bird's nest, I have always been grateful though this is the next to smallest P. O. in the state of Mississippi, and I do not enjoy being referred to as a hussy by my own grandfather."

But Stella-Rondo says, "Yes, you did say it too. Anybody in the world could of heard you, that had ears."

"Stop right there," says Mama, looking at me.

So I pulled my napkin① straight back through the napkin ring and left the table.

As soon as I was out of the room Mama says, "Call her back, or she'll starve to death," but Papa-Daddy says, "This is the beard I started growing on the Coast when I was fifteen years old." He would of gone on till nightfall if Shirley-T. hadn't lost the Milky Way she ate in Cairo②.

So Papa-Daddy says, "I am going out and lie in the hammock③, and you can all sit here and remember my words: I'll never cut off my beard as long as I live, even one inch, and I don't appreciate it in you at all." Passed right by me in the hall and went straight out and got in the hammock.

It would be a holiday. It wasn't five minutes before Uncle Rondo suddenly appeared in the hall in one of Stella-Rondo's flesh-colored kimonos④, all cut on the bias⑤, like something Mr. Whitaker probably thought was gorgeous.

舅舅突然出现在了走廊里，穿着一件肉色的女式宽大晨衣。

① napkin：餐巾。
② Cairo：伊利诺斯州南端城市，位于密西西比河与俄亥俄河汇流处的低洼三角洲。
③ hammock：吊床。
④ kimono：和服，宽大晨衣。
⑤ cut on the bias：斜裁。

"Uncle Rondo!" I says, "I didn't know who that was! Where are you going?"

"Sister," he says, "get out of my way, I'm poisoned."

"If you're poisoned stay away from Papa-Daddy," I says, "Keep out of the hammock. Papa-Daddy will certainly beat you on the head if you come within forty miles of him. He thinks I deliberately said he ought to cut off his beard after he got me the P. O. , and I've told him and told him and told him, and he acts like he just don't hear me. Papa-Daddy must of gone stone deaf①."

"He picked a fine day to do it then," says Uncle Rondo, and before you could say "Jack Robinson"② flew out in the yard.

What he'd really done, he'd drunk another bottle of that prescription③. He does it every single Fourth of July as sure as shooting, and it's horribly expensive. Then he falls over in the hammock and snores④. So he insisted on zigzagging⑤ right on out to the hammock, looking like a half-wit⑥.

Papa-Daddy woke up with this horrible yell and right there without moving an inch he tried to turn Uncle Rondo against me. I heard every word he said. Oh, he told Uncle Rondo I didn't learn to read till I was eight years old and he didn't see how in the world I ever got the mail put up at the P. O. , much less read it all, and he said if Uncle Rondo could only fathom⑦ the lengths he had gone to get me that job! And he said on the other hand he

舅舅的举动也很古怪,跑到院子里,并且在每个独立日喝酒,然后呼呼大睡。

① stone deaf：完全地聋了。
② before you could say "Jack Robinson"：说时迟那时快。
③ prescription：处方,药方。
④ snore：打鼾。
⑤ zigzag：曲折前进。
⑥ half-wit：弱智,笨蛋。
⑦ fathom：揣摩,彻底了解。

thought Stella-Rondo had a brilliant mind and deserved credit for getting out of town. All the time he was just lying there swinging as pretty as you please and looping out his beard①, and poor Uncle Rondo was pleading with him to slow down the hammock, it was making him as dizzy as a witch to watch it. But that's what Papa-Daddy likes about a hammock. So Uncle Rondo was too dizzy to get turned against me for the time being. He's Mama's only brother and is a good case of a one-track mind②. Ask anybody. A certified pharmacist③.

舅舅是一个头脑简单的药剂师。

Just then I heard Stella-Rondo raising the upstairs window. While she was married she got this peculiar idea that it's cooler with the windows shut and locked. So she has to raise the window before she can make a soul④ hear her outdoors.

So she raises the window and says, "Oh!" You would have thought she was mortally wounded.

Uncle Rondo and Papa-Daddy didn't even look up, but kept right on with what they were doing⑤. I had to laugh.

作者特别善于描写对话,在接下来的长篇对话中,读者可以看到"我"是如何上了妹妹的当,被妹妹利用,并被诬陷的。

I flew up the stairs and throw the door open! I says, "What in the wide world's the matter, Stella-Rondo? You mortally wounded?"

"No," she says, "I am not mortally wounded but I wish you would do me the favor of looking out that window there and telling me what you see."

So I shade my eyes and look out the window.

"I see the front yard," I says.

---

① loop out his beard: 捋着胡子。
② one-track mind: 死心眼。
③ pharmacist: 药剂师。
④ a soul: 此处指人。
⑤ kept right on with what they were doing: 该干什么接着干什么。

"Don't you see any human beings?" she says.

"I see Uncle Rondo trying to run Papa-Daddy out of the hammock," I says. "Nothing more. Naturally, it's so suffocating①-hot in the hour, with all the windows shut and locked, everybody who cares to stay in their right mind will have to go out and get in the hammock before the Fourth of July is over."

"Don't you notice anything different about Uncle Rondo?" asks Stella-Rondo.

"Why, no, except he's got on some terrible-looking flesh-colored contraption② I wouldn't be found dead in③, is all I can see," I says.

"Never mind, you won't be found dead in it, because it happens to be part of my trousseau④, and Mr. Whitaker took several dozen photographs of me in it," says Stella-Rondo. "What on earth could Uncle Rondo mean by wearing part of my trousseau out in the broad open daylight without saying so much as 'Kiss my foot,' *knowing* I only got home this morning after my separation and hung my negligee⑤ up on the bathroom door, just as nervous as I could be?"

"I'm sure I don't know, and what do you expect me to do about it?" I says. "Jump out the window?"

"No, I expect nothing of the kind. I simply declare that Uncle Rondo looks like a fool in it, that's all," she says. "It makes me sick to my stomach."

"Well, he looks as good as he can," I says. "As good as anybody in reason could." I stood up for Uncle Rondo,

---

① suffocating：令人窒息的。
② contraption：精巧的设计。
③ I wouldn't be found dead in：我要命也不会穿的。
④ trousseau：嫁妆。
⑤ negligee：妇女的长睡衣，随便的穿着。

please remember. And I said to Stella-Rondo, "I think I would do well not to criticize so freely if I were you and came home with a two-year-old child I had never said a word about, and no explanation whatever about my separation."

"I asked you the instant I entered this house not to refer one more time to my adopted child, and you gave me your word of honor you would not①," was all Stella Rondo would say, and started pulling out every one of her eyebrows with some cheap Kress tweezers②.

So I merely slammed the door behind me and went down and made some green-tomato pickle③. Somebody had to do it. Of course Mama had turned both the niggers loose; she always said no earthly power could hold one anyway on the Fourth of July④, so she wouldn't even try. It turned out that⑤ Jaypan fell in the lake and came within a very narrow limit of drowning.

独立日里没有人干活,我一个人在厨房做饭。

So Mama trots⑥ in. Lifts up the lid and says, "H'm! Not very good for your Uncle Rondo in his precarious⑦ condition, I must say. Or poor little adopted Shirley-T. Shame on you!"

That made me tired. I says, "Well Stella-Rondo had better thank her lucky stars it was her instead of me came trotting in with that very peculiar-looking child. Now if it had been me that trotted in from Illinois and brought a peculiar-looking child of two, I shudder to think of the

---

① you gave me your word of honor you would not: 你也拿名誉跟我担保过绝不再提。
② Kress tweezer: 克莱斯品牌的镊子。
③ pickle: 泡菜,腌菜。
④ the Fourth of July: 美国独立日,国庆日。
⑤ It turned out that . . . : 结果是……。
⑥ trot: 小跑,快步走。
⑦ precarious: 不稳定的。

reception I'd of got, much less① controlled the diet of an entire family."

"But you must remember, Sister, that you were never married to Mr. Whitaker in the first place② and didn't go up to Illinois to live," says Mama, shaking a spoon in my face. "If you had I would of been just as overjoyed to see you and your little adopted girl as I was to see Stella-Rondo, when you wound up with③ your separation and came on back home."

"You would not," I says.

"Don't contradict④ me, I would," says Mama.

But I said she couldn't convince me though she talked till she was blue in the face⑤. Then I said, "Besides, you know as well as I do that that child is not adopted."

"She most certainly is adopted," says Mama, stiff as a poker⑥.

I says, "Why, Mama, Stella-Rondo had her just as sure as anything in this world, and just too stuck up⑦ to admit it."

"Why, Sister," said Mama. "Here I thought we were going to have a pleasant Fourth of July, and you start right out not believing a word your own baby sister tells you!"

"Just like Cousin Annie Flo. Went to her grave denying the facts of life," I remind Mama.

"I told you if you ever mentioned Annie Flo's name

"我"怀疑妹妹的孩子是否是领养的,但是妈妈对"我"冷嘲热讽。

"我"提起了安妮舅妈的死,结果被妈妈打了一巴掌。

---

① much less：更不用说。
② in the first place：首先。
③ wind up with：以……而告别。
④ contradict：反驳。
⑤ she was blue in the face：她气得脸色发青。
⑥ stiff as a poker：固执。
⑦ stick up：此处指固执。

I'd slap your face[①]," says Mama, and slaps my face.

"All right, you wait and see," I says.

"I," says Mama, "I prefer to take my children's word for anything when it's humanly possible." You ought to see Mama, she weighs two hundred pounds and has real tiny feet.

Just then something perfectly horrible occurred to me[②].

"我"一直在怀疑妹妹带来的孩子，甚至怀疑到那孩子会不会说话。

"Mama," I says, "can that child talk?" I simply had to whisper! "Mama, I wonder if that child can be — you know — in any way? Do you realize," I says, "that she hasn't spoken one single, solitary word to a human being up to this minute? This is the way she looks," I says, and I looked like this.

Well, Mama and I just stood there and stared at each other. It was horrible!

"I remember well that Joe Whitaker frequently drank like a fish[③]," says Mama. "I believed to my soul he drank chemicals." And without another word she marches to the foot of the stairs and calls Stella-Rondo.

"Stella-Rondo? O o-o-o-o! Stella-Rondo!"

"What?" says Stella-Rondo from upstairs. Not even the grace to get up off the bed.

"Can that child of yours talk?" asks Mama.

Stella-Rondo says, "Can she what?"

"Talk! Talk!" says Mama. "Burdyburdyburdyburdy[④]!"

So Stella-Rondo yells back, "Who says she can't talk?"

---

① slap one's face：搧……耳光。
② Just then something perfectly horrible occurred to me. 就在这个节骨眼儿上，我蓦地想到一件非常可怕的事。
③ drink like a fish：牛饮。
④ Burdyburdyburdyburdy：（妈妈学小孩说话的样子）叽叽喳喳。

"Sister says so," says Mama.

"You didn't have to tell me, I know whose word of honor don't mean a thing in this house," says Stella-Rondo.

And in a minute the loudest Yankee[1] voice I ever heard in my life yells out, "OE'm Pop-OE the Sailor-r-r-r Ma-a-an[2]!" and then somebody jumps up and down in the upstairs hall. In another second the house would of fallen down.

"Not only talks, she can tap-dance[3]!" calls Stella-Rondo, "Which is more than some people I won't name can do."

"Why, the little precious darling thing!" Mama says, so surprised. "Just as smart as she can be!" Starts talking baby talk right there. Then she turns on me. "Sister, you ought to be thoroughly ashamed! Run upstairs this instant and apologize to Stella-Rondo and Shirley-T."

"Apologize for what?" I says. "I merely wondered if the child was normal, that's all. Now that she's proved she is, why, I have nothing further to say."

But Mama just turned on her heel and flew out, furious. She ran right upstairs and hugged the baby. She believed it was adopted. Stella-Rondo hadn't done a thing but turn her against me from upstairs while I stood there helpless over the hot stove. So that made Mama, Papa-Daddy, and the baby all on Stella-Rondo's side.

Next, Uncle Rondo.

I must say that Uncle Rondo has been marvelous to me at various times in the past and I was completely

"我"彻底地感到了无助,妈妈、祖父和孩子都站在了妹妹的一边,只剩下了舅舅。接下来舅舅也和"我"反目成仇了。

---

① Yankee:美国佬。
② OE'm Pop-OE the Sailor-r-r-r Ma-a-an:《大力水手》动画片主题歌。
③ tap-dance:踢踏舞。

unprepared to be made to jump out of my skin①, the way it turned out. Once Stella-Rondo did something perfectly horrible to him — broke a chain letter② from Flanders Field③— and he took the radio back he had given her and gave it to me. Stella-Rondo was furious! For six months we all bad to call her Stella instead of Stella-Rondo, or she wouldn't answer. I always thought Uncle Rondo had all the brains of the entire family. Another time he sent me to Mammoth Cave④, with all expenses paid.

But this would be the day he was drinking that prescription, the Fourth of July.

So at supper Stella-Rondo speaks up and says she thinks Uncle Rondo ought to try to eat a little something. So finally Uncle Rondo said he would try a little cold biscuits and ketchup⑤, but that was all. So she brought it to him.

"Do you think it wise to disport with ketchup in Stella-Rondo's flesh-colored kimono?" I says. Trying to be considerate! If Stella-Rondo couldn't watch out⑥ for her trousseau, somebody had to.

"Any objections?⑦" asks Uncle Rondo, just about to pour out all the ketchup.

"Don't mind what she says, Uncle Rondo," says Stella-Rondo. "Sister has been devoting this solid afternoon to sneering⑧ out my bedroom window at the way you look."

---

① jump out of my skin：让我震惊。
② chain letter：(要求收信人看过复写成一定份数,再分寄给其他人以不断扩大收信人范围)连锁信。
③ Flanders Field：一战时期美军在比利时的墓地。
④ Mammoth Cave：猛犸洞,位于肯塔基州,是一系列天然形成的地下溶洞。
⑤ ketchup：番茄酱。
⑥ watch out：小心。
⑦ Any objections? 有任何异议吗?
⑧ sneer：嘲笑。

"What's that?" says Uncle Rondo. Uncle Rondo has got the most terrible temper in the world. Anything is liable① to make him tear the house down if it comes at the wrong time.

So Stella-Rondo says, "Sister says, 'Uncle Rondo certainly does look like a fool in that pink kimono!'"

妹妹一句话,舅舅也开始对我发火了。

Do you remember who it was really said that?

Uncle Rondo spills out all the ketchup and jumps out of his chair and tears off the kimono and throws it down on the dirty floor and puts his foot on it. It had to be sent all the way to Jackson to the cleaners and re-pleated.

"So that's your opinion of your Uncle Rondo, is it?" he says. "I look like a fool, do I? Well, that's the last straw②. A whole day in this house with nothing to do, and then to hear you come out with a remark like that behind my back!"

"I didn't say any such of a thing, Uncle Rondo." I says, "and I'm not saying who did, either. Why, I think you look all right. Just try to take care of yourself and not talk and eat at the same time," I says. "I think you better go lie down."

"Lie down my foot③," says Uncle Rondo. I ought to of known by that he was fixing to do something perfectly horrible.

So he didn't do anything that night in the precarious state he was in — just played Casino④ with Mama and Stella-Rondo and Shirley-T. and gave Shirley-T, a nickel⑤ with a head on both sides. It tickled⑥ her nearly

---

① liable：有做某事的倾向。
② that's the last straw：最后一根稻草，来自谚语"The last straw breaks the camel's back"。
③ Lie down my foot：[俚]去你的吧。
④ Casino：由二至四人玩的纸牌游戏。
⑤ nickel：美国的五分钱镍币。
⑥ tickle：使逗乐。

423

舅舅的恶作剧式的报复,他把鞭炮一个个扔进"我"的卧室。

to death, and she called him "Papa." But at 6:30 A. M. the next morning, he throw a whole five-cent package of some unsold one-inch firecrackers① from the store as hard as he could into my bedroom and they every one went off②. Not one bad one in the string. Anybody else, they'd be one that wouldn't go off.

Well, I'm just terribly susceptible to noise of any kind, the doctor has always told me I was the most sensitive person he had ever seen in his whole life, and I was simply prostrated③. I couldn't eat! People tell me they heard it as far as the cemetery, and old Aunt Jep Patterson, that had been holding her own so good④, thought it was Judgment Day⑤ and she was going to meet her whole family. It's usually so quiet here.

"我"已经不能忍受了,决定马上搬到邮局里去住。

And I'll tell you it didn't take me any longer than a minute to make up my mind what to do. There I was with the whole entire house on Stella-Rondo's side and turned against me, If I have anything at all I have pride.

So I just decided I'd go straight down to the P. O. There's plenty of room there in the back, I says to myself.

Well! I made no bones about⑥ letting the family catch on⑦ to what I was up to. I didn't try to conceal it.

"我"开始收拾属于自己的东西,"我"与家人之间的关系要彻底决裂了,并且他们发誓以后再也不去邮局了。

The first thing they knew, I marched in where they were all playing Old Maid and pulled the electric oscillating⑧ fan out by the plug⑨, and everything got real

---

① firecracker:爆竹。
② go off:爆炸。
③ prostrated:沮丧的。
④ hold her own so good:保养得好。
⑤ Judgment Day:审判日,世界末日。
⑥ make no bones about:对……毫不犹豫。
⑦ catch on:理解。
⑧ oscillating:摆动的。
⑨ plug:插头。

hot. Next I snatched the pillow I'd done the needlepoint①
on right off the davenport② from behind Papa-Daddy. He
went "Ugh!" I beat Stella-Rondo up the stairs and finally
found my charm bracelet③ in her bureau drawer under a
picture of Nelson Eddy④.

"So that's the way the land lies," says Uncle Rondo.
There he was, piecing on the ham. "Well, Sister, I'll be
glad to donate my army cot⑤ if you place to set it up,
providing you'll leave right this minute and let me get
some peace." Uncle Rondo was in France.

"Thank you kindly for the cot and 'peace' is hardly
the word I would select if I had to resort to firecrackers at
6:30 A. M. in a young girl's bedroom," I says back to
him. "And as to where I intend to go, you seem to forget
my position as postmistress of China Grove, Mississippi,"
I says. "I've always got the P. O."

Well, that made them all sit up⑥ and take notice.

I went out front and started digging tip some four-
o'clocks⑦ to plant around the P. O.

"Ah-ah-ah!" says Mama, raising the window. "Those
happen to be my four-o'clocks. Everything planted in that
star is mine. I've never known you to make anything grow
in your life."

"Very well," I says. "But I take the fern⑧. Even
you, Mama, can't stand there and deny that I'm the one
watered that fern. And I happen to know where I can

---

① needlepoint：针绣花边。
② davenport：长沙发,长椅。
③ bracelet：手镯。
④ Nelson Eddy：好莱坞早期的歌舞演员。
⑤ army cot：行军床。
⑥ sit up：[口]引起注意。
⑦ four-o'clocks：紫茉莉。
⑧ fern：蕨类植物。

send in a box top and get a packet of one thousand mixed seeds, no two the same kind, free. "

"Oh, where?" Mama wants to know.

But I says, "Too late. You 'tend to your house, and I'll 'tend to mine. You hear things like that all the time if you know how to listen to the radio. Perfectly marvelous offers. Get anything you want free. "

So I hope to tell you I marched in and got that radio, and they could of all bit a nail in two①, especially Stella-Rondo, that it used to belong to, and she well knew she couldn't get it back, I'd sue for② it like a shot③. And I very politely took the sewing-machine④ motor I helped pay the most on to give Mama for Christmas back in⑤ 1929, and a good big calendar, with the first-aid remedies⑥ on it. The thermometer⑦ and the Hawaiian ukulele⑧ certainly were rightfully mine, and I stood on the step-ladder and got all my watermelon-rind⑨ preserves and every fruit and vegetable I'd put up⑩, every jar. Then I began to pull the tacks out of the bluebird wall vases on the archway to the dining room.

"Who told you you could have those, Miss Priss?" says Mama, fanning as hard as she could.

"I bought 'em and I'll keep track of 'em," I says. "I'll tack 'em up one on each side the post-office window, and you can see 'em when you come to ask me for your mail, if

---

① bit a nail in two：把一个钉子咬成两半，此处指恨得咬牙切齿。
② sue for：控告。
③ like a shot：立刻。
④ sewing-machine：缝纫机。
⑤ back in：早在。
⑥ the first-aid remedies：急救措施。
⑦ thermometer：温度计。
⑧ ukulele：夏威夷的四弦琴。
⑨ watermelon-rind：西瓜皮。
⑩ put up：此处指装罐，包装。

you're so dead to see 'em."

"Not I! I'll never darken the door to that post office again① if I live to be a hundred," Mama says. "Ungrateful child! After all the money we spent on you at the Normal②."

"Me either," says Stella-Rondo. "You can just let my mail lie there and rot, for all I care③, I'll never come and relieve you of a single, solitary piece."

"I should worry," I says. "And who you think's going to sit down and write you all those big fat letters and postcards, by the way? Mr. Whitaker? Just because he was the only man ever dropped down in China Grove and you got him — unfairly — is he going to sit down and write you a lengthy correspondence④ after you come home giving no rhyme nor reason whatsoever for your separation and no explanation for the presence of that child? I may not have your brilliant mind, but I fail to see it."

So Mama says, "Sister, I've told you a thousand times that Stella-Rondo simply got homesick, and this child is far too big to be hers," and she says, "Now, why don't you just sit down and play Casino?"

Then Shirley-T. sticks out her tongue at me in this perfectly horrible way. She has no more manners than the man in the moon. I told her she was going to cross her eyes like that some day and they'd stick.

"It's too late to stop me now," I says. "You should have tried that yesterday. I'm going to the P. O. and the only way you can possibly see me is to visit me there."

妈妈试图挽回局面,但是"我"已经决定离开,而舅舅则在旁边添油加醋。

---

① I'll never darken the door to that post office again：我再也不会踏进邮局的大门。
② Normal：师范学校。
③ for all I care：与我无关。
④ correspondence：信函。

So Papa-Daddy says, "You'll never catch me setting foot in that post office, even if I should take a notion into my head① to write a letter some place." He says, "I won't have you reachin' out of that little old window with a pair of shears② and cuttin' off any beard of mine. I'm too smart for you!"

"We all are," says Stella-Rondo.

But I said, "If you're so smart, where's Mr. Whitaker?"

So then Uncle Rondo says, "I'll thank you from now on to stop reading all the orders I get on postcards and telling everybody in China Grove what you think is the matter with them," but I says, "I draw my own conclusions and will continue in the future to draw them." I says, "If people want to write their inmost secrets on penny postcards, there's nothing in the wide world you can do about it, Uncle Rondo."

"And if you think we'll ever write another postcard you're sadly mistaken," says Mama.

"Cutting off your nose to spite your face③ then," I says. "But if you're all determined to have no more to do with the U. S. mail, think of this: What will Stella-Rondo do now, if she wants to tell Mr. Whitaker to come after her?"

"Wah!" says Stella-Rondo. I knew she'd cry. She had a conniption④ fit right them in the kitchen.

"It will be interesting to see how long she holds out," I says. "And now — I am leaving."

"Good bye," says Uncle Rondo.

① take a notion into my head：心血来潮。
② shear：大剪刀。
③ Do not cut off your nose to spite your face. ［谚］不要做害人害己的蠢事。
④ conniption：歇斯底里。

"Oh, I declare," says Mama, "to think that a family of mine should quarrel on the Fourth of July, or the day after, over Stella-Rondo leaving old Mr. Whitaker and having the sweetest little adopted child! It looks like we'd all be glad!"

" Wah!" says Stella-Rondo, and has a fresh conniption fit.

"He left her — you mark my words①," I says. "That's Mr. Whitaker, I know Mr. Whitaker. After all, I knew him first. I said from the beginning he'd up and leave her. I foretold② every single thing that's happened."

临走"我"还不忘记刺激一下妹妹。

"Where did he go?" asks Mama.

"Probably to the North Pole, if he knows what's good for him," I says.

But Stella-Rondo just bawled③ and wouldn't say another word. She flew to her room and slammed the door.

"Now look what you've gone and done, Sister," says Mama. "You go apologize."

"I haven't got time, I'm leaving." I says.

"Well, what are you waiting around for?" asks Uncle Rondo.

So I just picked up the kitchen clock and marched off, without saying "Kiss my foot," or anything and never did tell Stella-Rondo good-bye.

There was a nigger girl going along on a little wagon④ right in front.

"Nigger girl," I says, "come help me haul⑤ these

---

①   you mark my words：你记住我的话。
②   foretell：预言。
③   bawl：大声哭喊。
④   wagon：四轮马车。
⑤   haul：拖拉。

things down the hill, I'm going to live in the post office."

Took her nine trips in her express wagon. Uncle Rondo came out on the porch① and threw her a nickel.

And that's the last I've laid eyes on② any of my family or my family laid eyes on me for five solid days and nights. Stella-Rondo may be telling the most horrible tales in the world about Mr. Whitaker, but I haven't heard them. As I tell everybody, I draw my own conclusions.

But oh, I like it here. It's ideal, as I've been saying. You see, I've got everything cater-cornered③, the way I like it. Hear the radio? All the war news Radio, sewing machine, book ends, ironing board and that great big piano lamp — peace, that's what I like. Butter-bean④ vines planted all along the front where the strings are.

Of course, there's not much mail. My family are naturally the main people in China Grove, and if they prefer to vanish from the face of the earth, for all the mail they get or the mail they write, why, I'm not going to open my mouth. Some of the folks here in town are taking up for⑤ me and some turned against me. I know which is which. There are always people who will quit buying stamps just to get on the right side of Papa-Daddy.

But here I am, and here I'll stay. I want the world to know I'm happy.

And if Stella-Rondo should come to me this minute, on bended knees, and attempt to explain the incidents of her life with Mr. Whitaker, I'd simply put my fingers in both my ears and refuse to listen. 　　　　[1941]

"我"下定决心一个人住在了邮局里,和家里人决裂了。而镇子上的人也分为了两派,一派支持我住在邮局,而另一派则反对。

---

① porch:门廊,走廊。
② lay eyes on:[口]瞧见。
③ cater-cornered:对角线的,斜放的。
④ butter-bean:棉豆,牛油豆。
⑤ take up for sb.:支持某人。

【思考题】

    1. 尤多拉·韦尔蒂是一位典型的美国南方作家,她描写的南方与福克纳笔下的南方有什么不同?

    2. 这个短篇小说的语言有何特点?

图书在版编目(CIP)数据

欧美小说名篇研读 / 黄铁池，孙建编著.–上海：
上海教育出版社，2014.7（2016.8重印）
大学文科英汉双语教材系列
ISBN 978–7–5444–5409–4

Ⅰ.①欧… Ⅱ.①黄…②孙… Ⅲ.①小说研究–世界–双语教学
–高等学校–教材–英、汉
Ⅳ.①I106.4

中国版本图书馆CIP数据核字(2014)第161488号

丛书策划 张文忠
责任编辑 王　鹏
封面设计 陆　弦

欧美小说名篇研读
黄铁池　孙　建　编著

出　　版	上海世纪出版股份有限公司
	上 海 教 育 出 版 社
	易文网 www.ewen.co
地　　址	上海永福路123号
邮　　编	200031
发　　行	上海世纪出版股份有限公司发行中心
印　　刷	昆山市亭林印刷有限责任公司
开　　本	700×1000　1/16　印张 27.75　插页 1
版　　次	2014年12月第1版
印　　次	2016年8月第2次印刷
书　　号	ISBN 978–7–5444–5409–4/I·0037
定　　价	68.00元